I
THE CALDERA

"An intriguingly fresh magic system complements this whodunit in the best way."
CAITLIN ROZAKIS, bestselling author of *Dreadful*

"A cunning mystery set upon a surprisingly alien world."
BEN AARONOVITCH, bestselling author of *Rivers of London*

"A stunning debut. Paxman offers up high stakes adventure
and a mystery full of satisfying twists and turns, all wrapped
in a gorgeous layer of magic. Masterfully done!"
A. C. WISE, author of *Wendy, Darling* and *Hooked*

"Bursting with rich characters and explosive intrigue (literally),
Death on the Caldera produces a rare alchemy in its blend of
magic, murder, and mystery. A smart, thrilling debut!"
JULIE LEONG, *Sunday Times* bestselling author of *The Teller of Small Fortunes*

"Eminently memorable, *Death on the Caldera* is a classic murder-mystery
romp, with realistic characters and an enthralling magic system steeped in
intriguing mythos. This unmissable debut is a heck of a pageturner."
KRITIKA H. RAO, author of *The Surviving Sky* and *The Legend of Meneka*

"A captivating blend of classic murder mystery and adventurous fantasy, *Death
on the Caldera* brings a fresh, captivating voice to both genres. Filled with
powerful witches, unpredictable magic, and a suspicious yet endearing cast of
characters fighting for survival, this book is nearly impossible to put down."
CAMILLA RAINES, author of *The Hollow and the Haunted*

"A gripping murder mystery, combining political intrigue, volcanic
magic and witches that are truly creepy, *Death on the Caldera* is a thrilling
adventure that keeps you guessing until the very last page."
GENOVEVA DIMOVA, author of *Foul Days*

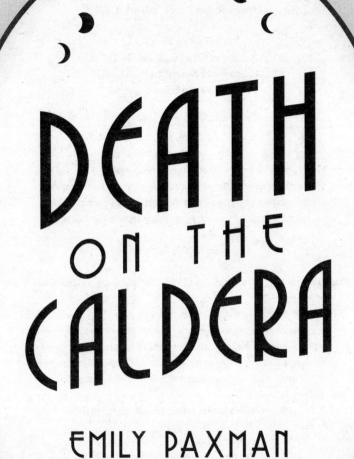

DEATH ON THE CALDERA

EMILY PAXMAN

TITAN BOOKS

Death on the Caldera
Print edition ISBN: 9781835411582
E-book edition ISBN: 9781835411599

Published by Titan Books
A division of Titan Publishing Group Ltd
144 Southwark Street, London SE1 0UP
www.titanbooks.com

First edition: May 2025
10 9 8 7 6 5 4 3 2 1

A CIP catalogue record for this title is available from the British Library.

EU RP (for authorities only)
eucomply OÜ, Pärnu mnt. 139b-14, 11317 Tallinn, Estonia
hello@eucompliancepartner.com, +3375690241

Typeset in Italian Old Style MT.

Printed and bound by CPI Group (UK) Ltd, Croydon, CR0 4YY.

to
Katie, Erika, Matthew, Marvin
Soprano, Alto, Tenor, Bass
Thank you for letting me join your choir.
I will always sing your praises.

· PART ONE ·
THE PASSENGERS

CHAPTER

1

As Davina Linde disembarked the train, a misty bank of fog rolled over her. Out of habit, she held her breath, then felt silly and provincial a second later. There was no need for such precautions here. Purposefully now, she let the gritty taste of the trainyard fill her lungs. After years of dreaming, she was finally visiting Pesca—the most fashionable, forward-thinking city in the world. And she'd be damned if she didn't make the most of it.

Her older brother Morel followed her off the train, stuck more firmly to her heel than a shadow. She didn't bother waiting for him and strode towards the baggage pickup as if she'd done it a hundred times before.

"Would you slow down? Gods, there are so many people here." Morel wormed his way through the press of passengers, earning puzzled stares from those around them. He looked like a bloody peasant, dressed in a loose tunic with his soldier kit slung over his shoulder. Davina had tried—and failed—to convince him they would blend in better if he donned the tailored suits and stiff-brimmed hats that were popular in Pesca. But he'd threatened to uninvite her from the trip if she didn't shut up about his clothes. Given the stakes, it was an acceptable loss.

Still, as they hailed a coach outside the trainyard's gilded gates, she couldn't resist a small dig. "Maybe it wouldn't be so crowded if people weren't stopping to admire your fashion sense."

He ground his teeth. "*Davina.*"

"Kellen is going to say something about it. I bet he orders me to take you shopping before I can even suggest it."

"I already told you, there isn't going to be time for that."

Yes, Morel *had* promised this visit to the most exciting city on the continent was going to be tedious and joyless. *Ha.* Well, even if that was true, it was still more appealing than enduring another second at home.

They had been travelling for over a week—first by ship, then train—to reach the capital of the Balterian Empire. Fifty years ago, the trip would have taken them through half a dozen smaller countries, each a broken piece of the last empire to sprawl across the continent. Commuting from Halgyr all the way to Pesca in so short a time would have been unthinkable, what with traversing so many borders and customs. But long before Davina's lifetime, Balter had pushed its way over the mountains, driving out the old inhabitants and unifying the southern caldera lands under their rule. Halgyr—mercifully—had been too far north to interest Balter, and so her nation escaped the onslaught. They were not within the same *sphere of influence*, as her uncle liked to say. It was the type of thing best forgotten when enjoying the efficiency of the rail line the Balterians had built through lands where the caldera villages used to lie.

Still, once they secured a coach, Morel promptly fell asleep, as if he'd been forced to cross the mountains on foot. In the precious quiet, Davina leaned out the window and drank in the briny night air.

The city of Pesca clung to the harbour like a jewelled necklace around a rich woman's throat. Rhyolite lanterns glittered on every street corner, casting a rosy haze over what looked like a dozen different parties. Late-night fish-and-chip shops hosted long lines of people eager for the cheapest catch of the day and street hawkers cried over the music pouring from their clubs, drawing in everyone from the seedy to the sophisticated.

The swill was so intoxicating, Davina wondered if someone was casting an enchantment over the night. If it weren't for Morel—who would surely ban her from every delightsome thing in existence if she misbehaved—she would have jumped from the carriage and gone dancing that second. Instead, she contented herself by rehearsing her plan, drawing a novel out of the pocket of her travel dress.

It was one of her favourite books—a sweeping romance by famed Balterian novelist Kira Westwick. More importantly, the cover image of a man with his shirt being ripped open by the wind had been enough to stop Morel from opening it and discovering her hiding place. Stashed inside the pages was an envelope addressed to the Pescan Ladies' Academy. It was the dullest college in Pesca, with wretched uniforms and mandatory classes in etiquette, but that was exactly the reason she might be allowed to attend. Davina had filled out all the papers, selected a major, even begged a note of recommendation from her old tutor. All she needed was the registration fee. And permission. But really, they were the same thing.

It didn't matter if Morel was right. Let this be the most boring trip ever travelled. What did she care if she waited a little longer? All she had to do was secure a return ticket to Pesca for the coming fall.

She was so absorbed, daydreaming about her future escape, that she didn't notice when the carriage pulled to a stop outside the Halgyric Embassy. Or that Morel had woken up from his nap.

"What are you looking at?" he asked as the driver came around to let them out.

Davina snapped the book shut over her papers. "Nothing."

"You aren't hiding something from me, are you?"

"Not hiding. Just keeping something private that doesn't concern you."

But Davina couldn't meet his eye as she stepped out of the carriage. And, as dense as Morel could be about some things, he wasn't an outright idiot.

She could feel him breathing down the back of her neck as they walked from the carriage into the embassy, but she kept her gaze fixed forward. If she showed a lack of confidence, it could undermine everything. The last thing she needed was for him to advocate against her now.

Morel handed their travel papers to the front desk. Once their Halgyric nationality was established, they were ushered into a waiting room in which Morel's attire no longer stood out. An aide took their names and confirmed what they'd expected: Kellen was working late and would be informed of their arrival.

As they waited, Davina stared at a doorknob across the room, determined to ignore her brother. Next to her, Morel twisted in his seat, clearly annoyed. He had far less authority over her life than he had opinions about it, and so long as Davina stood her ground, she could usually make him shut up. From the corner of her eye, she watched him shake his head and sigh, then shift from supporting his weight on one leg to another. His breathing grew more agitated until he *harrumphed* so loudly it broke her focus.

"Morel, honestly—" she started, but it was the acknowledgement he'd clearly been waiting for.

"Is this about university again? Is that what you're hiding?" He had to keep his tone civil, given the public setting, but one of the veins in his forehead still pulsed.

Davina's cheeks warmed. Her fingers curled tight around the novel. "So what if it is?"

"Davina… Father already said no." There was a shade of pity in Morel's voice, which was so much worse than anger.

Davina liked anger. Its burning dared a person to be brave. Pity was a candlesnuffer.

"Well, I'm not planning on asking Father this time."

"And do you really expect Kellen to overturn his decision? In the middle of… of *this*?" He gestured vaguely around them.

Davina guessed they could have spoken frankly about the personal aspects of their tragedy without tipping off the other people in the waiting room, but their family was trained to keep secrets. Even if Morel was terrible at it. As his voice heightened, a few quizzical faces turned their way.

"Is that why you wanted to come so badly? Some ridiculous scheme to get Kellen to send you to college?"

"No, that wasn't the only reason I came." Not that Davina could pretend her rationale had been totally altruistic. When the Halgyric court selected Morel to deliver news to Kellen, she leapt at the opportunity to escape with him. Sometimes she regretted leaving Uncle Sergei to attend affairs at home alone. But, by the gods, Davina had no interest in working with *him*.

"And it never occurred to you that using this trip for a personal errand might be a little selfish? Given our family's circumstances?"

Selfish? The nerve of him! Davina realised a long time ago that if she didn't secure her future, no one else would. She spun around, intent on giving Morel a piece of her mind, but before she could speak a calm, curious voice interrupted their argument.

"What sort of circumstances would those be?"

Morel's back straightened as if he were meeting a great general and he shot to his feet. Davina half-expected him to salute, which was laughable. There were only two years in age between him and Kellen. Perfect bloody Kellen.

Much as Davina hated to admit it, there was something about their eldest brother that demanded respect the moment he entered the room. He was dressed in a perfectly tailored suit that drew attention to his height and the elegant ease with which he carried his shoulders. Everything about him was sharp and modern, designed to match the niceties of Balterian society, with the notable exception of his hair. In all his time working at the embassy, Kellen never bowed to fashion by cropping it short. It hung to his shoulders in a cascading blond wave, the lucky bastard. Davina would never forgive him for inheriting the best hair in the family.

Morel lurched forward, as if he might hug Kellen, then clearly thought better of it and took a step backward. "We should talk in private."

"Yes, I imagine so. I wasn't expecting you." A small crease in Kellen's brow betrayed that he was more worried than his tone let on. If this were a normal visit, Morel would have sent word weeks ahead of his arrival with a serving man. But there had been no time to forewarn him. Davina and Morel *were* the harbingers of news.

Kellen surveyed the crowd around them, his gaze lingering on a few curious faces who had turned their way. "You have excellent timing. There's an art exhibition down the pier starting tomorrow," said Kellen inconsequentially, his hand sliding into the inner breast pocket of his jacket.

"What?" said Morel, who never picked up on these cues as fast as he should.

Davina sighed and stepped around so her head better obscured the motions of Kellen's hands. "Is it recent work or classical?" She propped up her eldest brother's falsehoods easily. Even if the exhibition was real, there would be no hope of seeing it. This conversation was all sleight of hand—the subterfuge of a magician with a much more important secret to hide.

"Classical, I believe. My clerk says the theme is... ah..." He paused as if seriously considering his words. In the meantime, he drew a thin vial from his pocket.

Davina had to credit him for his preparation. He must have suspected something the moment he learned his siblings were at the embassy.

"Realist portrayals of the Great Eruption," he said. "*Venri ai Soloz.*"

Fear only Soloz.

With the incantation spoken, he uncorked the vial and blew into it, disturbing the swirling mist inside. A foggy plume shot out and dispersed across the room, snaking into the eyes and mouths of everyone sitting there. Morel and Davina were no exception. The enchanted mist bore the sulphuric taste of the hot springs back home in Halgyr, and within seconds Davina felt it working its way through her mind, soothing her into a false sense of security. Muddling haze. Her family had used it for generations to protect their identities.

"Do you need something, Kellen?" she asked without thinking. Why in Soloz's name had she said that? Kellen must have brewed this concoction to make people particularly helpful. After years of exposure to muddling haze, she could withstand its impact better than most, but she still found herself acting like a damn simpleton.

"Here." Kellen pressed a clump of ruemoss into her hand, then did the same to Morel.

Davina popped the stringy lichen into her mouth. Ruemoss grew on the edges of thermal pools, making it resistant to the impact of mist blends. No sooner had she swallowed it than her mind cleared and all the depressing realities of their situation came flooding back. In the meantime, Kellen crossed to the desk where the embassy officers were blinking at him in stupefied compliance.

"If I may have the register?" he asked the man who had taken Davina and Morel's papers.

"Of course, sir." The clerk passed over a folder.

"Very good." Kellen leafed through it and pulled out what Davina could only assume were the records of their arrival, then handed the rest of it back. He locked eyes with Morel and Davina as he crossed the room back to them. "You'll stay at my apartment tonight. Neither of you were ever here."

Davina only nodded, but a furrow creased Morel's brow. "You aren't going to get that clerk in trouble, are you?"

"Of course not," said Kellen, even as he dropped the offending papers into the fireplace at the back of the room. "Now hurry up. The spell will lift in a few minutes."

Davina fell into line behind him. Even without muddling haze, she was expected to follow his orders. They left the rest of the room's occupants still slack-jawed. They would have no memory of the encounter once the mist wore off.

Kellen led them deeper into the embassy—up a flight of stairs, down more halls than Davina cared to remember, then finally to his private office. It was a small space for someone of his rank, but of course that was the entire point. Even at the embassy, no one knew precisely who Kellen was, and he couldn't go around muddling everyone he worked with. To them, he was just another diplomat, and a young one at that.

As they closed the door, he went to his desk and drew out a different vial. He went through the same ritual of activating its incantation; only this time, instead of targeting the people in the room, it seeped into the walls and windows. Until someone opened the door and broke the spell, no one beyond its four walls would hear a word they said.

Kellen dropped the empty vial back into his desk then turned to his younger siblings with a smile. "Well! It's good to see you both."

"And you." Now, without others watching, Morel didn't bother restraining himself. He threw his arms around Kellen in what must have been a bone-crushing hug.

Davina was slower to involve herself. She drew up to them, bracing for when Morel inevitably grabbed her shoulders and smooshed her into the embrace.

It was ridiculous to include her in these sentimental moments. Davina and Kellen hardly knew each other. She'd been nine when the court had sent him to Balter to attend university. He only returned home when business necessitated it and never bothered to get to know her. Too busy for younger sisters. And yet, in a matter of days away, he would have more power over her life than any other man.

"Now, what was it you were arguing about downstairs?" Kellen asked as they broke apart.

Morel grunted in disapproval, but Davina diverted the conversation before he could ruin her chance to pitch the idea of university to Kellen privately. "It's something we can talk about another night. In fact, we were only arguing because Morel was reminding me we had *more* important business at hand."

"Yes. Those circumstances." Kellen ran a hand backward through his long hair. "Did something happen back at home?"

Davina looked down at her shoes, waiting for Morel to explain. But as the silence dragged on, she looked up to see he was blinking furiously. Gods, he could get weepy about anything. Perhaps it was a good thing he'd brought her, after all.

Whatever sadness Davina was tempted to feel, she punched it down. Someone had to be strong enough to speak. She stared Kellen dead in the eye. "Father is dying," she said. "Congratulations. You're going to be king."

+ ✦ +

Since leaving Halgyr, Davina had spent long hours dreaming about the glamorous capital of the Balterian Empire. Would she get a chance to walk Pesca's famous theatre-lined waterfront? Tour the National Volchemistry Institute? Go for a drink on Lesly Pier? There were a thousand things she wanted to do, and she chafed at the knowledge that Morel was probably right. They wouldn't have time for any of it. But still she clung to those fantasies. They stopped her mind from drifting into darker corners.

Would she miss her father, once he was dead? Would she wish she'd done something about their relationship while he was alive, or would she always be angry at him for shutting her out? What responsibilities did the court expect her to take on, now power was shifting to the next generation? Was she going to have to marry soon? And what did Kellen—the man at the centre of this upheaval—think of all this?

Davina had hoped that coming to Balter would give her some hint about the future. A nation's regime change stood in front of her in the form of a sharply dressed, floppy-haired man. She watched him process the news and tried to get a sense of how her life was about to upend.

Father is dying. You're going to be king.

Kellen blinked. He placed a hand on his desk. "Ah… I see. He finally saw a doctor, then?"

There it was. The sum total of Kellen's emotional response. Davina couldn't fathom why she'd expected anything more. And yet she had. If anyone remembered the good days with Father— back when their mother was alive too—it should have been Kellen. But if even he didn't care, maybe it was useless trying to summon any grief of her own.

Davina glanced at Morel to see if he was ready to take over from her, but he was furiously rubbing away tears, so she did instead. The last letters Kellen had received from the family detailed how the king had experienced trouble swallowing of late. Since then, a host of physicians had been brought in, but what they found was too advanced to offer a hopeful prognosis. Cancerous growths coated the king's throat. Emergency surgery left him unable to speak, and worse still, hadn't slowed the disease. The court even hired a Balterian volchemist to examine him, who brought a wide array of sulphuric treatments. But when he suggested the king stop smoking, he'd been thrown from the estate.

Every day it grew harder for Father to eat on his own. Every day his skin withered a shade paler. He might be gone by the time they arrived back in Halgyr, or he might gasp out a few more months. No one was sure. But everyone agreed it was time for the crown prince to come home.

Wouldn't that be jolly? The whole family, all trying to avoid each other under the same roof again.

+ ✦ +

They only stayed in Pesca long enough for Kellen to wrap up appointments, organise his affairs and book train tickets back to Balter's eastern port city, Ealidor, from which they could sail north to Halgyr. Mercifully, Kellen's appointments bought Davina one day of leisure. He issued just one command to his younger siblings—Morel needed a shirt that tucked into his damn pants.

They tried to buy off the rack, but Morel's shoulders were so broad that every haberdasher in the city made it clear all items would need to be altered to the right length. That suited Davina fine. Kellen had entrusted her with more than enough money to pay for rushed tailoring, and she got the pleasure of wandering the city's famous High Street, poking into shops as she waited for the clothes to be finished.

She returned to Kellen's apartment laden down not only with Morel's new wardrobe, but also with a selection of outfits and accessories for herself. She and Morel were a study in contrasts. Stuck in a starched shirt and collar, he had never looked so miserable in his life, whereas Davina couldn't stop admiring her new cloche hat in every window they passed.

She threw open the front door with the hand that wasn't buried under packages, feeling lighter than she had in weeks. For a prince, Kellen's home wasn't a large residence—it had only four bedrooms and a maid who visited just once a week—but it was in a marvellously fashionable part of town. Exactly the type of place a young diplomat was supposed to be able to afford. If Davina got her way and came to Pesca for university, maybe she would live in a place like this. Though with her luck, she would probably be stuck in the dormitories.

Even Kellen had been expected to do a stint in his university dorm when he'd first come to Pesca as a student. The way they played this charade of being the same as their subjects felt ridiculous to Davina. For hundreds of years, the royal family of Halgyr had lived anonymously among their people. They only made their presence known under the cover of masks and long robes, looking like relics from a barbaric, bygone age.

The official names they used publicly were equally ancient. Kellen was the thirty-eighth Prince Matthias, son of Matthias the thirty-seventh. The title was always affixed to the crown's first-born son. Every subsequent child followed a similarly predictable pattern. Morel was the twenty-fifth Prince Lawrence, a name he shared with Father's stillborn twin brother. Davina, as the only daughter, got the privilege of being the thirty-first Princess Rochelle. Uncle Sergei carried the relatively obscure moniker of Prince Byron. There had been only seventeen of him.

The reasons for their secrecy were steeped in Halgyr's religious beliefs. Legend had it that Soloz—the ancient volcano god buried beneath the mountains and after whom the entire continent of Solozya was named—would rear up and rain fire down on the world if he ever learned the true identities of the kings of Halgyr. Discovery would mean destruction greater than the days of the Great Eruption.

Davina had a hard time believing any of it. It was difficult to quake in terror at the wrath of old gods when the nation of Balter was building trainyards and skyscrapers without bending the knee to any deities. But still Halgyr clung to its backward traditions. Her Uncle Sergei always told her it was less about Soloz now, and more a form of empathy. If the royal family blended in among the people, then they could know their needs properly and respond with the kind of compassion befitting just rulers. And now that international relations carried such sway, what could be more useful than sending the crown prince to Pesca, where he could infiltrate the Balterian Lords' Council as a low-ranking diplomat?

Davina hung her coat on a silver-gilded peg next to Kellen's front door. The political games of the modern age clearly called for hobnobbing with the rich and powerful. So much for living among the common man.

Waiting for Morel's tailoring meant that darkness had fallen, and Kellen was already home from work at the embassy. He sat with a book on volchemistry open, though he quickly snapped it shut when they entered. "How did you get on?" he asked.

"Fine." Morel headed to the guestroom, no doubt intent on ditching his new outfit.

"It was wonderful!" Davina knew Kellen only asked to be polite, but she couldn't restrain herself.

"Is the hat new?" Kellen asked.

"Yes! Do you think it suits me?"

"It's perfect. You could be a gangster's wife in that."

"Oh, you better not be making fun of me. I'm planning on wearing it every day." Davina checked herself again in a mirror that hung by Kellen's door.

"Every day until you can buy another one?"

She spun around, ready to be cross with him, but his smile

was relaxed in a way she hadn't seen these past few days. Even if Kellen wasn't sick with grief over Father's impending death, something clearly weighed on him. Yet for once he was listening to her. Teasing, even.

They weren't close. But that didn't mean they were opposite creatures, did it? She looked at his mother-of-pearl cufflinks and carefully kept hair. He clearly appreciated the finer things in life. Maybe this was the *in* with him she needed—a chance to plead her case by using the shared language of style.

"Can I show you what I bought?" she asked, testing the waters.

"Of course." He slid his book to the side and leaned forward.

Davina knew he had so many more important things to do than listen to her prattle, but for a few minutes he let her do just that. "I got a dozen new record stones." She emptied her bag to reveal a pile of quartz crystals, each one infused with a memory of a song. "They have so many here! I almost got a new crystophone too, but I guess I should wait until we get home."

"If you want to play one now, you can borrow mine," said Kellen, turning them over.

"Can I?" Davina felt her cheeks warm with excitement. She felt childish for enjoying the attention so much. But when had anyone other than Morel paid this much heed to her? And not a single lecture in sight!

"I also picked this up for Sergei. Won't it be dashing on him?" She pulled out a silk necktie that was destined for their crotchety uncle. Davina doubted he would touch it, let alone wear it, but spending Balterian finos had come naturally to her. "And, of course, there's the hat. Oh! I meant to mention—the milliner had so many wigs! She explained it all to me. Short hair is all the rage, but most of her customers are nervous about committing to a trend like that, so they wear their hair long in the morning, then pop on a short wig to go dancing at night. I almost bought one. She had one in the most delicious shade of red. But you'll never guess what it was made from!"

"Witch's hair?" Kellen asked.

"Yes! I was so shocked, I dropped the thing on the floor." Davina had seen wigs made of real hair before, but in Halgyr there had always been an understanding. The woman who sold her hair for the wig was probably still alive.

"You've seen them, then?" asked Davina.

Kellen reached for his book, a gesture that seemed to say it was time for the conversation to end. "Yes, they're quite popular. Like you said, the colours are stronger."

"I didn't know what to say to the milliner. This place is so wonderful and modern, and then someone comes out and casually offers to sell you a dead woman's hair," Davina went on, trying to recapture her brother's attention. He was drifting away, and yet she hadn't worked up to saying what she really wanted. The one thing that mattered.

Her eyes darted to the guestroom door. Morel still hadn't bothered them. What if this was her only chance? She had to speak now. "I really enjoyed myself."

"I'm glad." But Kellen didn't look up from the book.

"There's so much I could learn here. I've read about Balter, but it's different seeing the place. I... I don't suppose you'll be coming back to the embassy after your coronation?"

"Already plotting a return visit?" Kellen turned a page.

"Not a visit. I was thinking I could do what you did." She chose her words carefully, hoping it would flatter his ego enough for her plan to work. "Attend university, help out at the embassy. We'll need someone out here, won't we? I'm clever, like you. I could do it."

Kellen didn't lower his book, but in the drawn-out pause his eyes didn't move either. She waited as long as she could stomach for a response, but he gave her nothing.

"I've picked out a college." Her hands shook as she opened her purse and showed him the envelope she had stashed away in her romance novel. "The Pescan Ladies' Academy offers a very respectable education. I could study volchemistry. It could be good, couldn't it? Having someone in the family who knows how to use Balterian magic?"

"The court would never support you training to be a volchemist. Too many of them are afraid of it." Kellen's frown deepened but he still wouldn't lower that damn book. He held onto it like a shield.

Davina would have loved to grab the thing and toss it across the room. He couldn't say no. She'd worked too hard to get another no. "Literature then."

"You could study literature in Halgyr."

"Then governance!" Why did he have to make everything so difficult? "I'll study whatever you want. It doesn't matter."

"That's exactly what I'm worried about. I don't get the impression the educational aspect of this interests you." He arched an eyebrow, and for a few seconds she was cowed into silence. It wasn't fair that she knew so little about him, yet he could see straight through her. "I understand your admiration for Balter, but it isn't the escape it appears. Believe me, I would know."

"No! No, you wouldn't." Davina felt her temper rise to her cheeks. She'd meant to keep her head during this argument, but Kellen's casual disregard made each refusal burn more than the times her father had shouted her down. It was so easy for him to ruin her life, and yet he had the gall to think he could relate to her. "You're the bloody crown prince! You have a million opportunities back home. All the court thinks I'm good for is marrying off to some country noble, just so there are some backup heirs in case you and Morel mess things up. Is that all I'm good for to you?"

"No, of course not." Kellen let out a laboured sigh. "I completely agree. The court needs to modernise, but we can't expect every change to happen in an instant."

"I'm not talking about every change. Just me! No one needs me in Halgyr and I'm too young to get married." Gods, she hoped he agreed with that. "But I could do so much for the court here. Science, women's emancipation, it's all happening."

"Happening for *whom*, Davina?" She must have struck a nerve because he finally lowered his damn book. "What about that wig you saw? What we call freedom always comes at someone else's expense."

"Yes, it's terribly sad for witches here. What a pity!" She tossed her arms in the air. Here he was, sympathising with the most destructive beings on Solozya, but not his own sister. So typical. Hypothetical victims always mattered more to Kellen than those in front of him.

Both Halgyr and Balter had to deal with the witches somehow. Most power—the mist of Halgyr and the volchemistry of Balter—was accessible to all. Anyone could brew a sealing spell from spring water or hook up a quartz crystal to a crystophone. Their magic came from the continent's volcanic heartbeat, and whether a person could harness it was a matter of obtaining the right materials.

But the witches were unhampered by the limitations of volchemical science. It was said that a witch could do no small magic. When she lit a fire, she burned down a city. Never less.

Worse still, any time a witch used her magic, she shifted into a dark shadow-self that lived unconnected from her human consciousness. In Halgyr, centuries of laws prohibited women from owning land or most positions of influence, on the off chance they were hiding their witch self. Balter saw the problem as more specific. It wasn't all women they punished. Just the witches themselves. Once discovered, these untamed creatures were executed without delay.

It was easy to think both nations barbaric. All that mattered to Davina was which one gave her the most choices. Maybe Morel had been right to call her selfish before, but what was she supposed to do? Liberate the wicked women of a country she didn't belong to? She couldn't even free herself.

"I don't doubt you would excel at university. You're extremely bright and capable," Kellen went on haltingly. "But if we can wait until after Father passes—"

"Autumn registration is coming up. I need to send in the application now."

"I'm sorry, but *this* fall is definitely not feasible."

Her fingers tensed around her letter. "Why not?"

"It's too soon. But, once we get home, we can revisit the question for next year."

"Oh, don't lie to me! I'm not a simpleton." Davina stuffed the purchases she had so lovingly showed him back into her bag. Why had she ever thought she could connect with him? Hope really did make people foolish. "You're just like Father."

"*Davina.*" Kellen's jaw twitched.

She'd found another nerve. Good.

"I'm going for a walk. Am I still allowed to do that, *your grace*?"

"Of course you can go for a walk." He sounded so sorry for her, the hypocrite.

He was worse than Morel. Didn't he understand he had the power to change her circumstances? It wasn't some tragic accident that she was stifled back home, it was by design of the crown he was set to inherit. And to think there were people at court who were worried Kellen would come home filled with Balterian ideals and upend the old system.

Biting wind rolled in from the ocean, making Davina regret storming off without her coat. She rubbed her arms, wishing, as she had so many times, that her mother was alive. On nights like this, she liked to imagine the queen scolding her sons or husband for failing to listen. But in reality, her mother had been a timid, gentle woman. Maybe her tender hand would have been enough. Everyone said the king had been kinder while his wife lived. Perhaps her sons would have grown up with more sympathy, too.

Davina fished the letter from her pocket one last time. Her mother had done everything other people wanted and what did she get for it? An early grave was all. So, what was the point in listening to Kellen, anyway?

She opened it. It wasn't hard to add her signature and a forgery of Kellen's, too. It was even easier to take some of the leftover bills from her shopping trip with Morel, the Balterian finos sliding neatly into the envelope. Kellen had no idea how much she'd spent on the hat and trinkets. He'd never miss the money.

And wasn't money the same thing as permission?

Davina hailed a coach to the post office, where she handed over the envelope. Now she could wait on Kellen's timetable. They would talk at home.

When her acceptance letter arrived.

CHAPTER

2

RAE FREATH WONDERED if a witch had placed a curse on Ma.

She flipped to another page of her book, hoping to find something that described curses, but it was hard to say if the folk tales in *Lives of the Witches, Real and Imagined* were even true. Each entry had a box beneath it with either the word "verified" or "unverified" inside, which Rae had asked Ma about ages ago and learned it was a fancy way of saying "true" or "not sure". Most had the word "unverified", but Rae kept reading anyway.

The contents of their entire apartment were strewn across the floor and Ma was sorting spoons and socks with a fury that rivaled the caldera volcano. Usually, everything in their apartment was kept in exactly the right place, or else they might be overwhelmed by her mother's volchemistry ingredients: vials of mist, satchels of mountain plants, boxes of basalt, quartz and rhyolite—all of which Rae was forbidden from touching. Seeing the place a mess for once was fascinating. What had got Ma into such a state? There was probably a simpler explanation than a witch. But it wouldn't be half so thrilling.

"That will have to do," Ma announced suddenly.

Rae looked up, expecting to see piles that made sense—kitchenware on one side, clothes on the other, like Ma had created before they moved flats last year. But instead there were two jumbled mounds. Only when Ma pulled out her carpet bag and began to fill it with the contents of the smaller pile did anything become clear. "Rae, sweetheart, give me a hand," she said.

"Oh." Rae snapped her book shut over the entry on Ramona, goddess of witches. She'd read that one so often she had it memorised. *A being so vile and mysterious, not even the witches profess to know her will.* Didn't that sound marvellous?

But Ma was preoccupied with her piles and called out again. "Please, sweetheart. We need to get going."

Rae slid off her perch on the bed they shared and began to fold blouses and pinafores so Ma could slip them inside the bag. Were they moving again? Rae bit her lip. Ma was always on the hunt for somewhere *better*. Though what that usually meant was *cheaper*. The last flat had mildew down the walls. Rae shivered at the idea of returning there. Maybe they needed to, now that Uncle Larry was dead. They probably couldn't afford this apartment if he wasn't around to help with the rent.

"Going where?" Rae braced for the answer.

"It's wonderful news, actually. We're going on holiday."

"*Holiday?*"

"No need to sound surprised. Families like ours take holidays all the time." Ma took her volchemistry diploma out of its frame and shoved it in the bag.

Was that the sort of thing people brought on holiday?

"So why don't you gather up your favourite things and I'll add them?"

Rae stared at Ma, confused. She didn't own a bathing outfit

or anything else that belonged on a holiday. "Like a shovel? For building sandcastles?"

"No, we're not going to the beach. We're taking a train."

"Where?"

"Into the mountains, I hope." Ma frowned for a second, then tucked a small set of her volchemistry ingredients into a protective nest of stockings. "Get whatever you can't live without, Rae. Favourite things. There's room for a few."

Ma had already grabbed a collection of Rae's clothes—including some scratchy sweaters she would have much rather left—so Rae tried to think of what else she might want. She didn't own many toys. A few little wooden animals that an old beau of Ma's had whittled for her. A ragdoll. Rae gathered them up, along with *Lives of the Witches, Real and Imagined.*

Ma huffed when she saw the book in the pile. "Rae, that's too heavy. We can't take it."

"Then I'll leave the rest." Rae shoved aside her doll, clutching the book to her chest. "Or I'll carry it. I don't mind."

"You can't carry—oh, give it here." Ma relented and made room for the book. "I've told you a thousand times, it's just a textbook. I don't know why your father had it."

A textbook filled with old myths, illustrations, and stories. Rae's father had been a fisherman and there was no reason for a fisherman to own a collection of folk tales. He'd clearly bought it to read the stories to Rae.

That was the tragic thing about having a fisherman for a father. He could die at sea before he ever got the chance to read you anything.

They finished packing and Ma hefted the carpet bag to the door. "You ready to go?"

"But aren't we going to clean up?" Rae didn't particularly want to, but when had they ever left their apartment such a mess? There were still clothes and dishes piled on the floor.

"Ah…" Ma surveyed the chaos. "Actually! I have a little game we can play before we go. Let's throw everything around the room! Doesn't that sound fun?"

It sounded divine. "But…" Rae couldn't believe these words were coming out of her mouth. "Won't we have to clean it up when we come back?"

"Don't think too hard about it, sweetheart. See?" Ma grabbed one of the plates and tossed it at the sink. It smashed and fell to the floor in pieces.

Rae gasped. Witch's hair! What had happened to Ma? Maybe the clatter of broken pottery would be enough for her to recover her senses.

Then she turned to Rae with a forced smile and said, "Your turn!"

For ten minutes, they made a mess. Somehow, Ma managed to still give instructions while they did this. She didn't want chaos. She needed it to appear a particular way, though she wouldn't explain why when Rae asked.

Yes, make the clothes look like they're spilling out of the wardrobe, Rae.

Help me flip over the mattress.

Why am I cutting it? Well, have you ever seen inside a mattress? Sounds interesting to me! Let's see what's in there.

Ma really had lost her mind. Who cared what was inside a mattress? Actually, come to think of it, maybe it made a decent hiding place, precisely because it was so boring. But Rae and Ma didn't own anything worth hiding. Did they?

When they'd finished, the place looked as though it had been ransacked by a wolverine. As Rae stared at their handiwork, a realisation hit her. Whatever holiday they were leaving on was permanent. Ma hadn't used the word, but they were *moving*. Moving somewhere without half their things.

What could be so important that it was worth abandoning the little they owned?

Ma ran her hands down a silk dress, the only thing she'd left pristine in the closet. It was far prettier than anything else she owned, precisely because—as Ma frequently reminded Rae—it wasn't hers. The evening gown only came out when she dressed up for work at the hotel. Rae was under strict orders to keep her fingers off it, or else Ma could get in trouble with her boss.

Ma smiled. "You know, if I were a thief, I think I'd take it."

"But… but you *aren't* a thief." Rae tried to phrase that as a statement, not a question, but her mother still picked up on her need for a response.

"Of course not," said Ma. Then she unlatched the carpet bag and shoved the dress inside.

Rae didn't dare speak now. When they left, Ma pulled a vial of basalt dust from her travel dress and applied it to the pins in the door hinges. From there, she trailed the fine black powder down the hall of their building, until they were a few feet away.

"Stand back, Rae." Ma always kept a small obsidian knife at her side—the mark of a trained volchemist and the key to activating the volchemical bases. She unsheathed the knife and pointed the tip into the line of dust, twisting it back and forth in a quick rhythm. The entire line shivered.

"And what does basalt give us?" Ma asked. She tested Rae's volchemistry knowledge more often than the teachers at school.

Rae swallowed. "Motion."

"Exactly."

Ma gave the knife a final sharp twist and the whole line of dust reared up and flew forward, snaking up the hinges. The pins popped out as it slammed against the door, knocking it inward, as if it had been kicked open by a large man. Rae covered her mouth so she wouldn't scream. Ma had made it look like they'd been attacked in their own home. Why would she do that? Had something happened at work?

"Perfect." Ma grabbed Rae's hand and dragged her away. "Please keep up. We don't want to miss our train."

They hurried outside. Most of their neighbours were away working at this hour, but Ma clearly didn't want to be caught damaging the building. Once they reached the street, they hailed a carriage—the first carriage ride of Rae's seven-year-long life. She studied the thick upholstered seating, treasured the sight of the street from the vantage of the carriage window. The box made her taller than the top-hatted men who walked by. It would have been exciting if not for the lingering image of the door blowing off their apartment.

Rae sat in silent thought, too absorbed to bother swinging her legs along with the carriage bumps. Sometimes Rae wondered if all grown-ups hid the truth this often. There was no way of knowing, after all. She couldn't walk up to the other children in her class and ask, "What do *your* parents lie about?" No one would answer that.

Like, for example, if anyone asked Rae what her mother's job was, she had strict orders to say Ma worked at the hotel as a maid. Rae had no idea what she actually did, but she knew it wasn't *that*. And it wouldn't matter how the other children pried, Rae would never tell people what was "verified" or "unverified" about her mother's life. They were a team. The only family each other had.

She wished she had a similar shard of truth to hold onto now. Enough to know Ma trusted her, even if she was too little to understand why they'd left their apartment looking like thieves had blown through.

The closest thing to reassurance she got was when the carriage pulled up to the trainyard and Ma paused before opening the door. "Remember, Rae. If anyone asks, say we're taking a holiday together. That's why we're on the train."

Rae stared down at her shoes. She wanted to ask about the apartment. She couldn't. Instead, she settled for something safer. "Are we going on holiday at all?"

"Oh, of course! We're going to do lots of fun things together. More than ever before. We're going somewhere better. Truly better." Ma ran a hand gently over Rae's hair, which had been carefully braided for their journey. "We just… might not come back to Pesca anytime soon. It's a long holiday."

A long holiday. Not coming back. Listening to Ma was like trying to see through a window by clinging to pieces of broken glass. "A long holiday *would* be nice," said Rae.

"Exactly." Ma threw open the carriage door and together they stepped into the Pescan sun for the last time.

A busy throng pressed around them as they approached the towering gates of the city trainyard. It looked like another protest was going on. Ma had explained the whole thing to Rae ages ago. There were people in the city much worse off than them; people who'd been driven off their land when the Lords' Council decided to build a railroad between Pesca on the west coast, to Ealidor out east. Caldera Peoples, Ma had called them.

Rae had never walked so close to the protestors before. She squeezed tight to her mother's hand, instinctively nervous about what could happen if they became separated in the crowd. Most of the signs used words simple enough for Rae to read, painted in large block letters. Her gaze was drawn to them, as she tried to avoid looking anyone in the eye.

RENCHA REBORN!

NO SALE? NO RAIL!
GIVE BACK THE STOLEN LAND!

THE OLD EMPIRE WILL RISE

THE WITCHES ARE COMING

Rae sucked in a sharp breath. The woman holding that sign wore a violet wig that made her look like a storybook character. She'd never seen someone try to look like a witch before. The police killed witches, after all. But this woman stared out at the crowd, as if daring people to accuse her. Rae yearned to say something to her—at least compliment the wig—but a tug of Ma's hand swept her past the crowd and through the gilded gates of the trainyard.

They were funnelled into a hall flanked by brick walls. A line of clerks waited to stamp passengers' papers. Beyond that, platforms spilled off in every direction. For a moment, Rae expected there to be no tickets and that she and Ma would have to hop a train like outlaws. But Ma approached the counter like everyone else and soon they had directions to head to the platform at the very back of the yard.

They walked past several trains, until they reached the biggest of the lot. At the front, men shovelled massive chunks of basalt into the grinder. It took far more than the teaspoons of basalt dust Ma carried with her to move an entire train, and according to the porter waiting at the platform, this one was an express. It needed the largest grinder of them all to make top speeds through the mountains. Between the furrows of the tracks were piles of ashy grindings, waste left over from the basalt.

Behind the engine was a line of delicately decorated passenger carriages. Words were painted onto their oaken sidings with gold leaf.

"Contin... tin—no, contin... en..." Rae squinted at the letters.

"*Continental Rail*," said Ma, giving Rae's hand a gentle squeeze. "It's the name of the rail line."

"Oh."

With the way the protestors had been shouting outside, some part of Rae had imagined the train to be a metal monster. But these carriages looked genteel and inviting. Rae expected them to keep walking past the elaborate passenger carriages, but a porter motioned for them to step into one. Even he looked fancy, with his braid-trimmed uniform and starched gloves.

It was even better inside. The porter led them through a long dining carriage, set with pristine white linen and vases with fresh flowers at the heart of each table. Rae dropped Ma's hand and lunged forward, weaving around women in frilly dresses seated for tea. More than anything, she wanted to yank one of the tablecloths free and roll herself up in it, like a caterpillar in a cocoon. Tonight, she would grab a whole basket of linens and build herself a tent while everyone slept. Finally, the promised holiday had come.

"Rae! Stay close to me. This isn't our carriage." Ma's fingers closed over the back of her coat, dragging her to a standstill beside a shocked-looking gentleman with a walking cane.

"Oh." She should have expected that. This would be first class, and even if Ma pawned that fancy dress of hers, they wouldn't have enough money to afford a posh train.

"No, Mrs Freath. Your carriage number is clearly on the ticket." The porter showed Ma something and she squinted at the print.

"It's Genna Freath. No need for the Mrs." She snatched the ticket from the porter, who waited patiently with their luggage. "There has to be a mistake. I didn't ask for first class."

"The embassy's instructions were clear," the porter said mildly. "Besides which, this is the express. We have no second-class carriages."

Ma's knuckles whitened around the ticket. From her frown, the news didn't excite her half as much as it did Rae.

The porter lifted their tattered carpet bag again. "If I may?"

Her mother blinked, recovering. "Of course! This—this is a pleasant surprise."

"Very good, ma'am." The porter led them deeper into the train, and Rae resolved to ask her mother if they could try one of the pastries a waiter was now carrying out.

The sleeping carriage wasn't quite as sumptuously decorated, but there were two whole beds. Rae squealed and crawled into a bunk. "Can this one be mine?"

"Well…" Ma swivelled around their cabin like a rabbit trying to sniff out a trap. "I'm not sure if we're staying. Are there any other trains headed east today?"

"There isn't another until tomorrow night." The porter stowed their bag in an overhead compartment. "I assure you, ma'am. You are in the right place."

"I see."

"If you need anything else—" he began.

"No, we're quite well. Thank you." Ma shut the door on the porter's heels while Rae kicked off her shoes. Her own bed! And the sheets were butter-soft. She immediately untucked them and rolled herself into a sausage. Caterpillar time.

"No, sweetheart. We can't…" Ma stammered. "I'm going to talk to someone. See if we can get our tickets traded for tomorrow's train."

"But why?" Rae murmured from the comfort of her cocoon.

"No reason *why*. But I don't want to pay for overpriced drapes and—"

"Aren't the tickets already paid for?"

"That's the problem. I'm not sure—"

But before Ma could derail their adventure, there was a soft lurch as the train began to move out of the yard. Rae poked her head out of the bedsheets to see Ma gripping the overhead compartment for support. Like it or not, they were leaving.

Before Rae could waste time wondering what was wrong, Ma sat down on the bunk across from her. "Sit up, please. I need you to listen to me."

Rae squirmed into an upright position. From the focused glint in Ma's eyes, she knew what was coming. More instructions. More half-truths. "We're going to have a lovely time." Ma pulled one of Rae's hands free from the sheets. "But I need you to do me a favour, all right?"

"What is it?"

"I need you to tell me if you see someone. A man."

Oh. Was that how they'd got the tickets? Ma always had at least one gentleman hovering around her, desperate for attention. They were never good sorts. The last one—*Uncle Larry*, he'd made Rae call him—had even ended up dead. There had been a funeral and everything a month ago. Rae went and watched Ma cry, even though she'd never loved Larry. Ma had told her a thousand times. She loved no one but Rae.

And now there was another. When would the gentlemen of the world take the hint and stop bothering Ma?

"He's not dangerous, but I need to know if you see him," Ma continued.

Rae nodded, even though the first bit was the most obvious lie of them all.

"He'll stand out if he's here. He's tall, with long, sandy blond hair—"

"*Long* hair?" Rae had never met a man with long hair.

"To his shoulders." Ma made a sweeping motion lower than her own cropped bob. "And pale skin. Paler than most people. If you hear him talking, he'll have a northern accent."

How was Rae supposed to know what *that* sounded like? But she nodded, as Ma would expect her to. "And... if I do see him?"

"Tell me. I want to have a chat with him." Ma squeezed Rae's hand. "But he probably isn't here. I can't think why he'd want to travel at all. But just in case."

Just in case.

Rae held onto a lot of Ma's lies, *just in case* something happened. Something always did.

CHAPTER

+ ✦ 3 ✦ +

"You know, when we came to Pesca, Morel let me have my own compartment." Davina was trying a new tactic to get Kellen to let her enrol at university in Balter. She would remind him of how troublesome she could be until he wanted her as far from Halgyr as possible. It might not work, but at least she would get the pleasure of annoying him in the meantime.

"Well, I'm sorry to report that the embassy was only able to get two rooms. We'll manage." Kellen, of course, took the private berth. He needed the extra space for an office, since even Father's impending death wasn't enough to make him give up work.

As Morel hefted their trunks into the overhead compartment, Davina settled into one of the two bunks. She fiddled with the edge of her silk bedsheets, wishing she could enjoy them as they deserved. Since the royal family always travelled incognito, it was rare they indulged in tickets for a luxury train. But death wasn't something you sauntered up to casually. This new express line would see them home in record time.

Father is dying.

Davina's own words echoed in her bones. It was such a half-baked tragedy. If they arrived too late and he'd already passed by the time they reached Halgyr, would she be sorry? It would be easier to let him go without goodbyes. She didn't want to weep at his bedside as he slipped away. He hadn't earned her grief, yet it nagged inside, desperate to drag her down.

A gentle lurch beneath her announced that the engine had engaged. Outside her window, the gilded filigree work of the train-yard began to blur then vanish altogether. She pulled away from the glass, refusing to be sentimental about this parting. She *had* to come back to Balter. The future would be too bleak if she didn't.

Across from her, Morel looked just as melancholy, seated on his own bed and staring at his boots. She plastered on a smile and nudged one of his legs gently with her foot. Someone had to try to keep the mood bright. "Want to get something to eat? I think the chef said it's beef tenderloin tonight."

Morel rubbed the back of his neck. "I wish I could. Kellen has some business he wants me to go over with him."

"Oh." Davina's hands dropped into her lap. So, Kellen had assignments for Morel, but nothing for her. Admittedly, she wasn't sure she wanted to work, but sometimes she thought she would take forced labour over being constantly overlooked.

"But maybe this evening we'll grab dessert?" said Morel. "Or I heard there's billiards in the smoking carriage. It's a really fancy train."

When Davina was a child, Morel had cheered her up easily by taking her fishing along the river or teaching her how to swear behind their uncle's back. He'd been everything a little girl could want from an older brother. Now neither of them was young enough for such simple distractions to work, though he still tried. "Have you ever played billiards before?" he said.

"No." She faked cheerfulness again. "I guess that will be something new."

"I know this trip hasn't been what you hoped. Kellen... well, he mentioned that you talked about university." Morel took one of her hands in his, his fingers warm and calloused. For all his foibles, he did care about her. Cared enough he'd tried to warn her not to make a fool of herself by arguing with Kellen. "But even if it's not this year, maybe next? Some good has to come from Kellen taking the throne."

"I'm sure you're right." There was no point in telling Morel about the registration papers she'd sent in. With all his righteous worry, he'd only tell her eldest brother. "Well... don't keep Kellen waiting on my account."

"I'll be back as soon as I can. At least it's a good train."

"The train is perfect." It was the nicest thing she could think of to say.

Davina sat alone in her compartment for a spell. Ever since they'd left Halgyr, Morel had been her constant, pestering companion. She hadn't realised until now how easily he'd driven away her morbid thoughts.

Father dying.

Kellen, every bit as big of an ass, about to be king.

Gods, she was being dramatic. Davina unpacked her best dress, dusted her cheeks with rouge and rolled down her stockings. She didn't have much money on her, but this train had a smoking carriage that would be stuffed with gentlemen. Surely one would love the chance to shower her with drinks and push away her misery.

+ ✦ +

She tried the soldiers first.

A squadron of Balterian troops was on its way from Pesca to the eastern edge of the empire, where tensions still flared with the recently conquered Caldera Peoples. They were gathered around the billiard table, and when Davina sidled up, they were more than eager to show her their trick shots and brag about their new posting.

The group's most senior officer was a young captain by the name of Duncan Sewell and he seemed as good a candidate as any for an evening liaison. Though Davina wondered if perhaps she'd spent too much time flipping through romance novels. Books like that always made military men out to be gallant gentlemen. But, from the moment she'd said hello, Sewell had done everything he could to get a hand around her waist.

Was that sort of thing appropriate in Balter? Davina hadn't attended many parties anywhere. State functions in Halgyr were rare and ritualistic affairs, full of prescribed movements, dark cloaks and elaborate masks that kept even members of the court from knowing the identities of the royal family. There had hardly been opportunity for flirtation in that setting.

Here in Balter, there seemed to be no rules at all. Captain Sewell offered to teach her to play billiards, but even that turned into a ploy. The shape of the cue in her hands was unfamiliar, and every time she went to take a shot, he would come up behind her and try to place his hands over hers. "Let me help you!" he would say. And so, over and over, she'd been forced to knock him backward with her shoulder so she could try on her own. He made the whole experience rather tedious.

When she finally managed to sink one of the coloured balls into a pocket, all the soldiers whooped for her and Sewell squeezed her shoulder in a way that was too familiar. "I told you it wasn't so hard!" he said. "You'll be ready for trick shots soon."

"No, I don't suspect I will be." Davina handed the cue back to him. She didn't want to imagine what liberties he'd feel entitled to if she stayed for a full game. "I think I'd better turn in while I'm ahead."

"Oh, you can't leave." Captain Sewell frowned at her.

"I'm afraid I have to. My brother is expecting me for supper."

"Where?" The captain glanced around the carriage, clearly trying to suss out her lie.

"The dining carriage. Where else would he be?"

"Then let me walk you over."

"I'm perfectly capable of finding it on my own."

"Aw, be a sport." said the captain, his men chuckling behind him as he leaned in yet again. "Or is there no one waiting for you in the dining carriage? Hmmm?"

Davina felt herself scowl. Who was this man to call out her lie? She'd tell as many as she bloody liked, and he was an idiot if he thought he could make her ashamed of herself for brushing him off. If this was what women's liberation looked like in Balter, it was deeply disappointing. Why was she being forced to make excuses to a man she'd only met an hour earlier? Davina wished she could have told him exactly who she was—made him squirm with embarrassment when he realised he'd dared harass Princess Rochelle of Halgyr—but she bit back the ancient name. Even if the secrets her family kept frustrated her, this man certainly didn't deserve to be the reason she broke her vows of silence.

As she tried to come up with some other way to put Captain Sewell off, a deep, rich voice materialised by her ear.

"There you are, sister! Have you any idea what time it is?"

An impatient finger tapped Davina on the shoulder, and she twisted around to find a strange man at her side. He scowled at her and pointed to his wristwatch with such fury that she was struck silent.

"And now I find you galivanting with soldiers," he continued. "Father will not be pleased when he hears about this."

Oh. Sister, Father. It wasn't her he was trying to confuse, but Captain Sewell.

It would take an idiot to mistake this newcomer for any relation of hers. His hair was as dark as night and his eyes were ringed by the thickest lashes she'd ever seen. By the gods, he was prettier than her. She felt positively mousy standing next to him. But even if the physical difference between her and this man fooled the soldiers, the way she gaped at him—with her mouth half-open, like a dog salivating over its dinner—surely gave her away.

"I'm so sorry!" Whoever he was, he was offering her an escape. With some luck, Captain Sewell and his men would be too stunned to call out the ruse. "I really tried to get away—"

"Not fast enough." He gestured for her to hurry out ahead of him. "Time is money, you know, and I can't afford you wasting *mine*."

"Do forgive me." Davina rushed out of the smoking carriage, burying her face in her hands in what hopefully looked like remorse. In reality, she was struggling not to laugh. Maybe this man had a little sister of his own, because he sounded just like Kellen and Morel.

She raced down the length of the train, back to the passenger carriages, only stopping when she reached the door to her own compartment. By now, she couldn't restrain herself any longer

46

and she let herself laugh until her chest ached. A moment later, her rescuer caught up to her, a wide grin on his own face.

"Ah, there he is." She gave him an exaggerated swoon. "My gallant hero."

"Oh, hardly," he laughed, though he clearly didn't mind the attention.

She wondered how long he had watched her with the soldiers, waiting for a chance to insert himself. Or was she just flattering herself that someone so handsome might have been waiting for the chance to speak to her?

"You're well then, miss? Our soldiers didn't treat you too badly?"

"*Our* soldiers?"

"You'll forgive me for pointing it out, but that's quite the accent you have."

His smile was too delightful. Really, he was as presumptuous as Captain Sewell, but Sewell didn't have such adorable dimples in his cheeks.

"You could be from the northern caldera, though I'd guess… Halgyr?"

She nodded. "A clever guess. And you are?"

"Lord Carey the younger." He gave her a small bow. "I take my father's seat on the Lords' Council next year."

He spoke as though he were pitching himself to her, which perhaps he was. Clearly he'd saved her as much for his own benefit as hers, but, frankly, she didn't mind if his motive was to spend time with *her*. This might be the adventure she'd dreamed of having in Balter. When would she get the chance to entertain a dashing young lord again?

"Well, Lord Carey, I'm in a bit of trouble," she said at last. "I didn't lie entirely. I am here with my older brothers, but they're both busy with work. And if Captain Sewell sees me eating in the dining carriage alone, I can't imagine how I'll explain myself."

He nodded solemnly. "I can offer you my services, though I'll require something in return."

Davina shivered as he stepped closer. Was she really any safer with this man than with the soldiers? "And what would that be?" she asked.

He lowered his head so that his breath tickled her ear, and her heart leapt. "I have a frightfully boring friend with me. You must help me survive dinner with him."

As it turned out, Ambrose Carey was scheduled to have dinner with two other men and Davina could only guess at which of the pair was the bore. They both made decent candidates. One was a boisterous middle-aged man with a thick moustache who introduced himself as Lord Drawley, the most successful businessman on the Balterian Lords' Council. In his own estimation, anyway.

The other didn't introduce himself at all. He looked to be roughly Lord Carey's age, though his pale face was lined with a weariness that made it difficult to be certain. His clothes were the only clue about his identity. He wore the vestments of the Order of Chanri, a faith older than Balter itself. Davina had met her share of adherents in Halgyr, but there was something strange about meeting a Balterian who followed a religion that was typically followed by the Caldera Peoples.

She nodded to both men as Carey pulled out a chair for her, and her eyes lingered on the young acolyte. "It's good to meet you,

Mediate." Perhaps he would talk to her if she demonstrated she knew his proper title.

But he only furrowed his brow, forcing Carey to explain on his behalf, "Oh, Emeth's not a full Mediate yet. Still got a few more years' training."

"Oh really?" Then he must be on the younger side of her estimates. "So, what brings your jolly trio together on this fine train?"

Lord Drawley laughed far harder than her question merited. "Ah, a woman who gets straight to the heart of the matter. I like that."

"Business." Carey's reply hardly qualified as an answer and the wink he gave her seemed to say he knew as much.

"Oh, *business*? How very specific." She arched a brow.

"I mean, there's a, uh…" Carey began haltingly.

"We're part of a delegation from the Lords' Council," said Drawley. "We're setting up a new judicial office in Ealidor, which Lord Gamth will be directing. It's about time that place had some law and order. You could ask him all about it. He's seated with his mother at the back of the dining carriage."

Davina nodded as if this satisfied her and sipped her wine. There was obviously some other reason for their trip beyond that, otherwise Carey wouldn't have stumbled on his words. None of the three owed her an explanation about their plans, but so far it was all very typical. Men loved to keep her at an arm's length, never letting her know exactly how they spent their time. It was like some desperate bid to make their work appear more interesting than it actually was.

Maybe it was better not to know. She could imagine a host of romantic options while never confronting the reality of who Carey was or why he'd taken an interest in her. That was the pleasant thing about a train. She wouldn't know any of these people long enough for their lives to impact hers.

A first course of Pescan mussels in white wine sauce arrived and their party settled into the rhythm of suppertime chatter. Lord Drawley did most of the talking, often around a mouthful of the meal he should have been chewing. "Now that's Lord Raxton. Military man," he said, pointing at a broad-shouldered fellow who had taken up a table across the carriage. "Retired years ago, but there're rumours the Council wants him to check out the situation to the west of Ealidor. Might be more trouble there than the papers let on."

"Interesting. Miss Linde and I met some soldiers in the smoking carriage," Carey said.

Davina coughed into her drink.

"Really? They say anything to you?" Drawley's eyes lit up with interest.

"They seemed more invested in their billiards game, if you ask me," said Davina. "Though I would be too, if this was my last chance to have a good time before getting sent to a foxhole."

"Would you now?" Drawley shook his fork at her. "That fascinates me, miss. I can guess why everyone is on this train. All except you. Never dealt much with Halgyrics."

A tender mercy for the people of Halgyr, Davina thought. She shrugged.

"Take Lodi Barnaka." Drawley jabbed a thumb over his shoulder to indicate a woman in a hat festooned with enough feathers to fill an aviary. "Married five years ago, bloke dies six months later. There was a big tosh about it, since they had no heirs. Everyone thought she'd take his seat on the Lords' Council.

Another vote for women and all. Instead, she sold his title off to the highest bidder. Now you see her everywhere, spending the finos on whatever she fancies. What about you, Miss Linde? Got a story like that to share?"

"Oh, I wish I did. That's what every woman wants, isn't it? A dead, rich husband?"

Drawley broke into a deep belly laugh, while the silent, not-quite Mediate frowned, as if he worried she might be serious. Had the man taken a vow of silence or something? She'd never heard of such a thing in the Order of Chanri, but who knew? Morel had once told her the Balterians pecked at the stories of the old gods, only taking the bits that suited them, and remaking the legends to their likings.

The dinner conversation carried on in a similar manner for the next hour. Drawley would point out someone in the carriage, then regale the others with their history. This man had so little money, he was in danger of losing his title when fees were due next year. That woman was a famous dancer and acrobat, out on tour. And, judging by the uniforms, the pair at the back were army nurses, serving under Lord Raxton.

Davina wondered what Kellen and Morel would think if they found her seated with these strangers. Would they fly into a protective rage? But the threat posed by a handsome man like Carey might be blunted by the sight of his companions. Maybe Kellen and Morel would even be proud of her if she could report the gossip about troops moving around the Balterian Empire.

Would that make Kellen take her seriously? Actually, she bet she'd be rather good at politics. All that wining and dining and making people say things they shouldn't—it would fit right into her skillset. Why couldn't he see that? Even if her motives for wanting to stay in Balter weren't terribly selfless, what did that matter if she did the job well?

"My apologies, friends. But I think it's time for me to make a move." Lord Drawley's change in tone drew Davina back to the conversation. He threw his linen napkin onto his plate so it landed in the leftover gravy. "That Lodi Barnaka has too much money to her name. Maybe she'll be interested in our venture."

"But we have enough investors already, don't we?" Carey twisted around in his chair as Drawley headed towards the back of the dining carriage.

"Lesson one about business, boy," said Drawley as he threw them a parting wink. "You can *never* have too much capital."

Davina let out a sigh of relief, but she was far from the only one pleased to see him go. As Lord Drawley passed beyond earshot, the sour-faced not-quite-Mediate straightened in his seat, looked Carey squarely in the eye, and uttered his first words of the evening. "I don't like that man."

"Yes, Emeth. We've established that." Carey sighed, as if he were being dragged into an argument he'd had too many times already.

"Well, my opinion of him hasn't improved, despite your promises. He has nothing to recommend him," Emeth carried on. "No object other than profit. No scruples."

"And no manners." Davina lifted the napkin out of the gravy and tucked it to the side.

Emeth's gaze snapped on her, his dark eyes surprising in their intensity. "Yes. Exactly." He smiled, something Davina hadn't imagined him capable of five minutes earlier, and immediately ten years seemed to melt off him. A crease in his lean cheeks highlighted the sharp line of his jaw and Davina felt the need to fidget with the napkins again. He wasn't quite so handsome as Carey, but in that small change, he went from being a stone statue to a breathing man.

"Leave Drawley to me." Carey's voice pulled Davina's eye back to him.

The young lord fronted confidence but, even in their short acquaintance, Davina could tell it was an act. Clearly, Carey was the glue that had brought this group together and he was nervous about everyone playing their prescribed roles.

"I know he isn't the nicest sort, but he's got a head for business. I won't let him cross any lines if you just do your bit—"

"I'm here on this train, aren't I? You don't have to worry about my cooperation." Emeth lined up his fork and knife so the waitstaff could collect the dishes. "I think I'll retire. I'm missing the company of my books, and I don't want to keep you from your charming partner."

"Oh." Davina had got so used to the presence of the other men, she'd completely forgotten that, ostensibly, she was here with Carey because he was attracted to her.

"To your health, Miss Linde." Emeth raised the dregs of his wine in a salute.

She flushed, more flattered by the attention than she dared admit. For a brief moment, there were two young men smiling at her, until the quiet one stood up and left and she was alone with Carey. Instinctively, she searched the room for some sign of Kellen and Morel. Dinner wouldn't look nearly so innocent now.

"I apologise for my companions," Carey said. "But I did warn you."

"Yes, you did." Davina forced a laugh. His gaze felt so much more personal now than it had back when he'd rescued her from the billiards table. By Soloz, why was she letting him fluster her? She might lack experience in situations like these, but if there was one thing Davina prided herself on, it was her nerve. She had to reclaim it.

"Emeth at least means well," he went on. "We're old friends. Even before he took to the Order, he was like that. The poor man cares so deeply about everything, I don't suspect anything satisfies him."

"Oh, I didn't mind him." In fact, she found she liked Carey better for speaking well of his friend. They seemed so diametrically opposed—one the fine dandy, the other a sullen holy man. Taken apart, they were practically clichés, but together they gave her pause. Neither could be quite so shallow if they could see value in the other. "Was he highborn, then? You'll forgive my prying, but with the rest of you being on the Lords' Council—"

"Highborn?" Carey laughed outright. "That isn't the half of it. Before he renounced his house for the Order, he was a bloody Trudane."

"Oh!" Davina only knew a handful of names from the Balterian Lords' Council. There were more than four hundred voting houses, so she could hardly be expected to keep track, but a few were so important and influential that they regularly appeared in the newspapers in Halgyr. Ignacious Trudane had been Overseer of the Lords' Council for nearly ten years. In fact, now that she'd heard the name… "Wait, there was a big scandal, wasn't there? Something about Lord Trudane's son giving up his seat and—"

"Yes, that was Emeth." Carey shook his head. "I don't pretend I understand it, but part of me finds it admirable. He loved something enough to give up all this." He gestured at the fine furnishings that enveloped them.

It really was incredible if she stopped to think about it. Here they were, travelling across the spine of the continent, yet they were never expected to go without silver goblets or shrimp cocktails. Just how much had this Emeth given up to follow Chanri? Balter was something of an oddity on Solozya, with its elected Overseer of the Council and inclination towards women's liberation, but there were still plenty of obstacles to gaining power. The ruling lords only held onto their voting rights through exorbitant fees. Anyone who couldn't afford to fund their family's position swiftly lost it at auction when the payments that propped up the Balterian economy were due every five years. For the Trudanes to rise all the way to the position of Overseer, they must have had extensive holdings. Enough to buy up seats for their friends and influence the voting body. Davina couldn't fathom renouncing such power.

She glanced towards the table where Lodi Barnaka, the rich widow Lord Drawley had wanted to ingratiate himself with, was seated. Every indulgence the kitchens could muster was spread out before her: Pescan oysters, asparagus dressed in brown butter sauce, and the best wine from Korio's vineyards. Drawley wasn't the only man of importance hanging off her. The conductor himself was taking dinner with her—or perhaps even serving her. Who knew the limits to what her money could buy? Yet still she struck Davina as woefully short-sighted. Who would willingly sell off a vote in government? Neither money nor faith seemed strong enough reasons to Davina. Though perhaps she was being ungenerous. Emeth's decision surely spoke to a nobility of character.

That, or lunacy.

"You wouldn't by any chance..." Carey broke the silence

55

between them and Davina arched her brow, willing him to go on. He scratched the back of his neck and laughed. "By any chance… would you care to dance?"

"Dance?" At the back of the carriage a crystophone was playing a soft tune, but until now Davina had scarcely noticed the music. She turned in her seat and saw that a few couples were swaying on a small dance floor. She felt heat flood her cheeks as a *yes* and *no* warred inside her at the prospect. "I—I wish I could, but we don't have the same dances in Halgyr—"

"Oh, I can teach you." Emboldened, Carey rose from his seat. He proffered his hand, then drew it back just as suddenly, as if remembering the awkward situation he'd saved her from earlier. "Unless… I mean, it's been a wonderful evening, but if you're ready to turn in—"

"No." The thought of being alone in her room was enough for her to make a choice. "If you can teach me, I'd love to dance."

Carey's face relaxed into his signature grin and she wondered why she'd ever doubted her answer. He led her past the dining tables until they reached the section cleared away for dancers, where one of the porters stood to attention next to the crystophone. Carey whispered something to the man and the porter nodded.

"We'll happily play that song next, sir."

Davina watched in amazement as the porter selected a new quartz crystal from his bag and prepared to swap it for the one currently spinning. How important did someone have to be to request a specific song? If she asked, would the porter oblige her too?

The new quartz began to spin and a trio of brass horns warbled out a dreamy ballad, setting the stage for a honeyed, female voice to join in.

I only know the song when I hear you play it.
I only know my name when I hear you say it.
Baby, won't you whisper it to me?

Carey placed his hand gingerly against her waist. "This all right?"

"You can hold me a little closer than that," she laughed. "I'll need to follow your lead."

"Right, of course." His fingers strengthened against her spine and Davina swayed to the new rhythm. She smelled the piney notes of his cologne as he guided her into the first steps. "We begin on the left—well, my left, so your right. And it's a sort of one, two, three pattern. Forward, side, back. Forward, side—" Just a few steps in and their feet were already tangled. "Oh, damn. I guess when I go forward, you're supposed to go back. Sorry. Back, side, forward. Back, side…"

But Davina was laughing too much to heed his instructions anymore. "Oh dear, it seems you know this dance about as well as I do."

"I'm terribly sorry, Miss Linde." A flush darkened his cheeks.

"I'm not." She inched closer to him, letting the warmth that emanated from his body seep into her. "I'm very glad I met you, Lord Carey."

He smiled, those long, dark lashes sweeping not just over his cheeks, but through her heart. It was all too good to be true. The songs melted together as Davina grew sure of herself in his arms. Every so often, he would attempt to teach her another set of steps, and even though neither of them proved to be brilliant dancers, she never tired of trying with him.

She wasn't aware of how long they spent together until a familiar voice drifted above the din of merrymakers into her ear.

There was no mistaking her oldest brother's accent in this sea of Balterian voices. "Fine, a four-year-old will do."

Davina twisted out of Carey's embrace, searching for Kellen. Sure enough, she spotted him standing next to the dining carriage's bar, waiting for one of the bar staff to bring down a bottle of brandy. Should she dart out of sight while she still had the chance?

But a second later, Kellen glanced her way and waved clumsily. "Hullo, Davina!"

"What are you doing here?" It was such an infantile question, but all she could think of in this moment. He'd found her dancing with a strange man and now he would… wait, what *was* he going to do?

"Getting a drink." He held up his new brandy bottle, as if that were explanation enough. His typically perfect hair was rumpled over his ears at odd angles and dark circles rimmed his eyes, as if he hadn't slept in days. Yet she'd seen him perfectly collected just a few hours earlier.

The whole sight was so foreign that the truth refused to settle on her until she watched Kellen take a swig from his bottle without bothering to pour it into a cup first. "How much have you had tonight?" she demanded.

"Oh, this and that." He shrugged and inclined his head towards Carey. "What about you? Looks like you're having a good night."

"Morel said you were working."

"Yes. Heading right back to it now. Cheerio, Davina." Kellen tipped his hat to her and hurried out of the carriage, brandy in hand, as if *she* were the one who had discovered some lurid secret about *him*. She'd spent so much time worrying that Kellen or Morel might catch her cavorting with Carey, but Kellen was too bloody drunk to care.

"Was that one of your brothers?" Carey's hand on her shoulder dragged her back to her present circumstances.

"Ah, yes. Yes, it was." She hoped Carey didn't expect an explanation, because Davina didn't have one. She'd never in her life seen Kellen drunk before. Not after state dinners, not even in the safety of a meal with his family. He was such a controlled, calculated man. Davina had assumed, until now, that he never gave in to excess that way.

"He's a working man, then? I respect that." Carey went on inconsequentially.

But Davina wasn't listening to Carey. Kellen's indifference should have been a relief. Wasn't that what she'd always wanted? To be able to do whatever she pleased without the threat of someone shouting her down? If her father had walked in drunk to find his only daughter flirting with a foreign lord, she'd have been lucky to escape without a slap across the cheek. And yet, the incident nagged at her.

The selfish prick. The only reason she'd eaten dinner with strangers was because Kellen and Morel had been *too busy* with work. And yet here Kellen was, getting sloshed without her. If he wanted to spend his time grieving for their father and drinking himself into oblivion that was fine. But did he have to push her away to do it? Did he have to lie?

"I'm so sorry, my lord." She turned back to Carey with a smile, well aware that if she lingered here much longer she'd spill a host of secrets that were no one's business but her own. "I have a headache and need to retire."

Carey nodded slowly. "I often have a headache when talking with my family too."

"It isn't that—"

But he didn't force her to sustain the lie. "It's no matter," he said. "I'll see you to your berth." He lifted her hand and tucked it into his arm so he could escort her away.

He even kissed the back of her wrist as they said goodnight. It was all so perfect. And temporary.

She thought again of Kellen's slack smile when he'd seen her dancing with Lord Carey. If that hadn't bothered him, why in Soloz's name was he keeping her from attending university in Balter? Had the alcohol exposed his true thoughts or just impaired his judgement? Perhaps she would be in trouble come the morning. Once he regained his senses.

Davina locked the door behind her when she entered her compartment. Morel was inside, a sheaf of papers spread over his lap, completely sober.

"You're still working," she blurted out at the sight of him.

"I'm sorry." He rubbed his eyes. "Did you get dinner? I wanted to come, but Kellen needs me to finish these letters before we reach the port."

"Does he?" Davina didn't bother hiding the disdain in her voice.

"I know. It's too much, but he's going to be king soon." Morel shook his head wearily. "We all have to play our part."

There were dozens of things she wanted to say in response to that. To begin with, the nonsense about *playing a part* only seemed to apply to a select few. Where were her assignments? She was far quicker at paperwork than Morel. Kellen could claim all he liked that she would play a meaningful role in court, but it was clear he didn't give a shit about including her. And as for the urgency of their work, wouldn't Morel love to hear how Kellen was currently spending his evening?

But if she told him, there might be follow-up questions. Revealing Kellen's secrets would probably lead to him exposing her. And if dancing with Carey wasn't a problem now, why go out of her way to make it one later? Morel disliked anything that reminded him she was now too old to wear her hair in plaits. There was no sense in giving him a reason to be upset. She could keep Kellen's secret, and in return, maybe he would keep hers.

She might even be able to use this to argue her point. *See how well I managed myself in Balter? See how I protected you? Why not let me be your eyes and ears in the embassy?*

Davina settled to sleep that night, mind swirling with thoughts of Lord Ambrose Carey. Their liaison had been so pleasant, in part because it had all felt so transient. But what if that wasn't true? She could still convince Kellen to send her to Balter. Even if it took blackmail.

One way or another, she was going to escape her family.

CHAPTER

✦✦ 4 ✦✦

NIGHT FELL AS the train pulled into Korio, the last stop before it was due to climb into the mountains. To a Balterian train, Solozya's central caldera was empty land, home to nothing but the remnants of a dead empire—and from here, it would be a long, three-night journey between Pesca and Ealidor.

Dalton Rai lay flat on his stomach, thirty feet beyond the trainyard. For once, he wished he were thinner. The wheat stalks that camouflaged him were still tender with springtime. Next to him, Merrith wasn't helping. She shivered with cold, risking giving away their position even more than he did. On a damp night like this, she should have worn a coat. He planned to steal her one once they got to the east coast.

In the distance, the train hissed as the brakes released and the engine began its slow chug forward. Dalton eased himself up so he was propped on his arched toes, though he kept his back low. "You ready, Merri?" he whispered to her.

Merrith's whole body shook, but she still nodded as she got into a sprinting position. They'd planned this for so long and now they had one shot to get it right. They'd promised each other that if one of them missed the train, the other would jump off and stay behind too. But, once more, Dalton wondered if either of them would really give up on escaping Korio for the love of the other.

The engine drew closer and Dalton braced himself. The grind of the basalt engine grew louder, the slap of iron against iron a speeding heartbeat. As the train's nose passed, they both sprang. With any luck, the engineer never saw them.

Dalton launched himself forward. No looking back. He had to trust that Merrith was with him as he sprinted to keep pace with the speeding locomotive. Basalt dust from the grinders flew into his gasping mouth, but he fought the urge to cough. He couldn't afford any hesitation.

The train pulled further ahead, and he counted the carriages until the drab exterior of the luggage car came into view. He flung himself forward, closing his hand around a bar that ran along the exterior of the train. His shoulder wrenched as it bore the weight of his body being flung backward, but he kept his grip. The next seconds felt like years as he scrabbled to get his feet hooked on top of the carriage's waist rail.

With his weight on his feet and his chest pressed against the cold body of the train, he coughed hard to get the dust out of his lungs. Wind whipped the breath from his mouth as the train continued to gain speed, but he was part of it now. Bound towards better things. Unless…

"Merrith?" His voice came out as a croak as he twisted around, looking for her. Would it be safe to jump off the train at this speed if she hadn't made it? But a second later he spotted her, one carriage back, her arms wrapped around the rungs of a ladder. She'd grabbed hold of the caboose.

The sight sent energy surging back into his limbs. They would need to move fast, especially with her being so close to the train crew's accommodation. "You need to get to my carriage!" he called into the howling wind.

It was unlikely she heard him, but she nodded and pulled herself up the ladder, careful to keep her back below the sightline of the windows.

Dalton's climb was more precarious. He shuffled himself along the bar until he landed on the coupling, arms and legs aching. Carefully, he reached a hand into the exterior door and jiggled the handle. Locked. He swore under his breath. Now how was he supposed to get in? He would have to pull himself onto the roof and see if he could slip in through the trapdoor on top. But as he was formulating a plan, the door popped open.

He nearly flung himself from the train in that instant, but the face on the other side wasn't a guard or the conductor come to arrest him. It was Merrith.

He stared at her, dumbfounded, not quite taking in the grin on her face. "Some idiot left the door from the caboose open," she said. "Come on."

She grabbed his elbow before he had the presence of mind to let go of his handhold. It wasn't until she'd shut the door behind him and relocked it that he started to breathe more easily. They'd done it.

Stacks of fine trunks greeted them as they entered the luggage car. Dalton's fingers itched to pry them open and dig around for valuables, but he restrained himself. This would be their home for the next three nights and they needed to remain as inconspicuous as possible. He would have to wait until they were closer to their destination before helping himself to any goodies.

For now, he and Merrith nudged bags and suitcases this way and that until they carved out a narrow section along one of the walls for a hideout. They had just enough space to sit facing each other or to lie down, curled close together while they slept. Merrith unrolled a rough reed rug from her pack and spread it over the bare floor. It wasn't much, but it was enough.

"You want to eat tonight?" asked Dalton.

"I thought we agreed—" Merrith started, then stopped abruptly at the popping sound of someone unlocking the door that led to the caboose. Dalton scrunched a few inches lower. Had someone noticed them jumping onto the train?

But the footsteps came and went in a few seconds as the newcomer headed for the main passenger carriages. Dalton exhaled, resolving to get used to the sound. The Continental Rail employees would need to keep using the luggage car as a thoroughfare, but that didn't mean they were in danger. Not so long as they kept quiet.

Merrith let out a sigh as well, then carried on as if nothing had happened. "I thought we agreed we were going to save the food for tomorrow."

"You don't want to celebrate?"

"I told you. We shouldn't get cocky and eat our provisions early." Merrith focused on reshaping her pack so it resembled a pillow. "You're an idiot when you're hungry."

"So, you wouldn't want me to be an idiot tonight, would you?" Dalton grinned at her.

But Merrith wasn't having it. By Chanri, she had a scowl like a bear woken from a winter's sleep. "Don't you dare. If you go sneaking off—"

"I'm not going to go sneaking off!"

"The kitchens are off limits, you got that? Everything is off limits. No nicking passengers' scones or digging through their laundry. We stay where we are and we stay safe."

"So, what do you propose we do now instead?" Adrenaline pumped through his body. The thrill of jumping the train lingered and dared him to do something brave. Or foolish.

"Nothing." Merrith said flatly. "We wait."

"Nnnnngggg." He flopped onto the comfort of the old rug. By Chanri, it was going to be a long three days. Still, he wouldn't have traded Merrith being here for all the scones on the train. She was the closest thing he had to family.

They didn't have much to amuse themselves, but Merrith pulled out a knife and a small block of wood. Dalton's own whittling sat untouched in his bag, though it was pleasant enough to listen to the soft scrape of her blade against cedar. He was drifting off to sleep when the door opened again. Merrith's knife fell silent and Dalton's ears pricked.

"What was your name again, miss?"

Someone from the train company was leading a passenger into the carriage. Dalton and Merrith locked eyes. Passengers weren't supposed to be allowed in here during the journey. So much of their plan hinged on that. Dalton slid his elbows into position beneath his chest, ready to spring if they needed to flee—or fight.

"Kira. Kira Westwick, if you must know." The woman sounded tetchy. "It's a big crate. Nothing special to look at."

"Cargo, yes. Your section is this way." Boots drummed against the carriage floor as the Continental Rail employee led his companion to a spot on the other side. That was a lucky break. Dalton and Merrith hadn't tried hiding among the cargo crates. They were too heavy to move around.

"I see it." A new male voice filled the carriage.

A less lucky break. How many people were inside the luggage car now?

"Thank you, that will be enough," said the newcomer. "Miss Westwick and I can handle the situation from here."

"I'm afraid it's against regulation to allow you in here unaccompanied, Mr Braehurst."

"I said that will be enough." The man's voice took on a menacing note. "I assure you, my employer will compensate your passengers if any of their trinkets go missing."

In the silence that followed, Dalton crept onto his knees, ignoring the head shake Merrith gave him. He peeked around a trunk and tried to absorb the whole scene. All that was visible of the woman was her backside, but Dalton took note of her plaited blonde hair and that, unlike most highborn women, she wore trousers instead of a skirt. A man in a long black tailcoat commanded the rest of the room, his steely gaze fixed on a man wearing the distinctive red-braided jacket of a conductor.

The *conductor*. Whoever these passengers were, they were important enough for the conductor to be seeing to them.

Merrith smacked Dalton's thigh and he dropped back down. He would have to content himself with listening. They would be in a kettle full of trouble if the bloody conductor caught them.

"Very well, sir," the conductor stammered. "I'll wait for you outside."

"Good man." The gentleman in tails had won.

There were a few moments of silence as the conductor vacated the carriage. Once the door had shut, the woman cleared her throat in a scoffing *harrumph*. "Did you really have to make the man wet himself, Jarvie?"

"Open the box," commanded the man.

"On whose orders?"

"Mine."

"I don't work for you, Jarvie." Her voice was like clouded quartz—rich and beautiful, but with a hint that it held the darkest of memories. "I've got a very short list of people I'm allowed to show my wares to and you're not on it."

"You want me to report back to the boss that you were difficult?"

"Selnick knows I'm difficult. What I don't want him thinking is that I'm weak. Then he'll send even more of his goons to try and bully me."

Selnick? Dalton's mouth fell open and next to him Merrith softly gasped, then slapped her hands over her mouth. The pair—Jarvie and Kira, was it?—were too caught up in their own attempts to intimidate each other to hear something on the other side of a rattling train carriage, but Dalton now wished he hadn't been brazen enough to look at them. It was one thing to be arrested by the conductor, another thing altogether to get caught eavesdropping on the plans of the biggest crime lord in Balter. Magnus Selnick controlled everything from contraband Halgyric mist to solozite-loaded cannons, and every illegal thing in between. His name was as well-known in the empire as any of the Lords' Council.

"Smart girl," Jarvie said.

"Why are you following me, anyway? Is Selnick worried I don't know how to catch a train?"

"Maybe my timing is convenient."

"Ah, then you're here for someone else." Kira's footfalls drew a little closer to Dalton's hideout, which meant she'd come closer to Jarvie.

Curiosity ate at Dalton, but he fought his instinct to jump up and watch them.

"I'll make you a deal," she said. "You tell me which poor sap you're tailing, and I'll open the box for you."

Another proposition, another silence. And, like the conductor, the man called Jarvie chose to leave. "It seems I've said too much. A pleasure doing business, Miss Westwick."

"Isn't it always?" She followed him out the door. "Sleep well, friend. Let me know if you want to meet for breakfast in the morning."

"Not for all the gold on this train, Kira."

Once again, the carriage door swung shut and Dalton's muscles relaxed. Merrith shuddered, rubbing her arms to soothe herself. "We have to get off this train. If they find out that we heard—what are you doing!?"

Dalton threw himself over their suitcase fortress. "Making sure I don't forget which box they were talking about."

"Get back here!"

"In a minute." The crate in question bore a strip of green paint down the side. Was that Selnick's mark? Something like that would explain how Jarvie knew the box on sight. It was nailed shut, so Dalton silently thanked that Kira woman for winning the argument. Opening it would have required a crowbar, and he and Merrith hadn't been far from where the tools hung on the wall. Perhaps they should relocate?

"What if the conductor comes back? He's going to want to check they didn't steal anything. We have to get off the train!" Merrith hissed.

Dalton surveyed the box a little longer, kicked it, then wished he hadn't. Whatever was inside was incredibly heavy and the crate didn't budge an inch.

"Dalton!"

"Sorry, Merri." He crawled back into their nest, careful not to shift the surrounding luggage. "I dunno. I think we're fine. I'm guessing the conductor knows they're tied to Selnick and he's got no interest in sticking his nose into something that could get him in trouble."

"Unlike you."

"Well, it might be worth something."

"That money wouldn't be worth the trouble. This whole trip. I don't know, I…" Merrith was still rubbing her arms, but it didn't help her relax.

Dalton climbed back into their hiding place, embraced her, then stroked her arm. She curled into him, leaning her head on his shoulder. "I can't believe you talked me into this."

"It's for the best, Merri. There're jobs in Ealidor. Better ones than we've ever had."

"With our luck, we'll probably end up dead in a mine somewhere."

Maybe. Perhaps the work would be hard and pay little, but jobs weren't the real reason he was going. He'd taken pains not to mention this to Merri, but he had no interest in dying in a mine, working for a few measly finos. Something deeper called to him. Out east, there were people. *Their* people.

Balter had started to expand its borders from the foothills around Korio into the mountains more than a century ago, displacing those who'd lived there for thousands of years. Dalton didn't know enough of his ancestors' names to count back all those generations, but he still knew his lineage. Caldera Peoples were what the Balterians called those like him, but that empty wilderness used to hold so much more than a caldera. Rencha—

the last great empire—had grown up around the volcano at the heart of the continent. It had been the source of all Rencha's power and, ultimately, its downfall. Three hundred years ago, the Great Eruption destroyed its cities, scattering the survivors across the mountains.

No one knew what angered the great Soloz inside his volcano or why he'd destroyed the only people brave enough to worship him. It was a hard-learned lesson—Soloz offered power, not protection. Since then, most Renchans had worshipped Chanri and the other Glyn Folk who'd never done them wrong, but the damage was already done. Fragments were all that remained of Rencha, and Balter had been only too happy to finish the job, crushing anyone in its path as it spread across the continent.

Fifty years ago, Balter had conquered Ealidor. The old city was shelled to rubble with solozite cannons, but plenty of people escaped into the hills. And then the Lords' Council built this damn train line, right through the heart of a land that meant nothing to them but was home to the Renchans. Dalton and Merri's ancestors died fighting for Korio half a dozen generations ago. But out east? There were still skirmishes. Still hope.

Dalton's fist closed around a small shard of wood that hung from a leather strap around his throat—a sliver of petrified pine, sacred to Chanri. Even dead, it would live forever. He knew his fate. Better to die with hope than eke out a living in fear. But he didn't say so to Merrith. All she wanted was to survive and that was why she needed him. Without her, he'd be dead by now. And without him, she wouldn't ever live.

CHAPTER

+ + 5 + +

"BUT WHAT IF I flush and we're going over a bridge? Then what happens?" Rae gripped her mother's hand until her fingers ached. This was madness. Absolutely unthinkable.

"I already told you. It lands on the tracks." Ma was not taking the situation seriously. "Please, Rae. There's a line forming."

"But there're holes between the tracks! And on a bridge, what if— what if it fell through? It could hit something." Sometimes trains went over rivers, didn't they? And sometimes people rowed boats beneath bridges, too. Would the gods come down and smite her if her poop landed on someone's head? It could happen. No matter what Ma said about statistics and chances, logic said it *could* happen.

"We're not over a bridge. Go before you make yourself sick." Ma shoved her towards the toilet, but Rae braced her hands on either side of the stall. "You can't hold it for three days."

Rae's stomach did another flip. She looked to Ma for sympathy but got nothing but a stern jab into the stall. With a scowl, Rae slammed the door shut behind her.

Who would have thought a first-class train would be such a barbaric place? It didn't matter that the toilets were made of fine porcelain or that one lavatory carriage had twice as many as the whole floor in her apartment building. There was no plumbing on the train. These were toilets that led to nowhere.

Rae climbed onto the toilet and put her hands over her eyes so she didn't have to watch herself use the thing. She'd held out for as long as possible, even sleeping through the night without any accidents. But Ma wouldn't let her have breakfast until she'd done her business. What perfect torture! And to think people chose to spend holidays here.

After she finished, Rae scuttled out and Ma took her turn inside. There were people jockeying for a stall, so Rae went to stand outside the door to the ladies' lavatory. It didn't seem like a significant decision. She had stood around waiting for Ma countless times before. But as she idled and reflected on the horrors of plumbing-free trains, *just in case* caught up with her.

She hadn't been sure what to expect when Ma described the man they needed to watch out for, but he was too strange to go unnoticed. He really *was* that pale. With his height and ridiculous sandy hair, he looked like some ancient frost giant that had wandered out of the illustrations in *Lives of the Witches*. He dressed in a modern, pinstriped suit but clearly wasn't fooling anyone. Rae wasn't alone in staring. Several women watched him as he cut through the crowd.

Rae stifled a cry and ducked behind the safety of a nearby stranger as the man drew near. Was he looking for Ma? She braced herself for him to turn towards the ladies' lavatory and confront them right there, but he carried on down the train towards the sleeping carriages.

"If you wake me this early for breakfast tomorrow, I'm flinging you off the train, Morel," he groused to the man next to him, taking his time whenever he reached a vowel and stretching out the sound. Oh, so *that* was what a northern accent sounded like.

"Really? Whose bloody fault was it you woke up with a hangover?" said the other fellow, who had the same lolloping manner of speech.

They passed by without stopping and Rae's mind whizzed. Were they both after Ma, or just the sandy-haired man? She wasn't sure she could bear it if there were two villains on the train. Though if he *was* about to throw the other man overboard, there would soon be only one.

The door to the lavatory clicked open and Ma was at her side. "Ready for breakfast, sweetheart?"

Rae grasped Ma's hand and followed her numbly into the dining carriage. What would Ma think when she told her what she'd seen? Words failed Rae for long enough that a waiter had them seated before she could gather her thoughts.

Around them, the other passengers tucked into piles of eggs, sausages, and fried tomatoes. Her stomach roiled at the smell. What if she told Ma about the sandy-haired man and she immediately marched them off the train? What if they never got to eat breakfast at all?

It wasn't a real holiday. That much had been clear for a while. But it still broke Rae's heart that the good bits were slipping away so quickly. She wanted to pretend they belonged here for a little while longer.

The waiter brought Ma a coffee and Rae a glass of orange juice. Rae glugged down half of it, barely appreciating the sweet, tangy taste. Then her throat caught around some ragged floating bits and she gagged. Did all orange juice have solids in it? This was her first glass.

"Easy does it." Ma took the cup from Rae and set it back neatly on the table. "We have plenty of time to enjoy ourselves."

"Oh."

"How do you like the view?" Ma pointed out the window that adjoined their table. "I bet if we watch, we'll see a hawk flying over the mountains."

"Maybe." Rae stared out as well. When she'd fallen asleep the night before, they had still been in the outskirts of Western Balter, all flat farmlands and river deltas. Sometime in her slumber, they had climbed into the clouds. The dining carriage's large windows let in the spring sunshine, rising over the mountains. Growing up in Pesca, the mountains only existed in legends to Rae, but none of those tales had prepared her for the reality of this place. Here, there were rocks bigger than parliament; trees taller than the highest apartment building.

The sight was beautiful, but a shiver stole down her spine. What if Ma made them get off the train? How would they survive out here on the caldera, away from cities and water that came through pipes? And to think she'd been worried about train toilets a minute ago.

"Sweetheart, you're being very quiet. Is everything all right?"

It wasn't fair. Ma could always sniff out when Rae was hiding something.

"Well... um." Rae's eyes stayed glued to the window. She imagined herself teetering on the edge of those mountains. Another word and she'd slip off the ledge. A small confession and this whole dreamy world would come tumbling down.

But the waiter saved her, arriving with a menu tucked under his arm. "Ready to order?"

"I'm not hungry," said Ma. "Rae, what did you want?"

At a nearby table, a gentleman dug into a plate of waffles piled with cream and strawberries. Even the food was grander on this train than back in Pesca. "Could—could I have that?" asked Rae.

"Honey, maybe something a little smaller?" Ma said.

"I can speak to the chef about a children's portion," the waiter volunteered.

"That would be perfect," said Ma, though Rae didn't agree. "What will that cost?"

"Don't worry, Ma'am, it's taken care of," said the waiter, gathering their menus.

"Excuse me?" Ma placed a hand on the waiter's elbow. The night before, they hadn't bothered with the dining carriage, staying inside their sleeping compartment to eat sandwiches Ma had packed herself.

"Everything is to be deferred to the tab of an anonymous patron." The waiter threw her a wink. "Let me know if you would like something besides coffee."

The waiter hurried away while Ma gaped at him. The sandy-haired man had struck again.

Ma craned her neck, as if she thought someone might pop up from behind a table. Her hand closed over the quartz crystal that hung from her necklace. She even began to rise from the table. "Rae, sweetheart. Do you think you could eat nicely by yourself while I—"

"You're looking for him, aren't you?" Rae asked.

Ma sat back down at the table, leaning closer to Rae. "Pardon?"

"That man. He's..." Rae didn't want to speak the awful truth, but she wanted to lie even less. "He *is* here. I saw him."

The flush in Ma's face grew stronger. "You're sure it was him?"

"I saw him outside the lavatory. He walked by." Now that the words were out, Rae's hands stopped shaking, but she could have cried for the waffles and every other pleasant thing she was about to lose. "It was like you said. He even talks in a funny way."

"Did he approach you? Did he talk to you?" Ma reached across the table, grabbing Rae's hands.

"No. He didn't notice me." Why would one of Ma's gentlemen want to talk to her? They never did. Was he some sort of child kidnapper? But that didn't make sense. Why would Ma be given tickets by a child kidnapper?

Ma sucked her lips in all the way. If they weren't in public, she would have absolutely started shouting. For now, she kept her composure. Even though it wasn't close to the most important matter at hand, Rae couldn't stop her next question from tumbling out.

"Do we still get to eat breakfast?"

"Of course." Ma blinked. "I'm sorry, sweetheart. Did I frighten you? No, everything is fine. We're on holiday. Have all the breakfast you want."

"Thank you."

As they waited for Rae's breakfast to arrive, Ma grabbed her bag and rifled through it until she'd found a bottle of perfume. It was one she had brewed herself at the kitchen stove, using lavender oil mixed with some fancy mineral water. She always chanted strange words in a language Rae didn't recognise as she made it. Ma called the perfume her lucky charm. Gentlemen would jump at the chance to help her when she was wearing it.

When the waiter returned with Rae's waffles, Ma flashed him her brightest smile yet. "I've been thinking. I'll have the eggs benedict, if it isn't too much trouble."

"Of course, m'lady!" The waiter gave her a ridiculous, flourishing bow. Lucky charm perfume to the rescue.

"And if you don't mind…" Ma placed her hand on his arm and the waiter beamed back. "…after breakfast, I'll need directions to the compartment where Kellen Linde is sleeping."

+ ✦ +

Later that evening

Waking up hungover was among the least of Kellen's concerns, even if Davina had scowled at him the whole day. Morel had also been quick to pick up on the cues, and so had grumbled at him at every opportunity. Kellen still hadn't determined if this was because his siblings were genuinely angry with him or simply annoyed he hadn't thought to share the alcohol.

If they were worried he would arrive in Halgyr an inconsolable mess, they didn't need to be. Kellen excelled at picking his moments. Here, separated from the embassy and the Halgyric court, no one needed him. But as soon the train pulled into Ealidor, the court would doubtless send a delegation to meet them, and he would be ready. Kellen did his job and he did it well. Allowing himself the occasional moment of inebriation shouldn't be too much to ask.

Or so he'd thought. Now, as he pulled out his brandy for the second night in a row, a whisper of worry soured the taste of his drink. He'd made so few mistakes. How had this one turned out to be so bloody massive?

For a while, he tried to work. Morel had arrived in Pesca not just with news about their father's health but also with stacks of communications from the Halgyric court. Uncle Sergei was proposing a new tax on basalt imports, Dame Vedka wanted him to sign off the budget for the Gulwick's Day festival, and

Duke Maurice had questions about securing the future line of succession now the current king's health was failing.

Kellen couldn't stop himself from laughing when he read that one. The duke had no idea what he was asking.

A moonless night descended over their journey. Kellen lit his lamp and stripped down to his undershirt, letting the cool night air prickle his skin. A wise man would have immediately retired to bed, but instead he poured another glass of brandy.

His private compartment afforded him a small desk and so he sat there, tumbling into the same stupor in which he'd spent the previous night. He pushed aside the court documents and reached into his pocket, fumbling past an old envelope until his shaking fingers closed around two slips of paper. Before leaving Pesca, he'd had his steward at the embassy pull up every public record on Rae Freath. She was only seven years old, so perhaps he shouldn't have been surprised that her life could be reduced down to these two scraps. One was a school registration that indicated she was receiving some manner of education, thank the gods. The other was her birth record, the information overwhelming in its brevity.

```
Name: Rae Freath
Sex: Female
Mother: Genna Freath
Father: Unknown
```

What a marvellous lie. No, not unknown, just uninformed. Kellen could lose himself for hours, staring at that final line. How was he ever going to fix this?

A sharp rap on the door drew him away from his musings. He

swallowed another mouthful of brandy and recorked his bottle. What did Morel want now? Maybe he could talk his brother into a night-time drink and avoid another lecture from him. The knock sounded again and he grunted, getting to his feet.

"Coming!" He threw open the door, and only realised he hadn't bothered to refasten his belt when Genna's eyes immediately flew to the gap between his undershirt and trousers.

"Soloz!" He fumbled to tuck in his shirt. "Sorry, Genna, I wasn't expecting—"

She shouldered past him, entering his chamber. "Close the door."

Kellen hesitated. If Morel caught him with a woman inside his compartment, he would expect an explanation. And Kellen had no intention of exposing his history with Genna to anyone.

"I said close the door. We need to talk."

"I'm not what you would call ready to receive visitors," Kellen pointed out, hoping she would take the hint and leave. They needed to talk, yes, but not now. Not when he was half a bottle in and barely dressed.

Genna scanned him from head to toe. She didn't even attempt to hide her perusal. "I've seen you in less," she said.

He shut the door. "Fine. What do you want to talk about?" he asked.

"Shouldn't you put a sealing spell in place?" She moved slowly around the compartment, running a gloved hand over the small oak desk before taking a seat in his chair.

"Ah… yes."

Kellen took his time fiddling with the vials. It gave him a chance to collect his thoughts and remind himself that, yes, he'd meant for this to happen. They *had* to talk. As much as he dreaded this conversation, it was the whole reason he'd put them on the same damn train.

He finished the incantation and the mist sealed off the compartment. Genna watched him, completely unfazed. When he'd showed her this spell back during their university days, she'd been enchanted by his people's magic, so desperate for him to teach her how to work mist as well. Clearly, it was nothing but a trick to her now, and an old one at that.

Everything about her had changed. Back in university, she'd worn her hair long and flowing, as she hadn't been well-enough versed in the styles of the day to successfully spool it on top of her head like the wealthier girls did. There had been an air of naivety to Genna, coupled with a ferocious hunger to fix that problem. He'd loved that drive in her.

Clearly, she'd figured out the ways of the world since then. Her hair was razored to perfection, a bob skimming the edge of her jaw. Her figure was a little fuller than the present fashion allowed for, but the silk gown she wore had been cut both to emphasise her waist and to give the illusion of the boxier, fringed dresses Davina favoured. She'd kohled her eyes and painted her lips before meeting him and he wished he hadn't noticed. How he wished she didn't hold every card in this awful game they were playing.

With the incantation set, he dropped onto his bunk across from her. The overhang for the luggage compartment above his bed was too low for him to sit up straight, so he hunkered over and reached out to grab his bottle of brandy from behind her. His bare arm brushed against her shoulder and she shrank away, heat flooding her cheeks. *Ha.* Maybe he wasn't as helpless in this encounter as he'd thought.

"So, what can I help you with?" he asked, taking a drink straight from the bottle.

"How long have you been drinking?"

"Given the circumstances, not nearly long enough," he said.

She scoffed, unappreciative of the quip.

"How rude of me. I should have offered you a drink too."

"You can stop with the pleasantries. I'm not here out of choice," she said. "I'm assuming you want to see me. Otherwise I can't fathom why you've followed me onto this train."

"Actually, it's less a matter of me following you and more a matter of *you* accepting *my* help." He set the bottle down. "Or are you forgetting that you asked me for tickets?"

Her flush came back. "I asked for help to get out of Pesca. And I made it clear that, in return, I'd never bother you again."

"You know, it's strange. I remember that conversation differently."

Their encounter in the embassy had been brief but brutally unforgettable. Two days earlier, his secretary had brought him word that an old friend had asked to see him for lunch. No, not a friend. *Genna Freath.*

He'd been swamped with work, getting his affairs in order before he left Balter for what was bound to be his father's funeral. He couldn't really spare the time, but it was *Genna*. He hadn't heard from her in eight years. The more he thought about it, the more wonderful it sounded. He could take a break from his papers, catch up with her for an hour, then return to work, revitalised.

Instead, she arrived with a tiny photograph of herself holding a girl who looked strikingly like Davina had as a child—the same dark hair and large eyes, except with Genna's round nose. She didn't even need to speak the words "she's ours" before Kellen understood. Then came the threats.

Kellen rolled the bottle of brandy between his hands. "You insinuated that if I didn't get you out of Balter, you were going to expose me as the heir to the Halgyric throne," he reminded her.

If she did that, his whole family would be removed from power. And, for that reason, he'd never revealed who he really was to anyone in Balter. Not even her. How in Soloz's cursed name had she figured out his identity?

"Well, if you think I'm blackmailing you, then why are you forcing the issue?" she asked. "I don't want to be involved in your politicking. I promise, Kellen. If you leave us alone, I won't ever—"

"Because you've got my bloody daughter!" Brandy and hurt pulsed through him, making words he'd never utter under normal circumstances tumble out. "Did you know I saw her? When you boarded the train, she went tearing off and you had to chase after her, and I was *there*, Genna. I was in the dining carriage and…"

Kellen barely caught himself before he dissolved into a blubbering mess. Up until that moment when they'd boarded, he'd wondered if Genna might have played some elaborate ruse on him. Doctored the photo, perhaps. But then Rae had been there, bouncing like a grasshopper. *His child.* Yet he couldn't reach out and hug her.

He struggled for air. How drunk was he? Or was something else going on? He took a deep breath and his eyes watered. "Genna, you aren't wearing something, are you?"

She looked down at the sumptuous evening gown she had on. "Pardon?"

"A misting vial. Do you have one on you?" Now he was paying attention, he realised the air tasted completely wrong. There was more than the usual sulphurous smell of the sealing mist he'd cast. Something else lurked in the compartment, something blended with lavender and— "Is it… did you put something in your perfume?"

Genna's cheeks flushed. "Damn it, Kellen."

"I knew it! Gods. Now you're trying to drug me." Her perfume had clearly been mixed with muddling haze. Admittedly, he'd done similar things to Balterian dignitaries in the past. Of course, it became less effective the moment someone realised they were being muddled, but he was impressed Genna was bold enough to even try.

If he really wanted to be free of its effects, though, he needed ruemoss. He slid off his bunk and opened one of his trunks, digging around until he had the stringy lichen in hand.

"How is your perfume not muddling you?" Kellen asked. "You're wearing it right on your skin."

"It's a blend I designed myself," Genna said without meeting his eye. "It only affects men."

"Brilliant." He couldn't help but admire her ingenuity. "Targeted mist blends. That was your final project, wasn't it?"

"You remember?"

Kellen laughed. "You're many things, Genna. Forgettable isn't one of them."

Years ago, Genna had been his main competition in all their volchemistry classes. She'd even talked him into teaching her Halgyric mist concoctions, something he now regretted. He'd been such a cocky idiot at seventeen, thinking nothing would come of teaching a pretty girl how to brew mist.

She hunched lower in her chair. "Are you angry with me?"

"I don't know. This hardly changes things." He shrugged and swallowed the last of the ruemoss, all too used to the dry scrape of it against his throat. As the counter-spell took effect, another wave of realisation struck him. "Is that… is that how you figured it out?"

"Pardon?"

"Who I am." He'd attended a number of festivals in Balter. They held them whenever the Halgyric royals visited—or, more correctly, whenever they made their presence known. He always wore his mask and cast a muddling haze at those events, but if Genna had attended one, she'd have known enough to counter the haze's effects. "Did you come to a royal public appearance while taking ruemoss? I gave you some, didn't I?"

Genna nodded. "When you came back after the summer, you told me you had a work placement with the embassy. I was about five months along with Rae. I went to some silly parade and I took the ruemoss, only because I wanted to talk to you with a clear head. I thought you'd be working behind the scenes or…"

She broke off, dabbing her eyes gingerly so as not to smear her makeup. "And then there you were, in that ridiculous mask."

"How did you know it was me under—"

"Your hands." A half-smile broke through the gloom on her face. "I knew every inch of you. They were all I needed to see. And once I knew that, well…"

She gestured helplessly and some of Kellen's earlier rage died inside him. How betrayed she must have felt. He used to wonder what would happen if the girls he'd got involved with found out about his true rank. Would they become dizzy with glee, dreaming of marrying a prince? But he should have known Genna was too smart to believe in faerie tales. She'd have seen the real consequences of that revelation immediately.

He took his seat on the bunk again, drowning in how much that thought depressed him. When he'd come to Balter as a student,

Genna quickly became one of his closest friends. For most of that year, they'd swapped notes and argued over volchemical reactions. Nothing more. If only it had stayed that way.

Things changed when they went out drinking after mid-term exams. He'd kissed her, thinking she'd find it funny rather than romantic. But then she'd kissed him back and he couldn't bring himself to stop. Not for days. Not for weeks. It only ended because he headed home to Halgyr at the end of term and she stopped responding to his letters. He'd honestly been relieved. The court would never have approved the match, no matter what his feelings were.

He'd let her go so casually. She had been right to spurn him.

"Genna, I know… well, you must have been upset when you found out that I…"

"Lied to me?"

"Yes, that," Kellen admitted. "But you should have told me about Rae. I would have provided for her. For *both* of you. Maybe we couldn't have been together, but we could at least—"

"Well, you'll have to forgive me for not knowing that." There was a sharp snap in her tone that showed, even now, she didn't regret her decision. "I did what I needed to in order to protect my daughter. You're a prince, Kellen. Prince of the most secretive nation in Solozya. Your people erase memories all the time. Why not unwanted children?"

"You know I'm not like that."

"I don't know anything about you."

That wasn't true. She'd known him better than his own family at one time, but what could he possibly say now to convince her? They lapsed into a tense silence, broken only when the train lurched abruptly, nearly tossing Genna out of her chair. Instinctively, Kellen reached out and caught her shoulder, supporting her so she didn't tumble to the floor.

"What was that?" She winced at his touch as she repositioned herself in the chair.

"Hard to say. Trains have bumps."

"Rae might have woken up." Genna bit her lip, clearly weighing her options. "I'd like to think we've cleared the air. Can we both move on with our lives now?"

"Cleared the air?" Kellen bristled again. "Is that all you think is wrong? I still haven't met my own bloody child! You think I'm going to let her go so easily?"

"You will if you know what's good for you and that precious crown of yours," she fired back. "Don't test me, Kellen. I'll do what I think is best for my child—"

"*Our* child."

"And if that means telling people what I know—"

"Look, I know what you said. If I leave you the hell alone, you'll do the same for me. I agreed to your terms under duress back in the embassy. But, now that we're here, let me make myself clear."

"Yes?"

"I *will* pursue every legal avenue available to me to get access to my daughter. And I assure you, I have several. You won't be able to run, Genna. Least of all from me. And, let's be honest, you wouldn't have asked for *my* help if you weren't running from someone else."

The colour drained from her face. "That isn't your business."

"If it concerns Rae, it damn well is!" The anger he'd worked so hard to stifle throughout their confrontation bubbled out. "Did you really think so little of me? You assumed I would thank you for disappearing again and never letting me meet my own child? I'm not that kind of man and I am not that kind of father!"

"Oh, stop pretending!" She leapt to her feet, towering over him as he sat on the bunk. "You're no father. You think you can buy your way into her life with train tickets and free meals in the dining carriage? You're pathetic."

"Maybe I am, but it's all you'll let me give her." He got to his feet as well. "By the gods, Genna! If you wanted me to keep acting like an ignorant ass, you should have let me be one!"

She threw her shoulder into him, forcing him out of the way so she could reach the door.

"Genna, *please*. Wait—"

"I don't know why I thought it would be any use talking to you." She took hold of the door handle, then spun back around, levelling a finger at him. "You're going to leave us alone. Understand? Leave me and my daughter alone, or I will tell your court what I know. I don't want to hurt you, Kellen, but so help me—"

Before she could finish her threat, something ripped the night open.

Kellen flew backward, his head slamming into the luggage compartment above his bed. Genna toppled towards him and he barely caught her before they both collided with the floor.

His ears rang with a sound that pierced every register, from the low, deafening rumble of an avalanche up to the screaming hiss of metal tearing apart. His eyes swam, barely focused enough to see the suitcases tumbling out of the luggage rack towards them. Genna screamed. He tucked his arms around her and rolled them both out of the way. One of the bags exploded open right where their heads had been.

The compartment bucked until the room tipped on its side as the carriage skipped off the rails. The ground tore against the train siding as they skidded to a stop, jostling Kellen's throbbing body up and down. Glass shattered and either brandy or blood trickled into his ear.

For what felt like hours, but was probably only a minute, he lay shaking in the overturned carriage, Genna gasping for air in his arms. Discordant echoes reverberated through him. Every muscle in his body was tensed or bruised. Gradually, his ears stopped ringing and he became aware of his other senses, including the lingering smell of smoke.

"We have to get out of here." He tried to push himself off the ground, but his head span so badly that he almost vomited.

Genna's grip tightened around his hands, which hopefully meant she could hear him.

"There's been—" But what had happened? Had one of the basalt engines malfunctioned?

Genna coughed and streaks of tears ran down her cheeks. "Rae."

Rae.

Kellen dropped Genna, more abruptly than he meant to, then scrabbled past his overturned desk to reach the door, now hanging overhead in the fallen carriage. The lock had twisted stuck in the explosion, but he pounded at it until he knocked the door free.

The gods couldn't be that cruel, could they? Making him a father, only to take that away in a second? If he lived while that little girl died—

He had to find her. He hoisted himself through the door, into the hallway of the overturned carriage. All around him rang the shrieks of other passengers. There wasn't enough room to stand, so he pulled himself forward on his hands and knees over splintered wood and broken glass. His ears strained, desperate to pick up the cry of a child.

No matter what Genna said, he was *not* that kind of father. Kellen knew what it meant to lose a parent, not just to death, but to indifference. That Genna expected him to be no better than his own father was more than insulting. It was horrifying. After all, what if she was right?

What if he'd brought his child here only to die?

· PART TWO ·

THE SURVIVORS

CHAPTER

✦ 6 ✦

THE WITCH WOKE to the sound of her own scream. Smoke burned down her throat, yet she couldn't stifle the howl that pulsed through her ribs. It was as if she had been gouged in the chest with a hot poker, tipped with a charge of both life and death.

It seemed an eternity before her breath ran out and she was forced to inhale. A cough rattled her and she gasped for cleaner air, but there was none to be had in this ashen, hellish nightmare. Where was she? Night enveloped her, riddled with a distant chorus of moans. The witch ran her hand across the ground, but the stone texture beneath her fingertips made nothing clearer. Something terrible had happened. She could taste that in the burning air, but what?

She searched her memory for clues, but everything before her scream was a meaningless blur. All she knew was that this place couldn't possibly be safe. She pushed herself off her stomach and the ground creaked and twisted beneath her. Not so solid after all. This was ridiculous. If she wanted to get out of this strange place, she needed light.

The witch crawled forward, searching for something useful,

until she found a splintered wooden beam. How did this work again? Her hands held power, but how did she unlock it? She closed her palm over the end of the shaft and thought of fire. Surely this would give her a torch.

Immediately, the stick snapped to life. But so too did everything around her. Flames blossomed on every surface—the bedsheets, the overturned suitcases, the broken door. And on the man in the berth across from her. He howled as the fire burned him awake.

She screamed and plunged her hands into the flames, snuffing them as quickly as they had begun.

"I'm sorry! I didn't know..." Her stammering broke off as she realised with a wave of horror just how much she didn't know. Not that he was there. Or who he was. Or that using her powers would cause all that trouble. By Ramona, she didn't even remember her own name, though somehow the name of her goddess rang through her. Like a whisper, Ramona's voice seemed to hiss.

Congratulations, daughter. You're a witch. Good luck figuring the rest out.

Her breath grew ragged with worry. Her only hope of understanding what had happened lay in the man lying in front of her, so she crawled towards him. "Who are you?" she demanded, trying to feel brave.

He coughed, smoke still lingering from the blaze she'd caused. His features were *almost* familiar. Even singed at the tips, she recognised his stubby hair and blunted nose. He blinked into the gloom and she was met by sharp hazel eyes. Yes, the way he stared at her. That had meaning.

He cleared his throat, focusing on her face. "Who are you? Where's Davina?"

Damn it all.

The witch's head lolled backward, her body convulsed. All this time, she had waited to be free, and now it was already over.

+ ✦ +

Davina woke in a cold sweat, Morel hovering over her, shaking her arm.

"Davina? Oh, gods, please. *Please* wake up. Chanri and Tywith, please let my sister—"

She groaned and he let out a whoop, drawing her upright into a one-armed hug. "You're alive!"

"Of course I am," she muttered, blinking into the darkness. But her whole body ached, and why were they lying on the ground in the dark? There were lights on the train. Or there should have been. Her vision slowly cleared, and with it the severity of their situation. The whole carriage was on its side, trapping them against the exterior window. The smell of smoke filled the room, and nearby people were screaming.

Davina fought her own urge to panic. "What happened?"

"You fell over. One minute you were sitting up and then you went down. I thought something hit you or—" Morel sputtered out.

"I fell over and *this* happened to the train?" Davina gestured around them, then wished she hadn't. Her shoulder felt as though she'd dislocated it.

"No, I meant a second ago." Morel scooted backward on his knees so they could look at each other. "You came to see me after that fire almost got us. You looked all funny in the dark and I didn't recognise you and... don't you remember?"

Her eyes flicked from his face to the blackened edges of the bedsheets, then instinctively down to the stony floor beneath them. Something told her that had mattered too, but how? "No," she said. "I don't remember. Morel, move back."

He obediently slid a little further away so she could examine the rock. Had the carriage's side been ripped off? They'd clearly fallen off the tracks. She traced her hand along the rock until she reached a window frame, now filled with shattered glass. And beneath the glass, scrubby grass.

"Morel! Something happened to the train." Idiot! What use was pointing out the obvious? But she didn't know how to describe what she was seeing. "I mean, look at the stone! It joins all the way up to the frame. We're not on the ground. Something turned the train to—to stone?"

She stared at him, waiting for him to scoff. With a hard frown, he copied what she had done a moment ago, following the veins of rock until they reached the window. He paused over the sight of grass sticking up through the shattered pane, while everything else beneath them was made of solid rock.

"Move," he said.

She retreated as far back as she could into the corner of her bunk. It was too difficult to step around him in these cramped quarters. He traced one of the veins in the rock until it reached a spot right above her pillow where there was a shallow indentation. He laid his palm over the spot, covering it completely. Several veins in the rock radiated out from that point.

"Give me your hand." His voice shook as though he had seen a spectre.

"Why?"

"Please, your hand. I need to see—no, your right hand."

She reached towards him and he guided her fingers into place. He placed her flattened palm into the hollow, like she'd seen him do earlier. It fitted perfectly and little canyons encased each of her fingers. Was she imagining or remembering the feeling of placing her hand against the wall? Of something like a volcano rushing through her?

Her heartbeat rose into her ears. "Morel?"

"I need you to get out of the way. Squeeze past me."

A shiver stirred her skin. Was it cold tonight, or was everything starting to sink in? The train tilted and groaned beneath her as she staggered over the fallen debris and into Morel's overturned bunk. The door to the hallway loomed out of reach above her. How were they going to get up there? Morel would have to give her a leg-up, but could she pull him after her?

A crack pierced their tiny room and Morel swore as something flew back at him.

"What happened?" Davina shrieked, then saw the gun he held with his spare hand, spent basalt dust trailing out the back. "What did you do?"

"The best I could to destroy the evidence," said Morel as rock dust drifted onto her bunk, the telltale crevice blown open. "We have to get out. Before someone sees you here."

"Whatever for?" She wanted out as much as he did, but the way he said it made it sound as though it wasn't because of the smoke filling the carriage.

Morel stashed his gun in a side holster. He must have slept with it beneath his pillow. "Because I think you destroyed the train."

"No," Davina sputtered. "That's ridiculous. I wouldn't, and besides which, I could never—"

"That's the problem." Morel reached up and jiggled the handle of the door above them. Stuck. "No one knows what you're capable of."

CHAPTER

✦✦ 7 ✦✦

Lord Ambrose Carey struggled to breathe, his back throbbing from where he'd landed on the thin mountain grass. Stars spun above him. So many more stars than he'd ever seen before. They were far from the city lights of Pesca now.

He'd been out in the observation carriage when the engine went. Bright-blue flame had engulfed the locomotive. When the carriages started to jump on the rails, it had been as if a giant had struck the train, flinging him into the open wilderness.

He staggered to his feet, ears still ringing from the impact. Fire burned in the distance, where the train had ground to a smouldering stop. Carey tried to run, but his knees jittered with each step on the uneven ground. As he neared the overturned train, debris littered his path, mostly trunks and crates spat out through a hole in the back of the luggage car. There was no sight of the caboose anywhere.

"HEY!" a voice in the distance cried out, and Carey turned to see a man in a soldier's uniform sprinting towards him. It was the same idiot he'd rescued Miss Linde from the night before.

Miss Linde. Was she safe? What about Lord Drawley and Emeth, for that matter?

"You there! Are you injured?" The captain drew closer.

Carey stifled a cough. Dust from the basalt grinders drifted in the air, mixing dangerously with the small fires burning in the brush around them. "A little winded, but—"

"Good." The captain pressed a crowbar into his hands.

Carey fumbled the heavy tool. "What am I supposed to do with this?"

"People are still trapped inside," said the captain.

"So?"

"So, you're able-bodied! Get your ass in there, man! And if you see any of my men, tell them to find Captain Sewell."

"Right." Carey ran, if for no reason other than to avoid getting yelled at again.

A creaking overhead alerted him to the fact that a portion of the luggage car's roof was dangerously close to collapsing. He dodged around it, fighting a surprising sense of guilt. But no one would have been inside the luggage car. Surely he could leave that to crumble?

All along the length of the train, people were scrabbling to pull themselves out of windows or through holes punctured in the sides. The conductor stood alongside the smoking carriage, hollering at anyone who went past. Carey steered his path around him, eager to avoid another encounter with orders he didn't know how to fulfil.

The dining carriage burned furiously as basalt dust collected in a furrow where it had landed. As Carey tried to cut a wide berth around it, a boy in rags dashed out, stripping off his shirt. The boy screamed as he beat the garment against the ground, trying to extinguish the flames licking at his clothes and skin. The scent of burning flesh mingled with the ash in the air and Carey doubled over in a dry retch.

He kept running, ignoring the pain in his knees. Towards what, he couldn't say, but surely there was someone out here qualified to handle a tragedy. Where were the doctors and nurses? Did the train have medical officers? Considering what he'd paid for his ticket, he would have expected there to be someone, but no heroes emerged from the rubble.

He reached the carriage closest to the engine. The nose of the train was nothing but a twisted mass, the metal warped from the high heat of the explosion. There couldn't possibly be anyone alive in there. He was about to turn back when something struck him as odd about the chaos in front of him. The carriage closest to the engine was deformed, but not by fire. The wooden sides gave way to dark, black rock that extended along the entire carriage, encasing the side that had landed on the ground.

Carey took a cautious step. The rock went all the way to the front of the train, eventually merging with the engine. What in the name of the gods could have caused this?

Genna had to stack Kellen's desk and chair on top of each other before they could reach the doorway above her, and even then he'd had to pull her up after him. These damn luxury trains. If they had been riding something more economical, the compartments wouldn't have been so large and impossible to navigate.

Smoke from the engine filled the hallway, darkening the already impenetrable night. She had only her ears and memory to guide her. Kellen was several feet ahead of her.

"Rae is sleeping two cabins down," she called out.

"I know."

Of course he did. He'd bought the tickets, hadn't he? She'd been so furious when she realised how close together their compartments were to each other and that Kellen had managed to hide from her for a day and a half. Now, their proximity might save Rae's life.

She shouldn't have left her child. She never should have given in and gone to see him.

They reached the compartment and Kellen immediately began to wrench on the door, but the heat of the explosion had fused the hinges. The space was too cramped to kick it in either, no matter how hard they tried. Eventually, Kellen crawled towards the door that led to the next carriage.

"Where are you going?" Had he given up?

The carriages had been disconnected in the crash, so Kellen climbed out the door and onto the coupling. "Is anyone out there? I need help!" he shouted into the night. "You! Get over here!"

Genna turned back to the door, tracing her fingers along it. "Rae? Rae, can you hear me? We're going to get you out."

No response came. Genna swallowed but tears still leaked down her cheeks. If her daughter died on this godsforsaken train, she'd never forgive herself.

Kellen reappeared, dragging a man in a fancy tailcoat, who for some reason was carrying a crowbar. *A crowbar!*

"Do you know how to use—" Kellen began to ask.

The man shook his head, so, without another word, Kellen grabbed it. In a second he had it in the jammed door and raked back on it until the hinges squealed and broke. Genna dived into the open compartment, nearly toppling down into the cabin beneath before Kellen caught her shoulder.

"Please, let me," he said. "My arms are longer."

A new fear gripped her as she thought of him holding Rae for the first time. She'd spent years making sure they never met, but if her pride got in the way tonight and something worse happened...

"Fine." Genna moved out of the way and rubbed her tears away. "Rae! Rae, are you down there?"

"Mama?"

Bless the gods! Who or whatever protected her daughter, bless them. More tears ran down her cheeks, but she no longer cared. "I'm here, Rae. It's going to be all right."

"Grab my hand!" Kellen hooked his knees on either side of the door frame and dropped the rest of his body down into the compartment.

Genna heard rustling as he pushed aside fallen debris, then he let out a delirious laugh. "I think I've got her."

He pulled and a shrill scream sounded as he hauled Rae into the corridor.

"Mama! Mama!"

Genna tried to reach around and take her from him, but he held Rae fast. It wasn't worth fighting over. Not now. Instead, she smoothed out Rae's hair, feeling the cold sweat on her brow.

"Careful," Kellen said. "I think her arm's broken."

"You didn't pull it, did you?" Genna demanded.

"I don't know. We need to get out of here." He had to hunch over as he adjusted his body to hold the girl more safely. "Rae, I need you to hold onto my neck. Can you do that?"

She nodded, throwing her good arm around her his neck. Together, they crawled the length of the corridor, Genna at their heels. Outside, a brush fire had started, but Kellen ignored the flames and waited for her to climb down the coupling next to him. Before Genna could object, he grabbed hold of her hand and dragged her past the smouldering wreckage until they reached the shelter of a small grove of aspens.

Kellen laid Rae on the wet grass. Her eyes were fixed on him. Genna could worry about how to explain away his help in the morning. For now, they needed to survive the night.

"She needs a doctor," said Genna, carefully positioning Rae's fractured arm. During her volchemistry courses, she'd learned a few salves based on mountain plants, but what were the chances she'd find anything useful nearby? Did Continental Rail hire a doctor to oversee overnight routes?

Kellen got to his feet, his grip on Genna's fingers relaxing. She tightened her hold on him, jerking him back. "Where are you going?"

He dropped to his knees next to her. "I have to go back, Genna. My brother and sister are in there."

"Don't leave. Please Kellen, I need—"

"I'll try to find someone who knows how to set Rae's arm." He smiled at her, the way he always did when he was trying to smooth over bad news. The way he'd done at seventeen when he'd left her for the summer in Halgyr. Only now there was blood running down his temple from a cut above his right eye. She hadn't even noticed he was injured until now.

"I'll come back. I promise," he said. Their hands were still entwined and he pulled her towards him.

She was shocked at how easily she kissed him back. Her lips parted for his, like they had a memory all of their own, and her free hand flew to caress the line of his jaw. He tasted raw, a mix of the night's brandy, ash and sweat all mingled together. When he pulled away, she wasn't sure if she was more stunned it had happened or that it was already over.

What in Soloz's name had made him do that?

"There's a squad of soldiers. I—I think they brought nurses with them," said an awkward voice.

Kellen shot to his feet, whipping round to see who had followed them. It took Genna's eyes a second to focus on the figure a few feet away in the darkness. It was that idiot with the crowbar. He shrunk under Kellen's gaze. "A nurse could... help the child?"

Kellen nodded. "I'll send them to you, Genna."

"Thank you." She choked back her tears. Nurses should be enough, but some irrational part of her still wanted him to stay with her. "Go on then. Find your family."

Kellen took off, back towards the train. Genna returned to Rae, desperate to mask the flush spreading across her face.

Rae breathed raggedly and tears ran down her cheeks.

"Here." The gentleman bent down next to Genna, taking off his tailcoat and laying it over Rae's shivering form.

"Thank you." Genna said.

"Your husband is a brave man." His voice bore an embarrassing amount of awe.

In better circumstances, Genna would have laughed. "He's not..." Why was she bothering to explain herself to this man?

But he stared at her, waiting for her to go on.

"He's not brave, so much as reckless. He doesn't believe there's anything in this world he can't fix and that's what makes him such a damn fool."

The man chuckled, clearly getting the wrong message. Not that it mattered. "He'll be back. Now if you'll excuse me, there's someone I need to look for as well."

Genna nodded, relieved to be alone, and yet...

She squinted at the disintegrating train, hoping to spot Kellen in the madness, but he was too far away now. He was right. She should have let him stay an ignorant ass.

What trouble had they got themselves into now?

CHAPTER

✦ ✦ 8 ✦ ✦

At FIRST, THEY pulled bodies from the train. Then trunks and other supplies, to keep them from burning. It was more than the young acolyte riding the train could have prepared for. More than anyone could have prepared for.

Emeth worked silently in a line organised by Captain Sewell. A company of fifteen able-bodied men and women spent the night breaking open compartments where the locks had warped, then digging victims out from beneath fallen trunks and suitcases. Sometimes, he was lucky and found the occupants alive. Emeth would guide them north, to the sparsely forested hillside that sloped downwards from the tracks. They were somewhere high in the mountains of the continental spine that cut Solozya in two. Distant peaks flanked them in every direction. He couldn't be certain without a map, but if Emeth had to guess, he thought they must be within the central caldera. The crater surrounding the volcano's mouth was miles wide, but the inner geyser plain couldn't be too far off. A strange place for the gods to strand them.

Emeth took those with injuries to the centre of the camp, where a medical ward was forming around a pair of army nurses.

The conductor handed them the passenger list, so they could count survivors as more wounded came in. Mostly, they identified the dead by process of elimination.

To the east of them, the soldiers were digging a pit for the bodies.

Anyone lucky enough not to belong in either the medical ward or a grave was attempting to construct shelter out of the scrubby trees that ringed a forest clearing. Among the survivors was a dance troupe, led by famed acrobat Penny Aldridge. Emeth could remember his mother dragging him to see her perform a decade ago, before Penny took over her own dance company. Since the crash, she'd appointed herself in charge of the luggage. Unclaimed bags were building up, with so many dead, so she staked out a spot on the western side of the medical ward, across the tracks from the ruined luggage car. Her dancers gathered everything they could, intent on finding supplies.

After several hours, the nurses reported their final count. Forty-seven survivors, from a train with a capacity of ninety-six.

As Emeth carried a bag of croquet mallets towards the luggage pile—some people brought the most ridiculous things with them—one of the nurses ran through the group, checking faces and calling out for someone. When she turned her attention towards him, she let out a chuckle of relief. "There you are, Mediate."

"I'm not a full Mediate yet. Just an acolyte." Emeth glanced down at his robes self-consciously. Since all his clothing had been issued by the temple of Chanri, his sleepwear differed little from his usual robes.

"Is that so? Well, you'll have to do. One of the patients is asking for you."

"Asking for me?" Had something happened to Lord Drawley? Ambrose Carey at least was alive—Emeth had worked alongside him as they'd helped the soldiers pull people from the train. But they hadn't seen hide nor hair of their wealthy patron. By Chanri, if anyone actually deserved to die on this caldera, Drawley was the one Emeth could do without.

"Yes, someone needs to do rites for the dead," said the nurse.

Emeth swallowed. "I'm not fully trained—"

But the nurse grabbed his wrist. "Is anyone ever? Come along. You'll be fine."

She dragged him into the medical ward. People moaned softly around him, the looks of pain in their faces sending shudders through him. He'd visited the sick during his training, but this was different. He could hold himself apart from their tragedies. This, he was a part of.

The nurse took him to a spot on the edge of the group, where a teenage boy paced next to a body. The victim must have been past saving as she was already swaddled in linens from the train. Only her face was exposed, but there were enough clues to know she'd met a violent end. Blood, dark with the browns and purples of death, coloured the sheet across her abdomen.

"The Mediate's here, Dalton," said the nurse.

"I'm not—" Emeth tried again, but the nurse smacked him in the side before he could explain himself. She shot him a frown. To her, this was a lie worth telling. "I'm... not sure what I can do for her," he amended.

"You can bless her body, can't you?"

The boy stared at him with large, hollow eyes. Bandages were visible through the burnt remains of his shirt. He was lucky to be alive himself. But his matted hair and gaunt face suggested days, if not years, of neglect. The dead girl was likewise thin and ragged. The world had been cruel to this pair for far longer than one night.

"They're saying they'll chuck her in a mass grave with everyone else. But Merri—she deserved better than that." Tears overwhelmed the boy. "She deserved the whole world. She—she wouldn't even have jumped the train if I hadn't made her. She'd be alive."

"I'll leave you to it, Mediate." The nurse prodded him forward. "Let me take those mallets of yours to the luggage pile."

She pulled the bag of croquet supplies from his shoulder and trudged off, leaving Emeth with the grieving boy. What had she said his name was? Dalton?

When the Mediates prepared the body of one of their faithful back at the temple, there were days of ritual to give meaning and purpose to the death. This girl should be cleansed with spring water, her shroud made from a bed of pine boughs. But there wouldn't be time for any of that. Nothing but a few, pathetic words of wisdom uttered by a junior acolyte who had no real authority to intercede for the dead.

But as the boy stroked the girl's cheek, Emeth knew the nurse was right. It would be far worse to do nothing at all, even if the only hope he could offer was false.

He knelt next to the girl. "What was her name?"

"Merrith. Merrith Rai."

Rai. Lost one, in the tongue of the old Caldera Peoples. Did the gods have no mercy? These children were orphans and descendants of those who'd faithfully stayed in the caldera lands after the Great Eruption. If anyone deserved to make it through this calamity—

"How did she die?" Emeth swallowed back the anger that burned inside him.

"Well, the train. You know." Dalton fiddled with the bedsheet wrapped around Merrith's body. "We were hiding in the luggage car. I swear, we took nothing from anyone. We wanted a better life. The whole plan was to jump off before we reached Ealidor, and no one would care, but Merri…" The boy struggled through several sobs. "I got hungry, all right? When she fell asleep, I slipped off to the kitchens, thinking I'd surprise her with something. When the train blew, I got out before the kitchen burned up. But I should have been in the luggage car. I could have woken her, but she never had a chance. All the bags toppled on her and that was that."

"It's for the gods to know of things to come, not us," Emeth said.

The boy looked up, eyes swollen as he waited for Emeth to go on. The time had come for him to justify his presence—to try to soothe this aching heart. "Your Merrith might not have lived long, but she lived well," Emeth continued. "She had a true friend. When she reaches the high plateau, she will know Chanri, because she knew what friendship was. And Chanri is friend to all gentle creatures."

Dalton choked on his tears. "That was Merri, all right. Gentle. Good. Not like me."

"Chanri will guide her forward." Emeth placed his hand on the girl's forehead in what he hoped looked like an authoritative way. What a sham of a proper burial.

Still, Dalton lurched forward and threw his arms around Emeth. This was far worse than the tears—the embrace stifled him, a reminder of how transient any comfort would be.

"There he is!"

Emeth turned at a familiar voice. It was that boar of a man

Ambrose worked with. Through the gloom, Lord Drawley stumbled forward, his thick finger levelled not at Emeth, but at the boy. "See? Right next to the other rat they found in the luggage. I bet my life on it, Captain. That boy hasn't got papers or a ticket."

Dalton sprang to his feet, but he'd only ran a few steps before he doubled over in pain, clutching the bandages that encircled his burned skin. Captain Sewell was at his side in an instant. "You got a name, boy?"

"What's it to you?"

"Not much. You're under arrest," said the captain.

"Hold on, Captain!" Emeth was on his feet. "What's the point in asking about papers? No one has them after what's happened."

"Oh yeah? Then why'd he run off?" asked the captain.

"The guilty can't help but expose themselves," said Drawley.

"I get it, Mediate. You're a soft touch. That's fine in your profession." Captain Sewell took hold of Dalton and twisted his wrists behind his back. The boy howled, but Sewell ignored him. "Best leave me to handle mine."

Emeth watched, speechless, as the boy was carted away. He had no authority to stop these men. All he knew was facts that would condemn the boy. Drawley mistook his silence for acquiescence and tutted as he came to stand by Emeth. "Mark my words, there's something foul about this whole affair. I've ridden dozens of trains and I've never seen an engine go like that. And if that criminal was skulking around the cabins, that's the place to start."

"That boy is where it starts?" Emeth repeated. How many people did Drawley intend to have the captain cart away like dogs on a chain?

"Like I said, mark my words. Something's wrong here." Drawley threw him a wink, as if he believed them to be co-conspirators, then marched off into the night.

Ash fell from the sky and settled on Emeth's shoulders.

Chanri taught that ash was a blessing. Fire rejuvenated the natural world. It let plants burst to life that would never grow had the earth in which they took root not been razed. But what was the point of a fire if it burned away the young, and left the old and decaying unscathed?

"Oh dear. You look ill now, too."

Emeth didn't know how long he'd stood there, his thoughts swirling, but the nurse was back. She looked from Emeth's stricken face to the dead girl and the empty space by her side. "I see they came and took him. Shame about that."

"How did they know?" Emeth said sharply.

She laughed. "You think I told them someone jumped the train? No, I'm more than happy to let live. Someone saw a kid in tatty trousers. Didn't take them long to figure out how he got here." She bent down next to Merrith's body and tucked in the corners of the sheet. "Well, this one's ready for the next life. You take her feet, I've got her shoulders."

"I don't know if I should—"

"Really, Mediate. You worry too much. Now use those arms while we're all still alive."

He didn't dare disobey the nurse a second time. They faced each other as they carried Merrith's body to the mass grave. The nurse was middle-aged, her red hair streaked with grey, yet she gave off the impression of someone much younger. Perhaps it was because all her wrinkles looked as though they'd been etched by laughter. Even struggling beneath the weight of a dead body, she didn't frown.

"How do you manage it?" The words were out of him before he could think better of it.

She shifted the body matter-of-factly into the open grave, on top of a pile of others. "What?"

"Going on, faced with this." Emeth watched as a pair of soldiers expanded the width of the pit as more bodies were thrown in. "It's not your first time, is it?"

The nurse laughed, the sound jarring in the dead night. "Well, it's my first train explosion. But I've seen worse. I do my duty, Mediate. D'you know, it's a holy night tonight?"

Emeth blinked. "Is it?"

"It's the new moon." She pointed up at the empty sky. "On the new moon, Ramona descends to earth. This is her doing."

"Ramona? The witch goddess?" Emeth's training at the temple covered a wide array of gods and spirits, but most had concerned the Glyn Folk—gentle spirits, born after the time of the old gods, who focused on making the world a better, more liveable place for mortals. Ramona was primal. Old as Soloz. And hardly known for being a comforting figure. "You think she cares what happens in the lives of men?"

The nurse's mouth quirked. "Men, perhaps not."

"I'm sorry. I meant—"

"No need to worry. She won't set her beasts on you for rudeness. But what other goddess would find meaning in a train burning on a moonless night? This is her work. And knowing that…" The nurse smiled in her serene way. "I can do my part. Help the afflicted survive her."

"But not all do." Emeth stared at the pit in which they'd laid the young girl's body. Would Chanri find that small soul, wandering the caldera? Would she guide her to the high plateau?

"Well, we have to forgive the gods their chaos. And hope they do the same for us."

"Ashby?" Another figure came through the darkness. She also wore a nurse's uniform, her lapel embroidered to show she was head of the unit. "You finished with the girl?"

The nurse who had been speaking with Emeth nodded. "Yes, ma'am."

"Good," said the head nurse. "We've found some decent wood for splints. If you can start seeing to broken bones."

Ashby turned back to Emeth. "You'll have to forgive me, Mediate. My duty goes on."

"I'm not a Mediate."

"Ah, you're close enough." She trudged into the darkness.

She meant her words kindly, but they couldn't have been further from the truth. The real Mediates were all back in Pesca, safe from the wrath of the gods. He'd thrown his lot in with Ambrose and Drawley, so should he even be surprised to find himself abandoned on this caldera, surrounded by the avarice of the Lords' Council? The whole luxury train deserved to taste the hardship they had inflicted on the likes of Dalton Rai.

A moonless night. Ramona walking the earth. Prayers to such a goddess were pointless. She wanted no simpering devotion and she couldn't be entreated to do anything but her own will. A thousand years ago, she'd defeated Soloz, and no one had heard from either of the old gods since. So Chanri had taken up the mantle of guiding mortals, leading the Glyn Folk in good works. There were temples built along the north-eastern fjords of Halgyr all the way south-west to Pesca's harbour—all dedicated to Chanri's worship. But what power did she have if one of the old gods reared their head again? There was a darker will at work tonight.

The train smouldered in its grave on the hillside. Ashby was right. One god in particular had designed this exactly to her liking.

CHAPTER

✦ 9 ✦

ONCE DAVINA AND Morel broke out of the train, they spent the next couple of hours looking for Kellen. When they found his compartment empty, Morel suggested checking the dining carriage, but that yielded no results either. Finally, Davina spotted him propping up an old man as they staggered together from the train to the medical camp, a crowbar tucked under his other arm.

Davina rushed towards him. Who did he think he was, running around playing the hero? He looked absurd, bleeding and dressed in an undershirt, not that any of them looked any less ridiculous in their sleeping clothes. But Kellen was so bloody vain, it seemed worse finding him unkempt. She threw her arms around him the moment the old man was safely seated.

"Davina?" He caught sight of her right before she collided with his middle. "Ow! Careful, I think something landed on me there."

"Then why don't you see a nurse?" she demanded as Morel huffed up next to them.

He shook his head. "I don't think I'm a high enough priority. It's good to see you both."

"Good to see us?" Morel repeated. "That's it?"

"I assumed you were alive. You'd broken out of your compartment by the time I got to you." Kellen belatedly pulled Morel into the embrace.

"We could have been in the dining carriage." Morel snapped. "Or somewhere else! The observation carriage or—"

"The door was broken down from the inside. You could see it from the direction the splinters were facing," Kellen said.

Davina almost wanted to laugh. Bloody insufferable Kellen, he had to be right even in a crisis.

"Fine. Never mind that, we need to talk." Morel broke them all apart, gripping Kellen's shoulder. He dragged him away from the survivors milling around the medical camp and Davina trailed them, heart racing. Morel had promised her that if anyone had an explanation for why that rock crevice fit her hand so perfectly, it would be Kellen. "Something happened—"

"Obviously." Kellen gestured at the burning train. "There are still people stuck inside. If you'll come with me, Morel."

"You don't understand. The rock around the train… That was Davina."

"Yes, Davina could help in the relief effort too." Kellen ploughed on, unhearing.

"The rock!" Morel shook Kellen by the shoulders, making their older brother wince and grab the bleeding part of his head. "She did that. She *changed*."

Kellen didn't respond right away. Instead, he stared at Davina, making her aware she was biting her thumbnail, a habit left over from childhood. If even Kellen had to stop and think about this, it couldn't be good. "You mean…"

"We have to get away from here," Morel whispered.

What? He hadn't cleared that idea with her. Leaving meant running away from any hope of rescue. What did he think they would be heading towards in this godsforsaken wilderness?

"Before people start to ask questions," he continued.

"No." Kellen's regular air of authority returned to him. "That would cast suspicion on us. We're going to act like nothing's happened."

"Kellen!" Morel didn't shake him again, but he lurched as if he wanted to. "If we don't protect her now—"

"That's *exactly* what I'm doing." Kellen placed a hand on Morel's shoulder, stilling the volcano that was their middle brother before he could erupt again. "We're going to build an iron-clad case for why this whole affair wasn't Davina's fault, and that way, when Continental Rail sends someone to find us, she won't get accused of anything. Understand?"

Kellen's words sounded far more like a plan than Morel's daft suggestion of running into the mountains, so why hadn't Davina's pulse quietened?

"Do I ever get to find out what's going on?" Davina demanded.

"Yes." Kellen turned what was probably meant to be a reassuring smile on her, but his eyes kept darting about.

Brilliant. Even *he* was worried.

"Once things calm down and we have some privacy, we'll discuss this whole thing. We're going to be fine."

"Really? Because Morel thinks I blew up a train."

Both her brothers scowled at her. Davina hadn't meant to be flippant, but the last thing she wanted was to treat that idea as feasible. Because if it was…

"Perhaps…" Kellen scanned the landscape. For all the pandemonium of the train crash, they were still on an open rail line in the middle of the night. There was plenty of wide, empty space to get lost in. As if sensing this, Kellen turned back to her. "Perhaps we should tend to this now. Nobody is likely to notice if we're gone for a few minutes and our carriage has already been emptied. We can steal a moment alone in there."

+ ✦ +

At first, Kellen explained nothing at all. Instead, he had the nerve to start asking *them* questions. He wanted Morel and Davina to recount everything they remembered about when she'd woken up. Did they know how the bedding in the compartment had ended up burned? Where had the indentation in the rock been that was shaped like Davina's hand? Kellen scolded Morel for destroying it before he could see it, but Morel rolled his eyes.

"And what would *you* have done?"

"I'm not sure." Kellen touched the edge of where the bullet had dented the rock. "But this doesn't look any less incriminating."

The rhyolite in his hand cast a dim glow over the scorched surface. There was too much loose basalt around the wreck to make torchlight safe, and the mechanism that kept all the train's lanterns bright had been damaged. Kellen, like many other survivors, had broken one of the lamps off the wall and extracted the rhyolite from inside. He activated it with his own volchemical knife and a fresh vial of basalt dust. Its pinkish light lit up his knuckles like rays escaping the corona of a solar eclipse. Sun and moon were joined together in his hand. They were one and the same in so many of the stories Davina had grown up with, too; the two faces of Ramona, hanging in the sky. One of which, according to legend, her own ancestor had stolen.

A thousand years ago, Halgyr hadn't been a nation, but merely a man. He lived in the chaotic days when the old gods had walked the earth. They each ruled their own domains—Ramona the sky and Soloz beneath the ground. But neither was lord of the surface and so that was where they waged their wars. They cared little for the mortals that got caught up in their battles, until one day Ramona decided to take an ally—someone clever and quick. Halgyr, the mortal she recruited, crept into the volcano where Soloz slept and carved his face off him. It was an act so daring that Soloz never dreamed a mere man might try it. Once he'd lost his face, the mountains caved in and created the caldera on which they were now stranded, and Soloz was left to writhe within his subterranean prison.

In return for his help, Ramona granted Halgyr a kingdom. Then, with Soloz's face, she created a new race of creatures—the witches—designed to torment mankind and keep them in fear of her.

Do you see the sun? Davina's mother used to say. *That's Ramona's kind form. One of warmth and tenderness, which makes the crops in the fields grow and gives us light to see by. When she wears that face, she is every woman that ever cared for you. She is mother, sister and wife.*

And now do you see the moon? Yes, her other face. The changing, duplicitous one. The one she stole from Soloz and wears as if it were her own. It is dark and haunting, and some nights it's not there at all. It pulls the tide to and fro, and makes the ocean her plaything. She grins at you, mocking. Never trust the moon. Who can trust a woman with two faces?

Usually, when Davina reflected on the old legends, they felt like nothing more than superstitions, silly children's stories. Now, she might be the same sort of monster as Ramona. A two-faced woman.

A witch.

She swallowed. Kellen had fallen silent as he studied the way the rock curled around the broken windows. She couldn't stand it anymore.

"So, have you made up your mind yet? Am I a witch or not?" she demanded.

Kellen's hand dropped to his side, plunging them all into darkness. "*That* isn't the question we lack answers to."

"Davina—" Morel started, his voice riddled with tenderness that was so much worse than anger.

"One of you better work up the bloody nerve to tell me what's going on, because this isn't…" She wanted to keep her voice even and controlled, but it was impossible. She gulped for air, forcing herself to go on. "This isn't *fair*. How do you know more about this than I do? If I *am* a witch, shouldn't I be the one to—"

"Because of Mother." Kellen twisted around, the rhyolite making him shine like a ghost in the darkness. "Let me start at the beginning. I don't believe she ever wanted to tell me she was a witch, but she fell ill so quickly, she was desperate. Not for herself, but for you."

"Mother?" Davina repeated. "She was a witch? Have you known since she died?"

"Not exactly," said Kellen. "She handed me a letter a week before she passed away. Told me to keep it away from Father and Uncle Sergei. From everyone, really. And she made me promise not to read it until I was a man and could understand it, and— how did she put it?—*decide what was best to do with the information inside*. Yes, that was it. I would show it to you, but it's back in Halgyr. I certainly didn't think I'd need it now."

"And it said what? That she was a witch and so am—and I'm…"

119

Davina struggled to breathe. Morel placed an arm around her. As much as she would have liked to knock everyone away right now, she leant her body into his for support.

"It was more like she *used* to be a witch and you *could* be one. It's complicated," said Kellen. "Mother said she hadn't shifted into her witch self since she'd married Father and became queen. She'd given that part of herself up for him, or so she thought. It's hard for witches to slide between their human and enchanted forms alone. But one day, she was holding you as a baby and it happened. Then she gave you your witch name and you changed too."

"My name? I have another *name*?" Weren't two enough?

"Names have power. Especially with witches. They're like incantations," said Kellen.

"When we woke up here, you looked sort of... wrong," said Morel, pointing to a spot at the centre of the scorched bedsheets. "You were in the same nightdress, but with a different face. Then, when I said your human name—*Davina*—you buckled over. You switched back."

She flinched away from his hand. Her human name. His words spoke volumes. Some part of her was more monster than person.

"But why did I turn into a witch at all?" Her voice sped up. "How could that have happened, if we were asleep and—"

"That's the real question. For which I can think of two answers." Kellen shone the rhyolite over the rock again. His mouth had turned to a flat line, as he finally voiced aloud what he'd been considering since they entered the compartment. "Possibility one: someone used your witch name in your proximity, causing you to answer the call and switch selves. Since I was not in your room at the time, and I've never told Morel what your witch name is, that's highly unlikely."

"Morel," she repeated. "You told Morel... how long have *you* known?"

Morel's eyes fell to his feet. "A while."

"*How long?*" she repeated.

"I opened the letter before heading off to university," said Kellen. "You were only nine. Father had just told you about the royal family, and I couldn't imagine putting even more pressure on you."

Davina wished she could argue with him, but even she remembered what a little dunce she'd been when Father told her she was a princess. Most Halgyric royals learned their true positions at around the age of ten, when they were old enough to keep a secret. Her family let her in on the truth right as Kellen was leaving, hoping it would explain to her why her brother had gone to study in Balter. Her father immediately regretted telling her a year early. She'd spent a few blissful weeks trying to blurt the news that she was a princess from the rooftops. Only a scolding and an encounter with the strap from her own father convinced her to keep quiet. It had been a hard-learned lesson.

So that was why Kellen had never told her. He was trying to keep a little girl from getting whipped for knowing the truth. Or worse. But an excuse like that couldn't last forever. "Fine, so you didn't tell me as a child. What took so long?"

"Honestly Davina, I tried to make the best decision I could. All Mother told me was that you had a witch self, and that Father and Sergei would be terrified if they knew. But I had to ask someone for advice."

"Don't blame this decision on me." Morel pointed a finger at Kellen. "I always said we needed to tell her."

"Yes, and you *also* agreed it should be when she was of age and we had a plan; some way of training her." Kellen ran a hand back through his hair, matted with blood and grit. "Davina, I've dug through countless books in my spare time, trying to learn about witches, but your people don't tend to write manuals. Most texts are either old legends from home or they're Balterian guides about how to kill witches. From what I know, most witches learn to manage their powers through an apprenticeship under an aunt or a mother—someone they can trust with both their names and who'll use them only with their consent. Short of storming the High Coven and demanding lessons, I'm not sure how else to educate you."

Davina's mind raced for a solution—there had to be somewhere outside the High Coven where knowledge of witchcraft flourished, because yes, *that* place was out of the question. The stronghold of the witches, it clung to the north-western corner of the caldera amid jagged peaks, and its people were even less hospitable than the terrain. Balterians, because of their policy of executing witches, were treated as enemies, and since Halgyr maintained friendly diplomatic relations with Balter, Halgyrics weren't considered much better. Frustrating though it was, she knew Kellen was telling the truth. There hadn't been a good solution. No easy way of preparing her for this news.

But he hadn't earned her forgiveness yet. Her blood still boiled with the indignity of it all. She'd been his insect in a jar—something to be studied and contained, for fear she might bite. Well, he would feel her teeth now.

"So, I've been your research project all these years and you didn't think it made sense to tell me? Not even when I came to visit you in Balter! They could have hung me!"

As she shouted the words, an even grimmer realisation settled in. When he'd shut her down back in his apartment in Pesca, it hadn't been Balter's progressive politics he'd been trying to keep her from, and it hadn't been her choice of university he'd disliked. He'd known she could be executed if her true nature were revealed. So why hadn't he warned her?

"It wasn't my idea to let you visit Balter." Kellen threw an annoyed glare at Morel.

Gods, no wonder she'd had to beg for so long to earn the trip. Morel looked positively sick as he stuttered out his own excuse. "I'm sorry. It was only supposed to be for a week. And she wanted to go so badly—"

"What's done is done." Kellen waved a hand.

Davina, noticing Kellen's clenched jaw, realised she must have missed more than one argument between her brothers about her situation. She wasn't sure if she should be angry with Morel or grateful to him. Taking her to Balter against Kellen's orders would have stirred up plenty of tensions, all on her behalf. But then again, they might have avoided this whole mess if he'd listened.

"I suppose I should be thanking you," said Kellen. "If you hadn't let her come, there's a good chance we could both be dead."

"What do you mean?" Davina asked.

"We've reached possibility two," said Kellen. "When you turned into a witch on the train, it wasn't because someone used your witch name. You did it because witches change form out of self-preservation when their lives are threatened."

"What Kellen means is, you *did* turn the train to stone," said Morel. "But not because you were trying to destroy it. You were trying to stop the engine fire from burning down the carriage."

"You mean I saved us?" It sounded too good to be true.

"Possibly," Kellen said. "I can't imagine what would prompt you to launch an attack on a speeding locomotive that you, yourself, were riding. Though your lack of memory is concerning. I don't know if we'll be able to prove you didn't sabotage the train until we know what caused the crash."

"So, this could just be a big accident?" Davina asked, awash with relief.

"Well, why shouldn't it be?" Kellen beamed at her with his classic politician's smile.

Usually, she hated that look, but for once it worked on her. He sounded so reasonable, and she felt her pulse slow to a gentler rhythm.

"Accidents like this are rare, but they *do* happen," he said. "We'll talk to the conductor and he might be able to shed some light on what happened. Rocks on the track, something like that. I wager he'll sort the whole thing out."

"Oh, thank the gods." Morel fell back on his heels.

It was so tempting to share in his relief, but at the mention of the conductor her own suspicions came rushing back. "But he's going to think it *was* me," Davina pointed out. "Or… well, not necessarily me, but one of the women. No one is going to look at this train and think there wasn't a witch involved."

"True." Kellen pushed off his knees, doing his best to stand in the dark, cramped space. "So, we'll do our best to deflect suspicion until Continental Rail arrives to rescue us and we're on our way to Halgyr again. We might not use it often, but we've got more than enough means to buy our way out of trouble, should we need to."

"Maybe my witch self knows something." Davina had heard about memory gaps in witches before, but it was surreal to think she might be experiencing one now. If Morel hadn't sworn he'd seen her with some other woman's face, she'd have thought the whole thing impossible. "If we summon her, perhaps she can tell us how the crash happened?"

She got no reply from either brother. Instead, they exchanged a wary glance. "Kellen?" she pressed. "Morel?"

Morel shook his head and turned away, clearly terrified of the question. "I think it might be safer to wait until we're back in Halgyr," said Kellen.

"But why?" It was a simple solution.

"Davina, you're a *witch*."

To her amazement, he sounded frightened. Never in her life would she have guessed she could make Kellen fear her in any sense. He was too self-assured. Too confident.

"You might not have caused the crash, but you almost burned Morel alive," he said. "You're lucky the fire was contained in here, because you could have burned down the whole train. If you change forms now, you won't recognise me or Morel, and why would you trust us if we start to question you? You'll retaliate."

"But I saved our lives!" Did stopping the fire from the train engine count for nothing? "I wouldn't hurt you."

"You saved yourself. I don't think a witch's sense of self-preservation extends to her brothers," said Kellen.

"Besides, it wouldn't take much to cause trouble," said Morel.

Davina scowled at him, daring him to go on, but he didn't balk at the challenge in her eyes. "What if you ran away?" he said. "Or tried to use your powers and someone else saw you? Those Balterian lords aren't going to care if you're guilty of the train crash or not. They'll hang the first witch they find."

"I'd like to see them try!" She shouldn't have said that. Both Morel and Kellen withdrew a step from her, as if they thought she might burst into a demon at that very second. She would have liked to. Wouldn't it have been delicious to transform and prove to them she could solve this whole mess? But, try as she might, how could she? She didn't even have a name for the poor creature trapped inside her.

"You can't do this to me," she said. Which brother was likelier to break? Morel was the softer touch—the one who'd loved her and comforted her for a lifetime. But he'd kept this secret too. Kellen's opinion was law, no matter how Morel fought it outwardly. If she wanted to free the other half of her soul, it was him she had to convince. She grabbed hold of his arm, trying to force him to hear her. "You can't tell me I have these powers then not let me use them. What if I could get us to safety? Or fix the train?"

"Maybe. But *maybe* isn't good enough. It's not a chance worth taking. Something could happen to you."

Kellen shook her off and Morel came up behind her, attempting to pull her into an embrace. "Davina, we're both so sorry—" he began.

"Don't you dare!" She wriggled free of Morel's grasp, ignoring the pained expression he wore. If he wanted her on his side, he should have told her. He should have told her years ago. "And don't pretend you're protecting *me*. I can take care of myself. You're just cowards! You're both bloody cowards and—"

"Is there someone down there?"

The voice was ragged, as if the man approaching them had been running. Perhaps he hadn't been close enough to overhear what they'd been saying? But the sound of it was vaguely familiar, setting Davina's teeth on edge.

"Anyone in the train? We're counting heads."

"Yes! We'll be up in a second." Kellen called.

The asshole was getting exactly the interruption he needed, so he didn't have to deal with her questions. It wasn't fair. Why should he have such control over her? And yet, as much as she hated to admit it, they'd almost been discovered already. Maybe Kellen was right, and it would be safer to wait until they reached Halgyr to unleash the witch. Did she really *want* to give herself over to a creature that stole a portion of her memories? What if Kellen was right to be afraid? What if the witch took over and Davina never came back?

She might have stood there, letting these thoughts spiral, for hours, but Morel clapped her shoulder to signal he was ready to boost her up so she could climb out of the compartment. Kellen was already out, reaching a long, lean arm down to her. When she surfaced inside the upended hallway, she could see a shadowy figure at the end of the carriage. It must be the man who had called for them to join the head count going on outside. He was carrying a rhyolite crystal like Kellen. It glared in Davina's eyes, much brighter than her brother's.

"You'll want to come quickly. They're nervous about anyone they can't account for," he said.

Davina finally placed his voice. It was Lord Carey's friend— the sullen priest, Emeth Trudane. As her eyes adjusted to the light, she could make out the anxious pallor of his face.

"They?" she asked, while Kellen hauled Morel out of the compartment behind her. "Who are *they*?"

"The Lords' Council." He shook his head. "All the remaining lords have assembled and appointed themselves in charge now that... now that the conductor's dead."

"*What?*" Kellen nearly dropped Morel.

"His body's just been discovered," Emeth went on.

"But I saw him outside the dining carriage only an hour—" Kellen tried again.

Emeth waved his hand, as if expecting the objection. "That's the thing. He didn't die in the crash. There's a slash as deep as your finger through his throat."

· PART THREE ·
THE SUSPECTS

CHAPTER

+ + 10 + +

THE CONDUCTOR'S BODY was bathed in warm blood. All the lords of Balter were gathered around where his corpse lay, not far from the luggage carriage, shining rhyolite crystals on the poor man, so his blood sparkled wet and slick in the sea of pinprick light. No one was doing much more than staring, so it wasn't difficult for Morel to force his way into the circle and clear a path for Kellen to join. There was no mistaking that a murder had occurred.

Morel fought against the tightening in his throat. He'd never been good with blood. He could shoot a gun better than most men, but the thought of turning it on another person made him shiver. He wasn't built for tragedy, something his uncle reminded him of constantly. Uncle Sergei had been a spare son of the crown, just like him, and had been responsible for his military training. Still, Morel had never cultivated the detachment that truly mattered in a crisis.

At least this was one crime no one could pin on Davina. But that only begged the question of who *had* killed the man.

"How did it happen?" Kellen immediately knelt by the body.

"How should we know?" said one of the lords. "We found him like this."

"*You* found him?" Kellen asked. "All of you?"

The councillors turned to each other in a bluster of confusion.

"I only heard everyone else shouting—"

"I think it was—"

"The thing is, it was rather dark—"

"I found him."

The crowd fell silent as a young man stepped forward. His well-tailored trousers were torn and he had blood splashed liberally down his front. Weren't killers often discovered lingering at the scene of the crime? The man gestured to his shirt and stammered, "I—I tripped over the body. On my way to look for supplies in the luggage carriage."

"Morel, could I have your help?" Kellen asked.

"Help? Help with what?"

"The body. No one has moved it, have they?" Kellen looked up at the circle. "Compromised its condition? Aside from the…"

"Trip?" Morel raised an eyebrow.

The young lord across from him blushed so deeply that his cheeks burned through the cover of night. "It was an accident!" he said. "Then I checked for a pulse and…" He gestured helplessly at the dead man. "And then I told everyone what I'd found."

"Who else was nearby when you discovered the body?" Kellen asked. "Who did you tell first?"

"Ummm…" He glanced around at the other lords. "Sorry, I don't remember."

"Well, if anything comes to you, let me know. What's your name, sir?" Kellen asked.

"Carey. Lord Ambrose Carey."

"Thank you, Lord Carey. I'm sure we'll speak again."

"Hang on!" one of the lords howled. He had a row of stitches at his collar, marking him as a member of the Balterian military. Lord Raxton, if Morel wasn't mistaken. "Who gave *you* the right to speak to any of us about this? I vote we wait for the train company to get here and look into—"

"The conductor is *dead* and, as far as I'm aware, none of the other train staff survived the crash." Kellen was generally a patient, even-tempered man, but when he did speak with authority, he had an uncanny ability to silence his foes. "The only person left alive who had the knowledge and means to contact Continental Rail has been slashed through the throat. It's still two nights before the train is due to arrive in Ealidor and they realise anything is wrong. Then they'll need to send *another* train towards us. Rescue could be several days away. If you want to spend that time stranded with a killer and no plan, fine. Frankly, I'm not so willing to sit around and wait until they strike again. But, yes, by all means, vote on it."

Raxton grunted, but no other dissenting voices spoke up.

"I vote that we investigate the murder and find the culprit as quickly as we can," said Carey, waving his bloodstained hand. "I agree with the Halgyrics. We should figure out what's going on."

"Maybe so…" Lord Raxton clearly didn't like the direction things were heading, but, without any other support, he didn't want to make a scene. "But what gives you the right to stick your nose in this business?"

"Because *I'm* volunteering," said Kellen.

Morel had to resist the urge to swear. "Kellen?" Morel cleared his throat. "Could we speak for a mo—"

"And because my brother, sister and I were all on the opposite end of the train when this body was discovered." Kellen pressed on, ignoring him. "The Mediate found us there, so it couldn't have been us. We're the safest option you have."

"I vote with the Halgyrics," said Carey.

"Yes, we *know* that." Morel grabbed Kellen's shoulder, trying to force him back to his feet. "Can we *please* talk?"

"What's there to talk about? We're the logical choice." Davina's voice materialised at his elbow. His sister's face was paler than the moon, but there was an eager gleam in her eye. Finally, he realised what both she and Kellen saw this as—an opportunity to prove her innocence. The Lords' Council might suspect a witch, but *they* could distract from any rumours of witchcraft if they caught whoever had murdered the conductor.

Yet Morel still felt this was a mistake. It might help make Davina look innocent in the eyes of the Lords' Council, but whoever had sabotaged the train would know the engine hadn't been supposed to turn to stone. They would be looking for the witch who'd ruined their plans.

But he couldn't say any of this. There was a crowd of panicky lords around them that might turn vigilante if he didn't follow Kellen's lead. Kellen's eagerness to investigate the murder would also bestow a sense of order to the tragedy—something they all desperately needed right now.

"Well… put it to a vote, then." Morel said.

"OK," said Carey, eager to appear helpful, no doubt. "Who thinks we should let the Halgyrics investigate this murder?"

Unanimously, the lords of Balter raised their hands. Even Lord Raxton joined in. With that, Kellen rolled up his sleeves and began to examine the body.

"Someone fetch some water. I believe the stores were in the medical tent," said Kellen. "And, Davina, can you find me the passenger list? I want to see the list of who's survived the crash."

CHAPTER

+ + 11 + +

BY THE GODS, *what* was he doing? This wasn't what rational men volunteered for. Kellen had no qualifications to investigate a murder, but he couldn't imagine another course of action. He had to do *something*, or else the implications of their situation might come crashing down on him.

First Rae and her broken arm, then Davina's witch powers activating, now this. It was one too many things. No, it was *three* too many things, but what choice did he have? If there was some other way to handle this solution, he didn't know it, and so Kellen did the one thing he consistently did well.

He got to work.

As he waited for someone to bring water, he carefully began to remove the conductor's uniform. He paused at intervals to shine rhyolite over the body, hoping for a clue. A whisper of dawn was starting to break over the hills, but it was still dim. When he turned out the conductor's pockets, a nametag, almost entirely covered in blood, was revealed. He rubbed it and the name *Carson Neuwirth* became visible through the stain. Then, just below it, Kellen's fingers caught on a pair of more interesting items. A ring of keys came up, tucked next to a billfold loaded with Balterian finos. Kellen was no expert on the going rate of pay for a train conductor, but even he, a diplomat working in Pesca, had never carried so much money on his person. It seemed odd, considering they'd all been confined to a train on which Mr Neuwirth wouldn't have to pay for anything. Why wasn't the money inside his compartment? Had someone given it to him after he'd boarded the train? And why hadn't the murderer taken it?

Perhaps it wasn't too surprising that the murderer hadn't bothered with petty cash. This was a luxury express, after all, and most of the passengers who'd been on board didn't want for money. But the untouched keys were even more curious. It seemed that whoever had killed Mr Neuwirth hadn't done so to obtain anything from him. Not even access to the train's locked compartments.

Kellen hesitated for just a second before pocketing both, aware of Morel's eyes on him as he worked. Anyone who knew his brother learned quickly that Morel was nothing but lingonberry jam beneath the sharp crust of his exterior. But, standing close by, he made an imposing enough figure to keep people at bay.

"You really think those are going to be worth a damn?" Morel whispered as Kellen tucked the items away. "What do *you* know about investigating a murder?"

"I know it's better to give people a sense that's something's been done rather than letting them run around blindly," said Kellen. "I'm only holding onto these. When Continental Rail gets here, we can pass anything we find to them, then... well, Balter is supposed to have laboratories. They do things with this stuff. Fingerprinting."

Morel snorted, as if he found the whole idea of fingerprints to be superstitious nonsense.

Lord Carey arrived with water, and Kellen took it and applied himself to the task at hand. Carefully, he washed some of the blood away, revealing the slash across Mr Neuwirth's throat in stark detail. No other stab wounds appeared on the now naked torso, though there was a mark across his shoulders, as if he might have grappled with his attacker.

"Morel, what do you make of this?" Kellen called his brother over.

Morel's combat training quickly bore fruit. "Grabbed from behind."

"Really?"

"Sure. You can see where the elbow dug in there." Morel pointed to a red mark near the armpit. "But there's bruising coming up behind his neck, too. Looks like a fairly standard grab attack. He wouldn't have seen it coming."

"So, it was a quick death?" asked Kellen.

"Well, it should have been. Whoever did this cut him clean across the neck. Hit both carotids." Morel's eyes narrowed as he bent over the corpse. Then he shook his head, as if trying to rid himself of any curiosity. "So, you're looking for someone young and fit enough to overpower a man quickly. Someone with *blood* on them."

"Excuse me?" Kellen said, not understanding until Morel pointed to where Carey stood with the others.

"Look at him, Kellen!" said Morel loudly, walking towards the onlookers. "His hands are covered."

Carey's arms flew upwards in desperate submission. "I told you already! I was trying to check his pulse!"

"Who tries to check the pulse on a man whose head is half-detached from his body?"

137

"Morel, that's *enough*." Kellen rose and stood between the two of them. "We don't know enough to accuse anyone yet—"

"Then why is no one else covered in blood?"

"I'm covered in blood! Right here." Kellen gestured at the stain on his undershirt, caused by drips from where the brandy bottle had exploded against his head.

"That doesn't count! He's the only one who looks like he's killed someone. The only one who could have—"

"We don't know how long the conductor has been dead." Kellen threw an arm towards the fire still smouldering near the train. "I saw him an hour or so ago, by the side of the dining carriage. But whoever killed him could have burned the evidence and swapped their clothes in that time. Have you been keeping track of what everyone's wearing well enough to know that hasn't happened?"

Morel's face twisted with anger. "No. But I *will* be from now on."

"I promise, sirs. I wouldn't—I wouldn't begin to know how to…" Carey stammered. "I never even met the man!"

"You're under the same level of suspicion as everyone else," said Kellen with a benign smile. "No more."

"By Soloz," Morel swore, turning away.

At some point, when they were alone, Kellen would explain to Morel that he didn't think him foolish. There were plenty of incriminating signs that pointed towards Ambrose Carey, and yet Kellen also didn't think it could be him. Would the foppish man who didn't know how to use a crowbar really be capable of killing? There was a chance his incompetence had been an act, but Kellen was still waiting to see a sign of cold intelligence in the man before he could truly suspect him.

But until he was sure, Kellen needed to keep Carey compliant and trusting. "Could I have a private word, Lord Carey?" he asked, beckoning him away from Morel and the others.

Carey nodded and followed Kellen like a scolded puppy.

"You said you didn't know the deceased?" Kellen asked when they were out of earshot from those gathered around Mr Neuwirth's body.

"No more than anyone on the train," said Carey. "I might have said hello to him in the hallways. Might have... I don't know. I don't recall seeing him before tonight. I *did* see him alive after the crash. A couple of hours ago. Near the smoking carriage."

"Good." It was only a little information, but Kellen still clapped him on the shoulder. "You've been most helpful. Would you do something for me?"

"Of course! I want to see this matter resolved as much as anyone."

"Wonderful," said Kellen. "Could you deliver a message? I don't know if you remember, but when we met earlier this evening, I was with a woman and a young girl—"

"Oh, yes! I remember." Carey's face lit up. "What would you like me to tell them?"

"That I might be a while. Could you let Genna know I'll be there as soon as I can?"

Carey's eyes warmed with concern. "Of course, sir. Happy to."

"Thank you."

With that, the young lord jogged off towards the medical ward. For a second, Kellen was tempted to follow. It wasn't really his duty to solve the mystery of Mr Neuwirth's death. He should be consoling the people he cared about—Rae and, if he was honest with himself, Genna. Something instinctive had taken over when he'd kissed her in the aftermath of the crash. He'd known it would help to calm her if he did it, but afterwards he'd realised how badly he'd wanted it too.

He didn't have a right to her. And, after how he'd let her go all those years ago, it was ridiculous to think she might harbour feelings for him. But yet...

"Kellen?" Davina's bright voice over his shoulder interrupted his musings.

"Yes?"

She grinned at him, the one cheerful face he'd seen since the crash. "I've got the list. All the living passengers are marked."

"Wonderful." He reached to take it, but she pulled the papers back, the look of triumph on her face intensifying.

"*And*," she added, "I know who the conductor was speaking to before his death."

CHAPTER

✦ 12 ✦

Earlier that night

DAVINA HAD NEVER been so grateful for a man's death. She would send her condolences to whoever cared about the conductor, of course, but thank the gods! His murder exonerated her. Kellen had said he'd seen him beside the dining carriage only an hour before, so that meant she'd been awake and in control of her own body long enough to know that she couldn't have killed him. Kellen's story about her reacting to the engine fire by turning it to stone seemed much more plausible now. There was no reason to think she'd been trying to harm anyone.

She managed to get the passenger list from the two army nurses at their makeshift ward. With that, she'd gone through the living company and helped the lords complete the head count. Now the conductor was dead, there were forty-six survivors.

Some people were easy to rule out as suspects. Those who'd been heavily injured were gathered around the nurses. With the medical ward taking up the centre of the camp, they had all been seen dozens of times. Besides which, they were in no state to have murdered a man then made a quick escape. The nurses themselves had also been seen by dozens of people. It might technically have been possible for one of them to have snuck away and killed the conductor, but the window of opportunity would have been very narrow.

For the same reason, Davina ruled out the Mediate. She found Emeth Trudane helping the nurses, who swore he'd been with them for hours. At the moment, he was washing up so that he could assist one of them as she sutured a gash in someone's cheek.

Meanwhile, Fallon—the head nurse—gave Davina a full report. "We've sent him on a couple of errands, but he's never been gone for more than a few minutes. He's been on surgery duty with Ashby for at least an hour, right Ash?"

"Aye, ma'am," called the nurse who was now working with Emeth.

"Then that young lord came barking about the murder." Fallon shook her head. Davina could only assume she meant Carey. "And we sent him off to help gather the survivors together."

"Thank you *very* much," said Davina, making a note on her copy of the passenger list. "Well, Mediate. Looks like you're safe from me tonight."

She flashed Emeth a smile, but he seemed to have reverted to the sullen, silent persona he'd assumed during dinner the previous evening. All she got for her efforts was a furrowed brow. What an impossible man. She didn't know how Carey put up with him.

Carey.

She didn't want it to be him, even if the poor fellow had blood all over his hands. Yes, he was undoubtedly strong enough to take the conductor down and he'd admitted to being the first one to come across the body, but she just couldn't believe that the one person who'd brought her happiness on this terrible journey was capable of such an unspeakable act. And, if he was the murderer, why would he alert everyone to the killing when he still had the conductor's blood on him? Besides, there were plenty of other strong, capable men around.

The soldiers certainly had the physical strength and training necessary to murder the conductor. But it seemed that each of the five who'd survived the crash—Captain Sewell included—had a convincing story about what he'd been doing. First, they'd been rescuing people from the train. Once that had been taken care of, they'd split up. Two had dug the mass grave, far from the murder scene. Sewell and the other two had been busy guarding the scraggly beggar boy.

So her thoughts turned to the Lords' Council. Six members had survived the crash, including Carey. He technically didn't hold a seat yet, but since everyone knew he was his father's heir, the other lords paid him the same level of respect as a sitting councillor. He was by far the youngest of the group. Most of the others were middle-aged or well beyond. Lord Zerick had a white beard and leaned on a heavy walking stick for support everywhere he went, so Davina thought it unlikely he was responsible. Lord Solthus had broken his leg during the crash, placing him firmly in the medical camp at the time of the murder. That left Drawley, Raxton and Gamth.

Gamth himself was able-bodied, but his elderly mother had been on the train and had needed attention. He claimed to have been sitting with her when the news of the murder broke. Old dowager Gamth, however, had nodded off to sleep, so couldn't confirm his version of events. Davina made a note to ask her when she woke up, and kept looking.

She did confront Lord Raxton, who was less than impressed with her questions.

"Gods spare me the day my life ends up in the hands of some Halgyric mountain goat," he said when she asked him where he'd been at the time of the murder. "I was doing what men of my nature do. I was patrolling."

"Without your men?" Davina asked. "The soldiers all say they were rescuing survivors from the train or digging graves."

"Yes, well…" He scrubbed a hand across his chin. "What are you bothering us for, anyway? It can't have been a man."

"Why not?"

"Because half the bloody train has been turned to stone! We're looking for a damn witch."

"Hmmm… thank you for your time." Davina scribbled a few more notes then hurried away. Raxton had made an excellent point. If she wanted to deflect attention away from her, she needed to find someone who could be guilty of both offences—killing the conductor and crashing the train. And since everyone else assumed the stone wall was part of what had caused the crash, it wouldn't do her any good pushing men into the spotlight.

But the list of female suspects was tiny. The nurses certainly hadn't had the opportunity to kill the conductor, and hardly anyone else on the passenger list seemed likelier. Genna Freath was able-bodied, but she had stayed with her injured daughter in the medical ward ever since the crash. Penny Aldridge and her dancers were helping sort luggage, putting them closer to the murder scene, but many people had seen them throughout the night. Then there was *Kira Westwick*. Davina had to reread that name several times before she could believe it. Her favourite novelist, a passenger on *this* train! Davina would have loved to speak with the woman, though not to accuse her of murder. It didn't matter, anyway. Though others affirmed she was alive, Davina never spotted her in the darkness.

Kira wasn't the only one missing. Some fellow named Jarvie Braehurst hadn't crossed paths with Davina, either. Then there was Lord Drawley, who'd disappeared right after the Lords' Council had voted to let Kellen investigate. Perhaps he had something to hide? After all, he'd joined the conductor at Lodi Barnaka's table after he'd bid her and Carey goodnight.

Lodi Barnaka.

Yes! That rich woman that Lord Drawley had wanted to butter up after dinner in the hope she'd invest in whatever it was that he, Carey and Emeth were doing. She'd seen her sitting with the conductor as she'd danced with Carey. A decent lead at last!

Davina ran back towards Kellen.

The sun was bleeding over the eastern edge of the mountains when Davina rejoined her brothers by the body. Despite their circumstances, Davina felt strangely hopeful as she handed Kellen the list. All the surviving passengers who were able-bodied enough to have possibly killed the conductor were separated out into another list:

> *Captain Duncan Sewell, plus the four soldiers who served under him.*
> *Penny Aldridge and her team of dancers.*
> *The men she'd eaten with on the first night—Carey, Emeth and Lord Drawley.*
> *Two more Balterian lords without anyone to account for their whereabouts—Lord Gamth and Lord Raxton.*
> *Two nurses, Fallon and Ashby.*
> *Genna Freath.*
> *Kira Westwick.*
> *Jarvie Braehurst.*

Then, circled enthusiastically at the end of her list, was the real win: *Lodi Barnaka*.

"I saw her, Kellen," Davina whispered as she passed him everything she'd gathered. "Lodi was talking to the conductor on the first evening. I bet he was trying to get money out of her. That's what everyone wanted from her."

"Money?" Kellen's eyebrows raised.

+ ✦ +

Lodi was not difficult to locate. They found her making quite the commotion near the luggage pile. Several monogrammed bags were already gathered around her, but it was a large, gilded trunk of hers that Penny Aldridge was holding back that had really raised her ire.

"I don't give a whit about your policy!" shouted Lodi. "I'll take all my things and I'll take them now, thank you very much!"

"I'm sorry, ma'am, but we haven't searched your trunk yet," Penny said. Despite being no taller than Davina's chin, the leader of the dance troupe made for an unyielding figure with her sharp posture and tightly knotted hair. "We're withholding goods until we can confirm everyone has enough provisions to—"

"Provisions!" She snorted at the word. "I promise, I'm not carrying anything so common as *provisions*. Imagine the nurses using *my* silk gowns to make a bandage."

"They might need to," said Penny evenly. "This is an emergency situation. Everyone has to do their bit to help out."

"Why, I never!" Lodi's diatribe was interrupted by Kellen clearing his throat behind them.

"Excuse me, Ms Barnaka, is it?" Kellen asked.

Lodi swerved in their direction, her angry gaze softening as she took in Kellen's tall, lean frame. "Yes, sir?" she said demurely.

"Could I steal a moment of your time? I have some questions to ask you. Perhaps once we've spoken, I can help you resolve this matter with Ms Aldridge?"

Lodi sighed. "That's the first reasonable thing anyone has—"

"How do you know my name?" asked Penny, eyes narrowing.

"I've got the passenger list here. Forgive me, I should have introduced myself first. Kellen Linde."

"Hmmm." Penny shook the hand that was offered to her, but her shoulders remained tense.

There wasn't anywhere private to go. The train was lying on its side, dark as a tomb without its rhyolite lamps burning. Kellen and Davina's only option was to lead Lodi a discreet distance away from the other passengers, so they settled for a cluster of poplar trees on the eastern edge of the camp.

Kellen readied a notebook, which had a massive splotch of ink down the front. He must have pulled it from his study after the crash. As he did so, he furrowed his brow at Davina. "This investigation should be private," he whispered to her. "I'd rather—"

"I can take notes!" She opened her hands. Kellen wasn't getting rid of her that easily.

He hesitated for a second, then handed her the notebook, adding, "Try to stand where she can't see you. It might make her less suspicious."

Kellen strode towards Lodi, who had seated herself on a stump amid the poplars, carefully splaying her nightdress skirt so it fell elegantly down her knees. Kellen smiled at her and she let out a little hum of delight. Perhaps the best hair in the family wasn't *entirely* wasted on Kellen.

"I wanted to ask what you've been doing since the crash," he said.

"And why is that?" asked Lodi.

"We're trying to make certain all the passengers feel safe," he said. "You're in good health, Ms Barnaka?"

"Hardly! I don't know how anyone could feel safe. First the crash and then that wretched news about Mr Neuwirth." She dabbed at her eyes with a handkerchief. "And now everyone is trying to feel important by ordering us about. That *woman*! Making herself into a customs officer! It's an invasion of privacy."

"Most certainly." Kellen nodded sympathetically. "Have you been trying to get your things back, then? Since the crash?"

"Well, first I was trying to get *out* of the carriage. The service was very slow. The crash woke me up, but I hadn't the damnedest clue what was going. Not for nearly an hour. That horrid dancer got her hands on my trunk during that time, I suppose. But then someone *finally* found me. Gave me a good heave out of my unit."

"May I ask who it was?"

"One of the army boys. They were *so* helpful. It's a good thing we have them."

"Then afterwards?" Kellen prompted her to go on.

"Well, the soldiers helped me get my things out of my compartment. But it was only my travel kit, you see. Half my wardrobe is in that trunk. I need it back."

"So that's where you went? After you had your travel kit you—"

"Yes. I spent ages asking around, only to find out this Aldridge character is holding hostage all my—"

"She doesn't have an alibi!" Davina tried to whisper this to Kellen, but the woman shot up as if she'd been struck.

"What was that?" She craned her neck around Kellen, trying to spot Davina.

"Nothing. It was only—" Kellen tried.

"Is that girl *writing down what I say*?" The look of horror on Lodi's face would have been quite delicious if it hadn't also come with such a disgruntled huff from Kellen.

Davina tried to step back into the shadows, but Kellen was already losing control of the situation. "As I said, Ms Barnaka. We want to make sure everyone feels—"

"You can't think *I* had anything to do with this mess, could you? Why would *you* be asking? Shouldn't the conductor—Mr Neuwirth!" Lodi smacked a hand over her mouth as her eyes grew wide. "He's dead and now you think you've got the right to run things! Oh, you're as wretched as that Aldridge woman! All you people conspiring against me to—"

"No one is conspiring against you!" Davina snapped. Kellen reached towards her, but she knocked his hand away. He was being too delicate about this whole affair, anyway. "I saw you talking to the conductor on the first night. He sat right at your table and now he's *dead*. First, *you* turned the train to stone and then—"

"Gods save me!" Lodi swooned backward onto her stump. "Of all the uncouth, uncalled for, uncharitable... Oh, Chanri! Let the goddess save me from these madmen! Come to me, who is innocent of all offences laid at my feet and—"

"Ms Barnaka, no one is accusing you of anything," said Kellen.

"Surrounded by liars, as I am. Bereft of any friends."

"Friends like the conductor?" Davina tried.

"Davina, for the last time—"

"Someone killed him," Davina said, hands shaking. "Why not her?"

"*Someone* killed him? Davina…" Kellen's expression abruptly shifted from shock to pity. "Listen to yourself."

At that moment, Lodi blew her nose into an embroidered handkerchief and Davina felt her argument crumble. How could a woman who'd been demanding attention from everyone around her at every minute possibly sneak off and slash the conductor's throat? And all that white lace! Surely there would be blood on it. No doubt her heroic soldier boy would be able to identify the clothes she'd been in when he rescued her from her compartment. Her wardrobe was too distinct. Of everyone, she'd probably have the most difficulty hiding any incriminating evidence.

But Davina *needed* it to be Lodi. Lodi could satisfy the paranoia of Lord Raxton and everyone else who thought the crash had been caused by a witch. Otherwise, it was only a matter of time before they accused Davina herself of something.

But Kellen, she realised, wanted to catch the real killer. She couldn't decide which feeling plagued her more—his betrayal or her own mounting guilt. How could he forget her predicament so easily? But how could she justify her desire to pin the blame on Lodi to someone of his ideals?

"It *could* be her," Davina insisted. Gods, she sounded like a petulant child, even to her own ears. "Please, Kellen."

"Davina…" His pity grew more crushing with each second.

Mercifully, Penny Aldridge interrupted them, hurrying towards Kellen with a linen bag in her arms.

"I found it, sir!" Penny beamed at him.

"You did?" Kellen spun away from Davina, who felt her jaw drop.

Across from her, Lodi had fallen silent.

"Look at this." Penny unfolded the flap on the bag to reveal a row of glass jars. "Contraband Halgyric mist. Thousands of finos' worth, all stashed inside Ms Barnaka's trunk."

"My good sir!" Lodi was on her feet with a nervous laugh. "You are as surprised as—there's quite the logical explanation—"

Kellen turned back to her with a light smile. "I'd love to hear it," he said.

CHAPTER

·+ ✦ 13 ✦ +·

WHEN KELLEN HAD introduced himself to Penny Aldridge, he'd shaken her hand. Hidden in his palm had been a simple note, scrawled on a page he'd torn from his notebook:

Investigating conductor murder.
Check her trunk while we're gone.

He'd sized up the leader of the dance troupe correctly. Penny seemed like the sort of person who prized order and discipline, and Kellen had assumed that would make her amenable to helping him. Plus, she'd been putting up with Lodi's squawking at the luggage pile for over an hour. If anyone wanted to dig up dirt on the wealthy widow, it would be Penny. His trust hadn't been misplaced. She'd found at least part of the puzzle in the form of Halgyric mist, illegal throughout the Balterian Empire.

Halgyr's strongest mists were a closely guarded secret. The royal court didn't share the recipes with anyone, for fear the strange, mind-altering effects might be used against them. Balter, for its part, didn't want the stuff anywhere near its people. Its Volchemical Institute did recognise misting as a branch of volchemistry—much like petrology and biological volchemistry—but its study was confined to university laboratories, where only the simplest recipes were known.

But, if you knew where to look, there were underground parties at which people could dance while mist blends laced with rosewater wafted through the venue, making inhibitions looser. These mists were very popular among young Balterians. But, of course, they had to be sourced from the black market. There was serious money to be made by anyone who smuggled them.

Lodi fidgeted as the jars of mist were placed in front of her. If she was afraid of this revelation damaging her reputation, she really should have started talking much faster. The longer Kellen waited for her to explain herself, the more onlookers drifted towards where they sat beside the poplars. But for now, she was denying everything.

"Ms Barnaka," Kellen said. "You can't really mean to suggest that you're surprised by the discovery of mist in your trunk."

"And why shouldn't I be? They were in the luggage hold, not my rooms. Anyone could have flung them in there."

"*Flung them!*" Penny looked especially appalled at this lie. "That's ridiculous."

"Well, I don't know. That's my point! I never knew a thing about any mist being inside my trunk. That's why I was so... so shocked! Yes, shocked at the revelation."

"Of all the cockamamie—you wait here!" At that Penny stalked off.

Kellen turned back to Lodi, happy to have a moment to try to pry an answer from her alone. "I'm sure there are smugglers who use other people's luggage unknowingly. It's a terrible tragedy that you've been the victim of this."

"Yes! Exactly. The conductor must have put the jars there without my knowing."

"Now, hang on." Kellen feigned surprise. "What makes you think the conductor—of all people—would be the one smuggling contraband mist?"

"Well, he obviously…" But Lodi hesitated, clearly recognising her slip. "He… he had access to the luggage car! Yes, that. *And* he's dead now. So, someone must have known he was doing it."

"Ms Barnaka…" Kellen gave her a sorry smile. "It's my understanding you took dinner with the conductor, Mr Neuwirth."

"And no one is more surprised to hear this kind of thing about Carson than *I*."

"There!" With a triumphant cry, Penny appeared again, this time dragging Lodi's trunk. "Take a look at that!" She reached into the empty trunk, feeling around until her fingers closed on a latch. With a small tug, a false bottom popped open, revealing a row of velvet-lined alcoves, perfectly sized for transporting the four jars.

"A trunk specially designed for transporting mist that someone *accidentally* put mist inside of. Quite the coincidence," said Kellen.

"Everyone is making the most terrible assumptions!" But Lodi was shaking now.

"The interesting part in all of this is that the Halgyric embassy *does* get contacted regarding smuggling cases." Kellen regarded her evenly. "Some on the Lords' Council have tried to accuse us of bringing mist into Balter in the past, but we told them again and again that our sources pointed to someone working on *their* rail line. Alas, I don't think they ever looked into it."

At that, he pulled the ball of finos he'd found next to Carson Neuwirth's employee badge from his pocket. Lodi made a darting motion, as if she wanted to grab the money, but Kellen held it out of her reach. "Come now, Ms Barnaka. Would a few thousand finos really make such a difference to the likes of *you*?"

"It's my money! If you won't let me have the mist—" Lodi flushed with rage.

"Are times hard, Ms Barnaka?"

"They will be if I don't hand that over."

"Hard enough to drive a woman to murder?"

"I wouldn't murder Carson! Mr Selnick, however…"

"Selnick?" Kellen repeated. He read the newspapers, so knew the gangster's name as well as any man. "Dear me, you're mixed up with a dangerous sort."

"You can make fun of me all you like, but what was I to do? I've got debts, Mr Linde!" Her face flushed deeper. "My late husband's money didn't last forever. I'll own up to it. I might have spent a bit too liberally. Gambled a touch. But you can't accuse me of *murder*. What Carson and I did was simple."

"How so?" Kellen asked.

"He let me ride the Continental Rail trains as much as I liked. For free," she said. "And what I said about him going into the luggage car is mostly true. He would put the mist in when it suited him, then I'd carry the jars off the train wherever I disembarked. No one's ever checked my trunk, except that Aldridge woman—"

"Oh, gods." Penny was still standing close enough to listen in.

"—but it wasn't a situation I wanted to change! Selnick expects his shipments regularly and he pays regularly. It was…" Lodi seemed to struggle against tears. "It was perfect. Carson didn't deserve this. You might not understand, but he was a decent sort of fellow. Kept his nose down and did his job."

"Do you know anyone who might not have shared your opinion?" Kellen asked. "Did he have any enemies among Selnick's thugs?"

"Never! He was discreet. He was a *professional.*" Lodi gave him a cross harrumph. "Believe me, if I knew of any enemies of his, I'd gladly tell you all about them."

"She probably would if it meant saving her neck," said Penny.

Lodi got up and stood to her full height. "Carson Neuwirth was a friend. Though I wouldn't expect *you* to understand such a thing."

Penny opened her mouth as if she intended to argue, but Kellen raised a hand to silence both of them. "Thank you, Ms Barnaka. When we reach Ealidor, I'm sure the authorities there will be interested in this whole story."

"But you can't *tell* them!"

"I doubt I'll need to." He gestured at the crowd milling around them. Half the surviving passengers must have been listening in. Lodi let out a yelp and Lord Raxton took this as his cue to step forward.

+ ✦ +

Once Lodi's collection had been exposed, so too was her history as a gambler. Half her fortune had come when her husband died and she sold off his seat on the Lords' Council. The other half had been thanks to some large investments in Magnus Selnick's clubs. Ambrose Carey confirmed he'd seen her at half a dozen parties, then spent the next hour red in the face, as he realised he'd admitted he liked to frequent such dens of iniquity, too.

"If you'll come with me, Ms Barnaka," said Lord Raxton. "And as for that contraband mist—"

"As an ambassador of the Halgyric Embassy," Kellen cut in before anyone else could, "I do believe I have jurisdiction over our mist."

"You would *believe* that!" Lord Raxton bristled at that, but from the perspective of Balterian law, Kellen was more or less correct. He was one of the few people who were legally allowed to possess the mist. So instead, Raxton shouted at somebody who did have to listen to him. "*Captain Sewell!*"

"Sir?" The young soldier hurried to his side.

"Take this woman into custody. See she's kept with that caldera brat—"

"But I didn't attack the train! And the conductor? I would never! We did business together." Lodi tried to fend off the soldiers who moments before had been her heroes. To his credit, Duncan Sewell did apologise before tying her hands.

"Raxton, is this *really* necessary?" Kellen asked.

"I agreed to letting you handle the investigation," he said. "You let *me* administer the law. Consider me at your disposal, should another of your theories bear fruit."

Kellen couldn't tell if that was a begrudging compliment or a threat. Perhaps a bit of both. He considered arguing, especially as Lodi wailed her way towards the luggage car. This wasn't what he envisioned when he'd signed up to investigate a murder. What did he care for petty crime when they were in real danger? But he sensed he needed to allow Lord Raxton to assert some authority, or else he might find himself with a powerful enemy. The other lords were watching the proceedings with interest, and many had quietly followed behind Lodi and the military men.

"I don't like it." Morel approached Kellen, muttering the feelings his elder brother had decided to keep private. "Those soldiers shouldn't be detaining *anyone*. They aren't police. It's not an army's job to fight its own people."

"Much as I agree, we're the foreigners here. And we're already—"

"No, I get it. We're conspicuous enough." Morel glared at him in a way that communicated he thought that was very much Kellen's fault. He was probably right. "No sense pissing them off."

"Yes. Thank you for your ongoing support, Morel."

"Oh, shut up."

Behind them, Penny cleared her throat. "Shall I return to the luggage pile, sir?"

"Thank you, Ms Aldridge. I'll be sure to check in with you again."

"If there's anything suspicious, my girls will find it. We'll be in touch," she promised before hurrying back to her post.

By now, most of the crowd had dispersed. People had either followed Lodi or they were seeking out something to eat. Now they'd had a chance to go through the luggage, Penny's dancers were starting to sort out food for the survivors. Some provisions had survived the crash, and Kellen intended to grab Genna and Rae some breakfast once he'd had a chance to breathe. Hopefully, that moment would come soon. But first he had someone else to deal with. Someone who had been just as concerned with saving her own neck as Lodi.

Kellen checked in all directions to be sure no one was eavesdropping. "Davina—"

"She *was* hiding something." His sister's arms were folded over her chest, a perfect picture of distrust. "You can't blame me for thinking she might have—"

"No, of course not." Kellen wished he knew better what to say, but he'd never had the talent for calming her foul moods the way Morel did. "Everyone is under suspicion—including Ms Barnaka."

"Right, so… there's nothing more to talk about."

Kellen sighed. "*Davina.*"

"What happened?" Morel asked.

Davina huffed with frustration, pink flaming up in her cheeks.

"Among some very smart, *genuine* accusations," Kellen tried to break the news as softly as possible, "Davina may have suggested Lodi was the witch who'd turned the train to stone."

"Oh, Davina…"

"Stop acting so self-righteous! You didn't hear what people were saying." Davina glared at Morel. "Everyone knows there's a witch on the train. Do you want them to kill me?"

"Of course not," said Kellen. "But for the purposes of a murder investigation—"

"I'm sorry. I didn't think—no one's accusing you, are they?" Morel's arms were around Davina in an instant. Her arms were still crossed tight, but she leaned her cheek into his shoulder, struggling to keep her composure. There it was. The reason Kellen's siblings liked each other more than they did him. After Mother died, Morel had always been more patient with her, and thank the gods someone had been. The court had needed Kellen to take over so many of Father's duties, and he'd rather failed to step in and parent Davina the way he might have wanted to. Someone needed to be sure that poor girl grew up loved, and Morel had excelled at that.

Kellen tried not to resent the close bond they shared. But he couldn't help thinking that even if he tried to hug her, she wouldn't let him.

"No." Davina gulped in a breath. "No one's accusing me. Yet. But even if we find who did it, no one's going to believe they crashed the train too—unless it's a woman. So this is all pointless."

"That's not entirely true." Kellen stepped closer to them. "It didn't have to be a witch. I remembered something from my volchemistry classes."

"Volchemistry?" Davina raised an eyebrow. "The *science of gentle magics*?"

"Not all of them are so gentle," said Kellen. "There's solozite, for example."

Davina pushed away from Morel's embrace. "People *use* solozite in Balter? On purpose?"

"I thought they ran out of deposits." Morel clearly knew its history as a warfare tactic during the Balterian invasion of the caldera lands. "We're talking decades ago."

"But those cannons are gone? Aren't they?" Davina asked. Halgyrics feared solozite in the same way Balter feared the witches. The rare mineral held the raw power of the volcano god and was not something to be trifled with. Yet Balter had done far more than trifle—at least while they'd been able to mine it in sufficient quantities. Their cannons had fired massive chunks of solozite at the battlefield, transforming the ground where it landed. Not even the witches had been able to withstand that.

Davina's eyes were wide with shock that such a fabled, dark power might still be alive in the world. "No one uses it anymore," she said. "There were treaties signed and everything."

"I know. But if there's mist lurking around in people's bags, maybe there are some samples left over." Kellen shrugged. "It's an unlikely reason, of course. But it's one that doesn't single out the female passengers. We should try to circulate the idea around camp."

"But how would—" Davina attempted to ask, but Kellen touched a finger to his lips.

Lord Ambrose Carey emerged through the poplars, closely followed by Lord Drawley. Kellen hadn't seen much of the older man since the train had crashed, but the fuss over Lodi Barnaka seemed to have drawn him out from wherever he'd been hiding.

"Well, I never!" he thundered without any preamble. "That Barnaka woman. Never would have thought it of her. I can assure you, I had no idea the conductor was dealing in illegal substances. You can search my things, sir. You'll find me clean as the Glyn Folk."

"Thank you, sir." Kellen pivoted away from his siblings. "I'm sure Penny Aldridge and her dance troupe will be happy to assist you."

"But that's not all. I was thinking to myself..." Drawley pulled a handkerchief from his pocket and mopped sweat from his forehead. "I was thinking, why are you Halgyrics concerning yourselves with this murder business? I'm sorry for the conductor bloke as much as anyone, but the real mystery is the train, isn't it? Who crashed it? That's what you should be looking for."

"One would assume the same person was responsible for both the murder and the crash," said Kellen. "Anything that yields clues in either direction—"

"Yes, but the train! It's half-covered in ruddy rock, which means a—"

"Which could have been caused by a wide range of things. Solozite. Witchcraft." Kellen tried to drop the word with as little consequence as possible. "Hasty assumptions are only going to get us into trouble. I can assure you, Lord Drawley. I'm investigating all possible angles."

"Well... good." Drawley's moustache twitched. "Still, I talked to the other lords, and we voted. We think one of our own should be helping with the investigation."

Kellen exhaled slowly through his nose. He wasn't surprised, but it didn't make this development any less convenient. "But most of *you* weren't accounted for at the time of Mr Neuwirth's death," he said.

"Well, you lot were off cavorting in Soloz knows what corner of the train! People are saying you were too far away to have carried out the murder, but were you?"

"Fine." Kellen didn't have the energy to argue this, and they wouldn't get much further without the support of the Lords' Council. "Did you have someone in mind?"

"I… I volunteered, sir." Carey stepped out from the shadow of his companion.

"Brilliant," said Kellen. So long as it wasn't Lord Raxton, he could manage.

"Well, that's settled then," said Lord Drawley, grabbing Kellen's hand and shaking it. He turned abruptly and stomped off through the poplars.

"What? Kellen, *no!*" Morel stepped forward. "He's the most suspicious—"

"He really isn't," said Kellen. "And if you truly believe he might be the culprit, wouldn't you rather have him beside us so you can keep a close eye on him?"

"So he can knife us in the back?" said Morel. "And anyway, we don't need more people investigating this. I don't even know what *I'm* supposed to be doing. And Davina's one lead turned out to be a dead end—"

"Davina found more than one lead," said Kellen, pulling the passenger list out of his pocket. "She's confirmed something I've been wondering about for a while. Now that the conductor is dead, none of the train staff are among the survivors."

At Kellen's words, Carey spun in a circle. "Do you think someone's targeting the Continental Rail employees?" he asked.

"I need to speak with the nurses," said Kellen. "See if their bodies were found."

"By the gods," mumbled Morel. "You think they're *all* dead?"

"Well, it's the only logical—" Kellen began.

Davina threw out an arm. "Wait!" She pointed at the wrecked train. "But they're not the only thing that's missing."

"*Of course.*" Kellen followed her hand to the spot she was indicating. At the very end of the train, where a long shadow spread from the luggage car, down the tracks back towards Korio and Pesca, something *was* missing. "The caboose."

The very place where the train-company employees would have been sleeping was gone. The rest of the train lay on its side, staggered down the tracks like a fallen column from the old temples of Rencha. The couplings had broken apart in many cases and the dining carriage was smouldering into ash, but every other compartment could clearly be identified.

"Maybe they knew what was coming and detached it," said Davina.

"You mean you think *they* did this to us?" said Morel.

"Well, it makes sense," said Carey, jumping to agree.

"No, it doesn't," said Morel. "Who killed the conductor?"

"He could have offed himself?" Carey suggested.

"No. Someone grabbed him. Plus, if he had killed himself, you'd have found the knife he used nearby." Morel rolled his eyes.

Kellen had to concede that, though Carey might be easier to manage than Raxton, he was enough of a dolt to make their lives difficult entirely on his own.

"It also wouldn't explain why he was still smuggling mist right up until his death. What did he have to gain by destroying his only means of moving mist between the coasts?" said Kellen.

"Well…" Carey sputtered to a halt.

"I'm still going to check with the nurses," said Kellen. "But you make an excellent point about the caboose. You three should go looking for it. It must be somewhere down the tracks."

"The *three* of us?" Morel repeated.

"Yes, the caboose could contain any number of clues," said Kellen. He tried his best to give Morel a meaningful look—one that said *please get this idiot out of my way*. "And it might give us a better idea of how likely rescue is. If the rail workers are gone, we might…"

"Right." Morel spoke up before Kellen had to utter the unthinkable. Even if Continental Rail hadn't perpetrated the crime, the fact that the crew might have been targeted wasn't a good sign. "Well, if we're hiking down the tracks, we'll need water."

"Why do *I* have to go with them?" Davina asked, fixing Kellen with a look of suspicion.

"Because you've got a great eye for things that aren't quite right. I need you there."

Davina furrowed her brow, as if sensing something amiss.

It wasn't entirely a lie. Kellen did trust Davina to notice things Morel and Carey wouldn't. But truthfully, he wanted to get rid of all of them. He couldn't visit Genna and Rae if his siblings were around, and he was growing anxious over their wellbeing. It had been a while now since the nurses had set Rae's arm, and he wanted to know how it was healing. Thank the gods the pair hadn't left the medical ward since it had sprung up after the crash. Kellen hated the idea of them being alone while there was a killer in their midst.

"Well… all right then," Davina said, narrowing her eyes.

"Thank you," said Kellen. And he meant it. So long as he had the support of his brother and sister, it meant he hadn't lost control of this crisis. Now he only had to convince forty-three other people he could save them.

CHAPTER

✦ 14 ✦

THE SANDY-HAIRED MAN kept coming back. First, he'd pulled Rae from the train. That part had happened so fast that she hadn't even been sure it was him. Then he'd been there a few hours later when the nurses set her arm. He'd hovered nearby as the bone was straightened and splinted and she'd screamed. And when she'd started to cry, he'd been there, an arm around her Ma's shoulders. If only he would go away. Rae hated crying in front of strangers. But he stayed until the pain grew too exhausting and she fell asleep.

She woke up stiff all over, beneath a heavy wool coat. For a moment, none of the previous night existed. There was blue sky overhead and the smell of freshly burnt cedar. Birds sang in the trees and Rae wondered if this was what the High Plain looked like. Maybe they had all died on the train, and this was what was on the other side. But then she tried to move her arm, and it ached—and, as she sat up, she noticed her bottom was wet from the grass beneath her. Little hardships like these didn't belong in the afterlife.

Ma turned at her movements and her hands instantly fussed

over Rae's forehead, testing it for warmth and pushing away her hair. Rae swatted her with her good hand. "How are you feeling, sweetie?" Ma asked, undeterred.

"Ummm…" There were so many words for what had happened. But if she said those words would the pain of last night rush back? Would she find herself screaming or crying or clinging like she had a few hours earlier? That seemed so much worse than pretending none of it had ever happened. "Hungry," she said finally.

Ma sighed. "I don't blame you. I'm not sure what there is to eat. How's your arm?"

The nurse had tied her arm together with reinforced leather straps so she couldn't flex her wrist or elbow. She couldn't even remember how the break had happened. One moment she had been asleep in the train, the next she'd been half-buried beneath cases and bags, and the sandy-haired man was pulling her body free, her arm trailing uselessly behind.

"Fine." She wiggled her fingers and little stars of pain danced up to her elbow.

"That's good. You want to keep your blood circulating." Ma touched her fingers, but Rae winced and drew her arm away. "We're going to get through this. Everything will be all right."

A lie. Even more obvious than everything Ma had said about going on holiday, but Rae didn't bother pointing that out. Already, she was busy searching the crowd.

Searching for him.

Dappled sunshine fell through the budding branches of the trees that gave them shelter. A few feet away, a man lay with a blood-soaked sheet wrapped around his leg. Another had a bandaged head. Rae didn't like that she belonged here too, that someone had decided she was one of these people. The broken people.

"Here. The nurse said you should drink this when you wake up." Ma held out a small cup and Rae clumsily reached for it with her right hand. She gagged at the taste and spat some back, but Ma made her drink the whole thing.

"Buckwheat tea. It's a very special kind. The flowers only grow near geysers," said Ma.

"It's awful," said Rae.

"It should help your arm mend," Ma insisted.

Rae drank the last drops, her eyes watering. If this was what it took to get better, maybe she only needed one arm. "Can we have breakfast?" She needed to get the taste out of her mouth.

"We can try to find some food. And our clothes. You'll freeze out here without your coat."

Rae wasn't sure about that. They had the giant tailcoat. Had that belonged to the sandy-haired man too? Ma folded it over her arm then held Rae's hand as she got to her feet. For some reason, the world tipped and turned as she walked, even though it was her arm that was broken and not her legs. Ma tightened the sling and they started towards another section of the camp set up alongside the train.

They had only gone a short way when *he* came back again. Jogging through the other injured people, he stood out like a waving flag. The sandy-haired man was like a cat you'd once left food out for. You gave them one little scrap and they never left you alone. Ma's grip tightened over Rae's fingers, erasing any doubt she had that he was trouble.

"You're up." He slowed to a walk that matched Ma's pace as he reached her side.

"Yes, looks like we made it through the night," said Ma. "Did you find your family?"

"All well, gods be praised," he said. "And Rae? How are you? Feeling any better?"

Rae stopped in her tracks, forcing Ma to a standstill as well. He knew her name. The sandy-haired man came around so he was looking at her and dropped to his knees, bringing them face to face. Why did he know her name? Had Ma betrayed her by telling him?

"Is your arm doing better?" He wouldn't let her go without an answer.

"Ma gave me some medicine," she said, hoping that would be enough.

"How very sensible."

Rae remembered now that Ma had said he might try to talk with her. She shrank back against her mother's skirts. Ma was in the fancy dress, she realised. Rae had no idea why.

"We were going to look for breakfast," said Ma. Her fingers twitched in Rae's grip. "I suppose if you haven't eaten, you could join us."

"Actually, that's why I'm here." He hopped back to his feet, taking a bag down from his shoulders. "Most of the kitchen was destroyed when the dining car fell on the tracks, but the stores in the luggage car made it. It's not much. People are talking about rationing. Hard to say how long it will take the train company to realise we're stranded."

He lifted a pair of twilled, flaky rolls out of his sack and handed one to each of them. Pastry! Rae bit into hers before she remembered that Ma didn't trust him. But the buttery crumb was so smooth she couldn't bear the idea of spitting it out.

"Why? Where are we?" Ma asked. "When did we pass the last trainyard?"

"That's the issue. None of the crew is present, so no one knows." He shouldered his sack again and Rae took another bite of her roll. "We've sent a search party after the caboose and I need to speak to the nurses about the dead."

"By the gods, Kellen! When was the last time you slept?"

"Irrelevant. Couldn't if I wanted to. You heard about the conductor, didn't you?"

"Yes," said Ma.

Rae's face twisted upwards. Heard *what* about the conductor?

"Well, now that he's gone, someone has to get to the bottom of it."

"Someone has to—Kellen, no! Nobody's asking you to—"

"I might have volunteered."

"*Volunteered?* That is the most ridiculous thing I've ever—"

"What's going on? What happened?" Rae tugged at Ma's hand.

Ma let out an exasperated sigh. "This man is trying to find out what happened to… us." Ma chose her words in a way that told Rae she'd left something out. "He's trying to figure out why the train crashed."

"Guilty as charged," said the sandy-haired man, giving Rae a wide grin.

Why did this man smile so much? No one who had been inside an exploding train should look so happy.

"But I wouldn't mind a short break," he continued. "If the invitation still stands."

"Invitation?" said Ma.

"To eat with you."

He looked hopeful, like gentlemen always did around Ma. How could someone actually think about romancing her when both Rae's arm and the train were broken?

"Of course," said Ma, her smile thin. Ma had told Rae long ago that a man's attention was a dangerous thing, but it was also dangerous to bruise his pride. That had to be the reason she was playing along now. "It's probably time you two were introduced. Rae, this is Kellen Linde. We used to go to university together. Mr Linde is going to help us get to safety. Kellen, this is my daughter, Rae."

Mr Linde. Was she supposed to call him that from now on? Both of them looked at Ma, then back at each other. For once, the man didn't smile, and Rae shrank back against Ma's legs, but she nudged her forward. "Say hello, Rae."

"Hello, Mr Linde." Even with the rolls, she didn't like this. Something felt horribly wrong. Wrong in a way that couldn't be blamed on a train blowing up.

"Hello, Rae." The good humour returned to his face as he hunched over so his hand could reach hers. "It's a pleasure to make your acquaintance."

It was a lie. It always was with gentlemen. Rae's existence was an inconvenience to whatever they pictured themselves doing with Ma. Still, she took Mr Linde's hand, as expected. He shook it gently, as if he were worried she'd broken her right arm too.

Rae and Ma followed Mr Linde as they searched for somewhere to eat their breakfast. It was almost pleasant to see the mountains up close instead of through the window of a train. Almost. Rae would have preferred the whole experience if it had been done willingly.

They were stranded in the narrow, twisty part of the train route. Mountains loomed up on both sides of them, and the train tracks snaked through the valley. The southern side of the line tumbled down into sharp cliffs, but to the north was a small alpine meadow.

Most of the survivors had gathered here, sheltering beneath the spindly trees that dotted the landscape. A trickle of water was audible somewhere in the distance, though Rae couldn't see the stream it came from. Ma said there were rivers all across the mountains, which ran down from the snow caps. Spring had just arrived in the valley, so there were snowdrops littering the field and fresh green grass. It almost looked like the kind of place someone would go on holiday, just like Ma had promised.

Though why in Ramona's name would they go on holiday with Mr Linde?

They settled on a spot in which some bare rocks poked above the grass. Mr Linde sat on the largest boulder, but it was still too close to the ground for his long legs. He looked a bit ridiculous, which was maybe why Ma wouldn't meet his eye as she sat across from him. Rae tried to sit behind her mother, but she'd barely settled in when Mr Linde held something new out to her.

"You like sweets, don't you Rae?" he asked.

Rae stared at her mother, aware these were one of the many things she wasn't supposed to accept from strange men. But when Ma nodded, she opened her hand. "Yes."

"Wonderful." Mr Linde placed a small bag into her palm. It was done up with a silk ribbon and inside was an array of beautiful jelly fruits. They were almost too pretty to eat. Almost. They were stranded on a mountain with limited food, after all.

"Don't eat them all at once," said Ma, as Rae stuck the first one in her mouth. Sugar and juice burst across her tongue and it was hard to keep hating Mr Linde, even if he wasn't behaving that differently from the other men that had been in Ma's life. Larry had brought her cinnamon sticks once, but they'd made Rae sneeze. The difference, she figured, was that Mr Linde was rich like everyone else on the train and could afford better sweets.

"Where did you get those?" Ma asked.

"My bags," Mr Linde laughed. "I don't know if you remember, but I used to buy them all the time in college and—"

"And you thought you would take some home with you?" said Ma, with a smile. "To remember Balter?"

"Perhaps? Maybe I hoped to see you both on the train?" said Mr Linde. "Do you like them, Rae?"

Rae had barely had the time to try one flavour, let alone the whole bag. The man was being nosy far too early. She curled into her mother's side, unsure whether she wished him to go away or not. Ma sighed, brushing some of Rae's hair off her forehead with a soft sweep of her fingers. "She's a little on the shy side, I'm afraid."

"Takes after you, then?"

"Well, she *is* my daughter."

"May I ask you something, Genna?"

Rae kept her nose buried in the treats but listened to their voices.

"I don't know. Depends on the question."

"It's a simple one," said Mr Linde. "What makes you so certain I'm headed home?"

"I... I might have read it in the paper," she said after a moment's hesitation. "The day before I came to see you, there was an article about changes at the Halgyric embassy."

"There's no way the Balterian newspapers cared enough about Halgyr to report on *that*," said Mr Linde.

"No, I expect they didn't," said Ma, busying herself with straightening the fly-aways of Rae's hair rather than looking at him. "But Pesca's a big city. They've got papers for Halgyric expats."

"You read the *Halgyric Gazette*?" Mr Linde shook his head. "I don't even bother with… you've been keeping up with me, then."

Rae took a bite of a jellied strawberry. Ma said nothing.

"That's why you visited the embassy right before I left Balter."

Once again, Ma didn't respond to Mr Linde. Rae licked sugar off her fingers. Well, that was interesting. Ma had sought him out, not the other way around. Why had she been so surprised to see him on the train, then? Did she want to talk to him or not? And if *he* didn't know what was going on, why had he bought them tickets? Adults liked to pretend they had things figured out, but they could do the most ridiculous things when left alone.

"Well, I've finished my roll." Abruptly, Mr Linde got to his feet, dusting crumbs from his hands. "I should probably get back to work."

"Just stay safe, Kellen," said Ma. "Circumstances being what they are, you can't be too careful."

"I'll be fine. We all survived the crash, so the worst is over," he said, and took off towards the medical camp.

A giant lie. Or was it? Rae got the impression Mr Linde actually believed it. Looking at the scowl on Ma's face, Rae knew better than to agree.

+ ✦ +

That could have gone far worse.

Genna slowly chewed on half of her roll. She'd tucked the rest into her pocket. If food was going to be rationed, then that would mean hunger later, so she needed to hold onto something for Rae. She had her imperfections as a mother, but never in seven years had her girl gone hungry. It wouldn't start today.

She took the bag of sweets from Rae once she'd eaten three of them, promising her they'd be returned later in the evening.

173

Genna wasn't sure what she thought of Kellen buying gifts for Rae before they'd even met. But he also hadn't pushed when Genna had introduced him as nothing but an old friend, and that meant the world to her. Words were all it took to ruin things, and yet he hadn't told Rae who he really was.

All of a sudden, Genna's stomach twisted with worry. Had he said nothing because he wanted Genna's approval, too? But why? Surely he couldn't want to pursue her—not after everything they'd done to each other, could he? And why hadn't he followed through on his threats to demand access to their daughter? He'd worked out that she'd kept an eye on him over the years, and now he knew it hadn't been a coincidence she'd gone to him just as his assignment at the embassy ended.

He probably thought she was desperate to see him before he left. That wasn't entirely untrue, but it was hardly the whole story either. A series of things had lined up—Larry's death, the note about Kellen in the paper—until Genna had finally caved under the hope that her life could be different. All she had to do was force Kellen to help her get out of town, a deal he should have taken. He should have put them on a different train from him, then at least she and Rae wouldn't have been in this mess.

It was too late to wish for better now. There were more pressing concerns to focus on, like getting their bags back. She offered Rae a hand up from their picnic spot, then led them into the throng of people gathered around the luggage pile.

Genna moved carefully through the crowd, making sure no one bumped into Rae's arm. It amused her to see these wealthy people cast around for some semblance of comfort. For most, the explosion had struck while they were asleep, so these self-important rich people were stuck walking around in muddy dressing gowns. Genna smoothed out her neckline. Though her dress was a little ash-stained, she looked in better shape than most around her. Kellen had taken the real beating in the cabin.

A strange thought occurred to her as she and Rae made their way to where the dancers were sorting the luggage. What would she have done if Kellen had died on the train? Losing Rae would have been unfathomable, but Kellen? He was the first man she'd ever loved. He'd hung over her life for so long, haunting her in the depths of her daughter's eyes. But if he'd died—protecting her, no less—she'd never be free of him. There wouldn't be a single corner of Balter she could run to and find peace in. Somehow, she had to disentangle herself from him. Permanently. It was the only way she could live her life on her own terms.

Even soiled with soot, her measly possessions were easy to spot among the grand trunks. A miniscule woman came towards her holding a clipboard, the back of it marked with the logo of Continental Rail. Some things must have survived in the conductor's cabin. "We're checking all luggage now for provisions that can be shared," the woman explained. "Names?"

"Genna and Rae Freath."

"Ah, first carriage, cabin four? No baggage in the luggage car. One in the overhead?"

"That's us."

"Come this way," she said. "Do you consent to a search?"

Genna hesitated a second, counting the nights since they'd boarded the train. The warding mist should still be working. "Yes, of course," she replied.

"Thank you, Mrs Freath. If you'll come with me—"

"Genna? Genna Freath! What a pleasure, seeing you here! Well, if we can call anything a pleasure in these circumstances." A man with a cane approached Genna and Rae. He was dressed in smart clothes, his wide grin almost familiar.

"Yes?" she said hesitantly.

"We met once, back in autumn." He kept coming closer, even as one of the women handling the baggage began to unlatch Genna's case. "Lawrence introduced us at the Ribaldis' party. Jarvie. Jarvie Braehurst."

As he gave her his name, he grabbed her free hand and shook it vigorously. The reason for the grin on his face became all too clear. He'd been hovering by the luggage pile, waiting for this moment. Instinctively, Genna angled herself so her body obscured Rae. Why had she ever tempted the gods by coming on this train? She'd been followed, and now they were stranded with her pursuer.

"Good to see you again, Mr Braehurst." She forced herself to be pleasant. The spell *had* to work now. The dancer might make a wry comment at finding a large stash of money inside her carpet bag, but if *he* saw it, she'd be lucky to escape alive.

"Jarvie. Call me Jarvie. I was so sorry to hear about Lawrence. Good kid."

"Does he mean Uncle Larry?" Rae asked.

Braehurst's gaze snapped around and focused on the child. "Uncle Larry! That's him. You must miss him terribly," he said.

"I guess." Rae retreated behind Genna's skirt again, immediately regretting her question.

No, she did *not* miss Larry. Genna had only had him over to the apartment a couple of times, and he'd always tried to play the clown for Rae. He'd offer to throw her in the air or fly her around the room like a bird, and when she didn't react with enthusiasm he'd get angry and stomp around, demanding she be nicer to her

176

uncle. It infuriated Genna to watch him with her, but in other ways, Larry had been good to them. He'd bought groceries when Genna had to take Rae to the doctor when she'd had mumps. And, for all his bluster, he never hit or threw things. That was a rare quality for men in his line of work.

"I hope nothing went missing in the accident?" said Braehurst, making a move towards Genna's open bags.

The dancer who was searching through them jumped as another set of hands interfered with her work. "If you'll excuse me, sir! This process is private."

"It's all right," said Genna.

"I was wondering if—ah, there it is." Braehurst's hand closed around something inside. Genna held her breath, bracing for him to draw up the wad of finos. But instead, all that surfaced was Rae's ragdoll. He shook it so the arms flopped around comically. "Something to make the little one smile. We could use a smile today. Does dolly have a name?"

Rae snatched it from him. "Ramona."

Braehurst laughed. "Like the witch goddess?"

"She's got a good imagination, my girl," Genna said.

The woman inspecting the luggage refolded Rae's clothes and snapped the bag shut. She never opened the side pouch on the inside. Did that mean the warding mist had worked? Or had Braehurst noticed the bills through the thin fabric lining?

Perhaps he would leave them alone if she handed the money over, but then what would she use for her fresh start in Ealidor? No, Larry had died for that money. And the bloody moron had the nerve to hide it in her flat. She wasn't handing it back to one of Selnick's goons this easily. If Braehurst thought he intimidated her, he had another think coming.

"Are we done then?" Genna asked the woman.

"Yes, thank you."

"Thank you. Good day, Mr Braehurst." Genna curtsied goodbye and led Rae away with her. She marched them several feet away before she chanced a look over her shoulder. Jarvie Braehurst met her eyes and smiled.

Even if he hadn't found the money yet, he wasn't done looking.

CHAPTER

✦ 15 ✦

Davina didn't own a single pair of shoes suited to traipsing through the mountains, something that under normal circumstances she considered a point of pride. Before she, Morel and Carey left, she had managed to swap her nightclothes for a travel dress, but the footwear she carried wasn't so easily adapted to their environment. She had picked her sturdiest heels for the trek down the tracks but still had blisters within half an hour. Morel kept stomping ahead, annoyed with the slowness of her pace, while Carey gallantly offered her a hand over the rocky landscape, annoying her brother further. They were a terrible group to set on any task, which made Davina certain of one thing—Kellen didn't really care about the caboose. He just wanted to be rid of them. She'd upset him with the Lodi Barnaka accusation, and now he was punishing her with physical exertion.

She had to admit, though, that it *was* interesting the caboose was so far back. The train must have carried on without it for some time before the crash occurred, which was... well, it was damn inconvenient. Davina wondered how far they'd have to hike before conceding it had been lost forever.

Until then, she had to contend with yet another stone making its way inside her shoe. As she paused to remove the pebble, Carey came to a stop next to her. He was the other pleasant part of this enterprise. There were worse things than a walk through a mountain valley with a handsome man. It could have been romantic had they not had Morel scowling at them all the way.

"How are you managing, Miss Linde?" Carey asked for the hundredth time.

"Well enough," she said. "I bet you're wishing you hadn't volunteered to help the investigation now."

"On the contrary! I've been able to spend the morning with you." He winked and a blush would have flooded Davina's cheeks had she not already been red in the face from the hiking. "When the Lords' Council asked for a volunteer to help with the investigation, your involvement was one of the reasons I raised my hand."

"Only one of them?" Davina flashed him a grin. "You needed another?"

"Well, I would *like* to clear my name." His gaze drifted to Morel, who was a few feet ahead of them. "But also… Miss Linde, I confronted something about myself last night."

"Oh, did you?"

"Yes. After the train crash." He got a misty look to his eyes, which Davina found quite darling. "I didn't have a damn idea what I was supposed to be doing. No one did. And it was the same after the conductor died. But you know who did know what to do? Both times?"

"Who?"

"Your eldest brother. And I realised, that's what a real man does."

180

Davina let out a sharp laugh. Too late, she realised Carey meant his words with hand-over-heart sincerity. He gaped at her now as if she'd spat upon his hero's grave. "My apologies," said Davina. "It's only that… to me, he's Kellen. Nothing more. But I'm glad you find him so inspiring."

"I know the two of you have a complex relationship," he said.

Once again, she was grateful that the exertion of the walk disguised her flush. She'd almost forgotten how her first night with Carey had ended. How could he hold a good opinion of Kellen when they'd both seen him drunk?

"I don't mean to suggest he's perfect," said Carey. "But you should be proud that—"

"I am. Exceptionally." She cut him off before he could say anything that might anger her or, worse, draw some other feeling out. As a child, she *had* looked up to Kellen. During his visits home, he'd seemed so educated and modern, bravely disagreeing with her uncle and father over dozens of issues. But then he'd turned out to be just like them.

Yes, he'd *had* a good reason to deny her the chance to study in Balter. But in the end, he'd only traded one crime against her for another. He'd kept the fact she was a witch to himself. It cast their entire relationship in a new light. Had he let Morel deal with her all those years because he was afraid of her? Did he even like her? Honestly, why *would* he want to attach himself to a monster? Why would anyone?

"I've made you unhappy. My apologies, Miss Linde."

"No. It's fine. It's just… it's this dreadful business about the crash." Davina dabbed her dry eyes, trying to look convincing. "I haven't felt right since then."

"Well, of course not!" Carey took one of her hands in his,

buying her display of feminine weakness without question. "No one expects a tender heart like yours to endure such hardships."

"Thank you." She struggled not to snort with laughter.

Kellen might have sent her away from the murder investigation, but there were still things she could learn here. Ambrose Carey was a guileless man and he clearly liked her. With a little effort, she reckoned she could get him to tell her anything, and there were questions that nagged at her after her last argument with Kellen.

"It's all the talk of *witches*." She didn't have to fake the shudder that passed through her when she said the word. "Do you really think they could have done this? It's such a frightening prospect! I don't know if I could even exchange words with the other women on the train if I thought one of them might be hiding a witch self. Mind you, my brother Kellen…"

She looked ahead, to see if Morel was paying attention to her and Carey. His pace had slowed, but they still hadn't drawn level with him. Davina repressed a smile, knowing this whole plan relied on her trembling lip. "Kellen said it might even be volchemistry? But that's impossible, isn't it?"

"Volchemistry? I don't see how it could turn a train to stone. Unless…" Carey broke off, as if the idea had just occurred to him. "Well, I suppose it depends on what materials the saboteur had, you know?"

"But I don't. I never learned about volchemistry in Halgyr. Please." Davina slotted her fingers through his, drawing him closer. "I'm frightened."

"Well…" Carey cleared his throat, eyes falling to where their hands were joined. She slid a thumb over his wrist, and he broke. "If it will help you feel safer, Miss Linde, I'm happy to help."

He pulled their hands apart, then threaded hers through the crook of his arm, restoring them to a proper distance. He led her forward, as if they were promenading together down the wide avenues of Pesca. Never mind the gnats that followed their every move like a curious, hungry cloud. "So, volchemistry…" Carey stepped carefully along the uneven level of the railway sleepers. "We've known for a long time that all power comes from the continent's central volcano. Your own traditions teach as much, I'm sure."

"Of course."

"Our people discovered volchemistry two hundred and fifty years ago. Not long after the Great Eruption. There were so many refugees coming into our lands after it wiped out Rencha. My family can actually trace its roots back to a great-great-and-so-on grandmother who escaped the caldera." Carey sounded rather proud of himself for the association, which drew a smile from Davina.

"Yes, we got a number of refugees back then, too." There was no event more significant in the history of Solozya than the Great Eruption, which had reshaped the entire continent and its people in an instant. It wiped out one civilisation and gave rise to another. Halgyr was unique in how little the eruption had interrupted its history. Yes, there were stories of crop failures the year that ash blackened its skies, but the central caldera had been altered forever. Whole cities were buried under ash. The only reason the refugees had survived at all was because of the witches.

It gave Davina pause. Witches. She didn't know how they did it, but they were ferocious enough to survive a volcano.

"Honestly, I'm amazed anyone stayed in the caldera at all. Look at this place. Not what you'd call hospitable." Carey's nose wrinkled as he surveyed the terrain. To the north was dense forest and to the south nothing but steep cliffs. There wasn't a single sign of human habitation near them. Balter's expansion through the caldera lands had decimated what few Renchan villages littered this valley. It made the search for rescue an ominous prospect, should they not find the caboose.

"The refugees who came to Balter brought their own share of traditions," said Carey. "Most were used to accessing the volcano's powers from their time living in the lands that surrounded it. But the only volcanic materials near Pesca are the basalt flows north of the city. So that's where they—and us Balterians—started.

"A wide variety of igneous rocks have powerful properties, but we couldn't do anything without basalt. Grind it down and it gives motion." He reached into his pocket and pulled out a small vial of black dust. "Any person of means carries these around, along with a volchemical knife. The Renchans first figured out how to activate basalt with an obsidian blade. But every year, we find more uses for it. Add a little dust to rhyolite and it gives you light that burns steadier than a candle. Or sprinkle it on quartz and it captures memories."

"Or releases them, right? That's how a crystophone plays music, isn't it?" Davina's mind flew to the record stones she'd purchased back in Balter.

"Exactly. There are all sorts of things we can do now, but each of the volchemical bases does something predictable. Quartz for memory, rhyolite for light, sulphur for healing and so on and so forth. With basalt providing motion—or force, as some volchemists put it. Apply force to a volchemical base and all sorts of interesting things happen."

"You know a good deal about this." She gave his arm a squeeze and he grinned.

"Alas, far less than some," said Carey. "I took a few courses when I was at university, but I can't pretend to have a natural talent. It's just good, sensible stuff to be aware of."

"None of those things are going to turn a train to stone, though," grunted Morel, who had given up the pretence that he wasn't listening in.

Carey drew to a startled halt. "Oh. Well, no. Not quartz or rhyolite."

"But something else could?" Morel asked, cocking an eyebrow.

"Well, I don't know." Carey's arm squirmed in Davina's grasp, like a child being caught in a playground fib.

"Kellen mentioned something. Though I can't remember what." Davina tugged Carey's arm, trying to steal his attention away from the terrifying spectre of Morel. Not that he was co-operating.

"He mentioned solozite," said Morel.

Carey coughed again. "Yes, so... I suppose that could do something to the train. It's a transmogrificator. The Mediates in the temples say it's the thing most like Soloz himself. They say that, after Halgyr stole his face, he couldn't hold corporeal form anymore, so he changes the shape of things whenever he touches them."

"He doesn't touch *anything*. He's trapped under a mountain," said Morel curtly.

Carey laughed nervously. "I'm only repeating what they taught at the temple when I was a boy."

"Yes, let's *not* get into a debate around religion," said Davina. "What's important is the science. So solozite could turn a train to stone?"

"Yes, but it's incredibly rare! Do you know what the chances are of anyone carrying it?" said Carey. "Believe me, if someone had it, I would *know*. My father used to own a solozite mine, but it ran dry years ago. It would take at least a hundred pounds of the stuff to transform the train!"

"*A hundred pounds?*" Morel repeated. "You know the amount off the top of your head?"

"Well, yes, my family owned a mine! And don't look at me like that." His gaze darted between Morel and Davina. "I already said the mine is empty. We're not getting a hundred pounds out of it. And why would *I* want to blow up the train? I was headed towards Ealidor for business. This whole thing is damn inconvenient."

"What kind of business?" Morel pressed.

"I don't care to discuss it, actually," said Carey.

"It's all right, my lord. I'm sure we'll find the real culprit." Davina rushed in. "We don't think you turned the train to stone. Morel and I believe you, don't we, brother?"

Morel let out a frustrated growl. "Maybe. But you're hiding something, Lord Carey, and I intend to figure out what."

With that, he stomped on ahead, leaving Carey with his jaw hanging open. Davina had to nudge him on, in order for their journey down the tracks to continue. "Well," she said. "I'm sorry how that ended. My brother can be quite protective."

"I see that." Carey took a shaky step forward.

"But *I'm* grateful," Davina said, squeezing his arm. "For everything you told me. I feel much better now."

"Then it's surely been worth it." His smile was weaker now and neither said a word for several minutes, though they continued walking arm in arm down the line.

Carey had given her a lot to think about, though Davina wasn't certain how she planned to use the information. When they got back to the crash site, she could circulate the story of his family solozite mines among the passengers and end all talk of witches, but who would that help? When all was said and done, she liked Carey. She didn't want him to suffer unjustly. Perhaps she could use his tale to cast suspicion on his travel companions—Drawley and Emeth surely knew about his history with solozite, and either one could be smuggling it. But, foolish though the impulse was, even she wanted to find the real culprit.

"Oh, shit."

Morel's voice jolted her back to the present. The tracks climbed upwards ahead of them, but Morel had gone on so far ahead that he'd already reached the top of the hill. His back was ramrod straight, as if something terrible loomed ahead of them.

Davina dropped Carey's arm. Ignoring the scraping of her heels, she broke into a run. Her brother's silhouette obscured whatever had brought their journey to an end. She shoved Morel aside, only for him to lurch and desperately grab her by the shoulders. The effort was a little overblown, but she still gasped as she stumbled a foot closer to an open canyon.

Morel pulled her to the safety of the pine trees that flanked the railroad tracks. Below, the ground plummeted a thousand feet to a shallow, snaking river. The canyon gaped ahead of them, the shattered skeleton of a railway trestle crumbling into its depths. Splintered wood and twisted metal were all that remained of the iron highway they'd flown along the night before.

"What happened?" Morel picked up a broken wooden beam.

"The bump…" Carey muttered as he came up behind them.

"What?"

"I was sitting up in the smoking carriage when the explosion hit, and before it, there was a bump." Carey stepped away from the edge of the canyon. "That must have been this or... but how did we stay on the tracks?"

"Maybe someone did it after the train went by?" said Davina. It was the only possible explanation. "They must have come back."

"But where's the caboose? That was the whole point of this!" Morel threw the wooden shard into the canyon, sending it toppling into the river.

Davina held her breath, trying to steady her nerves. The trestle bridge had been burned from the centre and fire had eaten away at its supports. The destruction looked so strange, juxtaposed next to the sparkling river below. Sunlight danced down the canyon walls, illuminating layers of brown, orange and yellow rock, like a child's paintbrush had been dragged across the landscape.

"What kind of rock is this?" she asked.

"What does that matter?" asked Morel, but Carey caught her meaning.

He inched forward, craning his neck over the canyon wall. "Rhyolite."

"I thought I recognised it." Davina lifted a stone and saw its fine grain resembled the burning cores the train used in all its lights. "We must be close to the centre of the caldera, then, if there's something other than basalt around. Maybe it's a clue to where we are?"

"A clue?" Carey repeated.

"You own a *mine*. Do you know anything about the mineral deposits in the mountains?" she asked more pointedly.

"Well, maybe a little," said Carey, colour rising in his cheeks again. "Along the train route, there isn't anything terribly rare. Beck's Canyon is rhyolitic. We might be close to there. But, if we were, we'd be seeing evidence of quartz crystals too, like—oh."

At that, Carey reached down to the rubble surrounding them. A wobbly sphere had caught his eye, a crystalline window visible through the rock. "Quartz."

"So, we know where we are. What's near Beck's Canyon?" Morel asked.

Carey shook his head. "Nothing is near Beck's Canyon."

"Nothing? No one wants to mine all this?" Morel found another stone that looked as though it might hold a crystal.

"Well, they might have once, but this was a choke point during the caldera wars. Continental Rail built a trainyard on the other side of the canyon but it's abandoned now." Carey pointed at the empty expanse. "But there aren't any indigenous people in the region anymore. The nearest village is much further north, closer to the geyser plain."

Davina squinted and thought she might be able to see some buildings far beyond them. But even if there were any people in them, they wouldn't be able help them with such a gaping hole between them.

"This was intentional." Morel paced the rim of the tracks. "This was *all* intentional."

"Well, we knew that, didn't we?" Carey said.

Davina bent down over the bits of quartz Carey had found. One crystal had been split in half. Its clouded surface seemed to glow and she had to be careful not to cut her thumb on the jagged edge. "Quartz holds memories, you said," she looked up at Carey. "Is that only after it comes into contact with basalt dust?"

"I think so?" said Carey. "Why?"

"Damn." Davina set it down, only to pick it back up a second later. "But there's basalt dust everywhere. Look at the tracks!"

Black powder lay along the length of the train track in

furrows, left over from the grinders that had powered the train. Buried among them were the loose quartz stones, gleaming in that peculiar way that made Davina hopeful. "Maybe with the explosion and the basalt dust, some of them were activated? Maybe one of them recorded what happened last night?"

It was a far-fetched idea, but as Davina looked to Carey for approval, he slowly nodded. "We do have to be *very* careful when we mine volchemical ingredients. Solozite can explode if loose basalt gets on it, so… you might be onto something."

"Brilliant! Morel, open your bag."

"This is for carrying *water*. I'm not schlepping a bunch of rocks back to—"

"Oh, shut up and open your bag!" Davina didn't have to ask again. Much as it seemed to annoy him, Morel was used to falling in line behind his bossier siblings.

"Do any of you have a clue how to get memories out of these?" he asked as they dropped some promising stones inside his bag.

"Someone back at the crash site should," said Davina. "We've got half a dozen lords with us. One of them must have studied volchemistry. Either way, it's worth a try, isn't it?"

Morel shrugged, as if he found their efforts entirely useless. He might not be wrong. Whoever had stranded them in the mountains clearly knew their way around the landscape and wanted to make rescue as difficult as possible. It was a thought so overwhelming that Davina did all she could to push it aside.

The alternative was admitting they were all about to die in the wilderness.

CHAPTER

✦✦ 16 ✦✦

THEY HAD LEFT in search of a caboose and were coming back with a bag full of rocks. Morel couldn't think of a better metaphor for how disastrously everything had gone since... actually, when was the last time things had been good? Morel would have settled for things returning to how they'd been before the crash, but even then, he couldn't have pretended life had been going well. Father was dying, Davina was desperate to leave home, and Kellen was day-drinking inside his sleeping compartment.

Now, with the crash, those divides between the people he loved had only deepened. Father might pass while they were stuck out here, Kellen had them running all over the mountains, and Davina was understandably pissed off with the lot of them. Ever since Kellen had told him about Davina's witch powers, he'd imagined they would share the news with her in a quiet moment back home, presenting her witch name to her like they were bestowing a gift. It should have brought them closer, not broken the thin bridges that connected them.

But what was he supposed to do about it? Neither sibling was listening to him. Kellen wanted to solve this damn murder and

Davina was fawning over the daft lord who was their only suspect. Well, the only suspect unless—gods forbid—Kellen had dug up some other unsavoury characters while they'd been gone.

By the time they returned from their morning mission, the sun was high. Sunshades constructed from tablecloths and bedsheets that had been scavenged from the train compartments were strung between the spindly mountain trees. Morel scanned the company for any signs that rescue had arrived while he was away, but there were none. Instead, he saw people napping after their long night of rescuing fellow passengers. Those who were on their feet were busying themselves with a variety of odd tasks—sorting luggage, rigging up shelter, boiling a mishmash of surviving produce into a soup.

Carey took off to inform the Lords' Council of recent developments, while Davina went to find a pair of shoes that, to use her words, "did her the kindness of pinching her feet in a different place". That left Morel to report to Kellen alone.

It didn't take long to find him. He was interviewing the head nurse about those who'd died in the crash. A notebook was covered in Kellen's signature chicken scratch, but Morel didn't bother trying to read any of it.

"You can stop looking for the crew's bodies," said Morel, shouldering his way into the conversation. "The caboose is gone and I'm guessing they were in it."

"Oh." Kellen lowered the book.

"May I get back to work then, sir?" asked the head nurse.

"Certainly. Thank you for your time, Ms Fallon," said Kellen.

The nurse hurried off and Kellen fell into step next to Morel. Once they were out of earshot of the medical ward, he leaned in closer. "There's something else, isn't there?"

Morel grunted. "Real surprise, right?"

With that, he filled him in on everything they'd discovered. Kellen was particularly interested in the tales of Carey's solozite mine, which surprised Morel.

"But Davina turned the train to stone. We already know it wasn't him. At least, not because of the solozite," said Morel.

"True, but the conductor was a smuggler. If he was willing to transport mist, then why not solozite? This news might be more important than we think," said Kellen. "Now, show me those quartz crystals you found."

Morel let the bag fall from his shoulder. "Davina and Lord Carey thought we might be able to get some memories of the explosion out," said Morel. He still didn't understand the science, but the rhyolite that surrounded the quartz did emit a faint glow, so maybe activation was possible. "We'll need a volchemist, though."

"Luckily, we have one," said Kellen.

"We do?"

"Yes. Follow me."

Kellen led him to a spot on the edge of the forest, where numerous sheets were spread, giving the place the look of a tented city. Morel didn't recognise any of these people, but Kellen must have used the time to speak to some of them. Why else would he stride up to someone who looked the least likely person to be a highly skilled volchemist? A young woman with a child.

"Genna Freath?" Kellen called. At his voice, the tiny girl scurried behind her mother's skirts and Morel caught sight of a sling around her arm. The sight crushed his heart. The poor little bean. This wasn't a situation grown adults were equipped for, let alone a small child.

"Do you need something, Mr Linde?" asked the girl's mother.

"Actually, yes." Kellen gestured for Morel to come forward. "How are you at extracting quartz from rhyolite stones?"

The question clearly surprised her, but she stepped forward with a curious glint in her eye. "Depends on the density and what you want to use it for. I'm rusty in petro applications, but we could try refining the stones in the grinder, see if any have a high enough crystalline content to produce a clear projection."

"The basalt grinder?" said Kellen.

Morel resisted the urge to swear. They were going ask him to flip the thing the right way up so they could run it, weren't they? Fine. So be it. It wasn't like he had anything else to do in this damn valley.

"On a low setting," said Genna. "Enough to break up the rhyolite, without activating it. Where did you get the stones?"

"Well…" Kellen gave her a bracing smile. "Have I introduced you to my brother? Genna, please meet Morel Linde. He was looking for the caboose for us an hour ago when he found these."

"And?" Genna leaned forward, lips parted in anticipation of the answer.

"Maybe we should talk alone somewhere?" said Morel, aware of a small figure that had crept close while her mother was speaking.

"But I want to know what happened to the caboose too!" the little girl shouted. "It's bad news, isn't it?"

"It isn't all bad news. We have rocks." Kellen held one out to show her.

She scowled at it. "That doesn't make anything better."

Morel snorted. Wasn't it charming to hear all your worst thoughts come out of the mouth of a seven-year-old?

"Rae! Mr Linde is trying to help us." Genna bit her lip, fighting a smile. "I'll tell you the news soon enough, but Mama needs a chance to talk with him. If you don't mind, sweetie?"

"Where am I supposed to go?" she demanded.

"I don't know, sweetheart. Just give us a little room—"

"Mr Linde!"

Oh, what now? Morel turned around to find people running towards them. At the front was Lord Carey; Davina was a few feet behind.

Kellen's smile froze in place. "Yes?"

"The Lords' Council needs you," said Carey.

"Right. I'll be along shortly." Kellen tried to turn away, but the young lord placed a hand on his shoulder.

"They need you now," he said. "It's not about the caboose. There's another body."

Another body. Morel's blood chilled. "What?"

"Did someone succumb to injuries?" asked Kellen.

"I'm afraid not," said Lord Carey. "Another murder. Knife through the throat. And people remember seeing him walking around after the crash."

"Who was he?" asked Kellen.

"Jarvie Braehurst. Everyone's saying he worked as an enforcer for Magnus Selnick."

CHAPTER

+ + 17 + +

JARVIE BRAEHURST'S BODY had been found lying on the eastern edge of the camp. Most of the lords were giving it a wide berth, but they were quick to shuttle Kellen and Morel into position once they arrived, ready to investigate.

Kellen tilted the dead man's chin to the side, and blood stained a pair of work gloves one of the soldiers had lent him. They were hardly sanitary, but they'd have to do for checking the body. The knife wound through the victim's neck had begun to congeal. Sticky pools of blood obscured the details of his clothes and skin. Once he'd been cut, he bled out quickly. If Kellen had to wager a guess, it had been done with the same knife that killed the conductor.

However, there were differences between the killings. Braehurst was a bear of a man, the kind Kellen wouldn't have fancied his own chances against in hand-to-hand combat. It would have been much more difficult to use the advantage of surprise on a man so clearly used to looking after himself, and when Kellen pushed open Braehurst's bloodstained collar, he saw no evidence of the bruises he and Morel had found across the conductor's shoulders.

Behind him, Morel paced, arms folded tight over his chest. "What are you looking for?" he said. "It's obvious how he went, isn't it?"

"His throat's been slit, yes," said Kellen. "But what led to it? How did he get here?"

The body had been found by one of the army nurses, hidden a short walk from the train tracks in an outcrop of bushes. Now, she sat pale-faced on a dead tree stump. "I stopped everyone from meddling with it," she said, her voice still quaking with shock. "Of course, I touched him myself, checking for a pulse."

"And how did you find him?" Kellen scraped a finger around Braehurst's ear and a gritty texture came away, as if the blood had mixed with sand.

"The crows were making a fuss out here," she said, wiping bloodstained hands on her soiled apron. "They must have smelled it. Well, I've always liked crows, sir. Thought I was walking over here for a bit of birdwatching. Never thought…" She swallowed. "Never thought we'd lost another one. I wasn't expecting him."

The nurses had been steadfast through the initial tragedy, so Kellen thought it was interesting how Braehurst's death seemed to have rattled the woman. Perhaps it was because she'd tried and failed to revive him? Or maybe she knew the deceased?

"Did you see him alive?" He might as well ask.

A scratch of pen against paper confirmed that Morel had started taking notes for Kellen.

"Mmm, maybe?" The nurse picked at her nails. "He was wandering around the luggage pile at one point, I think. You might ask the girls stationed there. But he wasn't injured in the crash, so I didn't see him in the ward. I'm sorry, sir. I don't know what happened. I wish I did."

"And before the crash? You never met him?"

"Never," said the nurse. "I don't understand it. First the crash, now this. I suppose this means the engine going wasn't an accident. If you like, I can fetch some water to clean the body. Might help us figure out what happened to him."

"Thank you," said Kellen. "And what's your name again?"

"Ashby." She regained her composure as she left to fetch supplies. Perhaps it was the investigation that made her nervous, not the body.

"Found anything yet?" Morel asked once they were alone.

"There's a lot of dust mixed in the blood. It makes you wonder..." Kellen tipped Braehurst's head backward and his mouth popped open. Four gold teeth, all intact; a testament to how many times he'd been knocked down, as well the sort of replacements he could afford. "He wasn't killed for his money. They left a fortune in here. And look—" Kellen scooped out a finger full of blood-soaked gunk, lodged at the back of his throat.

"What's that?" Morel's brow furrowed.

Kellen ran it between his fingers. "Basalt dust or... no. It's too coarse. I think they're grindings from the train."

"Someone tried to choke him with grindings?"

"The way I see it, we've got two options," said Kellen. "Maybe he was murdered near the engine, then dragged here. In that case, the grindings would mean very little. Or we're dealing with a volchemist. Grindings are usually nearly inert, but I've heard of them sometimes activating."

"Carey said something about that too," said Morel. "But there isn't anything here to activate."

"There are the grindings themselves. When all's said and done, they're still basalt. Maybe someone made a dust cloud with them."

Kellen was straying into the realm of the theoretical now. He'd only got the chance to study volchemistry briefly during his time in Balter. He understood most of its industrial applications, in which grindings were never used. But that didn't mean they were useless. Somebody with more training would know how to activate them.

"We should check by the engine for signs the body was dragged," said Morel.

But when they scouted the region near the engine, there was no obvious trail. In truth, there was so much blood on the ground from when they'd pulled the dead out of the train, it was difficult to make sense of it. The same went for any hope of identifying the killer by their clothing. So many people were dressed in bloodied shirts that there was no point in searching for that kind of visual evidence.

"Should we assume volchemistry?" asked Morel as they retraced their steps to the body.

Ashby had returned too and was stripping the body down. "Volchemistry, did you say?" She splashed some water over the corpse, washing away the worst of the blood so they could see the stab wound in the neck. "That could be the case. We haven't been able to account for all our medical equipment since the crash. Anyone could be running around with one of our knives."

"You mean a volchemical knife?" asked Morel.

Ashby nodded. "Obsidian blade. We use them to mix medicines and such."

"That's good to know," said Kellen. It widened the suspect pool substantially. "How about the body? Any new insights now it's been cleaned up a bit?"

"Bruising over the sternum," said Ashby as they knelt down

beside her. Braehurst's clothes had been unbuttoned low enough for the nurse to open his shirt and show them where hands had pressed between his ribs before the knife did the dirty work. "There's a thumbprint there," she said, pointing to a mark at the base of his neck. "And that's the heel of the hand on his chest. I'd guess he was attacked from the front. Hand span is a bit larger than mine." She demonstrated, laying her palm flat against the set of bruises. Kellen's own fingers were too long.

"So, we're either after a large woman or small man," he said.

"If it's a man, I wouldn't think he'd be that small," said Ashby. "Had to be big enough to drop the bloke."

"Unless the basalt dust did most of the work," said Kellen.

"Do you want him prepared for burial?" said Ashby "He's going to start stinking out here in the open."

"I might need to take another look at the body," said Kellen. "But we'll need to get him away from the crows."

Peck marks marred the skin, but Ashby had found the body before the scavengers had done much more than pluck out his eyes.

"I'll get the soldiers to help me carry him closer to the camp," said Ashby.

"Not too close though," said Kellen. "We don't want to frighten everybody."

What if Rae saw the body, decomposing on the mountainside? Kellen had only known the girl for a day, but he could already picture her looking for it. Somehow *he* frightened her, but the idea of dead people and broken trains didn't. "Do your best to keep it safe," he said. "But don't let it distract you from tending the injured."

As the nurse left them, Morel turned to Kellen, an eyebrow raised. "So. A volchemist."

"It *is* a strange development." Back when Kellen had first suggested the idea, it had clearly been a tactic to draw attention away from Davina. Now it looked as though a volchemist might actually be behind the murders.

"And that Genna woman you were talking to is the best one on the train?"

Kellen jumped at the mention of her, which did nothing to wipe the knowing look off Morel's face. "Best one I know of," said Kellen.

"Right," said Morel. "So given that fact, she *should* be our main suspect, right?"

"Genna didn't do it," said Kellen, perhaps too quickly. "The nurses said she stayed with her daughter in the medical ward all night. She couldn't have killed Mr Neuwirth."

"Well, then aren't we lucky to have such a skilled ally?" Morel didn't actually sound pleased about it. He shoved the notebook back into Kellen's hands. "I better get that grinder working, like *she* wants."

"Thank you," said Kellen.

Once Morel left, Kellen flipped through the notebook, adding a few of his own thoughts and correcting Morel's spelling. It helped him put his thoughts in order and consider what options they had. Magic of all kinds seemed to be swirling around this case. Witchcraft. Volchemistry. Even Lodi Barnaka had been carrying Halgyric mist. But it wasn't the pleasure blends she was carrying that he needed now.

Kellen snapped the notebook shut. It might raise Morel's suspicions yet again, but the situation couldn't be helped. He needed Genna.

+ ✦ +

The sight of Kellen approaching wasn't a welcome one. Genna expected it, of course. Ever since Jarvie Braehurst's murder, a cold dread had filled her. He was so tied up in all things relating to Selnick that her own history was bound to come out at some point. Kellen was going to learn everything. And when he did, he'd demand she hand over Rae.

She was so worked up with fear that she was entirely unprepared for his actual words to her. "I need your help," he said.

Genna blinked. "With the rhyolite?"

"No, I need your perfume," said Kellen. "None of the lords are opening up about how they knew the deceased and I don't have the ingredients on hand to make a muddling haze."

"Pardon?" Genna caught sight of a girl behind Kellen. What was he doing mentioning her perfume in front of strangers? Or Rae, for that matter. Genna could feel the girl tucked into the side of her skirt, listening.

"Oh, my apologies," said Kellen. "Davina, I'd like you to meet Genna Freath and her daughter, Rae. Genna did some volchemical work for the embassy during my time there. Genna, this is my younger sister, Davina."

At least Kellen had thought up a decent lie before introducing them. But whatever gods had spared her embarrassment a moment ago suddenly abandoned her.

"I thought you said you met Mr Linde at university," said Rae.

"Best volchemist in our class," said Kellen. "That's why we hired her."

"You're too kind." Genna watched Davina's face, looking for any hint of suspicion. Gods, it was so obvious. Genna had never thought Rae looked like Kellen. But now she could see Rae's soft cheekbones, her wide eyes in this young woman's face.

"And she has muddling haze with her?" asked Davina, clearly unaware that anything of significance was happening.

"A little," said Genna. "I didn't imagine I'd need to work when I got on the train. But I don't feel comfortable handing it out. It's illegal outside the embassy. If the lords knew—"

"That's fine, you're going to come with me," said Kellen. "Davina, would you mind watching Genna's daughter? She has an injury and shouldn't be left alone."

"You're joking, aren't you?" said Davina.

"I know how to watch myself!" said Rae petulantly.

"Kellen, I don't know about this..." said Genna.

"It's our best shot at finding the killer before they can strike again."

"I don't know if the blend is strong enough to get a confession out of anyone," said Genna. "All it does is... nudge them a little. Make them more open."

"Please?" he asked.

Perhaps it was better to play along. Much as she didn't want her own secrets to come out, it would look suspicious if she was uncooperative. "Rae, you'll behave yourself for Miss Linde?" she said.

"I don't want you to go," said Rae. But the look she gave her was nothing compared to the utter outrage on Davina's face.

"Morel would be better at babysitting," she snapped.

"Well, he's also better at lifting heavy things," said Kellen. "And he's currently trying to right the train engine with the lords and the soldiers, so we can run the rhyolite through the grinders. But if you'd rather heft that—"

"Fine," said Davina, scowling. "What about you?" she said, turning to Rae. "Do you want to watch a bunch of men try to flip a train carriage over?"

"Yes!" Rae hopped forward, though she still cradled her broken arm carefully.

"Wonderful. We can laugh at them when they drop it."

"Davina!" Kellen called after her, but she ignored him as she took Rae's good hand and led her in the direction of the engine. Genna's breath caught as they walked away. Kellen's sister. Rae was casually wandering off with Kellen's sister.

"She doesn't know, does she?" she asked.

"No," he said. "I don't know how she'd take the news."

Genna swallowed, surprised at how hard such a little thing had hit her. By cutting Kellen from her life, she'd taken more than a father away from her daughter. She'd also denied her an aunt and uncle; a whole network of people who could have loved her.

"Let me get my perfume," she said, turning towards the shelter in which she'd left her belongings.

But Kellen had seen the tears at the corners of her eyes. "Are you all right?" he said, following her.

"It doesn't matter." She tried to keep ahead of him, but her vision blurred.

"I'm sorry," he said. "But I knew Davina would listen to me. If we had another option—"

"I said it doesn't matter!" She gulped for air. "Not everything has a hidden meaning to it. I'm tired, Kellen. I haven't slept in a day and a half, my daughter has a broken arm, and I don't know how we're getting out of this damn valley. Isn't that enough?"

He cleared his throat, as if he meant to console her, but no words came. What could possibly fix a situation like theirs? His gaze dropped from hers.

"Of course," he said eventually. "Of course that's enough."

Who did she think she was fooling? She collapsed into Kellen's chest and his arms tightened around her. Memories flooded through her, the smell of his body so familiar, so reassuring. But he'd lost the lanky boyishness in his arms he'd had eight years ago, and he made no attempt to kiss her forehead as he would have done back then. This man. He was the last person she wanted to hold her while she cried. And he was the only one who could.

She let herself cry for a few minutes, determined to squeeze every tear out. She already knew she didn't want to do this again—not in front of *him*—so it was better to let the well run dry. Finally, she regained her composure and broke away from him.

"All right, perfume," she said, brushing her cheeks dry and tucking her bobbed hair behind her ears. That would be the end of it. "I'll need to be with you while you question the lords. I designed the blend to work on myself and I'm not sure what effect it would have if you wore it."

"Are you saying I don't have the assets to pull it off?" he said, thrusting out his chest. "Some men prefer my build, you know?"

She smacked him on the arm, but despite—or maybe because of—her earlier tears, she laughed. "Very true," she said. "I meant it's more to do with body chemistry."

"Noted," he said, falling into step next to her. "How much do you have left?"

"Only a little," she said. "It's expensive to make." She didn't add that, now Larry was dead, her supply of contraband Halgyric mist had dried up.

"I have ruemoss and the rosewater mist we confiscated from Lodi Barnaka, which I might be able to turn into some kind of muddling haze," said Kellen, scanning the landscape. "If we're stuck here, we may need to look for more ingredients out on the caldera."

"Well, you've already found geodes…" She unlatched her carpet bag and dug out a small bottle of perfume. She dabbed what little remained onto her wrists and neck.

"Oh, that's strong," said Kellen, digging in his pocket and pulling out the ruemoss. "I better take this before I end up helpless to your charms."

"Yes, we don't need a repeat of last night."

"Was the kiss really that awful?" said Kellen, putting the ruemoss into his mouth.

"Well, you *were* drunk."

"In my defence, I was tired, I'd just found out my daughter had broken her arm, and I didn't know how we were going to get out of this damn valley."

She smacked him again, for parroting what she'd said earlier, and his grin grew wider.

"One more project together? For old times' sake?" He held out his hand for her to shake, and she found herself taking it with a smile. But it was tinged with sadness. Every laugh they shared, every touch that made her feel warm and comforted would mean nothing when this was all over. Kellen would never pick her over his country. All she was to him was a youthful fling.

Losing him had torn her apart once. And here she was, giving him the chance to do it all over again.

Emeth heard the news about Jarvie Braehurst's death from Drawley as the supper hour was approaching.

"You! Get over here. This is bad business. A bad, bad bit of business," said Drawley, clamping a hand over Emeth's arm and dragging him from where he'd volunteered to help the cook—

one of Penny Aldridge's dance troupe—distribute stew to the surviving passengers. There was so little a priest was good for here, but serving food was one service he could provide.

"Sir, there are people waiting—" Emeth tried to protest, but Drawley waved a hand.

"There are far more important things afoot. Murder, man!" Drawley marched him towards a rocky outcropping where Ambrose Carey was waiting for them. "There's been another damn murder. And that Barnaka woman can't have done it. The guards were watching her."

"Who is it?" asked Emeth.

"Does the name Jarvie Braehurst mean anything to you?" asked Ambrose.

Emeth shook his head automatically. He'd renounced his father's way of life and associates years ago, so it didn't feel like much of a lie. But every noble family in Balter had dealings with Magnus Selnick and his thugs at one time or another, as there was no other way to get hold of contraband Halgyric mist or the last remnants of solozite on the continent. Emeth's father had let Selnick move goods through their estate lands, and the family had taken a fee for it. Braehurst's name had showed up many times in the account books that Emeth used to pore over.

"You're a lucky boy," said Drawley. "He was one of Selnick's lot. Those Halgyric rubes are now investigating his death along with the conductor's. One more thing for them to bungle."

"I think they've conducted themselves quite sensibly," said Ambrose.

Drawley snorted his disdain. Even Emeth had to admit that Ambrose's opinion of the Halgyrics was more swayed by the pretty girl they'd brought with them than reason.

"They don't know our ways," said Drawley, squeezing Emeth's shoulders. "Those Halgyrics, they're religious sorts, aren't they? They'll listen to you. Gods. I had nothing to do with this business. Bought a few things from Selnick once or twice, but I paid my tab."

"And my family hardly had the money to get involved with Selnick," added Ambrose.

Was Drawley actually concerned that suspicion might swing his way? How ridiculous. In their short acquaintance, Emeth had pegged Lord Drawley as a man who was all thunder with no strike. But instead of pointing this out, an idea struck Emeth. His testimony would likely be meaningless for these men, but it could help someone else.

"I might be able to help you," said Emeth. "Take me to the Halgyrics."

Kellen and Genna spoke to all the lords they could find, asking them if they had any connections to the deceased. Thanks to Genna's perfume, almost every one of them volunteered a lurid history. It turned out that very few of them had a problem with buying from Selnick. Lord Gamth even admitted that Braehurst had been sent around to his home to collect payment once. But it was obvious that each man they spoke to had been genuinely shocked by what had happened. Genna had claimed her perfume wouldn't produce confessions, but Kellen imagined it might at least hint at a guilty conscience. Most of the lords had strong alibis as well, having been within sight of many others in the camp for the past several hours.

"Gamth is worth looking into further," said Genna. "And we still haven't heard from Lord Drawley or Lord Carey."

"That's true," said Kellen. "Let's get their testimonies out of the way. Then we'll follow up with the dancers who've been looking after the luggage."

They were only halfway back to camp when Lord Drawley and Lord Carey came blustering towards them, with the reedy man in priest's robes who'd informed him of Mr Neuwirth's murder walking behind them. It took a moment for Kellen to place which of the Glyn Folk the young acolyte served, but eventually he spotted an insignia on the hem of his robes that showed his devotion to Chanri.

"Mr Linde!" Lord Drawley's booming voice drew Kellen's attention back to the matter at hand. "I understand you're running an investigation, and I wouldn't mind helping out. My good man here says he knows something pertinent."

"Yes, of course." Kellen tapped Genna on the shoulder and she passed him the notebook. "If you can answer a few of our questions?"

"Oh, there's no time for that! We know where you ought to be looking—" Drawley began.

"It won't take long." Genna smiled and the three men twisted around to her.

Kellen repressed a laugh as their eyes grew foggy in her sway.

"Did any of you know Jarvie Braehurst?" she asked.

"Not I," Lord Carey volunteered eagerly.

"Well, I did. Bad business about his death," said Drawley, the perfume destroying any resistance he might have had to the truth. "I did some business with Selnick. Absolute travesty what he charged, but I paid my bill. I'm no idiot."

"And you, sir? I missed your name?" Genna turned the full force of her perfume on the young acolyte. He staggered backward, as if pushed by the force of mist that hung around her neck.

"Ah, yes… Emeth." He rubbed his eyes.

"Did you know Mr Braehurst?"

"My father had some dealings with him."

Lord Drawley turned, his moustache bobbing in surprise. "You never mentioned that, Trudane."

"Trudane? Emeth Trudane?" Now Kellen knew where he recognised the man from—a combination of newspaper clippings and conversations, not with him, but with his father. The Trudane succession crisis had been one of the great scandals of the past few years. All the Lords' Council had buzzed over who might take Lord Trudane's spot, since his son had sworn himself to Chanri's ministry. That he still associated with the Council at all was very interesting.

Emeth stared back at Drawley, caught off guard by his own words. "I'm sorry, my lord, I didn't think it important," he said. "I tried to put my father's contacts behind me. Braehurst certainly wasn't someone I wanted anything to do with."

"And why not?" asked Genna.

"Because he was a hard, evil man," said Emeth. "Everyone knew he was a monster. Like Selnick. There are people who work for gangsters out of desperation, and then there are those who enjoy hurting people. I don't know why we're bothering to mourn a death that the gods themselves would applaud."

Emeth broke off, blinking rapidly. Perhaps he wouldn't have revealed such a deep abhorrence for Braehurst if Genna hadn't been wearing mist. Kellen didn't doubt he was wrong, but the contrast between his testimony and the other lords was stark. Perhaps it was because, at their cores, they didn't object to the existence of crime lords, but this man clearly did. No wonder he'd run off to join the temple.

"And where have you lot been for the last few hours?" Kellen asked.

"Yes, where were you?" Genna added.

Right. Kellen returned to his notebook. He needed to let her do the questioning if they wanted the perfume to work.

"Well, I was part of the party that went to find the caboose," said Carey, shrugging. "Then I talked to the other lords. Grabbed a bite to eat. That sort of thing."

Lord Drawley hadn't been so industrious. "I've been doing nothing, really," he said. "Wondering when you'd all be back with news about the ruddy caboose."

"I was helping the cook set up for supper," said Emeth. His robes even bore the slop stains of the stew he'd been serving.

"Very well," said Kellen. "What did you want to tell us?"

"Go on, Trudane," said Drawley.

"*Emeth*. It's just Emeth," he said, but he stepped forward. "Earlier, I went to visit the boy the soldiers took captive. If you ask me, that was all very rashly done."

"How so?" asked Genna.

"He's hardly more than a child. Accusing him of destroying the train was absurd."

Lord Drawley made a sputtering sound.

"I wanted to make sure he had water and sustenance," he said. "And he told me a remarkable tale. He wanted to bargain with the soldiers guarding him, but they wouldn't listen. He saw Braehurst. Back when he was in the luggage car, before the train exploded. He saw Braehurst threatening a woman."

"Threatening a woman?" Genna repeated.

"You should ask the boy about it," said Emeth. "I believe he knew the woman's name, too. And, if you can, would it be possible

211

to talk some sense into the soldiers? The boy's word might prove useful, and since he was tied up, we all know there isn't any possibility he killed Braehurst or the conductor. Guarding a starving boy and a wealthy widow seems rather pointless, given our current problems."

"Of course," said Kellen. A new female suspect, which was rotten luck. They'd have to interrogate witnesses who'd be resistant to Genna's perfume. Worse still, every time the investigation circled back to the female passengers, Kellen found himself confronting the Lords' Council's original theory.

A woman might not need the help of volchemistry to overpower a man like Braehurst. Perhaps Davina wasn't the only witch on the train.

CHAPTER

✦✦ 18 ✦✦

It turned out there were good parts to being stranded in the mountains after your train exploded and ruined your holiday. As the sun arced a course towards its night-time bed beyond the harbours of Pesca, Rae fought against the sleepiness that was making her eyes feel heavy. She couldn't fall asleep now. Not when things were finally getting interesting.

She sat next to Miss Linde, watching as the men attempted to wedge a fallen tree beneath the engine and use it as a lever. When they began, there had been lots of laughter and posturing as the lords lined up and bragged about how well they'd boxed in college. Miss Linde leaned over and whispered in her ear that they were all a bunch of ninnies. Aside from the soldiers, there was only one strong-looking chap in the mix. The rest were wisps of men, overwhelmed by their impressive tailcoats.

They grunted and huffed, but for all their exertion they succeeded only in snapping the tree in two. Davina laughed and Rae followed suit, enjoying the scowl the big fellow threw the pair of them. This was the best time she'd ever had with a babysitter.

Miss Linde had remembered to fetch them dinner, but other than that, she didn't seem the least bit bothered about what Rae was up to. Even though Rae had a broken arm, she let her climb over the boulders on the southern bluff and toss rocks onto the train tracks. There had been plenty of times when her mother had to work, and Rae had been left with nannies who shrieked and tutted and insisted she sit and do everything exactly *just so*. Miss Linde seemed about as interested in issuing discipline as Rae was in receiving it.

"You aren't helping." The brawny man walked towards them as the crew took another break to discuss how they intended to tip the engine back onto its wheels.

Rae slid into Miss Linde's shadow. She hadn't considered that they might actually make the men angry. It seemed like a joke a moment ago, but now—

Miss Linde was unfazed. "Maybe I'm no help," she said. "But at least I'm not breaking my back trying to do something ridiculous."

"It's your fault we're at this. You and Kellen. Everyone's sold on his plan to get the damn grinder going."

"That's Kellen's idea, not mine," said Miss Linde. *Kellen.* Rae knew that name. It belonged to Mr Linde, but she wasn't supposed to use it, even though her mother did.

"Fine, but I'm not wasting any more time on this," said the man. "If Kellen comes by, tell him I'm going to dig latrines. We can't use the ones on the train, and if we're staying here, we're going to need somewhere to go to the toilet."

"Thank goodness!" Rae spoke up without thinking of whose company she was in.

Miss Linde turned in surprise, as if she'd forgotten Rae was with her. More frighteningly, the big man noticed her. His stare was obsidian-sharp, and Rae quivered at the sight of him. His shoulders were even broader than Larry's had been and he was almost as tall as Mr Linde. "Who's your friend, Davina?" he asked.

"Oh, this is Rae," said Miss Linde. "Kellen made me take her, so he could work with her mother. She's a volchemist or something."

"He didn't ask for your help?" he asked.

"Apparently not." Miss Linde didn't sound happy. Was this why she'd ignored Rae so thoroughly? Was she upset that she hadn't got to work with her brother, instead of Ma?

"Did you feed her?" he asked. "It's past dinner."

"Of course I've fed her, Morel! I'm not an idiot."

Morel. Rae mouthed the name silently to herself, wanting to remember it. She recognised him now. He'd been with Mr Linde when he'd brought the bag of rocks to Ma, though he hadn't said much then. None of the gentlemen who'd courted Ma had ever come with so many people before, but somehow she'd already met Mr Linde's brother and sister. How many more Lindes were there?

A slight smile creased Morel's dour face. "How's my sister treating you?"

"Very well!" shouted Miss Linde.

"Fine," mumbled Rae.

"How's your arm?" He bent low and Rae scooted away.

"Don't touch it," she said.

"I wouldn't dream of it. It's sore, then?"

She nodded, uncertain why he was still talking to her. Ma wasn't even nearby to impress.

"I broke my arm once on deployment." He pointed to a snaking scar that wrapped around his right forearm. "Not even for something exciting. One of my boys' guns misfired, and it spooked my horse. She tossed me."

"Did it hurt?" Rae almost wished she could remember what her own break felt like.

"You bet. Hurt like hell, and they made me drink this awful potion."

"Ma gave me one too!" Rae leaned forward, amazed that he'd sworn in front of her. Grown-ups always pretended they didn't know rude words when she was around. "I hated it!"

"Ugh, sorry to hear it," he said. "I wish it didn't work, but it does. Rotten drink cut my healing time back by half."

"But you've still got a scar."

"Yeah, I guess." He raised his arm. "Maybe you'll get one. Then you'll look like a brave soldier."

Rae grinned at the idea. "Is that what you are?"

"No, he's a snivelling coward," said Miss Linde.

Mr Morel gave his sister such a huge grin that it was a wonder to Rae he'd ever looked serious. "She's just jealous she's never done anything exciting enough to break one of her bones," he said.

Miss Linde rolled her eyes. They probably could have gone on like this much longer. They sounded like children, prodding at each other in the same way as the twins in Rae's class at school used to. Rae found the dynamic fascinating, having grown up an only child, but their chatter was cut short by a curt voice a few feet away.

"Hey, Morel! Are we doing this thing or not?"

The voice belonged to a woman with a long, golden braid. She carried a shovel over her shoulder and Rae could only guess she planned to help the gentlemen dig toilets, since a small group was gathered behind her. She watched Mr Morel with a keen eye, and at her command he got back to his feet.

"Coming, Kira."

"*Kira?*" The bored tone was now gone from Miss Linde's voice. "As in Kira Westwick? *You're* Kira Westwick? Sorry, I saw your name on the passenger list and I've been wondering—I'm your biggest fan actually—"

The woman with the shovel turned away, but Mr Morel furrowed his brow. "You know Kira?"

"I wish I did!" Miss Linde lurched to her feet, beaming at the blonde woman. "My copy of *Drake's Descent* is in my bag. It's absolutely brilliant. You're really her, aren't you? Are you on book tour or—"

"I wouldn't call *this* a book tour." Kira swung the tip of her shovel in an arc that seemed to indicate the whole sorry valley they were stranded in. "You're a fan, then?"

"I… well…" Miss Linde stuttered with an uncertainty Rae hadn't imagined she could possess until now.

Did this woman write books, then? She didn't seem very excited about it, but then again, Rae had never heard of the book Miss Linde was so fond of. Clearly she'd never written anything as good as *Lives of the Witches* if she'd rather go and dig toilets than talk to a fan.

"Well, if we make it through this, I'll sign your book." Kira fell into step alongside the other men waiting to dig the latrines. "Come on, Morel."

Mr Morel gave his sister one last, quizzical look, then turned back to Rae. "I'll see you later, little one. Keep taking your medicine." He waved and, as he left, Rae felt an odd ache in her chest. Miss Linde might have let her do what she wanted, but it was rare adults ever treated her as though what she had to say mattered. Mr Morel had done it so easily. Was that what it might have been like growing up with a father?

Rae hugged her knees tight to her chest while Miss Linde sat next to her again, now wearing a slight frown. Was she upset by the way the author lady had treated her?

"Are you bored?" Miss Linde asked suddenly.

"Umm…" Wasn't everyone?

"I want to look for something, so that means you'll need to come with me. Unless you'd rather go and dig toilets with my brother—"

"I can help you." Rae jumped to her feet. Even if Mr Morel was nice, she'd had enough of toilets. "Are we going to *investigate*? Like Ma and Mr Linde?"

"I'm just planning to look for something."

"For the investigation?"

"Maybe." Miss Linde shrugged, doing a terrible job of pretending this wasn't exciting.

She walked them down the line of fallen carriages, leading them to one close to the back. "I think this was the smoking carriage." She hopped onto the coupling, then yanked on the door. It fell open on broken hinges, revealing nothing but dusty darkness inside. Miss Linde looked down at Rae. "This is your last chance. You can still follow Morel—"

"I want to see what's inside too."

"All right." Miss Linde reached down so she could hoist Rae up by the armpits. Rae bit down on her cheek as the pressure of Miss Linde's grip strained against her sling. But she made it, and Miss Linde gestured for her to be the first one through the door. Rae's heart thudded at the possibility of an adventure.

Miss Linde flicked at one of the lamps, but it didn't light. "Worth a try, I guess," she said.

Rae nodded, not that anyone could see her. Only slivers of the setting sun filtered through the smashed windows overhead.

She walked slowly, letting her eyes adjust to the gloom. The sight of the world turned sideways and tumbled together was fascinating. The bar counter must have been fixed to the ground because it now hung in the air, its cupboards flapping open and filled with broken glass. The furniture lay in a jumble, obscuring their path.

"Do you think there are any bodies inside?" Rae tried to keep the tremor out of her voice. Perhaps she wasn't as brave as she'd thought. This was the type of thing the witches in her book faced without flinching. She stepped around a fallen chair, careful not to touch anything. Broken glass crunched beneath the stiff soles of her boots.

"They got pulled out last night." Miss Linde climbed over the furniture. "We should tell the men to grab some of the furnishings, though. It might be nice to have a chair back at the camp."

"But we aren't going to be at the camp much longer, are we? Ma said someone from the train company will come looking for us."

"Oh… right, of course." But Miss Linde didn't look at her as she spoke. Maybe she was distracted by whatever secret task had prompted her to enter the smoking carriage in the first place. She slid a table into the corner, so she could climb on top and reach the bar counter.

Still, she might be easier to get information from than the other adults. "Were you with Mr Morel when he went to find the caboose?" Rae asked.

"Ah, yes." Miss Linde reached into one of the open cupboards, then flinched. "*Shit.*"

"You shouldn't say that," said Rae, though she was secretly thrilled she had.

"Well, I hurt myself."

"You touched glass, didn't you? It's everywhere."

"I guess it is."

"Like witches' eyes."

"What?" Miss Linde nearly slipped from her perch on the table. She really should be more careful.

"See? The floor is sparkling." Rae swept her finger through the air, tracing the dim evening light that shone through the window and danced across the broken glass on the floor. There was barely any moonlight tonight, just enough to make the stars on the ground shine.

"And witches' eyes... do you think they sparkle?"

"Philomena's did," said Rae, eager for the chance to share her passion. Ma had grown tired of the topic long ago, and everyone else always told her to hold her tongue when she wanted to talk about witches. "She was a really powerful witch from over three hundred years ago. When the volcano blew, she led a group of refugees into Halgyr, but she refused to enter the cities with them. So, she lived wild in the woods for a hundred years."

"How do you know about that?" Miss Linde was no longer searching the cupboards. It was gratifying to hold the attention of someone who'd previously ignored her. "Aren't you Balterian?"

"I guess," said Rae.

"Then how did you learn about witches? I hardly hear about them in Halgyr, and everyone's afraid of them in Balter."

"We have this book," said Rae. "It belonged to my father. Ma gave it to me to remember him by."

"And you're old enough to read it?" Miss Linde suddenly had an awful lot of questions.

"Ma has to help me with some of the big words."

"And your father… what did he have to do with witches? Did he hunt them or—"

"No!" That much Rae did know. Not because of anything Ma had told her, but because, deep in her bones, she knew her father couldn't possibly have been cruel like that. He hadn't left them with some vulgar book about killing witches, but one full of faerie tales. "He was a fisherman. He died at sea."

Rae didn't dare say it out loud, but that was all she'd ever been told about her father. It pained Ma to talk about him, so Rae didn't press for details as much as she would have liked. Once she'd asked Ma if her father had bought the book, thinking he'd read it to her as she grew up, and Ma had only cried, unable to answer yes or no. But the tears had been enough for Rae—her father had intended to love them all his life. And if he were here, he'd tuck her in his arms and read her stories.

"Oh, I'm sorry." Miss Linde returned to rifling through the cabinets.

"It's all right," said Rae, relieved Miss Linde had turned away. Her eyes itched and she had to rub them. It must be the dust in the air. Or maybe it was the image of Morel smiling at her that swam in her memory. Most days, it didn't bother her that she and Ma were alone. They had each other, and some people couldn't say that.

A silence fell over the cabin. Rae held her breath, until her cheeks burned and the overwhelming feelings of the day settled a little further down inside her.

"I lost a parent too, when I was little." Miss Linde's voice caught Rae off guard. She climbed down from her perch on the table, something tucked under her arm. "It never quite leaves you. We should get back to the camp before it gets too dark."

"Did you find what you were looking for?" Rae asked.

"Ah, yes. Crystophone." She held it up for Rae to see. "And a handful of record stones. It's bent, but we can make it work."

"Music would be nice," said Rae. Anything happy sounded good right now.

"I think your ma and my brother are going to pull it apart."

"Oh, for the *investigation*!" Rae reached for Miss Linde's hand. "We did it, then? We found a clue?"

"Something like that," said Miss Linde, smiling as she led Rae out of the carriage. "Maybe now we've found a clue, my brother and your ma will want to see us."

"You think so?" Rae asked. Being with Miss Linde had turned out better than she'd thought it would, but even a nice evening exploring a toppled train didn't make up for the fact that her arm was broken and her mother was off with some strange gentleman instead of comforting her.

"They'd better."

Together, they headed back towards the camp, the crystophone tucked under Miss Linde's arm. They must look like a team of adventurers, and Rae almost felt glad she'd met her. Ma's gentlemen had never come with brothers and sisters before. It made Rae wonder what would become of Miss Linde when the sandy-haired man inevitably grew tired of Ma and left.

CHAPTER
19

For the first time since the train crashed, Dalton Rai felt something akin to hope. It wasn't a full hope—that had died with Merrith—but he felt a surge of not only *wanting* something, but also *believing* it could happen. And all this wanting and believing was focused on the conversation he was having with Ms Freath. She was going to get him out of his bonds and away from the soldiers. He just knew it. All he had to do was everything she asked.

The Mediate who'd helped bury Merri had brought Ms Freath around with another gent. They were looking into the Jarvie Braehurst murder and Dalton was only too happy to tell them all about that. Someone was finally listening to him, and he had the Mediate to thank for it.

"It was after the train passed Korio. That's where Merri and I jumped on." Dalton didn't bother trying to hide how he came to be on the train anymore. "We got behind some of the luggage and were settling in when we heard the conductor come in with some people."

"The conductor? He was involved with this too?" asked Ms Freath.

"Yes, ma'am," Dalton said. "There were three of 'em total. The conductor, Jarvie Braehurst, and a woman. But Braehurst made the conductor leave them alone. He put up a bit of fight, but I think he must have known who Braehurst worked for, cos he said… what was it? Braehurst said his employer would take care of things if something went missing. And she even mentioned Selnick."

"Still, both our victims were there." That was the other bloke. Dalton hadn't caught his name, but he had the most uppity Halgyric accent this side of the caldera. Still, if he was working with Ms Freath, Dalton would help him because *Ms Freath*! Who could possibly do anything other than what she wanted? "So, who was this woman?" said the man. "Did she survive the crash?"

"Oh yes, sir. I know she did. I even took a peek. Merri wanted to have my hide for it, but I figured I needed to know. Anyhow, he was trying to scare her, asking about a big old box she'd brought with her. It was marked with green paint. I checked that too, after they left, that is."

"And what did he say to her? We need every detail." Ms Freath knelt so that she was level with him and he was hit with another whiff of her perfume. She even smelled fantastic, which was odd. He usually hated lavender. Gave him headaches. But didn't it suit her?

"Well…" Dalton blinked through the haze. "Braehurst said she should open her box up for him, but she didn't. Then she told him to sod off and stop following her. But he wasn't following her, see. He said he'd come for some other reason and then she got all friendly and curious. Said that if he told her why he was there, she'd open the box for him."

"And did he?" Ms Freath's voice raised in pitch. "Did he tell her?"

"No, he backed off. She won that one. But that don't mean they didn't go at it again later. You have to talk to her," said Dalton.

"She's the lady wearing britches with the long, blonde hair. Name's Kira Westwick."

The Halgyric fellow scribbled the name down. "Thank you very much. You've been helpful."

So, were they done with him? He leaned forward and raised his hands, to remind them he was still tied up with ropes. By the gods, they had to help him. If they didn't—

But the Halgyric was speaking now, turning to the soldiers as if he were their general. "Captain Sewell, I don't think it's a good use of your men's time for them to guard this boy or Mrs Barnaka. They're hardly threats to our camp. Meanwhile, there's an actual killer on the loose. Given our limited resources and the boy's cooperation with the investigation, I think it best you untie them."

The soldiers went to Lodi first, guns still trained on Dalton.

"It's about bloody time!" Lodi cried.

They'd always treated her better than they had him. One had even fetched her food, whereas Dalton would have starved without the Mediate. He'd be furious if he told his story and all it achieved was Lodi's freedom.

"Sir, I wouldn't be so sure." Captain Sewell shifted his weight between his feet. "You can't let criminals go willy-nilly. They're the sort that take advantage of a crisis. Try to get away with things while everyone's distracted."

"We need a night watch to guard the camp," said the Halgyric. "That takes precedence."

"Captain, if you please?" Ms Freath stepped in.

"Fine. But I don't like it," said the captain.

"I'm not gonna cause any trouble. I promise. I want out of these mountains, same as everyone." Dalton held out his hands to be untied, and when the captain didn't hop to it, the Mediate stepped forward to loosen the bands himself. He'd been lurking behind the couple investigating the murder this whole time and Dalton was grateful for him now.

"I'll take the boy, if you're finished with us, Mr Linde?" said Emeth.

"For now, yes. If I have more questions for him, I'll come and find you." Mr Linde—that must be the Halgyric man's name—snapped his notebook shut and headed off with Ms Freath, no doubt looking for Kira Westwick.

"Thank you, sir. And ma'am?" Dalton called to Ms Freath, and she turned her lovely face to him once again.

"Yes?"

"If you need anything, I'm your man. Whoever did the killings probably wrecked the train, right? I'd do anything to… well, I'd do anything." He couldn't put Merri's death into words, even though it gnawed inside him. Some griefs were too big to swallow in a day.

Ms Freath nodded, then strode off after the Halgyric. What an odd pair. She was clearly Balterian—her dusky skin made her a dead ringer for the people in the fishing towns in the south-west of the country—which meant that she and that fellow were from opposite ends of the continent.

"How do you reckon those two shacked up together?" Dalton asked Emeth as the Mediate untied his wrists.

"I don't know," he said, his lips folded inwards as if the question bothered him. "You sensed a familiarity between them too, then?"

"Well, just assuming," Dalton admitted. "I mean, she could have any gent she wanted, couldn't she? But she's here with him. *Finally!*"

Dalton's hands came free, and if his ribs hadn't still been throbbing from last night's burns, he would have somersaulted down the mountains. For now, he contented himself in throwing his arms around Emeth. "Thank you, Mediate," Dalton wheezed. "Thank you for getting me out of that."

"It's—it's nothing." Emeth's back was rigid, as if he didn't know how to take a hug.

"Merri would have liked you." They were alike, in so many ways. Uptight and proper. By the gods… Merri.

"You must be freezing," said Emeth, dragging Dalton back to reality. "I have spare robes you can borrow."

"Thanks, but I don't think I'm worthy to wear a holy man's clothing."

"Few who wear them are," said Emeth. "There are clouds gathering over the mountains. Let's keep you warm."

Dalton relented, allowing Emeth to lead him towards the camp. Ahead, Lodi Barnaka was already reuniting herself with her wardrobe, which was still stashed near the luggage pile, but Dalton turned away from her. He'd heard enough of her bellyaching for a lifetime. The Mediate took him to a spot next to the medical ward where he'd stored his modest possessions. Emeth passed Dalton an oversized robe and it was all he could do to mutter a chorus of thank-yous. Nothing he did was enough, and he knew it. The Mediate wasn't even done. After getting him clothing, he led Dalton to the food line, where there were still a few bowls of soup up for grabs.

"Don't eat too quickly," Emeth warned. But it was hard to heed advice like that when it was the best meal Dalton had eaten in weeks. It probably wasn't much by the standards of the bigwigs on the train, but when was the last time someone let Dalton eat stew made with meat *and* bone marrow? He only slowed when he burned his tongue, knees jittering as he waited for the dumplings to cool.

As the sun dropped behind the mountains, so did the temperature. Dalton watched as little fires popped up around the camp, trying to keep the cold at bay. Emeth must have eaten earlier. He sat silent and stoic at Dalton's side, brow furrowed as if he were working through the problems of the day. Dalton didn't have the energy for that. Once this disaster was over, maybe he'd take the time to ponder all the details, but not here. Not when his ribcage was blistered, his wrists were sore from rope burn and his head throbbed with—

"Lavender," he said suddenly. "I… I *hate* bloody lavender."

He rubbed his temple, trying to drive away the headache. The Mediate turned towards him. "Pardon?"

"Oh, nothing. It's just something that Ms Freath had in her perfume. Didn't bother me at first, though. It was so odd, like…" Dalton turned to see Emeth staring at him with intense, dark eyes. "Sorry, I natter all the time. You should ask Merri about it. I can go off about the stupidest things and—well, I guess you can't ask Merri—"

"No, Ms Freath's perfume. What were you saying about it?" Emeth asked, as if something was clicking into place for him.

"Well, I don't know! I liked it when she was around, but once she'd left—"

"It gave you a headache. By the *gods*!" Something had the Mediate mightily excited. "You see what this means, don't you? That wasn't perfume. She was wearing mist. We let those damn Halgyrics lead the investigation and they're using mist."

Mist? Dalton had heard about Halgyric mist before, but always in these quiet, wondering ways. It was the stuff of legends. Back before the Great Eruption, the Renchans had used it, though they'd never had all the versions available in Halgyr. He'd mostly heard of it causing visions and spiritual experiences. Actually, that was probably why the Mediate knew about it. Some temples still used mist when they could get their hands on it.

"I felt funny when I talked with her," said Dalton, cottoning on to the Mediate's argument. "Like… nothing could go wrong if I just did as she asked. Like I could trust her."

"Exactly. Gods, they're clever. Clever and dangerous."

"Should we tell someone, then? Do you think they did it?"

Emeth paused, the same crease coming back to his brow. "That's a difficult question. Who would we tell? I don't trust the Halgyrics, but I trust the Lords' Council even less."

Dalton felt relieved hearing the Mediate doubt his countrymen. It meant he saw his nation for what it really was. The Balterian Lords' Council would justify any kind of wickedness if it served their interests. They'd waged war through the mountains, all to get a port on the eastern side of Solozya. Any one of them could have killed Braehurst for money. As for the train… Well, Dalton wasn't sure how the train came into it, but surely one of the lords could have a reason to blow it up. Probably money again. Balter would have to repair the rail line, right? Maybe one of the lords owned a rail company and wanted the Council to give him a stack of cash to fix the line?

"Besides, mist only alters perceptions." Emeth steepled his fingers beneath his chin. "It would take something stronger to turn an engine to stone."

"The soldiers were talking about that. Saying maybe…" Dalton swallowed hard. "Maybe witchcraft."

"A definite possibility."

That was all the Mediate said in response, though Dalton wished for more. They might have agreed about the Lords'

Council, but the Mediate was still Balterian. He would have been raised on tales of witches murdering as they saw fit. Well, they weren't gentle creatures, that was for sure, but they were also the only reason anyone had survived the Great Eruption. The whole central caldera should have been entombed beneath lakes of lava and ash. But, on that fateful day three hundred years ago when hell had rained from the sky, anywhere a witch's life was endangered, she instinctively transformed and saved herself. Pockets of Rencha had been spared. Anyone who lived near a witch benefitted from her protection. Any village who'd driven witches out died inside a stone coffin.

Since then, the witches had been the Renchans' protectors. Once Balter had started to use volchemistry to fight their wars, only they were strong enough to fight back. They lost, of course. But they were allies, at least out of necessity. Balter never suffered a witch to live and Halgyr barely tolerated their existence. What friends did witches have other than the Renchans?

"Emeth? Emeth Trudane!"

A new voice cut through the night and some dandy in a tailcoat marched towards them. Emeth was already rising from his perch, clearly recognising the fellow.

"Coming!" he called, then turned to Dalton one last time. "I'm sorry, but I'm needed elsewhere. You'll be all right, then?"

"Sure." Dalton poked at the remains of his stew.

What did *all right* even mean on a night like this? Dalton doubted any of the other passengers would welcome him into their campsite. He picked at the border stitched around the cuff of the robe the Mediate had lent him. Red for Chanri, guardian of gentle creatures.

The Mediate had given him a lot to think about tonight, but

somehow the threat of a witch echoed the most through Dalton's mind. He didn't want to believe it was true. Back when Merri had been alive, he'd dreamed about fighting Balter alongside the witches. But if a witch had blown up the train, it would mean one of Rencha's protectors had killed Merri.

CHAPTER

++ 20 ++

Emeth would have liked more time to think over everything he'd discussed with Dalton. There was an innocence to the boy that no one else on this mountain shared. But Ambrose Carey wanted his attention now and, nominally, he was the man paying him to be here. It wouldn't do to upset the temple's benefactor—and at least it wasn't Lord Drawley.

"Have you got a moment? We haven't had much time to talk since, well…" Ambrose threw an arm out towards their surroundings. "All this."

"True," said Emeth. "But there's been rather more need for action than words of late."

"Maybe so, but Drawley's livid that you lied about knowing Braehurst." Ambrose never masked his emotions well, and sure enough, he sounded put out. It was such a small lie that it amazed Emeth anyone could take exception to it. "And he didn't care for when you helped that boy."

"I was helping with the investigation. Am I supposed to bend reality to your patron's wishes? There's no way the boy was involved in the murders."

"I know. Of course he isn't. And I wouldn't say anything, it's just…" Ambrose glanced over his shoulder and Emeth shook his head. No one at the camp was interested in what either of them was doing, and paranoia like this only drew attention. "The boy is Renchan. I know that hasn't got a thing to do with the investigation, but Drawley's getting anxious now. He's worried you'll side with the Caldera Peoples when we reach Ealidor, like you did with the boy."

"Is he, now?"

"But I told him you're a man of honour. We gave your temple quite the generous donation and you're not one to break your word," said Ambrose.

"Yes, honour." Because there was *such* honour in what they were doing. "Well, why don't you point out how easily I gained that boy's trust? All the better to exploit his people when the time comes."

"See, that's what I mean. You say things like that—" Ambrose stammered.

But Emeth was tired of being cowed by self-important men. Especially one who used to be his friend. "If you want your damn solozite, Ambrose, then leave me to manage affairs my way. You'll get your mine. I just pray you're not foolish enough to start another war with it."

"Would you keep your bloody voice down?" Again, Ambrose swung around, peering over his shoulders for onlookers. "We don't need anyone knowing what we're up to."

"It's not that clever or shocking a scheme, Ambrose."

Emeth regretted his involvement in the plan in so many ways. There had been dozens of attempts over the years to open a new solozite mine—rumour had it that the foothills in recently conquered Eastern Balter held a large deposit of the rare mineral. The only issue was that it was entirely in treaty territory. Balter couldn't hope to wage a war with the Caldera Peoples over it without heavy casualties. Their military supplies of solozite were too low, and no doubt the moment they engaged, the Caldera Peoples would call in the witches to defend them.

Their only hope of opening a mine was diplomacy, which the nearby clans had no interest in. Why would they countenance the promises of the men who'd driven them from their lands? It was a small mercy they didn't just dig up the solozite and try to use it themselves. But that didn't stop fools like Drawley and Ambrose sinking money into ridiculous ventures.

Ambrose's brilliant idea had been to appeal to them through their faith—*he knew just the bloke!* A former member of the Lords' Council who'd taken off to the Order of Chanri and, better yet, was a dear friend. Sharp as obsidian, too. No doubt he'd have ideas for how to win them over. Wouldn't he be the perfect fellow to bridge the divide?

Emeth had tried to refuse. But the Mediates at the temple saw the situation differently. Funds were low and Ambrose was willing to give quite the generous donation for just a few weeks of his old friend's time. Emeth's superiors decided to sell his services, like he was some common plough horse. He was still reeling from the revelation that, even among the priesthood, he wasn't seen as anyone but the son of Ignacious Trudane—Overseer of the Lords' Council. That lineage of blood-soaked avarice would follow him to his grave.

"You can trust me, Emeth," Ambrose said. "We're going to keep the solozite in safe hands. No arms dealing."

By Chanri, if only Emeth could believe him.

"But if people hear us talking about the deal right now…" said Ambrose, tightening the grip on his cravat. "The deaths of the conductor and Braehurst have changed everything. What witch goes around stabbing people?"

"One who doesn't want to be found," said Emeth.

"It's rumoured around camp that the Halgyrics think it could be a volchemist. And that means anyone with solozite—"

"Ambrose, you don't even have any. Not yet," said Emeth. That was the whole bloody point of opening a mine, wasn't it? Or was Ambrose a better liar than his bumbling suggested? If he'd actually managed to get his hands on solozite already… Well, that opened up a whole host of complications. "Unless you found something?"

"No! No, of course not." Ambrose flapped his hands anxiously. "It's just—"

But before Ambrose could muster any feeble defence, a figure ran towards them in the darkness. "Lord Carey!" The voice had the signature lilt of Davina Linde.

Ambrose—of course—melted at the sight of her. Emeth could see him taking in her unkempt hair and flushed cheeks. Somehow, she was even more beautiful in the aftermath of the train crash than she'd been when Emeth had met her in the dining carriage. The sweet coquette was gone and Emeth got the impression he was now seeing a more honest portrait of the girl. Ferocious determination burned behind her eyes—enough to put the ambitions of the Lords' Council to shame.

"We've done it!" she said, beaming at Ambrose. "Ms Freath wore down one of the quartz stones and now we can play images."

"Already?" said Ambrose. "But how?"

"I found a crystophone," she said, with a delicate shrug. The movement was so practised that Emeth had to stifle a laugh. But some twitch in his face must have shown, because her gaze swung around to him. "Oh! I didn't see you there, Mediate."

"I'm not actually a—" Emeth began.

"Mr *Trudane* then, if that's what you prefer."

When he scowled at her, her smile only widened. *Bloody hell*, this was why he didn't talk to her. But since he'd already made the mistake of drawing her attention, he might as well follow this through.

"Am I to understand you used volchemistry to extract memories from the crash site?" Emeth asked. "That's quite ingenious."

"Oh, no. Not the train crash," Ambrose said. "The quartz came from where the trestle bridge—"

"Lord Carey, would you like to join the investigation team as we view the images?" Davina cut in, her smile growing more strained.

"*Bridge?*" Emeth looked between the pair of them. "Where's there a bridge?"

"If you'll excuse us, Mr Trudane," she said, grabbing Ambrose's arm.

"Sorry, Emeth. Duty calls." Ambrose gave him a feeble wave before the girl hauled him away.

Emeth had half a mind to follow them, or at least repeat his question. If they'd managed to extract images from quartz, he'd love to see what they'd recorded. He wanted to know who'd blown up the train as much as the next person. Plus, if he knew what bridge they'd found, it could help him work out where they were stranded. He might finally know how long it would be until rescue arrived.

Or it could mean just the opposite. If there was activated quartz near this bridge, something had happened there. Something the Halgyrics were keeping secret. And just as when Emeth had discovered them using mist in their investigation, he arrived at the same conclusion.

They were the ones who were up to something.

CHAPTER

✦ 21 ✦

IT WASN'T EASY for Genna to find a place to project the images without attracting attention. Kellen had said he didn't want people to panic, but she thought it more likely he didn't want whoever caused the train crash to know what they'd discovered. In fact, Genna wondered if he'd have told *her* about the destruction of the trestle bridge if he hadn't needed her expertise.

Once Davina brought them the crystophone, Genna had been more than happy to get to work. It had been a welcome distraction from questioning people about Braehurst's death. If they kept digging around, Kellen might learn that he'd been sent to tail *her*, and if he knew that… She didn't think he'd actually accuse her of anything so heinous as blowing up the train. But being involved with one of Selnick's thugs wasn't a good look, no matter how she presented it. Kellen would know what she'd had to do to keep Rae provided for. And he'd think that made *him* the worthier parent.

Gods, what if there was some truth to that?

Rae was nestled sleepily into Genna's side. She squeezed her shoulder for comfort and the little girl sighed. Rae was trying desperately to stay awake until they played the images, which Genna hoped her daughter failed at. Her child didn't need any more material for nightmares.

Their small group had assembled at the shadowy edge of the treeline. The location was slightly removed from the rest of the camp, which suited their purposes. Davina went off in search of Morel and Lord Carey. Even though they wanted secrecy, Kellen thought the young lord's geological knowledge might prove useful. Besides, it would keep the Lords' Council nominally involved.

Kellen, in the meantime, fetched the materials Genna needed. Penny Aldridge provided him with a white tablecloth and a set of candles from the dining carriage. Genna had him string up the tablecloth so they could use it as a screen, then set about arranging the candles and the mirror in her make-up compact so the light they provided angled into the crystophone. She then spent a long time fiddling with wires and wishing she had a pair of pliers as she tried to reconfigure the apparatus so it could project images as well as sounds.

Eventually, Davina returned with Lord Carey and Morel. The whole group seemed in high spirits, though Genna kept her back to them as she worked. She'd only exchanged a handful of words with Kellen's siblings, and even less with the young dandy the Lords' Council had assigned to them. She was wary of forming deeper acquaintances, especially with Morel. Every so often, she caught him looking her way, a stitch in his brow as if he were trying to work out how she'd wormed her way into their midst. As if *she'd* been the one who meant to do that.

She was so determined not to meet anyone's eye that it caught her off guard when the quartz crystal began to hiss. Apparently, she'd found the right angle. The wire pressed beneath her thumb caught on a groove in the quartz as it spun around on the cranked mechanism.

"Oh, gods!" she cried out, and the Lindes all turned her way.

"Is it working?" Kellen asked.

"Give me just a second…" She brought one of the candles over, focusing the beam of light into the magnifying glass she had affixed to the end of the crystophone. A disc of cloudy light lit up on the tablecloth screen. "Yes, I think that's it."

A silence fell over the group as the three siblings and Lord Carey crowded around her. Genna poured a vial of basalt dust into the crystophone's power chamber, twisted her obsidian knife into the fine powder, then sat back to wait like the others.

The basalt snaked down the chamber, coating the surface of the quartz. As it came into contact with the wires, a shrill hum filled the air, and then there was a pop like lightning as the magnifying glass caught hold of the images emitted by the quartz. A beam spread out over the sheet and there it was—the bridge, still standing strong, viewed from the perspective of the very rhyolite canyon it straddled.

For a few minutes, the group watched in hushed silence as the scene unfolded. First the tableau was empty, but gradually the sound of an approaching train echoed out of the crystophone's speaker, then the nose of the engine came into view. As it sped across the bridge, Genna noticed the caboose was already missing. Kellen hadn't told her about that, and it brought up a host of questions.

The train drew closer to the other end of the bridge, nearing the side of the canyon they were now stranded on. As the luggage car passed the end of the bridge, a figure came into view.

A stately woman with loose red hair peeked out from the back door of the luggage car. She looked like none of the survivors, yet there was something unnervingly familiar about her too. She extended her arm over the canyon, and with a flick of her wrist the entire bridge reared up, twisted to the side, and fragmented into shrapnel.

Next to her, Rae sucked in a gasp and dug her fingers into Genna's skirts. For her part, Genna wanted to cover her daughter's eyes before she saw anything worse, but nothing else happened. The train jerked but didn't fall off its rails. Instead, it sped on, the woman still aboard. After that, there was nothing but empty terrain, which gradually faded as the mountain's memories came to a close.

"Well." Kellen's voice broke the silence.

He looked pale. Maybe it was just the darkness playing tricks on her eyes, but all three of the Linde siblings had a haunted glow about them, especially Davina, who was bracing herself against Morel's shoulder.

"That settles it!" Carey clapped like he'd just seen a good show at the theatre. "It was a witch after all. Oh lords, what a load off that is!"

"Is that how it looked to you too, Genna?" Kellen asked. "You didn't see any hint of volchemistry or—"

"It's not like she threw a load of basalt out the back of the train," said Genna. "It's as Lord Carey said. That's witchcraft."

"Has anyone been wearing those clothes?" asked Carey.

"Clothes!" Life suddenly sprung back to Davina's face. "Can you play it again, Ms Freath? We could recognise her by the clothes—"

"Looked like a dark robe to me. No one's wearing one of *those*," said Morel.

"A robe or a nightdress?" Kellen rubbed his hand across his chin.

"Well, it must be a nightdress, because that's how she'd blend in, isn't it?" said Carey enthusiastically. "Make it look like she was just one of us."

"Who says she stuck around to get caught?" asked Davina.

"Well, she must have, because people are still ending up dead," said Carey.

"Right." Davina's cheeks flushed and she took a steadying breath. "I... of course, *right*. Well, I suppose that means all your interviews today were useless."

"I suppose it does," said Kellen. "Damn..."

"But that's not really a surprise, right, Kellen?" Genna wasn't sure if she should be contributing to this conversation. But something felt off about the way everyone but Carey was reacting to the revelation. It frankly troubled her that she was agreeing with a man who came off as a bit of an idiot while the more intelligent people recovered from shock. "We always knew it had to be a witch. Look at the front of the train."

"Of course. We always knew that." Kellen said it so quickly that he *had* to be lying. For some reason that hadn't been a foregone conclusion to him, which was ridiculous. What could cause the engine to turn to stone other than wild magic? What did he know that she didn't?

She stared at Kellen, unsure whether she wanted to call him out or not. But, before she could make up her mind, Rae tugged on Genna's arm. "Why would they do that? Why would...?"

But then the words died on the little girl's lips.

Genna didn't know how to comfort her. Rae's obsession with witches had always been rooted in a desire to know more about her father, so Genna had never thought much of it. But somewhere in all of that reading, she must have developed a warped view of them. They weren't violent rebels to her, just pictures in a storybook.

"I don't know, sweetie." Genna pulled her daughter close to her. "I'm sure there are lots of witches that would ask the same question. Just because one bad witch hurt the train, doesn't mean they all—"

"Two," said Rae.

"What?" Genna said.

"*Two*. There's going to be two," said Rae. "Witches travel in pairs."

Genna gaped at her daughter, while, behind her, Carey started to laugh. "What a droll girl! Did you see another witch in the picture show, little one?"

Rae scowled at him. "No. I didn't have to. That's just what they do."

"She's right," said Kellen, pacing next to the crystophone. "They can't shift between their human and witch self without someone else being there to say their secret name. So, they usually travel with a companion who knows it. And that's easiest if they're both witches, of course. *Damn*."

"What's so bad about that? Won't it narrow things down even more?" asked Carey.

"It would. Except our best suspect is a woman travelling alone," said Kellen.

"Well, that could be an act," said Genna. "Someone else might be working with her. It really could be any two women."

"But you've got a suspect! It's all almost done." Carey dropped into a squat so he could look Rae in the eye. "See? There's nothing to fret about. Your mother and father are going to figure this all out."

"Lord Carey!" Genna sputtered. But Rae turned away from him without comment. The misunderstanding didn't seem to bother her. Plenty of men had been mistaken for her father during her life. But what about the others? She spun around to see if Morel and Davina had overheard Carey, but they were several feet away, whispering fiercely to each other. Genna hadn't noticed they'd stepped away, but thank the gods they had.

Watching their lips, she was able to make out shreds of their conversation.

Morel was speaking, his hands placed on Davina's shoulders. "We were by the canyon when Braehurst was murdered. No one is going to think that you—"

"I'm not talking about Braehurst." Davina tried to shake him off. "I'm talking about a bloody hole in the ground and—"

"Would you excuse me, I…" Kellen was staring at his siblings too. Yes, he was *definitely* paler than usual. "Lord Carey, shall we resume this investigation in the morning? Could you keep this confidential? We don't want news getting out to the wrong people."

"Of course!" Carey nodded. "Your secret is safe with me. I should check in with the soldiers, anyway. I signed up for night watch."

"Excellent." Kellen clapped him on the shoulder, finally managing to shuffle him away. Now the only inconvenience left was Genna herself. Kellen gave her a pained smile. "I'm sorry, but I need to talk to Morel and Davina. If you don't mind—"

"It's fine, Kellen. Rae needs to go to bed." Genna bent over the crystophone and began to pack up the components. Clouds loomed to the west, and she didn't want the evidence they'd found to get damaged by rain.

"I'm sorry, Genna. I really am."

His sincerity was worse than being ignored outright. Whatever exchange was passing between his siblings, it was yet another secret that she wasn't privy to. There were so many aspects of his life that she'd never be involved in, and she felt foolish for having been sucked into his world yet again. All day she'd run around playing detective with him, as if they were still university sweethearts. Now, he was pushing her out in the way a man of his position would always have to.

But the way his sister had blanched at the sight of a mysterious witch blowing up the trestle bridge haunted Genna as she put Rae down to sleep. Her daughter shared just as much blood with Kellen as Davina did. And, for the first time, it struck Genna that there might be far more dangerous things to be than the crown prince's bastard child.

CHAPTER
✦ 22 ✦

Nothing Morel or Kellen said could convince Davina not to worry. The witch in her was capable of stealing her memories, and Morel had been asleep when the crash happened. Who was to say she hadn't headed to the back of the train and torn the bridge to pieces? It didn't even matter that the clothes didn't match hers. No one was dressed like the witch, so why couldn't her witch self hide clothing too?

She had no way of knowing. Morel had only seen her as a witch in the dark very briefly, so while he said he didn't *think* she'd had red hair, he couldn't be certain either.

"First everything was on fire and then it was dark, so... I don't know," he said helplessly. They were speaking in hushed tones, away from Genna Freath and her daughter. Davina wished for the privacy of a closed room, locked with sealing mist, but there wasn't anywhere to go. The best they could do was whisper and pray the night watch didn't catch them.

Kellen tried to calm her with his usual optimistic bullshit. "It *can't* have been you, Davina. It doesn't make sense. Why would you want to destroy the train?"

"So? You haven't found anyone here who *does* want to destroy it," said Davina.

"You were coming back from the bridge when Braehurst died. There was no time to kill him. You've got to be innocent," he insisted.

"Witches travel in pairs," she shot back. "You said so yourself. What if Mother told someone other than you about what I am? What if they're in league with me and *they're* the ones who killed Braehurst and Mr Neuwirth?"

"Mother never told anyone," Kellen said staunchly.

"How would you know?" Davina demanded.

"Because she told me she didn't."

"Oh, please! You were thirteen, Kellen. Do you really think a grown woman would tell all her secrets to a thirteen-year-old boy?"

His face contorted in a way that showed she'd hit a nerve, but he didn't retaliate. Of course he didn't. Kellen would rather die than own up to any real emotion. Instead, he chose the safest route. "Maybe we should all get some rest. There's going to be a logical explanation for all of this, Davina. And when we find it, it won't have anything to do with *you*."

It must be wonderful to live in such a state of confident denial. Lucky Kellen.

Davina didn't know how she was supposed to sleep. But finally she agreed, because what else could she do? She and Morel made their way back to Genna and Rae, leaving Kellen to pack up the crystophone and the evidence it contained, and they all silently made their way back to the camp. Davina lay down between Morel and Rae, certain she wouldn't catch a wink. But the past day had left her ragged with fatigue. Eventually, the night won and she dozed off.

+ ✦ +

Kellen and Morel had both signed up for shifts with the night watch, but their turns weren't due yet. For now, Kellen lay next to Genna, staring at the sheet that had been strung up over their small patch of grass. He needed to sleep. It had been almost two days since he'd woken up on the train, believing his biggest problems were an illegitimate child and a hangover.

A few feet away, Morel started to snore. Thank the gods someone in their party was getting some sleep. Kellen's own mind was consumed with swirling questions. How was he going to approach Kira Westwick, knowing the woman might be a witch? How was he supposed to accuse her of witchcraft without the Balterians lynching her?

And if the killings didn't stop, how was he supposed to keep the whole group from descending into a rabid witch hunt and targeting his own sister?

His turmoil was interrupted by a cool hand sliding into his. Genna. He twisted on his side so he could meet her eye. Her lips were parted, as if she wanted to say something to him, so he waited. But nothing came. They shared a minute of silence, as if agreeing on the same awful conclusion. Nothing either of them could say would make the world any less horrifying.

He tightened his grip on her hand, running a thumb over the callouses she'd developed from years of using her volchemical knife. She let out a tremulous breath and he found his own body mirroring hers. He pulled her close, so her head rested against his bicep.

"Kellen…" Her voice was hardly a whisper. "We shouldn't."

"I know." He couldn't blame this on alcohol now, but the warmth of her body seemed to seep right into him. Even after all these years, he could tell she saw through him in a way no one else ever could. He'd forgotten the bliss of it—of being known by someone. Even if she was furious at him, which she had every right to be, she *knew* him.

How could he have ever let her go? Why had he been so careless? Perhaps it was asking too much of a teenaged boy to have expected his younger self to recognise what he'd had in her, but if he could go back, he would have held on until…

Until when? Did he actually plan on doing something with this feeling now? It had returned to him, but for what? He was still bound towards Halgyr, ready to take up a throne his court would never allow her to share with him.

"I…" Genna cleared her throat. "I'm not saying I'm glad any of this happened."

He raised an eyebrow at her. "An auspicious start."

She rolled her eyes, but a smile played on her lips. "But I will say… all things considered, I'm glad Rae and I didn't have to do this alone. It's… well."

"You're welcome," he said, unable to restrain a grin.

"Don't let it go to your head," she said, brushing a lock of hair back from his face and tucking it behind his ear. "And thank you for not saying anything to your family about Rae. I know we probably should at some point, but… until I know what she and I are going to do when we reach Ealidor…"

"Of course," he said. "Take all the time you need." And that, right there, was why he couldn't kiss her, no matter how much he wanted to. Genna didn't need a lover. She needed stability for herself and Rae. Right now, in the aftermath of the train crash, he offered that, but in the long run?

She slid her hand away from his hair, down the length of his neck and shoulder. For a second, he thought she might bridge the gap between them and nullify all his doubts. But as she rested her palm against his collarbone, she pushed herself gently away, rolling back towards her daughter.

Their daughter.

Kellen let her hand go.

+ ✦ +

A few hours later, the witch woke up.

She pulled herself into a sitting position, careful not to disturb whoever was next to her. She took a quick look and recognised him immediately. After all, he was the only man she could recall. But they weren't on a train together anymore. Instead, they were somewhere in the woods, protected by a sheet strung between poplar trees. And they weren't alone. On the witch's other side was a small girl, cradling an injured arm as she slept, and next to her a couple huddled together for warmth.

The witch studied the group, hoping they'd teach her something about herself. Were they family? Friends? Or was she their prisoner? She liked to think the presence of the child meant they were safe. After all, the man from the train hadn't tied her up, so that was encouraging. Perhaps she should wake them; explain to them who she was and that all she wanted was to exist, and not to live hidden inside a feeble, human shell.

Her hand hovered over the shoulder of the man who'd been with her on the train. He had seemed more surprised than angry when he found her. If she could trust anyone, why not him? But then again, why risk it? Why give him the chance to destroy her?

With a start, the witch realised there was something she wanted besides the right to live. She didn't want to be alone. She pulled her knees to her chest, holding in tears. Leave or trust these people. Why couldn't she bring herself to do either?

Sister.

Her breath caught. The voice echoed in her mind so clearly, but no one around her stirred. The witch mouthed her reply, unwilling to risk detection.

Is someone there?

It was only a moment before words seeped into her mind again.

Then you are awake, sister. Good. We're waiting for you.

There were other witches nearby! She crawled away from the tent, following the instructions that continued to come from the ghostly voice.

Keep your back low. We're waiting for you on the southern side of the tracks. You'll be protected by a warding spell once you reach our fire, but don't let the night watch see you before then. There's little we can do to help if they do.

The witch wasn't certain which way was north or south in this dark valley, but she reasoned that whoever was calling her must be on the other side of the railway tracks, otherwise they wouldn't have mentioned them. She counted three guards patrolling the edge of the camp, but so long as she kept quiet, she doubted they'd notice her sneaking off. The witch waited until there was a gap in their circuits, then slipped past them.

She picked her way over a rocky landscape, slippery with rain. Twice, she nearly fell. Damn impractical shoes. Her human self had terrible taste in footwear. As she passed the train, she took a minute to survey the jumbled mess. She'd been inside there, not too long ago, hadn't she? She might have taken a closer look to see if she could find more clues or memories, but the warnings the voice had given her urged her forward.

Once she'd crossed the tracks, it was easy to pick out a fire burning in the distance. The flames shone an eerie shade of blue, suggesting it hadn't been started by natural means. Whatever enchantment had conjured the fire must have also rendered it invisible to the night watch. She crept down the hillside, until she could make out figures gathered around the fire. There were two, both women. At the sound of her approach, one turned and smiled.

It was clear that she, too, was a witch. Her orange hair sparkled in the firelight, brighter than a phoenix feather, and her skin was so pale that the moon glowed on its surface. How old she was, no one could guess. Nothing about her seemed bound by time or nature. Her companion was less brightly coloured—raven haired and with dark circles beneath her eyes—but equally otherworldly.

"There you are, sister." The pale witch held out a hand, beckoning her forward. "I'm so glad you came. Ramona be praised that you have some loyalty to our kind."

"I suppose." The witch fell back a step. Even though she'd risked so much to come here, her confidence wavered. But it was too late to turn back. She might as well try to get some answers. "Who are you?"

The pale witch laughed. "You're bold, asking for names. Tell me, child. If I wandered over to your campfire tonight, would you tell me your secrets with so little thought?"

"You mean my name?"

"Yes. Your name. You give me your name, and I'll consider giving you mine," said the pale witch.

"But I can't." She shuffled back a step. "I'm sorry. I don't mean to offend you. But I can't give you my name. I—I don't know it."

The pale witch's eyebrows flew upwards. "You don't know it?"

"I don't know anything. I woke up on a train the other day and then I woke up here. That's all I know, I promise you."

"Hmmm." The pale witch stood and began to pace around the fire. She reached her companion, still hunched over in silence, and prodded her with her foot. "And what do you think?"

The dark-haired witch raised her head, revealing a scowl. She ran her hand over a large ring with a black inlaid stone. "I don't like it either, but... I sense no falsehood."

"Congratulations, girl. You convinced my scryer," said the pale witch. "That you've reached adulthood uneducated is a tragedy, but it's not unheard of. Especially if you're from Balter."

"Am I from Balter?" the young witch asked.

"Most likely, but I'll be certain in the morning. First, some introductions. Since you don't know your name, I'm afraid we're on the back foot, but that also means it's bad manners not to give you mine. So welcome. I'm Hess." She held her hand out to shake, a strangely ordinary gesture. "And my scryer is Allonia. Though I'll thank you not to share that with any of the Balterians."

"Balter..." They'd mentioned that place a few times now. A hazy memory filled the young witch's consciousness of a trainyard, salty harbours and... a hat shop? These recollections must have been rooted in her human life. Perhaps she'd be able to break down the barriers in her memory after all, though how long would it take? "I came from there. I think."

"Of course you did. You were on the train." Hess sounded almost amused.

"You mean the one lying on its side?" So these people *could* answer her questions. "What happened to it?"

"You," said Hess without a hint of emotion.

"I don't understand."

"You will in good time," Hess said in a motherly voice. "For now, I want to help you. I'm afraid it's not safe for us here—especially for someone like you, who doesn't know her own name. We haven't much time, but if you'll take a seat, I might be able to help you survive a little longer."

Hess gestured to the ground. The witch hesitated for just a moment before sitting down. At the very least, she should listen to what the older witches had to say. They might feed her lies, but lies could be tested and disproven. Anything would be better than remaining ignorant.

"First, I want to make one thing clear. You are in trouble here. And not because of that nonsense with the train." Hess shook her head as if the crash were a passing triviality. "Most of the people who survived are Balterian and they'll kill you if they discover you're a witch."

The witch nodded, even though that wasn't true. The man in the train carriage last night hadn't tried to hurt her.

"Which leads me to my next point. It's the most important thing I teach every witch I train." Hess crouched down on her knees so they were nose to nose. Each of her words was sharper than a spear point. "*You. Are. Mortal.* I've lost dozens of talented girls to a misguided belief that it would take a whole solozite cannon to kill them. A good witch hunter won't try to beat you with raw magic. He'll come at you from behind and restrain your hands. He'll kill you with inconvenience, make it difficult to cast magic or to breathe. He'll wear you down until you die at a knife's blade."

The witch shivered, instinct telling her that this time Hess had told the truth. "Then, how do I fight back?" she said.

"However you can," answered Hess. "It's natural to recoil from your powers. But you can do incredible things."

Like that fire she'd cast in the train compartment. She might have killed someone if she hadn't put it out. Quietly, she wondered how the witches managed to cast such a small fire. Perhaps the Scryer, who was still rubbing her ring, had done it. Was that obsidian set into the silver? Maybe witchcraft wasn't the only magic they could command?

"But while there are grave consequences to your magic," continued Hess, "this isn't the time for caution. Allonia and I should be able to protect ourselves. There's no one else worth worrying about."

The witch's mind flicked back to the group she had left beneath the sheet in the woods. The man from the train, the couple huddled together, but most of all, that child. "No one?"

"They're Balterian. Your people live in the caldera, where their talents are respected. The High Coven would welcome you as a lost daughter, so don't spare a thought for any of these people."

"But if they're our enemies, then why don't we—" she began.

"It's a difficult thing to kill in cold blood," Hess sighed.

"I wasn't going to ask that! I meant, why don't we *leave*?" the witch asked. "If we're in danger here, isn't there somewhere else we can go?"

"There is. And we will. As soon as we can." Allonia, who had stayed silent for most of the meeting, spoke. She stirred the coals in their ghostly fire. "We stayed for you, young one."

"For me?"

"Once we realised you were on the train, we had to find you," said Hess, smiling. "But if you don't know both your names, we can't leave yet. You'll never be able to manage your powers otherwise."

So there was someone who cared about her. Even if they'd

never met her before, these witches seemed sincere. They wanted her. It was more than she'd dared hope for.

"I'm sorry I don't have it," the witch said.

"Any other memories? Fragments we can work from?" Hess asked, but the young witch hesitated. It was one thing to listen to these women. Another entirely to trust them with the few scant truths she knew about herself. At her silence, Hess went on. "Human memories would be valuable too. It might help us discover who knows your witch's name."

"I haven't got any of those." She supposed she could have mentioned waking up on the train and seeing the man in her compartment. The one she had been beside tonight. But she didn't trust Hess not to hurt those people. Luckily, her words were close enough to the truth that Hess didn't press further.

"The memories *will* come." Hess reached out and took her hand, squeezing it like a mother reassuring a nervous child. "It might not seem that way, but you and your human self are one soul. She's with you now."

Indeed, at Hess's words, a shadow seemed to stir in the witch's consciousness: a frightened girl, who knew so much more about all the terrible things going on in her world than the witch did.

"You're only separated by experience and memory. As your thoughts and feelings line up with each other, so will your memories. It's only a matter of time," said Hess.

But the witch couldn't picture it. She looked down at the wretched shoes her human self had chosen. Under no circumstance could the witch imagine purchasing and wearing such useless things. The girl who loved those shoes had a lifetime of memories to draw from—memories that stretched like a chasm between the witch and her human self.

"Whenever you transform, look for her. Look to see if she's left you any clues," Hess instructed. The witch nodded, even if she doubted it would do any good. "What about your human name? Do you know it?"

"I think so." She could still hear it ring off the lips of her travelling companion. *Davina*. Did she trust these women enough to share that name with them? Even as she turned the idea over in her mind, she found she couldn't do it.

Hess chuckled. "Don't worry. I don't expect you to say it. In fact, you can't. We can only ever give the name of our current form. Now, stand up so I can take a better look at you."

The witch obeyed, and Hess walked a circle around her, taking in everything from her coat and skirts to those awful, impractical shoes. It took a moment for the young witch to puzzle out why, but eventually it all made sense. When she woke up in the morning, whatever form she was in, she'd still be in these clothes.

"Good," said Hess, once she was finished. "I'll come for you when the time is right. For now, we need to blend in with the rest of the survivors. I'll do what I can to keep you safe."

"Thank you."

"When this is all over, we'll take you with us. It's time you met our people and learned who you are."

"Again, thank you." It was a lofty promise, but was it a comforting one? The witch wanted to believe the best of these women, but how was she to account for their words about the train? It was ruined, lying on its side. Surely no one but a monster would do such a thing?

"I need you to go back to your camp," said Hess. "Allonia's beckoning spell will wear off soon. It's the only reason you were able to shift into your witch self to begin with."

"You mean, I only woke up tonight because…"

"Because we called you. Yes. Once the spell fades, you'll revert to your human self. So, make sure you're somewhere safe before that happens."

The witch didn't need telling twice. She rose and scrambled back up the rocks, stumbling on the slick surface, and flitted past the night watch as she returned to her spot beneath the sheet. Hess's promise burned inside her. Trusting witches was a dangerous game, but wasn't she one too? She would be better off with them.

She crawled into her space between the little girl and the man she'd met on the train. The moment she was in place, he rolled towards her, still sound asleep but seeking the warmth of another human. A friend.

The witch shut her eyes, uncertainty dancing within her once again.

When this is all over, we'll take you with us.

Away from whatever it was Davina had here.

CHAPTER

✦ 23 ✦

THERE WAS ONLY a two-hour interval between Morel's turn on the night watch ending and Kellen waking him up before dawn. Morel shoved himself off the ground, accepting the rain and cold with dreary resignation. He'd camped in worse while stationed in the mountains, though he'd take the darkest foxhole in the caldera over this if it meant his sister and brother were safe at home.

Kellen's smiling face did little to reassure Morel as he shifted out of his spot next to Davina. His brother looked like hell. True, everyone did, but it showed on Kellen differently. His pale face looked worried and creased. Dirt and blood matted his long hair and the shadow of a beard covered his chin. Morel couldn't remember ever seeing Kellen unshaven before.

"Come on. We've got work to do," said Kellen, offering Morel a hand up.

"What now?"

"An interrogation. That beggar boy gave me the name of someone who knew Braehurst, but I never had a chance to pursue the lead yesterday."

"And you want my help? I thought that… friend of yours. The one from the embassy? Wasn't she helping you?" Morel wasn't sure what words to use to describe Ms Freath. He'd sensed a familiarity between the woman and his brother that set his teeth on edge. Kellen had even fallen asleep next to her, clearly oblivious to the implications.

It wasn't the first time Kellen had latched onto a beautiful girl to get through a tragedy. Back when their mother died, Uncle Sergei had lashed Kellen ten times across the knuckles when they'd found him cavorting with one of the scullery maids. But Sergei's methods had never produced much repentance or fear in Kellen. Still, Morel would have liked to think his brother knew better here. The stakes were higher and, frankly, why would he want to drag a woman with a child into the whirlpool of their lives?

"Genna deserves a chance to rest," said Kellen, his gaze lingering on the pair, sound asleep next to Davina. "And her daughter needs her. Besides, now we know we're dealing with witchcraft, I'd rather we kept things within the family."

"Right." Morel still wasn't sure what to make of what the quartz from the canyon had revealed. He didn't believe for a second that Davina could have destroyed the bridge, but he had no idea what their next course of action should be. The more they poked around for answers, the guiltier his sister appeared, and he worried that any new discoveries they made would only create more danger for her. But with someone still killing the passengers, they *had* to investigate.

"And if you don't mind," said Kellen, "I want to be delicate about the whole witch and bridge business. We don't want to give away what we know."

"Of course," said Morel. "Who are we interviewing?"

"Someone by the name of Kira—ah, let me check my notes." Kellen reached for his notebook, but Morel grabbed him by the arm.

"Westwick?"

"Yes." Kellen's eyebrows flew upward. "Do you know her?"

Morel's mouth was dry with thirst, but he tried to swallow back the nerves bubbling in his stomach. That was the same woman Davina had recognised from her books. He didn't like the way these coincidences were adding up. "Yes," he said. "I'll take you to her."

A routine job. That's what Selnick had called it. He'd lulled her into a sense of security with promises of easy connections and easy pay, and gods, hadn't she wanted something in her life to be *easy* for once? What a fool she'd been. Kira Westwick should have learned a long time ago that *easy* never came without a price.

Even before the sun came up, she'd woken knowing the job had hit another hitch. It came in the form of a pair of bickering voices, disturbing her from her slumber as they argued over—of all things—which one of them would wake her up.

"You're the soldier here. And you know her." The voice was unfamiliar, but the accent was so strong that it had to be one of those Halgyrics. The tall one, she reasoned, since she'd already met—

"And you don't see how that makes this even more awkward?"

Morel Linde. So, the gamble had backfired. He'd brought his brother around and she'd be lucky to get out of this encounter without ropes around her wrists. Kira pushed herself off the ground. Time to see if luck was on her side.

"No need to squabble, gentlemen," she said. "I'm not one to idly sleep through two men joining me in my bed." She stretched, careful to arch her back so her chest stuck out. Morel's ears reddened, but the other one only scowled. Not at her, but at his brother.

"Thank you, Miss Westwick," said the tall one. "My name is Kellen Linde. I understand you've met my brother."

"Yes, I helped him dig toilets." Of all the various relief efforts undertaken, that one had struck Kira as the least idiotic. They couldn't keep shitting en masse all over the mountainside. So, she'd joined, hoping that if she appeared helpful and proactive, she might avoid suspicion.

She'd also hoped Morel Linde might spill some secrets about how his brother's investigation was going, not that it had done her any good. His lips were as tight as his ass.

"Very good. If you'll come with us?" Kellen beckoned her forward, and after a second of hesitation, she followed. Odds were someone had told them something about her and Jarvie. They'd taken tea together the night before the engine exploded, but that was hardly a crime. Internally, she'd rehearsed the story she used whenever someone suspected her of a connection to Selnick.

Kira Westwick. Rugged adventurer and novelist, on tour with her latest book. This one is about a woman who gets lost in the mountains and falls passionately in love with a man who lives in a cabin at the edge of the caldera. Did you want a signed copy?

Jarvie might not have come across as an obvious fan of hers, but if they went through his bags, they'd find a signed copy of one of "her" books. They were actually written by Magnus Selnick's wife, who loved penning sultry tales of poor peasants getting locked into tight spaces with each other during winter storms. Kira only read them when she needed a laugh. Every so often, Selnick sent Kira on "tour" as the face of the books—a front to carry stolen goods of one variety or another. He liked to use rich women as his runners, convinced they got less trouble from customs officials than most. Kira, however, had only ever masqueraded in the role. She got paid the same rates as Selnick's other smugglers, no matter how many books she'd supposedly sold.

She'd promised herself she would get out of the business soon, but it was hard to turn down a pay cheque, especially one that came along with a first-class train ticket. All she had to do was smile and sip wine for a few days, then she'd have her money. Now, it seemed, she'd been caught in a trap aimed specifically at Selnick's associates. Jarvie and Carson were both dead, and even Lodi Barnaka had been caught by the Halgyrics.

But Kira knew she was smarter than all of them. There was no chance they'd be ensnaring *her*.

The Halgyrics led her to the edge of the camp, far enough away that they were unlikely to be heard without raising their voices, but close enough for a shout to enlist the help of the soldiers. She searched the brothers' faces for some hint about how much they knew.

"Morel, if you could take down notes? And mind your penmanship." Kellen passed his notebook over, ignoring the eyeroll Morel gave him in return. "Miss Westwick?"

"Yes?" She tucked a stray piece of hair behind her ear, like an idiot. She only did things like that when she was nervous.

"Please start by explaining your relationship to Jarvie Braehurst."

"Minimal. We chatted in the dining carriage. He asked me about one of my books, the dear man. I'm sorry to hear what happened to him."

That last bit wasn't a lie. Jarvie's death was an inconvenience. If these morons didn't pin the blame on her, there was a good chance Selnick would, especially given her other failures.

"You never worked together?"

"Never." Technically true. She'd met Jarvie at Selnick's parties, but since she did her job well, they'd never crossed paths professionally.

"What if I told you someone has claimed otherwise?"

Kellen kept his face glassy and unreadable, while Morel scowled at her like he thought her a traitor. As if her existing in proximity to him and not baring her soul after a couple of hours' acquaintance was a personal offence. Dramatic.

"Well, I'd be incredibly surprised," she said. "The work of a writer is solitary. Though I do hire a guide occasionally to take me through the mountains. It makes for the best inspiration, and my readers depend on me to bring a kind of realism to my—"

"You were seen having dealings with Braehurst." Morel clenched the pen he'd been handed until his knuckles blanched. "We aren't interested in lies!"

"Morel! Enough. I can handle the questioning." Kellen gave his brother a withering look. "Notes and as little commentary as possible. Thank you."

So, there was a crack between the two men. Kira was good at working cracks. Sure, Morel hated her now, but strong reactions were easier to exploit than tepid ones. Her smile widened.

"I told you we conversed in the dining carriage. He asked me to sign a copy of my book. I don't know if his luggage survived the crash, but if it did, I'm sure the book will be there."

"This book. Do you have a copy?" Kellen asked.

"In my bag, yes." The damn thing survived the crash. Unlike other items.

"I'd like to see it after we're done here. As well as Braehurst's copy, if possible."

Did she have a right to object?

"For now, can you tell me what you know about the young man Dalton Rai?"

"Rai? That could be anyone." She waved a hand. "That's what the Caldera Peoples call orphans, isn't it? Lost ones?"

"So, you speak some ancient Renchan?" Kellen asked.

"Well, I do my research. For my books." Something about this questioning set Kira's teeth on edge, but whatever Kellen knew about her, he wasn't showing his hand yet. "I appreciate their culture, but I haven't a thing to do with them."

Kira had grown so used to denying her mother's side of the family that the lie came naturally.

"There wouldn't be any shame in that," he said, smiling as if she'd confessed to something. Well, so what if she had? There were no laws prohibiting her mother's people from riding public trains. Not yet.

"But you don't have any personal connection with Dalton Rai, is that correct?"

"None that I know of. Is he a fan?" She could only hope.

"I'm afraid not." Kellen shifted his weight forward so that he leaned closer to her. With his superior height, he made an intimidating figure, though Kira had stood up to worse. Jarvie, for instance. She wouldn't let this self-important beanpole frighten her, even if his voice took on a sharper edge. "We have an eyewitness who's told us that Braehurst harassed you about the contents of your cargo. Cargo you were moving on behalf of Selnick."

"An eyewitness account? Is that this Rai character you mentioned?"

"He was hiding in the luggage car and overheard you. He claims you argued with Braehurst."

"If he was in the luggage car and you think Selnick is involved, then Selnick no doubt paid him to be there." Damn it, Jarvie! He'd no doubt hired the little whelp to spy on her.

"Perhaps, but the fact remains that he saw the conductor, Mr Neuwirth, let you into the luggage car, where you conversed. Our source knew both you and Braehurst by name, despite having been imprisoned since the train crashed and, therefore, unable to get your name off the passenger list. Which makes me ask—how do you know Jarvie Braehurst?"

There had to be a way out of this. The Halgyric must mean the kid that the soldiers had been guarding until recently. The boy was raggedy and Renchan himself, so he shouldn't be difficult to shift the blame onto. What could she say? That he'd seen her talk with Jarvie in the dining carriage and decided to pin something on her? That this was how he'd learned her name?

But she was taking too long to decide. There was a good solution, surely? A perfect lie that would make her troubles go away. But the boy wasn't a variable she'd prepared for. No doubt that ideal lie would come to her hours from now, when it was too late. The length of time it took her to speak would be enough to confirm the falsehood.

She had to tell the truth. Or at least part of it.

"I didn't kill Jarvie." She crossed her arms over her chest, doing her best to match Kellen Linde's posture. Somewhere in her periphery, she heard the scratch of pen on paper, signalling that Morel was eagerly taking notes. "We had very few dealings, and whenever our paths did cross, we stayed on friendly terms."

"The boy said he threatened you," said Kellen.

"Well, who didn't he threaten? Jarvie sometimes overstepped his territory. But I never bore him ill will. Selnick's men are all trained to do that. It's how they make sure you stay sharp in the field. Ask around, and you'll hear that we took tea together and stayed on good terms until he died. I know nothing about who killed him and nothing about the train."

"And the crate you were transporting? The one marked with green paint?"

"All legal goods, as far as I know. Sometimes Selnick needs to move a family heirloom and he asks me to accompany it on its journey to keep it safe. To my knowledge, nothing is contraband."

"Care to prove that?" Kellen clearly didn't buy her story, but, for once, her bad luck had turned to good.

"Oh, I'd be more than happy to, but unfortunately my luggage went missing." It was all she could do not to laugh. Yet, if these men didn't kill her for what had happened in this valley, Selnick surely would. "In fact, if you locate it, I'd be very much obliged. And to my knowledge, you can't arrest me for transporting a crate that isn't here."

But what to her had been her trump card only made Kellen's eyes glint with excitement. "Interesting," he said. "Braehurst was spotted loitering near the luggage."

"Excuse me?" Damn it damn it damn it!

"You said it yourself. He liked to overstep his territory. So, what's to say he didn't intercept your crate, open it, and, when he compromised the contents, you took matters into your own hands—"

"I had nothing to do with it!"

"And then there's Carson Neuwirth. He'd seen you with the goods, so you had to get rid of him, too."

A wild calculation raged in Kira's head. If she said more, it might exonerate her of murder and destroying the train, but it would get her locked away for another crime and make Selnick her enemy in the process. She wouldn't survive a prison. Not with so many willing to do his bidding inside.

"Morel, if you can take Ms Westwick into custody—"

But as Morel and his great, bear-like arms came closer with ropes in one hand and a pistol aimed at her in the other, a dam broke inside her. So long as she wasn't restrained, she had hope. Even if it meant escaping into the mountains. "Jarvie never had my crate," she said. "I don't know who does, but if Jarvie had got his hands on it, he'd still be alive."

Kellen held a hand up for Morel to stop. "And what makes you so certain of that?"

Kira swallowed. "I'll tell you. Even help you find the ruddy crate. But only if you have him back off. You're both Halgyric. You don't have any right to prosecute me for whatever business I did with Selnick. It's got nothing to do with your country."

Kellen tapped a finger against his chin. Watch him report her to the Balterian military instead. A smile broke across his face, as if the idea amused him. "It's true that most of the things you lot smuggle would be legal in Halgyr. Mist, for instance."

"Most. Not all," said Morel, clearly less forgiving. "It could be weapons."

If only it were something so mundane. Kira trusted her cargo in her own hands and no one else's. Perhaps that was why she was willing to tell these men what she'd been carrying. Until they found her crate, everyone on the mountain was at risk of a sudden, violent death. "Do we have a deal? I help with your investigation and you two stop badgering me?"

"I can't make any promises, but the more you cooperate, the more likely we'll vouch for you when the Lords' Council arrives with its own questions." Kellen's compromise was clearly the best offer she would get. Still, she waited until he nodded to his brother. "Put the gun away, Morel."

Morel holstered his pistol, his sharp eyes never leaving her face. "Fine."

"I don't know who took my shipment." Kira clenched her fists to keep her fingers from shaking. This was the first step towards selling out. She would have to come up with a whole list of names from Selnick's organisation to give the authorities and pray that was enough to keep her out of prison. "But if Jarvie had it, he'd have opened it and then there's no way anyone would have been able to get the jump on him. I was moving one hundred and fifty pounds of raw solozite. Whoever has that might as well be the caldera god himself."

CHAPTER

·+· 24 ·+·

DAVINA WOKE, SHIVERING from a mixture of sweat and the morning rain seeping in beneath the sheet they'd used for shelter. Her heart drummed out a warning against her ribs. Something had gone wrong during the night. Very wrong. If only she knew what it was. She reached out for Morel, but her brother was gone.

Davina pushed herself up on her elbows, nudging Rae and making her whimper in her sleep. But there wasn't time to check if she'd hurt the little girl's arm. Desperately, Davina searched their camp for some sign of Morel, but there was none. She was unsurprised to see Kellen had gone too, the flattened grass next to Genna Freath the only sign he'd slept at all.

Where were her brothers? She pressed the heels of her hands against her eyes, trying to force the panic in her stomach to settle. What had happened last night? No memory came to her.

A small hand grabbed her elbow, drawing one of her hands from her face.

"Miss Linde?" Rae blinked at her in confusion. There was a sharpness to the child's gaze that was so familiar. Did that have something to do with last night's events? "Are you all right?"

"Of course." Davina snapped to her senses. She couldn't give the little girl reason to question her. By Soloz, the child knew more about witches than Davina did.

The sound of their conversation was enough to rouse Rae's mother as well. Genna jolted upwards and looked, much like Davina had done, for the man who should have been asleep at her side.

"Kellen's not here," Davina blurted out.

Genna looked startled at her blunt tone, and heat flooded her cheeks.

"Actually, I was hoping you might know where he and Morel have gone."

"Sorry, your brothers never consulted me." Genna smoothed down her hair, although, after sleeping outdoors in the rain, there was little that could be done to make it look less rumpled.

Davina swallowed back her disappointment. Last night, they'd seen the bridge torn up like a piece of paper by an unidentified witch. A witch that could have been *her*. Given the danger she was in, she should be his first priority.

But why had she thought Kellen would take her welfare seriously? When had he ever? Gods, he'd spent more time with this Freath woman since the train crashed than his own family.

"I'm sure it has something to do with the investigation," said Genna, reading the hurt and frustration on Davina's face.

"No doubt."

"We should get something to eat, Rae." Genna helped her daughter to her feet, casting a wary eye in Davina's direction. "You could come with us, if you like."

"Thank you." Davina couldn't imagine eating right now, but the last thing she wanted was to be left alone with her thoughts.

Any company was better than none, and what other options did she have?

Though as it turned out, she'd underestimated the number of people that might want her attention. She had barely joined Genna and Rae in the queue for morning porridge when Lord Carey wove his way through the crowd towards her.

Even from a distance, his gaze was intent on her face. What could he want? She ducked behind Genna and hoped he took the hint to leave her alone. He couldn't see her in this state. It wasn't just her matted hair and torn clothes. What if he sensed the turmoil inside her? The witch, trapped in the back of her mind, screaming to break out?

But there was nowhere to hide. He pressed on towards her, a false smile plastered on his face. She steeled herself, determined to give him nothing but the coy, sweet girl he expected. "Lord Carey." She dipped her chin to him as he approached. By Soloz, wasn't this a strange place for formalities? But these small performances helped her slip into the role she needed to play.

"Miss Linde." Carey offered a hasty bow, not that it did much to restore the decorum of his appearance. "Did you sleep well?"

"Did anyone?" Davina bristled at the question. He couldn't know what had troubled her during the night, could he?

"I suppose not." He shifted his weight between his boots, as if he sensed the awkwardness in the air. He gave Genna a stiff smile. "If it isn't too much trouble, could I borrow Davina from you?"

Davina wished one of her brothers was here to say "no" to the request. Predictably, Genna didn't care and shrugged her shoulders to signify as much. "I'll ask the cook to set aside for a portion for you," she promised.

"Don't worry yourself. I'm not hungry." Davina gave up her

spot in line and followed Carey to a rocky hillside several paces away.

As they walked, Davina cast a glance over her shoulder, trying to will Morel and Kellen into her line of sight. What were they so busy with? Wouldn't Morel feel silly when he realised that, the moment he'd disappeared, a handsome young man had swooped in to steal her away. A man he suspected of murder, no less. He should be here to protect her honour against potential threats.

But he wasn't. He'd abandoned her.

"Are you feeling well, Miss Linde?" Carey's eyes roved over her face, confirming what an absolute mess she must appear to onlookers. "I know yesterday was difficult for you."

"No more than it was for anyone." She had to do a better job at pretending that was true. While Carey's attention had seemed thrilling a couple of days earlier, scrutiny was the last thing she needed now. "Thank you for asking, though. You're too kind."

"Well, I consider you one of the closest friends I have in this valley, if you'll forgive my boldness."

"I'm flattered."

When would he bring this conversation to an end? The night they'd danced together on the train now seemed like a lifetime ago, yet she got the sense he was trying to summon that familiarity they'd developed.

"I rather thought your brothers would come and find me this morning," he said. "We've got a lot of investigating to do and the Lords' Council has questions. I'm delaying telling them about the bridge, but you wouldn't happen to know where I could find Kellen, do you?"

"No idea." Davina let out a snort. "I haven't seen him this morning either."

"Ah, yes. I suppose we both have questions, then." Carey's shoulders deflated at her response and Davina wished she could tell him more. He alone seemed to see how they were treating her, and it made her forget for a second how isolated she felt out here. Something in her expression must have showed her hurt, because he reached for her hand. "You're sure you're holding up?"

"Of course I am." She should pull her hand away. Even if he was being kind, she couldn't trust any of the Balterians anymore. Carey had been thrilled to discover this tragedy was the work of a witch last night. What would he do if he knew the truth about her?

"But you're worried, aren't you? How is the rest of your family? Are they well?"

"The rest?"

"That darling niece of yours? Her arm is healing, yes?"

"Excuse me?"

"Her mother didn't say anything about the investigation, did she?"

"The Freaths. You're talking about the Freaths?"

"Of course. Your brother's…" But the confusion on Davina's face gradually worked itself onto his as well. "They are married, aren't they?"

"Kellen and Genna? Heavens, no."

"Oh!" His face bloomed red and Davina forgave him for all his previous awkward questioning. "I'm so sorry! I only thought, well, given the child—"

"No, they haven't any history like that." Davina laughed. "He saw her after the crash and recognised her from the embassy. She's done work for them. Probably the one lucky break we've had since the crash."

"Really?"

"It's an honest mistake. You needn't worry about it."

She expected a reaction to her words. A self-effacing chuckle, perhaps. Instead, Carey stood silent and stiff, gaze fixed on a faraway point as if he were working through some great equation.

"Miss Linde... I know it isn't my place to pry, so you'll have to forgive me..."

"Yes?"

"But... are you certain Ms Freath's presence is a happy coincidence? Your brother seems rather familiar with her."

"Well, they knew each other at university, too." Davina recalled Rae's insistence that this was the real link between their families. But the idea that Kellen had engaged in some deep, torrid love affair during his youth was romantic nonsense. Not upright Kellen.

"*Miss Linde.*" Carey's ears darkened to a deep crimson and she realised now he wasn't embarrassed for himself, but for her. A deep pity filled his eyes, and at the sight of it bile rose in Davina's throat. "As a friend, I feel it my duty to tell you. Your brother was the first fellow I helped after the crash. He was with Ms Freath and they were trying to break into the compartment where their daughter was. I lent them a crowbar."

"Well... Kellen was trying to help out after the crash—"

"He kissed her. Quite passionately." Carey couldn't meet her eye. "She was in her evening gown. Your brother was half-dressed. They'd clearly come from his cabin."

"No, that's ridiculous. He wouldn't..." But Carey's words tumbled and rearranged themselves a hundred times in her head. *Their* daughter? In *his* cabin? He'd kissed her. Was that what Carey actually saw? He'd kissed her. Their daughter. No, not Kellen.

"What do you know about this Freath woman? Really?" Carey stared at her.

"She's a talented volchemist. Kellen said he spotted her after the train crash and…" Davina faltered. If Carey had really seen him kiss her, then that meant Kellen knew Genna was on the train before the crash. And when she thought about it, didn't it explain other little details? There should have been three rooms for them to travel in, but somehow Kellen had misbooked. Kellen, who never dropped a decimal when he was doing his arithmetic. What if, instead, circumstances had necessitated he gave the room away?

"No." She fought Carey's words with all she had. "No, he might know Ms Freath, but Rae—I mean, the girl has nothing to do with him. Her father's dead."

"And that explanation doesn't strike you as… convenient?" Carey didn't miss a beat.

Davina took a deep breath. Wouldn't that be the simplest thing to tell a child? A child who'd objected when Kellen had introduced Genna as having worked with him at the embassy.

I thought you said you met Mr Linde at university.

Kellen had left for college when he was sixteen. How old was Rae? Come to think of it, if Genna and Kellen went to university together, didn't that mean she'd had Rae when she was quite young? Hadn't he introduced her as the best volchemist in his class? Exactly the kind of girl who would have grabbed his attention.

Rae's father was dead. And all he'd left her was a book about witches. And witches were something of a research project for Kellen, thanks to Davina herself.

"I—I have to go." Davina darted away without another word to Carey.

"Wait! Miss Linde—"

But what time did she have for his questions? She was a witch. Kellen might have a child. What next? Would they find out Morel had orchestrated the entire train crash? Did she know anything about her family or herself anymore? Or was she being too quick to believe Carey? But if anyone wasn't telling the truth, it was easy to identify the most likely culprit. Kellen was an effortless liar. He'd been raised to be that way, and unlike Morel, he'd never struggled with pulling off the double life of prince and politician. Why wouldn't he lie about other things when it suited him? After all, he'd kept her witch powers a secret.

Whatever hope she'd held out disappeared when she made her way back to the food line and saw Kellen there next to Genna, his mouth moving rapidly as they talked in hushed tones. Next to them was Rae, tugging at her mother's hand. For the first time, Davina saw it. The way the girl's mouth twisted to the side when she was thinking. The sharpness of her gaze. The fervour with which she read about witches, for goodness' sake. Her interests might have been different, but she could intellectualise as well as her father.

Rae didn't know, but how could that be? Why had Kellen left his own daughter ignorant and abandoned? Davina had never considered herself the maternal type, but she knew the horror of growing up without a parent. How could Kellen have inflicted that on someone else when he'd suffered the emptiness of a broken family too?

Her bones vibrated with indignation, but she had nowhere to take her pent-up anger. If she'd been her witch self, she would have rained fire and ash down on the entire caldera. What nerve he had! He'd even made her babysit her own niece, without so much as a word of warning. It was like their feelings were nothing but a joke to him.

Perhaps he felt her eyes boring into him, because he turned away from Genna and looked directly at Davina. He smiled at her, as if his furious younger sister was the most convenient thing in the world to him. Well, he wouldn't find her half as calm and sweet as she'd been yesterday, when he'd last dropped news of this magnitude into her life.

"Davina!" He jogged towards her, brazenly confident. "It's good you didn't go far. There's a crate with green paint—"

"How could you?"

He drew back a step at the sharpness of her words. "Excuse me?"

"You know what I'm talking about," Davina snapped. "Or have you buried all thoughts of your own daughter? So you can forget about her whenever you like?"

For a split second, she expected him to roll his eyes and deny her accusations. Or to grow stern and tell her she didn't understand what she was talking about. Instead, he was silent, his mouth falling open as all the bluster left him. Every tired line showed on his face, and yet that added helplessness somehow made him look younger, in a way that caught her off guard. In a flash, she saw what she'd never dared believe before. Beneath the smooth manners and authority, Kellen didn't have a clue what he was doing. He was as much an abandoned child as any of them.

"How…" He painstakingly found his voice. "How did you find out?"

"Lord Carey told me he suspected something."

"Damn him. Of course." Kellen attempted to run his fingers back through his hair, but they were soon caught in the tangles.

"I'm so sorry. I know you deserve an explanation, but there's a missing crate—"

"Oh, isn't there always?" Whatever pity she'd felt for him a moment ago vanished as, predictably, he encased himself in another layer of stone. "There's always some reason. There's always something pulling you away so you never have to deal with me or Rae or—"

"Davina, we don't have time for this!" he yelled.

Her own spirit stirred. Good, let him shout. He waved his hands at her in some desperate plea for obedience, eyes darting around to see if they were attracting attention. Carey, for one, was approaching the edge of their conversation. But what did she care if she exposed Kellen? He was a prince. He didn't deserve two secrets.

"Don't we? What could possibly be more important than your own daughter?"

"What on earth makes you think us having this argument is the best thing for my daughter's happiness?" he shot back. "I have other priorities, Davina! But you are so bloody selfish, you can't imagine a world where I don't have time to scream at you over some dreamed-up offence—"

"Oh, yes. Because running about—*playing the detective*—that's done so much for everyone. Bravo Kellen, what a hero you are."

"In case you haven't noticed, we could all die up here! Since the day I found out Rae existed, I've done everything I can to protect her, but it's never enough, is it? It's never going to be bloody enough for anyone!"

"Then why in all these years have I never met her?"

"Because *I* met her for the first time yesterday!" Kellen's face was red with anger. "Is that enough? Is that the explanation you need? Now, by the gods, can we get back to work?"

Davina wanted to fight back with some brilliant retort. Soloz, what she'd have given to be the one who had the last word right now! But the gravity of his own words stunned her into silence. He hadn't known.

And so instead of Davina, a different voice ended the argument. "Please, Kellen." Genna was struggling to cover her daughter's ears. But she must have known her efforts were in vain. Rae's face had gone pale as the table linens they'd pulled from the dining carriage. Despite her broken arm, she thrashed against the grip her mother had on her, but her eyes never left Kellen. She stared at him with horror.

And that look she gave him? Davina knew it was all her fault.

Tears rolled down Genna's cheeks. "Please. Please stop."

"Genna..." Kellen staggered towards them. "Rae, I'm so sorry—"

But whatever he might have said was drowned out by a raw, howling scream. Rae's shriek cut through every excuse and pretence the adults around her could muster. There was no explanation. No apology. Only the cry of a child who understood all too well what had happened to her.

There were more people gathered around them now. How could there not be? A cry like Rae's wasn't something anyone could ignore. Genna trembled, her face buried in Rae's neck, while Kellen crouched low next to them, hugging his knees. He looked as though he was restraining himself from reaching out and holding them.

Far too late, Davina wished she could whisk them away from this exposed, barren valley. She should have shielded them from nosy onlookers. She should have thought of the child.

Her niece.

"Rae…" She bent forward, attempting to comfort the girl, but she was one cloying hand too many. Rae twisted away, kicking hard, and broke Genna's grip on her. She tumbled forward, and as her injured arm collided with the ground, she let out another sharp shriek.

"Go away!" Rae dragged herself to her feet, tucking her arm against her chest.

Davina shrunk back, hands flying to her mouth. She'd done it again. Made everything even worse than before.

"Just go away! You—you lied! My father's dead! He isn't—I don't have…" She fought for air as her mother reached for her again.

"Sweetheart! You're going to hurt yourself—"

Genna was cut off as Rae slapped her arms away. "You lied worst of all." With that pronouncement, the girl turned on her heels and ran.

Kellen lunged after her, but Genna grabbed hold of his arm. "Please, Kellen. Let me."

"You really expect me to sit idly by and—" Kellen sputtered.

"No, I expect you to do your duty and find that crate before someone winds up dead." Genna's face still bore tear tracks, but the line of her mouth was firm. She placed her hands on either side of Kellen's face, forcing him to look at her.

His hands curled around her wrists. "And how am I supposed to believe you'll ever let me see her again?"

"Gods, Kellen." Genna closed the gap between them, kissing him abruptly. Now Davina really wished they were all somewhere else. Kellen's shoulders tensed, his eyes wide with shock, but the moment didn't last long. Genna released him, somewhat roughly, and regarded him with a frown. "Now get to work. I'll join you if I can."

With that, she took off after Rae. Even with the head start, the girl was still visible in the distance, struggling against her short legs and her injury. Kellen stared after them, stunned to the spot. "What the hell did she do that for?"

If Kellen didn't have an answer, then Davina certainly didn't. She tried to turn away while he was still distracted by Genna and Rae, but her movement caught his attention. His hand was on her shoulder in an instant, and when he spun her around to face him, it was not his usual diplomat's smile that awaited her.

"Kellen, I'm sorry, I didn't know…" Davina wished she didn't sound so weak and frightened. She wasn't the one who'd cavorted about and ruined her reputation, so why was she being made to feel guilty?

"We don't have time for apologies. I need you to come with me." Even when he was clearly in the wrong, he somehow got to be right.

She nodded and let him steer her away from the crowd. Some people made attempts to ask questions. Carey inched forward, attempting to ask how the investigation was going, but Kellen threw him one glare and he sputtered like an empty basalt grinder.

Kellen led her to an outcropping of bushes a short distance from the camp, towards the east. She braced herself for him to start yelling again, but, instead, he immediately began to push aside the juniper brambles. "Start searching."

"Right, but I don't know—" she started.

"A crate." Kellen wouldn't even look at her. "With green paint on the side. It went missing after the crash."

"Then it could be anywhere."

"Morel's taking a few others back down the tracks, to see if it got thrown out during the explosion."

"What's inside?"

"I was going to explain all of that," Kellen said tersely. "But that was before you drew the attention of the entire camp to our position. Get to *work*."

Davina finally followed Kellen's lead. If she upset him now, there was no saying what he might do once this fiasco was over. Once they got home, he'd probably marry her off to some old, loathsome baron, just to get her out of court. After all, Kellen was going to be king soon.

King—and with an illegitimate child. By Soloz, what was he going to do about that? If the court knew—

She blinked, surprised to find tears forming. Why was she crying now? She coughed, trying to clear her head as she moved on to a patch of sagebrush, but the pestering itch only intensified.

"Do you smell something?" Kellen asked abruptly.

"What?" Now that he mentioned it, there was a shift in the mountain air. Davina breathed in the morning dew and tasted the acrid notes of sulphur.

But they were nowhere near Halgyr and its hot springs. There were geysers and pools at the centre of the caldera too, but she didn't think the train route went this close to them.

"It's strange," Kellen said, as if voicing her thoughts. "You would think—"

But a tremor tore through the underbrush. Kellen's words were swallowed up by a deafening cascade of granite that hurtled towards the camp. Boulders rocketed towards them, large as houses. Rock dust blew in the air, clouding their sight lines. Through the haze, Davina felt Kellen yank her forward, urging her to run, but they'd only gone a few feet when the ground buckled beneath them.

The force threw her to her knees. One of those great chunks of granite would surely crush her to death. But when she looked over her shoulder, she saw the rocks falling into a widening chasm, filling with water. Where solid land had been only a moment ago, a river had formed. In the end, it wasn't the boulders she needed to fear. As more of the ground collapsed, the churning river sucked Davina and Kellen down with it.

She clawed for a grip on the rocks, but they had become like loose shale, sliding out beneath her. As she and Kellen slid further down into the chasm, a surge of water lapped her ankles, and in the distance she saw the train tracks buckle and the engine rear up like a spooked horse. She wasn't the only one about to die. This would be the end of everyone in the valley.

That was Davina's last thought before the witch took over.

· PART FOUR ·
THE CONDEMNED

CHAPTER

✦ 25 ✦

THE WITCH SPRANG to life, called by a force far stronger than the scryer's spell of the night before. Her magic surged on instinct, desperate to preserve her life. She didn't need instructions to know what to do. As the gravel slipped out beneath her, she dug her fingers further into it. She sensed a strange current coursing through the ground, most likely a wild magic someone else had cast not too far away. The witch seized onto that pulse, letting it fuel her for a second, then pushed with all her might against it.

Veins of solid stone radiated out from her fingertips. She wove together granite, basalt and obsidian into a tangled web, gathering up the disparate chunks that had been sent flying and reworking them into new forms. A slew of water soaked her, but she plunged a fist into it and it skittered away, rearranging into a spray of pebbles.

The earth continued to rumble, but she'd created a stable shelf for herself that the water couldn't break away. As she caught her breath, she spotted a pair of hands clinging to the edge of her solid perch. She watched as a tall man with filthy blond hair pulled himself up to join her.

Everyone will try to kill you.

Hess's words from the night before came back, and this time the witch didn't recognise the man. He could be anyone. Maybe he was the one who'd cast the magic that had caused all this destruction?

The witch backed away, digging around in the back of her mind for anything Davina might have left her. The man must have been with Davina when she transformed. The witch tried to bring to mind something that might guide her reactions, as Hess had counselled her to do, but all that came was hot frustration. Above all, the man's face inspired anger. If he was no friend to Davina, the witch knew she shouldn't trust him either.

He stared at her awestruck, his expression wavering between fear and comprehension. "Da… I mean, is that you?"

"Don't say her name!" The witch raised her arms protectively.

"No! No, of course not." He got to his feet much too quickly. He should have been disoriented. By Ramona, she was struggling to stand upright, though perhaps the magic she'd cast had taken something out of her. She took a deep breath, hoping to regain some composure, but before she could, the man had his hand on her shoulder. "Come on."

"What are you doing?" She tried to claw at him, but he was stronger than her and her fingers found nothing but air. Too late, she realised she couldn't transform him unless she could touch him with her hands. So, this was how ordinary men killed witches. "Let me go!"

"We have to fix this." He turned her around so her face pointed towards a horde of screaming people, but who were they? Her last memory was of slipping past patrolling guards, and she didn't recognise any of this new crowd. There was no reason to trust these people. Especially when this man was restraining her like this. Everything Hess said was proving true.

"I said let me go!" She tried to bite him, but that only made him tighten his grip over her.

"Damn it, we don't have time for this." He dragged her towards the edge of their safe perch. She screamed and flailed against him, but he pushed her downwards, until her hands were plunged into the crumbling dirt. Out of desperation, she shot out another wave of magic, forcing more of the soil to turn to solid rock so he couldn't throw her off the cliff.

She kicked as hard as she could, but he seemed to know that all he had to control was her hands. Clearly this man had studied how to hunt witches. But why was he prolonging her death? Was he trying to drag her to somewhere he had a weapon he could use to finish the job? He tried to call out to her several times, but she couldn't hear him over the din of the avalanche. They wrestled along the crumbling mountainside, and she grew more and more exhausted as she was forced to generate more rock to save herself from tipping off the edge again and again. Finally, they reached the twisted remains of a train track.

The train! Even in her frenzied state, that small moment of recognition helped anchor her. She was still by the train. Still on the caldera. There might be other witches nearby to help her fend off her attacker. He pulled her across the tracks, and she secured those, turning the rushing water to stone just before the river dragged the engine and carriages into them. What was he doing? That could have killed him too.

As they cleared the train tracks, his grip weakened and she threw her shoulder into him. He tumbled off and rolled a short distance. Now was her chance, but once again, he was the first to his feet.

The witch staggered, heaving for air. She expected him to assault her again, but, instead, he turned and stared out through the rock dust towards the west. "I think we did it," he said. He spun back around to her, smiling despite the blood dripping from the side of his mouth. Good. She'd managed to land a hit on him at least once, then. "Morel and everyone who headed west should be fine. We have to find Genna and—"

But before he could do anything else to her, the witch lunged at him. He wouldn't get the upper hand again. This time her fingers burned to strike. She had the satisfaction of seeing the terror on his face as his left arm came up just in time to protect his face.

"DAVINA! STOP!"

+ ✦ +

Kellen struggled to breathe. A sharp sensation unlike anything he'd felt before sped up his arm. His hand spasmed and pain radiated from there throughout his whole body, as if he'd been touched by evil. Perhaps he had. And it had attacked him in the form of his own sister.

A few feet away, Davina shook her head, coming to. She touched a spot on her cheek where a chunk of rock had flown up and hit her, and her fingers came away red with blood. Her cheeks no longer caved in a sharp line, as they had a moment earlier when he'd confronted her witch self, but he still shrank away from her, cradling his hand.

"Kellen?" She coughed on the dusty air. He could barely hear her whisper above the distant shouts. Everyone in the camp was awake now. "Are we safe?"

Another spasm shook his body and all he could choke out in

reply to Davina was a gasp. Gods, he was going to vomit at this rate. What had she done to him?

"Kellen?" Davina crept closer to him. "Is everything all right? Are we safe?"

"I'm taking care of something." He crawled away. If another avalanche struck, she might transform, and he wouldn't put it past her to attack him again. The rumble of the mountain had subsided, as if whatever dark force had started the calamity was now silent. But how could he trust her? How could anyone ever trust her again?

"Something happened. We were sliding away…" Davina spun around. They were mere feet from the new cliff edge, a deep gulf separating them from the eastern slope. Directly across from them, the railroad tracks were snapped in half and now climbed up into the sky. The chance of being rescued was now further away than ever.

"It stops right in front of us!" Davina squealed. "It nearly got us."

"It did." Kellen gritted his teeth, but it wasn't enough. No matter what he tried, he couldn't force the throbbing heat to subside.

"Pardon?" She turned back towards him.

"It did. We were sliding off the edge. You turned into a witch and made our side of the chasm solid again."

"Then I saved us!" Davina gasped.

Kellen could hear the glee in her voice, but he couldn't give her his attention now. Even though she wasn't a witch anymore, the spell she'd cast hadn't stopped. The pain was growing worse. Each heartbeat was like a jab to his left elbow, and the heat in his hand had grown so intense that he was no longer sure where one finger ended and another started.

What was wrong with him? There were no burns or abrasions, but perhaps the rock dust in the air was obscuring his view. As he tried to brush away the chalky residue that coated his fingers, he understood. His left thumb and index finger were warm to the touch, but when he rubbed the other side of his hand, he felt the texture of granite.

She'd turned part of his hand to stone.

For a second, he could only stare. She could transform a train and the earth, so why not a human? He was about to thank the gods that he'd managed to stop her before she killed him, when he noticed the grey colour was spreading up from his knuckles towards the base of his fingers. Calling on her human self had slowed the magic, but it hadn't been enough to kill it. Another surge shot into his elbow. Like venom from a snake bite, the spell was travelling.

Kellen fumbled for his boot, where he kept his volchemical knife. He'd carried one since university, even if he didn't need it often. But his right hand shook as he raised the obsidian blade and it fell from his grip. The pain was too strong and his own revulsion too intense. He couldn't do it.

"Davina..." He could barely speak, but she was at his side already. She must have drawn closer while he'd been distracted. Her face was pale with a mixture of confusion and fear.

"Kellen?" Her pitch rose as he awkwardly pressed the knife handle into her palm. "Did you get hurt?"

"You could say that." He grimaced as he extended his hand towards her. "Do you see my left hand?"

"Yes."

"I need you to cut off my fourth and fifth fingers."

Davina dropped the knife, scuttling away. "You what? No!

Why would I—"

"Do you want me to live, Davina?"

"What kind of a question is that?"

Gods, she couldn't even say "yes". If they had more time, he might have pointed that out, but his life depended on getting through to her.

"When you were a witch. You—you made a mistake. You didn't know who I was and you thought I was attacking you." Every breath was laboured, but now, more than ever, he needed her to understand him. "So you struck back."

"No! No, I wouldn't—" She buried her face in her hands.

"Please, I'm begging you. The spell hasn't stopped. Look." The stone had spread past his upper knuckles now. "If you do it now, I might get to keep the rest of my hand."

"What if—what if it doesn't work?" Tears ran down her face. "What if it's inside you and keeps killing—"

"Trying something is better than nothing."

"You could turn me back into a witch. I could reverse the spell..." But the words died on her lips, as Kellen shook his head.

"You don't recognise me as her. It's more likely you'd finish the job. Please. This is the only hope I have." He slid his left hand towards her, using his right to pull away the fingers they might be able to save.

Still shaking, Davina picked up the knife. She raised it above her head, then hesitated. "I don't think I'm strong enough to do a clean cut," she admitted.

Kellen twisted his head to the side so he wouldn't have to watch. "Then saw."

He felt her position the blade behind his knuckles; heard her

293

mutter a prayer as she got into position. Kellen bit down on the collar of his shirt, bracing himself.

The fabric muffled his scream as Davina threw the weight of her body against the knife.

One. Two. Three times.

Finally, the bones snapped.

CHAPTER

✦ 26 ✦

As Rae ran across the caldera, twigs and pebbles fought their way into the cracking leather of her shoes. Dew hung filmy in the air. It made her escape over the rocky terrain slippery and treacherous. The landscape assaulted her senses, a cruel reminder of how very real the world was. It was as if it mocked her for believing the thoughts that tumbled through her head.

The world has changed. Everything is a lie.

Rain slapped her cheek, perfectly ordinary. No, the world wasn't the liar. It was her mother and father. It was everyone who should have told her the truth.

Her arm throbbed with every step, begging her to stop and tend to the broken bone. As she reached the edge of the train tracks, the morning drizzle mixed with the furrows of basalt dust left behind by the train's grinder. Her feet wobbled in the sludge and she was forced to slow her pace. It wasn't long before she heard the thrum of footsteps behind her.

"Rae! Sweetheart, slow down!"

"Go away!" she shouted back, but experience had taught her that Ma never listened to demands like that. She was at Rae's side in a matter of seconds, hands pressed on her daughter's shoulders as she surveyed her arm.

"I know you're mad at me," said Ma. "I'm not saying you shouldn't be. But you can't run away like that. Not when your arm is like this. If anything happened to you—"

"I can take care of myself!" Rae would have gladly run away again, but her last attempt had left her exhausted. She didn't have the energy to fight Ma now with anything but words. "You knew. You—you knew this whole time he was my father, didn't you?"

"Of course I knew." At least Ma wasn't denying it, not that Rae would have believed her if she had.

"He—he said he didn't know," said Rae. The words Mr Linde had shouted at his sister were burned into Rae's mind, though she only understood parts of them. "Why didn't he? What happened to him?"

"If you come back to the camp with me, I'll tell you everything." Ma was already bargaining.

Much as she hated losing like this, Rae nodded and gave up her hopes of running off. Where would she even go? They were trapped by the wide, empty hills. She offered Ma her good hand and together they walked back towards camp.

"Like I said, I met him at university. We… well, I guess we fell in love." Ma said it like she didn't quite believe it had ever been true. "I know it's hard to picture, Rae, but we were so young. No one knows what they're doing at seventeen."

I will.

But Rae didn't voice her dissent. Ma was talking, and for the first time in days or even years, she might be saying something that was true. So Rae kept silent and listened.

"When the year ended, he went back to Halgyr, where his

family was from. I realised I was pregnant that summer and by then…" Ma shrugged, as if that answered every possible question. "He was gone. And I was on my own path. With you."

"So, he didn't die?" Rae asked.

"Of course not. How could he be here if he'd died?"

Rae hadn't thought up a way yet, but witches could do some incredible things. *Witches.* A cold chill settled in her. "And—and my book? The one on witches? If he didn't leave it for me when he died, then—"

"Gods, Rae." A smile broke over Ma's face. How could she smile about anything right now? "Yes, that belonged to your father. I don't even remember when he left it at my dormitory. He's terrible at picking up after himself. Far too lost in his own thoughts to keep his desk organised. You're a bit like him that way."

"I am not!" She had nothing in common with Mr Linde. How could she? He was too tall. Too… everything. "So, he didn't leave it for me? It was never for me?"

That silly smile disappeared. Good.

"I never said he left it for you, sweetheart. I don't know why he had it, but if you want—"

"It isn't fair." Rae swallowed hard, trying to stop her tears. She couldn't keep crying like a baby, even if her world broke into pieces. All those lovely, terrible things she'd imagined—her father going off to sea, him planning to read her tales from their book, only to go down with his ship before she was born. That man wasn't some messy student who couldn't keep his papers straight. And to think she'd thought that book meant something! She'd never meant anything to him. He hadn't even known she existed.

"If you want, you could ask him why he had that book yourself," Ma pressed.

Rae ground to a halt, tearing her hand away. "I'm *never* talking to him."

"Rae—"

"I'm not talking to anyone! Including you." Rae struggled against another wave of tears. And, even though she'd promised to never speak to her mother again, she was determined to get in the last word. "You lied. You—you lied about how we got the train tickets and going on holiday and Mr Linde. You lied about everything."

Ma reached for her again, trying to pull her back towards the camp. That place was another lie. No one was safe out here. Eventually, Ma settled for wrapping her arms around Rae's rigid frame. Her fingers wove through the knots in her daughter's hair as she whispered choruses of, "I'm sorry. I'm so sorry."

Rae didn't believe a word of it.

But whatever weaknesses Genna Freath had as a mother, one thing could be said of her. This time, she was holding her daughter when the world exploded.

CHAPTER
+ + 27 + +

Genna didn't so much hear the avalanche as feel it reverberate from the soles of her feet to the tips of her fingers, which were still wrapped protectively around Rae. In the distance, granite cascaded down the mountain. For a few seconds, it seemed like terrible luck. Avalanches weren't unheard of in these mountains, though they rarely occurred this late in the spring.

Then she saw it wasn't snow that rushed downwards, but chunks of a nearby peak, no more than a mile in the distance. Could someone have caused that? If someone had blown up the train and turned it to stone, then why not? Genna stared in horror and clutched Rae close. At least they would die together. And maybe it was for the best that her child died having known her father, for one imperfect day. Perhaps the gods were punishing Genna for failing to tell her sooner.

Then abruptly, the rocks hurtling towards them dropped off, as if they had reached a chasm and poured into it. It made no sense. The train tracks followed the valleys through the mountains and there were no gaping crevices here. Genna and Rae should have been flushed out like moss in a gutter pipe.

The ground still twisted beneath her feet, but Genna mustered her courage. She lifted Rae to a spot she could support her on her hip. Rae dug her fingers into Genna so deeply that it hurt, but at least she wasn't trying to run away. She stood up slowly, seeing for the first time the people fleeing for the west. No doubt they were screaming, but any noise was drowned out by the crashing rocks.

She should follow their lead and run, but she couldn't. She remained rooted to the spot and scanned the eastern horizon for some insight into how this had happened. The ground was sinking as a rush of water broke a new channel through the pass, taking some of the fleeing survivors with it.

Genna squeezed Rae tight and ran. It didn't look like a natural avalanche, nor could she blame one of the caldera's many volcanoes. So a much simpler explanation existed. Someone must have activated the missing shipment of solozite. A hundred and fifty pounds of the stuff would have easily transmogrified part of the mountain to water, and once that had been done, the entire peak had collapsed.

Trees creaked and tipped towards her as the earth in which their roots were planted fell away. Those who'd sought cover beneath their branches shrieked and scattered. It seemed they'd be safer running west along the train tracks. As Genna headed for them, the basalt dust flowed in a steady stream down to the newly formed crevice behind her. It rushed out like sand beneath her feet, tripping her and sending her sprawling as the ground continued to writhe. Holding Rae made it impossible for her to catch her fall, so she slammed knees-first into the rocky ground.

Suddenly, the shaking stopped. Genna stayed where she was, braced for another tremor. But as seconds became minutes, she worked up her nerve and stood. The avalanche had ended. For now, they were safe.

"Rae?" Genna attempted to pry Rae's fingers from her arm. "Are you all right?"

"No." Rae shook her head, quaking in Genna's arms, the cheeks she buried into her mother's side wet once again. But if she was speaking, that was a good sign.

"Let me take a look at you." Genna tried to set her down, but Rae wouldn't let go of her. It made examining her injuries more difficult, but she seemed no worse off than before. There were no new broken bones or even bruises that Genna could see. All told, they'd come out of this in better shape than they had the train crash. Except...

"Kellen." Genna sprang to her feet again, taking Rae by the hand. He'd headed off with his sister to search the eastern side of camp, just as this had happened. They'd have been right where the crevice formed. "We have to find your father."

She expected more resistance to the idea from Rae, but the girl's eyes only widened. Maybe the same fear had seized her too—that she'd lost something valuable right after swearing she didn't want it.

Where had Davina and Kellen gone? The eastern side of the camp was a large place to get lost, but she didn't have to wonder for long. Most of the survivors had fled away from the sinking eastern fringes, so when Genna heard the agonised shriek of a man ring out from near the locomotive, she knew who it belonged to.

"Kellen!" Genna dragged Rae forward, but she could only go so fast with a child in tow. If he was dying—by the gods, if he died after all they'd been through—she would never forgive him or herself.

His sister came into view. Her face was buried between her knees and blood shone fresh against her arms. Genna followed the trail of blood from Davina's hands to where it dripped on her skirt and onto the discarded knife at her feet. Kellen lay prone next to her, and judging by the angle of his arm, that pool of blood had come from where his hand used to be.

"What happened?!" Genna let go of Rae and ran the rest of the way on her own. With a bit of luck, Rae might turn around and not see too much.

Davina jumped as Genna slid in next to her and turned over the mangled remains of Kellen's hand. The knife had done a horrific job of tearing through the tendons at the base of his fingers, taking a chunk of his palm with it. Genna ripped some fabric from her dress and wrapped it over the stump, since this idiot girl obviously didn't have the presence of mind to do it herself. "I said what happened?"

"I…" Davina stammered. "I don't know."

"Rock fall. Crushed… had to amputate." Kellen gasped for air, clearly going into shock.

Shouldn't they have waited for a nurse before making any decisions about amputations? Something else must have caused them to take such rash action. Trust Kellen to find the energy to lie, even while he was bleeding out.

Genna tied off the fabric, the best she could do on her own. She tilted Kellen's chin towards her and his eyes rolled like billiard balls. He couldn't walk to the nurse on his own now. "Rae, get over here," Genna shouted. "I want you to hold his hand up while Miss Linde goes to fetch a nurse."

Davina startled. "What was that?"

"A nurse! Before he bleeds out."

302

Davina flushed scarlet, but at least she got to her feet and took off towards where the remaining survivors had fled. After the avalanche, Genna could only guess at how many more people might be injured, but surely this much blood merited attention?

"Rae, I said come here. He needs you to hold his hand up." Genna moved down to Kellen's legs, angling his body so they were lifted higher than his head. It was the best she could do to treat shock. She knew only rudimentary first aid, thanks to the basic medical training in her volchemistry courses. If only she'd spent more time studying biological applications. She'd have to hope this was enough to keep Kellen alive.

"I don't want Rae to see me like this," Kellen sputtered. He chose the most ridiculous things to worry about.

"Too late." With a scowl on her face, Rae took her father's hand and raised it up high.

Kellen winced, turning away from her. His eyes wandered for a moment, but eventually they found Genna's face. She reached down and brushed his hair from his forehead, trying not to panic at the cold touch of his skin. "That's right, look at me. Breathe with me, Kellen. In... and out. In... and out."

"Genna." He raised his good hand, stroking her cheek with one of his long, elegant fingers. It was strange how such an ordinary thing felt so precious now. "I love—"

"Don't you dare." Her thumb traced his temple, still crusted with blood from their night on the train. "Don't say another word. Just in... and out. In... and out."

She didn't dare blink. Her gaze was the only thing he seemed capable of holding onto.

"In... and out."

She repeated it over and over, until Rae began to copy her

rhythm. Then, finally, Kellen found it too. The colour returned to his cheeks as they breathed, all three of them together for the first time.

+ ✦ +

Mercifully, not too much of the camp had been destroyed. The ground to the east now sloped towards the newly formed river, numerous trees had toppled over, and some of the bodies in the mass grave had become exposed due to the avalanche. Gruesome though the sight was, at least the crevice hadn't cut directly through the main camp. Genna tried to keep Rae from looking at it when they walked back to camp, accompanied by the two nurses carrying Kellen's prone body on a makeshift stretcher.

The river had settled, forming a long, narrow band of murky water that ran all the way from somewhere deep in the northern woods down to the cliffs in the south. It was just wide enough to make it difficult for rescuers to reach them from the east. Penny Aldridge hurried to do a head count, and Genna relayed to her the names of everyone who'd been searching for the solozite. She didn't tell Penny exactly what they'd been looking for, and thankfully the leader of the dance troupe didn't pry, though she did have a suspicious look in her eyes as she regarded her.

Not that Genna had time to worry about that. Someone else needed her.

The head nurse, Fallon, treated Kellen herself. A few of the other survivors had suffered falls and bruising, but most of them had been further away from the avalanche than Davina and Kellen. So, thanks to his blood loss, he took priority.

Genna stayed at his side through the whole procedure, as the nurse cleaned the wound and relieved his pain with a concoction of mountain plants. Genna let him squeeze her hand with his good one as Fallon carried out rudimentary surgery to clean up what Davina had done with the knife. It wasn't until he'd fallen into a fitful sleep that his grip relaxed, but Genna couldn't find it in herself to let go. For two days, he'd thrown himself at every misfortune that had befallen their train. And look where it had got him.

Fallon was even more upset by the amputation than Genna. As she packed up her tools, she chided Davina for taking matters into her own hands rather than bringing someone to her brother. "I might have been able to do something to save the fingers," she said. "You'd be amazed at what advancements we're making in medicine these days."

"I'm sorry," Davina muttered quickly before slinking away.

Biological volchemistry had been the least interesting subject to Genna as a student, and she hadn't kept up with the field since she'd left university. Were there ways to regrow bones now? But it was silly to focus on what might have been. Knowing Kellen, there would have been some other reason behind the hasty amputation. Once he was conscious, she intended to ask him.

Fallon rolled up her emergency kit, the tools now slotted back into position. "What's your relationship to him?"

"Ah... old friend?" Genna tried, but the nurse arched an eyebrow. Too much of their history was now known around the camp. Genna shrugged in defeat. "He's my girl's father."

"You'll watch him, then? Until his brother shows up? I don't trust that sister of his. Too flighty."

Flighty. That was putting it mildly. Davina's blood-soaked hands had made Genna very suspicious.

For now, Genna simply nodded. "Yes, I'll wait for him."

That seemed to suit Fallon. She trudged off towards whoever needed her next, leaving Genna to sit with Kellen. Rae settled in next to them, frowning. Genna didn't know what to say to her. How did you comfort a child over a father she'd never known? All she could hope was that, in the silence, Rae was working out her own thoughts.

She carefully lifted his head and placed it in her lap, something she hadn't done since they were at university. How fitting that it had taken losing his fingers for Kellen to stop and sleep. As she stroked his hair, memories came back of the boy she'd held like this eight years ago.

Even back then, he'd never known how to do things by halves. The classes they'd shared should have been a low priority for him. As a governance student, he'd only been taking volchemistry as an elective. He could have treated the course as a chance to slack off and skate by unnoticed, and perhaps if he had, their worlds would never have collided. But when Professor Igthus posted their first round of marks, he came in sixth in the class and had absolutely no intentions of settling for such a performance.

He'd asked around until he found her. Genna had come in second, and he begged her to study with him. She'd been startled by his boldness and his wide, cheeky grin. It also struck her as odd that he didn't seek out the one student who outranked her as a study partner instead.

"Because you're a woman," he said flatly. "Which means you had far more working against you. I wouldn't be surprised if Igthus marked you down on purpose. Just so he didn't have to acknowledge that a woman came top of his class."

And he was right. Just a few weeks after they began to study together, the marks shifted so that Kellen leapt into first, while

Genna kept her spot one place below. She almost wanted to slap him for using her so perfectly, but instead they struck a deal. She'd keep tutoring him if he taught her about misting and the other Halgyric practices that Balterian universities weren't equipped to teach.

So what if she never made it to the top of the class? Igthus wouldn't let her have that spot anyway, even if Kellen wasn't there to get in the way. At least she got *him* out of the deal. For better or worse, it made them a team. There were rumours about the two of them sleeping together long before it ever happened, but with the entire girls' dormitory whispering about her behind her back, what could she do but rely on him more? No one else was as kind to her. Even without Kellen around, none of the other girls wanted to draw a charity-case scholarship student into their circles. They were there with firm instructions from their parents—obey the rules and find a young lord to marry before their programme ended.

Kellen had taken her to parties, where they drank too much, and to workers' strikes down at the fishing docks, where they handed out leaflets to disenfranchised Calderans. He could spend an entire weekend doing nothing but reading book after book, then the next organising a university social event with the same fervour. About the only thing he never did was sleep.

As he lay in front of her now, she realised just how little he'd changed. He should have mellowed as he aged. She followed the newspapers enough to know the embassy kept him busy, and she'd assumed that meant he'd settled down. But once they were on the train, it had become evident that his behaviour was as extreme as ever. Of course he'd drunk himself silly after learning he was a father. Of course he'd run into a burning train to pull out survivors. Of course he'd pursued a murderer when it was asked of him. But his luck had finally caught up with him.

Heavy footfalls drew her out of her morbid thoughts and she turned, unsurprised to see Morel approaching. Davina was at his side, and from the blush on her face and the scowl on his it was clear she'd explained everything to him. Genna tipped her chin upwards to show Morel that he didn't scare her. She'd moved on from the shame of bearing a child out of wedlock long ago. For her, nothing had changed.

"Genna Freath," said Morel stiffly. "I understand you're the mother of my niece?"

"That's what they tell me."

Morel bristled. "You think this is funny?"

"Not even a little." Genna turned away. How they must hate her—she was, after all, living proof of all the mistakes their brother had made. These secretive Halgyrics were never going to take kindly to news of a child wandering about with the crown prince's blood in her veins.

"This complicates things." As if on cue, Morel dropped to his knees next to her. He traced a finger along the top of Kellen's bandaged hand, his frown deepening. "You said it was... an avalanche?" Morel looked up at his sister for confirmation.

"Yes." Davina's eyes never left her shoes.

"And you've been watching him?" He looked at Genna with a glare as hard as quartz. She shifted away, more uncomfortable than she dared admit.

"If you need me to leave, I will," she said. Since Rae was born, she'd known this would be the outcome if she ever approached Kellen and his family.

"That might be for the best." There it was. Morel's mouth

never lost its hard line, and, for a moment, Genna wanted to yell at him for being so cruel. How could he push her away so easily, with Rae sitting nearby? She had no claim to Kellen, but what about the child? She had braced herself for this rejection for years, yet somehow it still stung.

Her hands shook as she eased Kellen's head back onto the ground. Was this goodbye? Or would he fight for her when he woke up? Maybe it would be better if she never found out. He'd never choose her over his throne. Morel was making things simpler. Once she'd gone, he'd tell Kellen they had to cover the whole thing up. Hush the affair. In a sense, he was an ally. He might be in favour of letting her skulk off to live in obscurity.

"Come along, Rae." She got to her feet awkwardly, one of her legs having fallen asleep. But, as she reached for her daughter's hand, Morel placed a hand on her shoulder.

"I think the girl—Rae, I mean—should stay with my sister. We need to talk alone," he said.

The nerves along Genna's spine prickled. "Why's that?"

Morel glanced over his shoulder then leaned in close to her ear. "The luggage girls came to talk to me," he whispered. "I need you to tell me how you knew Jarvie Braehurst before people start to talk around camp."

CHAPTER
+ + 28 + +

Of the surviving passengers, Morel had been furthest from the train when the avalanche struck. He and Kira were halfway to the broken bridge, searching for the crate. He and Kellen needed as many people to look as possible, but neither of them was mad enough to trust Kira alone. As the one with a gun, Morel had taken her west, while Kellen went to enlist Genna and Davina in the search. They'd also informed the beggar boy who'd told them about Kira and Braehurst, reasoning that he couldn't have stolen Kira's possessions while he'd been tied up, just as he wouldn't have been able to kill anyone. Morel hoped the decision didn't come back to haunt them, as the boy had been more than happy to search to the east of the camp.

Two hours into their search, Morel and Kira hadn't come across anything promising. They could have searched the valley for days without finding anything, he'd thought, though Kira insisted the task wasn't impossible.

"It's a large shipment," she said. "No one's going to be able to lug a hundred and fifty pounds of solozite that far from camp."

"Unless it fell out the back of the train." There had been

310

some damage done to the back of the luggage car, Morel remembered. And wouldn't that be the best-case scenario? He could only hope.

But that hope vanished when the mountain began to shake. They were too far away to see where the explosion had occurred, but the timing betrayed the cause. As the pine trees swayed overhead and a distant rumble resonated through the grey skies, Morel and Kira both fell silent. It was too convenient. Whoever had the solozite must have noticed that people were searching for it and activated the shipment while they had the chance.

"I told you that little whelp in the luggage car was no good," said Kira as they began to jog back towards the camp.

"For the last time, it wasn't him!" But Morel was losing confidence in that claim every time he made it. At this point, everyone was a suspect. Though the boy didn't strike him as a trained volchemist.

When they saw the newly formed crevice, a river of water surging at its base, it confirmed all his worst suspicions. The saboteur had cut them off from the eastern rail line. They were trapped in these mountains, at least until they could find a way across the chasm.

By the time they made it back to camp, the tremors had come to an end and people were on their feet, arguing over what had happened. Most people were blaming it on witchcraft, just as they had the train crash. And, if it hadn't been for the timing, he would have suspected a witch too. It was the simplest solution—except Kira had admitted to transporting solozite. Why would she do that if the story wasn't true?

For now, all Morel wanted was to make sure his brother and sister were safe. In the pandemonium, he spotted a circle that comprised most of the Balterian lords. No doubt Kellen would be with them, taking over the situation like an over-eager idiot.

"You…" He glared at Kira. "Don't go anywhere."

Kira snorted, tossing her curly golden ponytail over her shoulder. "There's nowhere else to go."

How right she was.

All the lords were shadows of the men they'd been back in Balter. Days without pomade to straighten their hair and of sleeping in suits that were built for business rather than roughing it made them look haunted. Morel approached the circle, looking for Kellen. But as he drew closer, he realised he wasn't there. Morel was about to turn around when Lord Zerick spotted him and waved frantically. "Get that man. I want a word with you, Linde! We demand an explanation!"

"About what?" said Morel. "I don't know anything about what happened. I just got back—"

"Exactly! That's the rub." With his broken glasses and rough, unkempt beard, Lord Zerick looked positively savage. "You Halgyrics disappear then another catastrophe strikes!"

"Where are my men?" A rabid Lord Raxton pushed his way to the front.

"Pardon?" said Morel. Where was Kellen and why wasn't he fielding these questions? This was what he was born for, and if he wasn't here—the implications were unfathomable. Not only should he leave, Morel *had* to. "I'm sorry. I don't have time for this. My brother—"

"And that's another matter!" A red-faced man with an absurd moustache took his turn now. Morel recognised him only because Kellen's investigation notes had contained his name— Lord Drawley. One of the richest men on the Council. "I don't appreciate the character of your family! You think you can trust a man, and then all his sordid affairs come out—"

"Please, my lords, we should stick to the matters at hand." Lord Carey spoke up and it pained Morel to have this buffoon as the only one on his side. "Mr Linde, I heard your brother had you out searching for something. All we want to know is what you were looking—"

"I want to know a lot more than one thing, Carey," snapped Lord Drawley. "Raxton is right. We need to know where our soldiers are. They're the only ones on the passenger list who didn't check in for the head count."

Every moment he spent here was another in which he didn't have answers about his missing brother. Morel threw up his hands in apology. "I'm sorry, but I don't know what you're talking about. I have to—"

"Our *men*, you fool!" All the voices blurred together. "All our soldiers are gone. You free that beggar boy, and the next thing we know, the soldiers are missing and there's a massive river."

The soldiers. If that included their captain, that meant there were five more dead, in one fell swoop. If they didn't let him look for Kellen soon, he was going to believe the worst.

"My lords, I don't have the answers to your questions—or the time. Good day." Morel turned his back on them. He didn't need a clutch of self-important men badgering him. Did this count as an international incident? Even without knowing about their royal status, the lords were treating the Lindes as representatives of all Halgyr. It was everything Morel had worried would happen. Kellen had involved them too much and now they were too conspicuous for comfort.

But he'd only gone a few feet when yet another person ran

towards him. She was the tiny woman who'd been looking after the luggage, not that Morel remembered her name. But now his family had been thrust so firmly into the middle of all this chaos, she thought she had a right to talk to him. Damn Kellen! Why had he done this? And where were he and Davina?

"Mr Linde?" She offered a curtsy as she met him, her posture alarmingly perfect. "I need to tell you something."

"Oh."

"And given your brother—well, I assume you must be leading the investigation now?" she asked. Morel felt the blood leave his head. By the gods, what had happened to Kellen? The woman took his horror-struck silence for an invitation to go on. "It's about Jarvie Braehurst. I mentioned to your brother that he'd spent a lot of time hanging around the luggage. If you ask me, he was looking for something. And Lord Carey's saying that all of you were looking for something a while ago."

"Ah… yes." How had that become common knowledge?

"Well, he was tailing someone," said the woman. "There was a woman. When she came to collect her luggage, Braehurst shoved between us and rifled through her bag."

"If you're referring to Miss Westwick—"

"I don't know anyone called Westwick," she said. "But I do know the woman he harassed. She's the one with the little girl. The one who's with your brother now."

"With Kellen?" Morel grabbed her by the shoulders. She squeaked, and he realised he'd frightened her. But he couldn't take another second of this flailing around, unsure if his family had survived the avalanche. "Where is he?"

"I can take you to him." A small, familiar hand closed around his arm.

Morel gasped in relief as he spun around to see Davina at his side. It didn't matter that her hands were caked in blood. She was alive. He pulled her into a tight embrace that she didn't return, but he didn't care. So long as they were together, there was hope.

"Thank the gods," he sighed.

Eventually, she gave him a squeeze back. She buried her face into his neck, and he expected to hold her while she cried. But then her voice hissed in his ear.

"Morel... it happened again."

CHAPTER
+ + 29 + +

"I DIDN'T KNOW Jarvie Braehurst." Genna couldn't look Morel in the eye.

"Don't lie to me," said Morel. "People are panicking, and they're going to start jumping to conclusions, especially if that woman from the luggage pile tells the others what she saw. If you want me to help you, we need to get on the same page as soon as—"

"Help me?" Genna could have laughed. "That's rich. That's absolutely *rich* coming from you—"

"What do you mean? I've never done anything to you."

Morel spoke as though he could promise her protection, but Genna had known enough of his type over the years. People like Braehurst, in fact. But instead of working for Magnus Selnick, this man was the royal family's enforcer.

"I don't know what happened between you and my brother," he continued. "But I'd like to think he *didn't* knock up a woman who then tried to murder all of us, including her own daughter. I don't want to believe that. So convince me to help you."

"This is ridiculous. I didn't..." Genna cast around for an escape, but Rae was still with Davina, almost like a hostage. *Want to see your child again? Convince the big scary man you shouldn't be locked up for all your past wrongdoing.* But Genna doubted this man would see it her way. He was a soldier, so though he'd know what it was like to be hungry while stationed in the wilderness, he wouldn't understand the crushing helplessness of being hungry in a city, where everyone around her had plenty and didn't care that she and the child who depended on her were starving.

"I've never hurt anyone," she said. "Everything I've ever done has been to protect my girl and myself. So, forgive me for not welcoming you with open arms the moment you lot decide to show up."

"Show up? Davina told me Kellen never knew about Rae." Morel crossed his arms over his chest. "Which makes me wonder what else he didn't know about."

Not that Kellen hadn't tried to find out. Back in his cabin, he'd guessed she was running from someone.

"I didn't murder Jarvie Braehurst. I didn't…"

"Then why was he going through your luggage? What was he looking for?"

"Money. What are Selnick's men ever looking for?" Genna tried to word her story in a way that kept further questions to a minimum. "I was seeing a gentleman a few months ago. His name was Lawrence."

Poor Larry. He hadn't been a great man, but he didn't deserve being made into her scapegoat either. All he'd been was greedy and foolish, and among Selnick's lot, those were hardly vices. "He worked one of Selnick's clubs as a bouncer. It wasn't the most honest work, but he had it, and I wasn't going to complain about a man who helped keep the lights on."

"*He* worked at one of Selnick's clubs?" Morel raised an eyebrow.

He might look like a brute, but not all of Kellen's perceptiveness had passed him by. "And how did you happen to cross paths with someone like that?"

"You have something against a girl going out to dance once in a while?"

"You're lying." He said it with such authority that it silenced her. "Lodi and the conductor were smuggling mist for Selnick. You know how to use *mist*, Genna! Kellen told me the two of you did all your questioning for this investigation while you were wearing some sort of perfume. What Balterian knows how to use mist? You…" He broke off. "You learned how from Kellen. By Soloz."

It wasn't a question. Genna felt a prickle of guilt, despite herself. "We were study partners. I—I just liked knowing things. I don't see how anyone can call themselves a real volchemist without studying the traditions of people from all over the continent and—"

"But after you graduated, had Rae, and needed a job, you used it, didn't you? Someone's got to work at those parties to keep people from overdosing." He shook his head and she realised this was the betrayal that had truly stung.

"I was trying to feed my daughter," she said weakly, but it didn't help.

"You sold Halgyr's secrets, rather than tell Kellen. Why would you…?" But this question didn't take him long either. "You knew? I mean… you *know*?"

"Excuse me?"

"Your old lover." Morel raised an eyebrow. "You said his name was Lawrence? What a coincidence."

She was about to ask him what he meant, but then it hit her

who she was talking to. Kellen wasn't the only one with a secret name and identity. Morel was Prince Lawrence. Second son of the Halgyric crown. He was telling her—smartly, covertly—that he'd realised she knew who Kellen really was.

"I…" She dropped her voice as low as she could. "I've never told anyone."

"And I suppose you want me to thank you for that?" he said.

"Actually, *yes*." Her temper flared back to life. "I loved your brother, Morel. I really did. But I'd never have let myself get into that situation if I'd known back then. So don't act all high and mighty with me, because I did protect you. All of you. Even though Kellen never did the courtesy of telling me anything."

"But he couldn't." Morel looked stricken in a way Genna wasn't prepared for. There was something unexpectedly tender about this surly young man. "I bet he wanted to, but he had to—"

"It doesn't matter. That's not what we're here to discuss." She'd had years to stew on the matter, and during that time spent many sleepless nights imagining the problem from Kellen's point of view. Of course he'd been bound by tradition and duty. But the secrets the Halgyric royals kept were there to preserve their own rule, and Kellen was the ultimate beneficiary of them. He might not have initiated the custom, but it was ridiculous to pretend he had no say in its continued existence.

She didn't need Morel to explain Kellen's tortured loyalty to his people. If there was one thing she could say for Kellen, it was that he'd never tried to justify himself. He understood what he'd done. There were lies that shouldn't exist between people who loved each other, and back then, he *had* loved her.

And maybe even did now.

"If you really want to know about Larry…" She took a deep

breath, willing herself to go on. "…his eyes got a little bolder than his fists. He tried to make off with the house winnings one night, after some high rollers lost an awful lot of money at cards. It only took a day for Selnick to figure out who'd robbed him. They killed him."

"I'm sorry," said Morel, the accusatory tone from earlier now gone.

"I am too." Genna smiled ruefully. "To make things worse, he hid the money in my apartment. When I found it, I thought… I thought I could escape. I'd never held that many finos in my hands before, and I thought…."

"But Braehurst followed you."

"I guess Selnick was watching me closer than I thought." Of all the things she'd done, taking that gamble was the one she regretted most. "I tried. I really tried to play it safe. I got Kellen to book the tickets rather than using the cash I had, thinking that might throw the gang off the scent. Selnick marks his bills, of course. But if I'd known I was endangering all of you—"

All of a sudden, Morel clapped a hand on her shoulder. The gesture was friendly, but her knees buckled under the unexpected force. Still, when she steadied herself enough to look at him, his large, brown eyes were painfully sincere. "We'll get out of this. *Together*. If anyone questions you, I'll vouch for you."

"I… thank you." What else could she possibly say?

"I just know we're so bloody close to figuring out *something*. Kellen thought that box of solozite was important, so I bet if we find who took that, we'll have—"

"Mr Linde!" said a frantic voice.

"Oh, balls," Morel muttered under his breath and Genna suppressed a laugh. "*What?*"

Morel whirled around to find the quaking form of Lord Ambrose Carey.

"I'm sorry, sir," he said. "But you need to come now. The Lords' Council wants to talk to you."

"I've already spoken to them," said Morel, who clearly thought that should be good enough.

"I'm afraid there's—ah… well, there have been developments." Carey's eyes darted around, a picture of nerves. "I don't know how it happened, but they know about the bridge. It's all anyone in the camp can talk about. Everyone knows we're stranded."

CHAPTER

✦✦ 30 ✦✦

MANY YEARS AGO, Ambrose Carey failed so many of his classes that he had to be held back a year at preparatory school. Under normal circumstances, he might have been expelled, but his father had just enough money and influence to make the problem go away.

"Take it as an opportunity, boy," his father told him. "When things go wrong, look for the opportunities. That's what smart people do. And even if you aren't one for books, there's bound to be something smart about you. There's *got* to be."

Even at fourteen years old, Carey had thought his father mad for suggesting there might be something to be gained by falling a year behind in school. But a remarkable thing happened. In his new class had been Emeth Trudane—as clever as he was prickly, and as friendless as he was rich. For the first time, Carey recognised an opportunity. He chose the desk next to Emeth and resolutely tried to strike up a conversation in every class they shared. It took some patience, but eventually he wore Emeth down. Finally, Carey had found his strengths— an easy-going personality and the ability to put up with those who got into ranting arguments with their professors. Not even Emeth could withstand his friendliness. A few years later, Overseer Trudane helped Carey's father pay their family membership fees to the Lords' Council, thus achieving the power and influence he'd always wanted. And Carey was even passing his classes, thanks to Emeth's tutelage.

These days, Carey prided himself on being a man who recognised opportunity. Though he had to admit, ever since the train crash, it had been difficult for him to muster such forward-thinking optimism. But someone else had clearly seen an opportunity in their current situation. What else would motivate Kira Westwick to whip the Lords' Council into a paranoid fury?

"She's telling everyone we're going to die out here on the caldera," said Carey, leading Morel to where the councillors were gathered near the train tracks. "Now that the bridge has gone and the avalanche has cut us off from the east."

"How does she even know about that?" said Morel.

"I was going to ask you the same thing," said Carey. "Did you mention it to her when you went off together?"

"Of course not," Morel snapped.

"It's the only explanation that makes sense! I certainly never said a thing about it."

Kira was standing on one of the train couplings, so she could be easily seen by everyone gathered around her. Most of the survivors were here now: anyone who was well enough to leave the medical ward; Penny Aldridge and her dancers; even Lodi Barnaka was standing in front of the train, weeping into a handkerchief for no discernible reason. Their eyes were all trained on Kira.

"Five miles!" she shouted. "That's how far we are from Beck's Canyon. Five miles. And none of the Halgyrics thought it might be worth telling us that. It never occurred to the idiots that Beck's Canyon might *mean* something to one of us. No, they'd rather die in these mountains."

"That's a lie!" Morel called out. A dozen faces whipped around to him. "My brother has been trying to keep you from all getting murdered—"

"And a brilliant job he's doing at *that*," Drawley snorted.

Carey ducked his head. Gods, he was starting to understand why Emeth hated that man so much.

"A whole troop of soldiers gone!" continued Drawley. "No one's seen them since the mountain collapsed."

"And what about the bridge?" said another voice. "Why didn't you tell us about that?"

"We were *trying* to find the saboteur. It's a lot easier to catch someone out when things aren't common knowledge," said Morel.

"That's all well and good, but there isn't time for this investigation." Kira put a hand on each of her hips. "We're cut off to the east and the west. We've only got one choice if we want to find safety. We have to head north."

"*Towards* the volcano?" Morel shook his head. "That's insane."

"Begging your pardon, miss," said Carey. The survivors all turned to him, making him wish he'd stayed silent, but it was too late now. "That would be incredibly dangerous. The central caldera is ringed with dozens of geysers and the ground is very unstable. Without a detailed map, you'll probably—"

"You don't need a map. You've got *me*." Kira swung her shoulders back, ponytail whipping over her shoulders. "I'm from Renchan stock. I'll get us out of here safely."

There was another chorus of mutters, but this time they were more appreciative. It all seemed incredible to Carey. It had barely been two days since the Lords' Council had imprisoned a teenage boy for being Renchan, but the irony of this seemed lost on everyone else.

Everyone except Morel Linde. "She's a smuggler! She's not interested in waiting for Continental Rail to come and rescue us because she knows they'll hand her over to the Balterian authorities. But if she can escape through the mountains—"

"Exactly. Let's *escape! Through! The! Mountains!*" With each word, Kira thumped a fist against her other hand and a cheer broke out from the crowd.

Carey realised Morel was right. Kira had found her opportunity. The soldiers were missing and Kellen Linde was unconscious. Aside from Morel, no one else was capable of resisting her, so now she was on the offensive.

"Why are we waiting around for someone to come and rescue us?" she shouted. "There are villages north of here. If we find one, we'll have food and water. It'll mean the rail company will find us alive. If they're coming at all."

"Couldn't if they wanted to! The bridge has gone!" The shouting mounted again, and it seemed as though the decision had been made before Carey could even grasp how it had happened. They were to pack up all the supplies they could carry and head north towards the central caldera. The investigation—such as it was—would be put on hold until they'd found somewhere safe where they could wait for help.

Carey was helpless to stop any of it. People were already loading tinned oysters, mustard, and the few other non-perishables that had survived the crash into bags. Walking sticks were fashioned for those who still had injuries, as even those in the medical camp didn't want to linger.

"Every day, we lose someone new," said Fallon, the head nurse, when Carey asked her if she thought leaving was a good decision. "Who's to say this valley ain't cursed?"

She didn't seem to be the only one who thought the gods may have turned against them. Carey, of course, wanted to get Emeth's perspective on the matter. His old friend was one of the few people he fully trusted. But Emeth's level-headed calm was nowhere to be found these days. He was still as eager to serve as ever, but his hands trembled as he stuffed potatoes and onions into a bag. Sleeplessness ringed his eyes and he gave the impression of a man haunted by the gods rather than someone who followed them.

"How am I supposed to know if it's the right decision?" Emeth said. "Moving is probably useless. Whoever is killing people can do it here or in the central caldera. I doubt they give a damn about where we are."

"Then you think we should stay?" Carey asked.

Emeth's nose wrinkled. "Did I say that?"

"Well, if there's nothing to be gained by leaving, then why should we?" asked Carey. "No one is taking the time to look for clues anymore! There must be something nearby. Those soldiers couldn't have vanished into thin air."

"*Ambrose*. The soldiers are probably at the bottom of that— that *river*." A shudder went up Emeth's spine as he looked over his shoulder towards where the water had carved its way through the landscape. "I confess, during the avalanche, I thought we were done for. Truly, I did."

"Then..." Carey struggled for words. He often felt foolish in front of Emeth, but never before had he felt hopeless too.

"Perhaps it's a good sign? We lived, so maybe the gods are merciful?"

Emeth laughed. "Does this look like mercy to you? No, it's not mercy. It feels more like… *interference*. What do you have against Kira Westwick, anyway? She seems no worse than any of the others who've tried to lead us."

That much was true. Just the day before, Carey had idolised Kellen Linde and the decisive hand he'd brought to their situation. But he'd turned out to be as flawed as any of the lords. No wonder Davina had been so stunned to hear Carey sing his praises. He should have been wiser. Less trusting. But even so, for all the Lindes' foibles, there were other considerations.

Carey cast a furtive look over his shoulder. "It's just… she's a *woman*."

"That's a bit regressive, isn't it?" said Emeth.

"I don't mean it like that! I mean, what if she's a witch?"

At that, Emeth's eyes flicked up from the sheet he was folding. "Do you mean you think all this is down to witchcraft? Did the Halgyrics come to that conclusion?"

"Well, doesn't it have to be? The engine that's been turned to stone, the crevice, the bloody bridge…" Carey made certain he didn't mention what they'd seen on the crystophone, but it had been obvious there were witches among them for some time. Emeth surely saw that.

"That would make sense," said Emeth. "But if it was witches, who's to say they were in our company? They could be roaming the mountains. Plenty of witches would like to see Balter driven out of these lands, and by attacking the railway—"

"See! That's another point! Why would we go deeper into the caldera when the people living there aren't going to want anything to do with us? It's dangerous."

Emeth shrugged. "Perhaps. But isn't staying dangerous too? No one is coming. If we want to live, we have to do *something*. You might want to put yourself to use, Ambrose." With that, he shouldered his bag and trudged off towards where Penny Aldridge was divvying up the supplies.

Kira would be leading everyone north the following morning. Dusk was already settling, so it wouldn't do to trek into the mountains now. Perhaps Emeth was right, and he should focus on helping everyone prepare for the journey. But Carey knew they'd lost the one person they could truly rely on. The man they needed was lying unconscious, missing half his hand.

Davina hugged her knees to her chest. Under Morel's orders, she was stationed at Kellen's side, ostensibly watching Rae while her brother and Genna packed up their gear for the trek north. Davina hadn't cast so much as a sideways glance at Rae since taking up her post. Her eyes couldn't leave Kellen.

How she would have liked to turn her face away and run! Instead, she stared, transfixed by the once-white bandages around his hand that had grown gradually darker as his blood soaked the fabric. Perhaps she would have indulged her cowardice if it hadn't been for the child at her side. If this girl could watch the sweat prickle over her father's brow so stoically, then Davina could do it too. She owed it to him.

Had she really tried to kill her own brother?

Even hours later, the shock of the revelation had not worn off. Her ears rang from his screams as she'd hacked away the evidence of her crime. His hand had been crushed by a rock, he'd told everyone, still protecting her. She didn't know why he'd bothered. She deserved to be executed, like the witch she was.

She was dizzy with a host of horrible thoughts, all related and yet fragmented.

I deserve this.

Why did he lie for me?

It's his fault. He should have told me about my powers sooner.

Thank the gods it was Kellen and not Morel. If it were Morel...

What kind of monster weighs the worth of her own brothers' lives?

He said I stopped the avalanche. Shouldn't that count for something?

If only Kellen had told me sooner!

He lied, the bastard.

I deserve this.

She didn't know how long she sat in her stupor. Time slipped by without her noticing, until Morel returned and placed a hand on her shoulder. Davina shuddered at his touch. She didn't deserve tenderness from anyone.

"How's he doing?" Morel asked, bending over Kellen.

"The same as before."

"The nurse said his hand was crushed," said Morel, turning back to her.

Davina shrugged. She'd already given him the real account.

"You don't think... do you think Kellen might have lied to you, too?" he said.

"Morel! You can't talk about that in front of—" But when she whipped around, Rae had gone. No one was watching Kellen except for her. Brilliant, now she'd lost the child too. Could she do nothing right? "Where is—"

"Genna took her a little while ago. They're checking to see if Rae's strong enough to wear a small pack. But when you had to..."

Morel wasn't capable of summoning the words for what she'd done, so instead made a sawing motion with his hand, which was so much worse than speaking about the thing. "Do you know if what he was telling you was true? I mean with Kellen, you never know."

Davina shook her head, turning away. "I felt his hand. His fingers were hard and grey and..." But if she went on, she would be sick.

"Sorry, but after everything I've been told today..." Morel traced his fingers through the dirt beneath them, picking up pebbles then squeezing them in his fist. "All we can do is wonder. How much is he still hiding from us?"

It was a wretched question, but not the first time the thought had crossed her mind. All through their teens, they'd been trained to live double lives, acting the part of royalty one moment and a commoner the next. But there had been another lesson in that— Uncle Sergei used to make them swear they'd never keep secrets from their own family. Someone had to hold your truth, or you'd lose track of it. Of course, even as a child, she'd sensed his real motive. What Sergei meant was that he didn't want them lying to *him*. But some part of her must have listened. She felt gutted now. Not one of the three of them held everyone's truth anymore.

Kellen was the most obvious problem, but she couldn't vouch for herself either. She'd forged Kellen's signature and mailed an application, desperate to attend university in Balter, not to fulfil some academic ambition, but because it was the pathway to greater freedom from the dull strictures of life in Halgyr.

What hurt the most was the deadened look on Morel's face. If any of them had been honest, it was him.

"So... you're going along with Kira's plan after all?" She'd heard the broad strokes. Every bird in the sky had, after the shouting match Morel had got into with her. But now her brother merely shrugged.

"I don't know what else to do. We're running out of food and water, plus it's stupid to split up. I might have voted for the plan myself if it hadn't been Kira proposing it."

"We leave in the morning?"

"Yeah. I just hope he's awake by then." Morel placed a hand on Kellen's shoulder. "And that he doesn't make a damn scene when he hears the news."

Davina snorted. "Oh, you know he will."

With that, Morel began to rise, but Davina caught him by the sleeve and dragged him back to her.

"Last night," she said. "Something strange happened. I'm not sure what, but when I woke up, I felt *wrong*. And then there was everything that happened with the mountain."

Morel's eyebrows flew upwards. "Do you think *you* had something to do with it?"

"I don't know." But that was, of course, exactly what she was afraid of.

Over Morel's shoulder, she spotted a new visitor. Lord Carey was hovering near them, his expression absolutely stricken. As Davina's gaze drifted to him, Morel followed her line of sight until he'd spotted Carey as well. The young lord seemed to be agonising over something.

Morel squeezed her hand. "We'll talk later."

"Did you need something, Lord Carey?" Davina asked, rising to her feet.

"Oh, well… I don't know. I just wanted to float a theory. Miss Westwick…" He took a tentative step towards them. "…you don't suppose *she* could be the witch, could she?"

"No," said Morel flatly.

"She was far from the camp when the crevice formed. Someone must have cast that spell."

"She was with me when the avalanche happened," said Morel. "And everything points to her just being a common smuggler. I should go and talk to Penny. See what she wants me to carry on the hike tomorrow. You got your assignment yet, Carey?"

"I'll be there in a minute."

Carey's eyes were trained on Davina and she felt a flush spread through her cheeks. Morel surely wouldn't leave them together now, would he? But he simply nodded and walked away.

Davina turned her back to Carey the second Morel left. The heat in her face was growing and she didn't want him to see her like this. Not when she felt caught between tears and screaming, incapable of doing either. She sat at Kellen's side again, trying to ignore the crunch of footsteps coming towards her.

"I'm sorry." Carey lowered himself onto the ground next to her.

Davina shook her head. "For what."

"For everything I said. About your brother being married when he wasn't. I shouldn't have—"

"None of this is your fault."

"But it isn't yours either. There was a misunderstanding. Nothing more." He placed a hand over hers and, against her better judgement, she looked up at him. He was so open and honest, it cut her to the bone. How could he think well of someone like her? "When your brother wakes up, you'll get a chance to talk through your quarrel, and all will be well."

"I cut half my brother's hand off." Davina snatched her hand away from him.

"But that was a brave thing you did. You only did it to save him from—"

"He'd never have been in that position if it wasn't for me."

"He was injured protecting you, then?"

"Right... of course." It was the only explanation that would make sense to Carey. How sweet of him to invent circumstances that cast her as an innocent. "Still, all my life, he's never trusted me. Never let me know him. I always thought him such an ass for the way he treated me, but after today..." She struggled for breath, and this time the tears came too thickly for her to flick them away unseen, try as she might. "He was right. I don't deserve trust. I've caused him nothing but pain."

"No, Miss Linde. You can't be blamed for what happened. Your brother will see reason." He took her hand again, and this time she didn't have the will to shake him off.

"Yes, he will. Reason isn't on my side, Lord Carey. And he'll see that plain as day."

"It isn't on his, either. No one seems to be in the right. And when that's the case, wouldn't you say forgiveness is the best step forward? For both of you?"

Davina swallowed. "How can I forgive him when I can't even forgive myself?"

"Well... I mean..." Carey meant so well and was trying so hard to cheer her up. Of course, he didn't have a real solution for her situation, but who else would sit with her at a time like this and still think her wonderful? As he failed to find his words, a smile broke over her face. She laced her fingers through his, and drew his hand towards her mouth so that her lips skimmed his knuckles. "What did I ever do to deserve your kindness?"

Now she wasn't the only one flushing. His eyes lowered, giving her a view of those thick, dark lashes of his. "I couldn't say, my lady. You make me want to be kind to you."

She pulled on his arm, drawing him closer. His mouth was waiting when it met hers and Davina let herself melt into him. Right now, she would have given anything to feel something besides her own crushing guilt, and Carey was offering himself so willingly.

Stubble pricked her chin. It wasn't quite the perfect, romantic ideal she'd dreamed over the years, but the warmth of his tongue still made her stomach swirl. He cupped a hand around her waist, holding her close to him. But all too soon, a curl of dread seized her. The blissful forgetfulness was already slipping away as reality crashed in around her. What was she doing, kissing a man while sitting at Kellen's side? She didn't deserve this.

And yet she kissed him harder. Her hands slid down his jaw and her lips pressed against his neck, searching for some deeper feeling; something that could make her forget herself. He groaned as her fingers toyed with his shirt and danced close to his collarbone. His mouth found her ear and it was almost enough.

But it wasn't. Nothing could be.

As suddenly as she'd started this, she broke away. Carey blinked, as if coming out of a spell, and she was careful to smile at him. Even as she flicked away her tears, she kept her smile in place. "Thank you." She smoothed out the lapels of his jacket, trying to restore some decorum to this man who deserved so much better than her. "Thank you for believing in me."

"Always, my lady." His eyes shone back at her. Davina almost wanted to try kissing him again. It had been, for a moment, a wonderful distraction. Instead, she hurried off to find Morel and Genna. She needed to pack as much as anyone. Most of all, she needed to go through Kellen's bags to find any misting supplies he might have brought with him.

She couldn't afford to escape the present right now. Her brother needed her.

CHAPTER

+ + 31 + +

It took until midnight for the medication that Fallon gave Kellen to wear off. He came to with a dull ache, and instinctively tried to flex the fingers on his left hand. Only half of them moved and a jab of pain arced across his palm. It cut through the numbness of the dark hour, bringing back a jumble of memories: Davina picking up the knife; Genna holding his gaze while she ordered him to breathe; a woman flying towards him, so like Davina yet more like a monster.

But almost as soon as he pictured her face, she slipped beneath the haze of sleep and drugs. He tried to focus and remember. What exactly had happened? And how had he ended up here, lying on his back in the middle of the mountains? He tried to close his hands into fists, but only one of them cooperated.

His fingers.

Davina.

The knife.

Understanding settled in, dull and grey. Those moments should have been vivid in his memory, but it was as though his brain was protecting him by blacking out the full range of details.

There had been something to do with a mountain and a crevice tearing through the earth, but he couldn't quite picture it. Genna had held him and brought a nurse to him. Even Rae had been there. But he couldn't recall her touch, nor anything the nurse had done. He bent his index finger downwards, and touched the bandage wrapped around his palm. There must have been some surgery or stitching; something to stop the bleeding. But he was missing the better part of the previous day.

Had he ever felt this useless before? Something like this had haunted him the day his mother had died. He had been a prince, the most privileged boy in an entire nation, but he'd still lost his mother. Nothing had been enough; none of the experimental treatments she'd been given; none of the prayers they'd offered; no amount of love or longing could have kept her with them. It hadn't been enough.

And neither had he.

But hadn't his mother believed in him? As she died, she'd even given him that letter that told him Davina was a witch, proof she trusted him more than anyone else. He'd thought he'd found his purpose then. What would she think if she saw him now? Stranded out on the caldera, next to a daughter he had no history with and a sister he'd driven to maim him. She should have given the letter to Morel. She should have trusted anyone else.

The letter.

Kellen sank towards sleep. What was the point in staying awake, fretting about these things? He twisted to his side, scraping against twig and gravel as his body shifted. Every movement echoed off the hills into the silent night.

The letter.

His eyes flew open. It was almost as if he'd heard a voice. He reached out with his good hand and it landed on Genna's shoulder. So, she was the one asleep next to him. He tried to gently shake her awake, but the tempo of her breath never wavered. A sick realisation settled in. After days and nights of horror and trauma, no one was writhing in their sleep. No one was twitching against the gravel; no one was snoring.

It was quiet. So quiet.

Kellen sat up, his head swimming in protest. But when he moved, something else flitted in the darkness. *Someone*. He saw the flick of a skirt go by.

"Genna?" Kellen grabbed her shoulder again, but it was like shaking a doll. "Genna!"

"Kellen?" On his other side, Davina sat up.

He flinched as she reached for him, but she'd said his name, so didn't that mean she was her human self? But if something was wrong, what if it happened again? What if she transformed? "You're awake," he said.

The reflection of the moon bouncing against the whites of her eyes was the only hint of light in the darkness. "I've been awake all night."

"There's something wrong. Genna won't move." Kellen reached across Genna and his hand found Rae, but, like her mother, the girl didn't stir.

"I *knew* something was going to happen. Get up." Davina scrambled to her feet, then offered a hand to Kellen. He didn't take it, even though he was clumsy with all the drugs still in his system. "Morel and I took the last of the ruemoss. He's on night watch."

Kellen's mind raced to catch up, adrenaline fighting against the fog of earlier. Ruemoss. He'd taken some himself earlier, back when Genna had been wearing her perfume and they'd been questioning suspects about Braehurst's death. It must have been enough to ward off the spell seeping through the air. "How far off do you think Morel is?"

"I don't know. There was a light off in the distance a moment ago—"

"Brilliant." Kellen ground his teeth. Divide and conquer. It was so obvious. From the pinch in Davina's eyebrows, she must have sensed they'd made a mistake too.

"We have to find him," Davina said.

"And leave Rae and Genna?" Kellen gestured to them, still lying next to him. "Why didn't you give them ruemoss?"

"There wasn't enough. And we can't leave Morel out there!" Davina stamped her foot.

"Then you find him. I'll stay here—"

"I'm not leaving you!" Her voice shook.

"Fine." Kellen could only hope that, wherever Morel was, he was being vigilant. "I think we're the ones in danger, anyway. I saw someone."

"Do you think it's the witch we saw on the crystophone?" Davina spun around in the dark, looking about.

"Maybe."

It was the easiest explanation. He couldn't smell Halgyric mist in the air, and he knew no other volchemical recipe that was capable of sending a large number of people into a deadened slumber. And that voice he'd heard in his mind, prompting him about the letter…

Kellen took a step back from his sister. He could think of one witch who'd want to know what was written in that.

He angled his body so he was between her and where Genna and Rae lay. Something must have shifted in his expression because confusion flickered on Davina's face. "Kellen?"

"I think you should go and find Morel." He didn't know what else to try. He had to get her away from here.

"I'm not leaving you! If something happens—"

"You're not the only one who's worried about witches, Davina."

It took a moment for the meaning of his words to register. Then shock, hurt, and anger all registered on her face. "I'm not going to hurt you. I swear, I only—"

Whatever promise she intended to make, however, there was no need. Fifty feet from them, the howl of a woman punctured the night. Kellen and Davina looked at each other, then tore off into the brush, pursuing the sound. Branches tore at his skin, and his injured hand smacked into a tree, but what else could he do? He would rather die knowing the truth than live with another failure.

In the distance, the shrieks grew lower and more guttural, until they faded to silence. By the time they reached the body, it was too late. A woman lay at Kellen's feet, blood coursing from slashes across both her neck and chest. He and Davina bent over her, but when he studied her hooded eyes and narrow face, nothing about it was familiar. She matched none of the survivors on the train. Worse still, she wasn't the red-haired witch they'd seen destroying the bridge in the crystophone projection.

As if they needed confirmation, he heard the confused rumblings of dozens of people waking up at once from behind him. The spell had been broken.

One witch was dead, but another was surely out there.

CHAPTER

✦✦ 32 ✦✦

DAVINA COULDN'T MOVE. Kellen said something about running back to fetch one of the nurses and asked her to stay by the body, and she must have murmured something that assured him she would. But Davina couldn't have left the witch's side, even if she'd wanted to.

She had no idea who this person was, and yet... An echo stirred in Davina's memory. That dead sunken gaze—had she seen it before? Had she met this witch while she was in her other form?

Boot soles thumped their way towards her. Davina looked up, expecting Kellen, but instead it was Morel who barrelled forward. As he spotted the body at her feet, the colour drained from his face.

"You—you didn't—" he stammered.

"Of course not!" Davina snapped. "It's *me* here, isn't it?"

Morel's great shoulders shuddered as he made his way towards her. "Thank the gods."

"I'm fine, Morel. I'm..." But her words faded as he drew her into one of his crushing embraces. A week ago, Davina would have told him off for fretting so easily, but the longer this went on, the clearer it became—Morel had been right to spend his entire life paranoid about their family's safety. She pushed back against his arms enough to force him to look at her. "That light you followed. Did you find out what it was?"

He swallowed and shook his head. They didn't have time for a longer conference than that. Others from the camp arrived hot on his heels. Even if they hadn't heard the witch die, the sound of Kellen and Morel running about must have been enough to alert them. Kira Westwick broke through the bushes, nearly tripping over the body in her haste. She let out a shout that was soon matched by the gasps of others who arrived—Carey, Lord Raxton, Penny Aldridge. Davina lost track as the number of survivors grew.

Lord Drawley pushed his way through to the front of the throng and the young acolyte followed with a lantern. "Hold it down low, boy!" Drawley bellowed out as Emeth dutifully cast his light onto the dead witch.

Whispers repeated the same conclusions Davina had made earlier. No one knew the woman, which meant she must be the witch self of someone who, until recently, had been among them.

Lord Drawley let out a violent whoop of pleasure. "Well done, man!" He strode forward and thumped Morel on the back, knocking Davina from his embrace. "Bravo! Got her right in the neck, I see."

Her brother shook his head. "I didn't kill—"

"Oh, Morel, don't be so modest." Davina pinched his arm, hoping that would make him shut up. "What he means is he deflected one of her spells right back onto her. She practically killed herself."

Morel stared back at her, his jaw hanging slack. *Please let the big idiot cooperate.* The last thing they needed was more suspicion to come their way, and that's what Davina could sense would happen if she let them examine the story too closely. There was still another witch out there. There was still plenty of opportunity for the survivors to accuse her. After all, hadn't she been the one discovered next to the corpse?

"Wake everyone up!" Drawley clapped his hands. "We're counting heads. Once we know who's missing, we'll know who did this to us."

Davina held Morel's arm to steady herself. If they identified this woman and worked out who her companion had been, then perhaps the identity of the second witch would be revealed. Then the puzzle would be complete, except...

Except if that was the case, why had the witch been murdered under the cover of night? Where was her real attacker, jumping in to claim the credit that was currently being given to Morel? The second witch couldn't have wanted her companion dead, so who had killed a witch but didn't want anyone else to know about it?

"All right girls, gather up." Penny Aldridge frantically gestured for the dancers to present themselves in formation. "Minnie! Has anyone seen Minnie?"

Davina scanned those in the crowd for traces of blood on their clothes. This had been so far from a clean kill that there'd be no way the killer would have escaped untainted. But, in the darkness, the only person she could see clearly was Emeth, still holding the lantern, and he was spotless.

Kellen rejoined the circle, bringing the rest of the able-bodied survivors with him. He was leaning heavily on Genna and his breathing was laboured. On Genna's other side was Rae, and behind them came the nurse, Ashby.

"There's a body, I'm told?" She pushed her way through, her face grim but composed.

"Better than a body. A traitor!" Lord Drawley seemed only too proud to hold court. "You know, I might have said a few things to you Halgyrics, but we've done all right with you, eh? You're coming through for us at last."

"What do you mean, sir?" Kellen asked.

"Your brother. Dispatched one of these monsters for us."

Kellen straightened, his face a picture of confusion. But Morel tilted his chin towards Davina and that was enough. Kellen smiled. "Well done, brother."

"If you don't mind, I'd like to get the body ready for burial." Ashby slid her arms beneath the dead witch's shoulders. "Miss Linde? Can I ask you for another set of hands?"

"Of course." Davina grabbed the ankles.

"Don't forget about us when you're counting heads," said Ashby, throwing Morel and Kellen a wink.

They carried the body just a few yards from the circle before laying it down. Davina was about to walk back when Ashby held a hand up to her. "They said your brother killed her?"

"Ah, yes. He reflected a spell."

The nurse's attention was fixed on the slashes across the dead woman's chest. "Did he now?" she said. "They're doing such interesting things with volchemistry these days." Ashby lifted one of the witch's hands and laid it gently across her chest—an oddly kind gesture to extend to someone who'd helped cause the train crash, but then Davina spotted her sliding a ring off the dead woman's finger. Ashby turned to her with a brazen grin. "What price do you suppose a witch's ring would fetch on the black market?"

344

"Well, I don't know," said Davina. It was time to get back to the circle and the safety of her brothers.

"I should ask that Kira Westwick. She knows all about unsavoury business." Ashby stroked the ring. "A minute before you go, girl. I need one thing from you."

"Yes?" Davina hesitated.

Ashby traced her finger over the ring again. "My name."

Something tugged at the hidden corners of Davina's mind. She wanted to run. She knew she should. But instead of escaping, her eyes followed Ashby's finger as it circled the ring's dark stone over and over and over.

"My name, girl. I know you know it."

Davina opened her mouth, meaning to explain how confused she was. But something else came out. "Hess?"

Ashby's face broke into a grin, but it wasn't her face anymore. The jolly nurse was melting away. The grey and silver in her hair burned bright and red, and her once-flushed skin now glowed like moonlight. It was the witch who had destroyed the bridge.

Hess grabbed Davina's wrist, dragging her away from the body, and the safety of Morel and Kellen.

Laughter tinged her voice as she swept her thumb across the ring again. "Well done, girl. Now come with me."

· PART FIVE ·
THE ARBITERS

CHAPTER
✦ 33 ✦

A DEAD WOMAN lay at Rae's feet.

It couldn't be right. For years she'd believed that witches were misunderstood—that they were heroes, if you only looked at things the right way. Could this woman really have been so wicked that she'd blown up the train? But so many things had turned out to be lies lately. Maybe the kindness of witches was another one? After all, she'd based her beliefs on a silly book left to her by a man who didn't give two hoots about her. Why shouldn't the book be full of lies too?

"Better than a body. A traitor!" The man with the big moustache boomed louder than all the other grown-ups around him, sucking up their attention.

Mr Linde was asking him a question now, not that Rae cared. Ma was anchored to his side, propping up Mr Linde. When he'd fetched them earlier, he'd been tripping and stumbling around like a drunkard, though Ma said it was the medicine that was making him loopy. Rae still couldn't believe that fool with his floppy hair and funny accent was her father.

She turned away from them, back to the body. If she ever saw her classmates again, they wouldn't believe the stories she had to tell them about everything she'd seen out here. The dead woman stared up at the night sky with frozen horror, blood congealing on her neck and chest. Had Uncle Morel really killed her? What kind of man would do something like that? He'd been so gentle with Rae when he hadn't known she was his niece. And it didn't make sense. He had a gun on his back, not a knife.

"Miss Linde? Can I ask you for another set of hands?" One of the nurses picked up the body, interrupting Rae's view. Miss Linde was quick to help her, and all too soon they were carting the dead witch away. Rae clutched her jacket close with her uninjured arm. Miss Linde. Aunt Davina. Was she supposed to call her that from now on?

Rae followed them as they took the body away from the group. She chanced a look at her mother, but Ma was too involved in the grown-ups' discussion. They were busy counting the women. Well, Ma could vouch for her. Rae crept closer to the spot where the nurse had laid the body.

She saw the whole thing. Not all the details of their conversation reached her ears, but she heard enough. Aunt Davina answered the nurse's questions then almost got away. But instead, she said a name. A new one. Hess. A name Rae had read about in the book her father had left her.

Rae screamed.

The nice nurse who'd bandaged her arm was gone, replaced by a striking face that she'd seen before in illustrations. Aunt Davina turned towards the sound of Rae's cry, but Hess dragged her away. So, that was the answer. Witches *were* villains. And they were kidnapping Aunt Davina.

Rae came to her senses and ran towards them. There wasn't a

moment to lose when a witch was involved. Ramona's teeth! She didn't even like Miss Linde. Was this what it meant when people did things because it was *for family*? It didn't matter how little Rae loved these people. If she lost Aunt Davina now, that would be losing a piece of herself.

Behind her, someone asked who'd screamed and the discussion became a confused torrent. She picked out the sound of her mother's alarm when she realised Rae was no longer where she should be, but she couldn't stop now. The distance between Rae and the group widened, but she was gaining on Hess. The witch hurried as best she could, but Aunt Davina was fighting her, trying to free herself from her grip. Rae was within ten feet of them when a pair of arms caught her by the middle and lifted her off the ground. She gagged for air as she felt the rough embrace of a man with a bandage wrapped around one of his hands.

"Let me go!" She thrashed against Mr Linde's grip, expecting it to be easier to break because of his injury, but he dropped to his knees, so he could use his whole body to restrain her. "There's a witch!" she shouted. "There's a witch and she took Aunt Davina—"

"I know! Morel will get her."

Why did Mr Linde have to be so stubborn? Didn't he understand it was his sister he was losing? Then, out of the corner of her eye, she saw Uncle Morel fly through the trees, grabbing his gun from where it hung on his back. Rae twisted in her father's grip, aching to be there too. Someone should warn him.

He wasn't the only one following the witch. Dozens of legs tore through the bushes ahead of her. Someone let out a whoop, declaring that the hunt was on, and Rae saw one of the younger gentlemen speed past.

"Let her go!" Uncle Morel aimed his gun.

Hess reeled back her arm. She must have known he wouldn't shoot while she was holding his sister. Unintimidated, she brought her palm down onto the ground. A force like a thousand basalt engines reverberated through the earth, wrenching the trees from their roots and sending them falling backward into everyone who had dared to follow her.

Uncle Morel dived to the side as a massive pine tree careened towards him. But the young gentleman next to him wasn't as quick.

+ ✦ +

In the darkness, Davina only saw their faces for a second. Morel and Carey drew to a stop. Her brother pulled out his gun, but Carey had nothing but his good intentions to save him. Then the trees lurched up from the ground, their roots a mass of tentacles that clawed at the sky. They pulled up the soil that used to hold them in place, creating a wall of debris between her and the people she loved.

Davina screamed and tried to run towards them, but Hess held her fast. Then something smacked her over the head and everything went dark. As she passed out, Davina willed her witch self to take over, but that instinct never triggered.

Hess wanted her alive.

+ ✦ +

Idiots.

Genna couldn't believe how many of the survivors ran towards the witch. The moment Davina and the nurse went missing, it was obvious what had happened. There was no need to count heads now that the second witch had revealed herself.

Kellen, she could forgive. In fact, Genna was grateful. He'd gone after a foolish child. And he stayed put once he had his arms around Rae. Genna almost understood Morel, too. He had combat training and a weapon. Besides, he clearly loved his sister enough to risk his own life, even if the attempt was rash.

But all the lords who'd run down the hill like sportsmen chasing a fox? Imbeciles, every last one of them. It shouldn't have come to this. They should have let the witch go.

The young man didn't have to die.

One of the trees broke Ambrose Carey's back, and he went quickly, jabbering out a message of love he wanted someone to pass on to Davina. If they ever saw her again. The young acolyte knelt down beside him and listened to his final words, his face an ashen pallor.

Carey's death saddened Genna more than she'd expected. He hadn't been the most useful man, but he'd been sweet and earnest. She thought of that first night, when he'd laid his tailcoat over Rae, extending what little kindness he could to an injured girl. Now the acolyte was struggling against tears as he buried his friend in a shallow grave. Until now, so many of the dead seemed to have died alone, but Carey had clearly been loved by those around him.

By the time someone was able to fight their way through the tangled mess of fallen trees, the witch had disappeared and it was too dark to follow her footprints. For several minutes, Genna simply sat by Kellen's side as Rae, trembling with tears, curled up in his arms. Kellen made no sound at all.

Kellen and Rae had been far enough away from the witch when she launched the trees and they'd only been hit by a few spindly branches. There were scratches down Kellen's arms, but when compared to everything else, they were trivial. Morel was in worse shape. He'd managed to dodge the largest sections of the trees, but there was a nasty gash down his back and one of his feet had got caught in a root as he'd run, resulting in a dislocated knee.

Now they no longer had the nurses, the group's attempts at medicine were rudimentary. Penny Aldridge had experience with dance injuries, so she volunteered to pop Morel's knee back into place, but even once that had been done it was still too swollen for him to walk on. Genna searched for supplies, unable to deal with Kellen's silent resignation any longer. She searched the body of the dead witch and found the medical kit that definitively identified her as Fallon, the head nurse.

Kellen lurched away when Genna pulled a bandage from it to wrap around his arm. "How do you know we can trust anything from in there?" he said.

"Please, it's just a piece of cloth," said Genna, ignoring his grumblings. "And besides… the care she gave you yesterday helped."

"Which does beg the question…" Kellen held out his arm, letting her wrap the bandage around him. "If the witches blew up the train, why did they work so hard to keep everyone alive afterwards?"

Genna frowned. It was strange to hear him attempt to exonerate the witches after everything they'd put his sister through. It made her wonder. Was it just a coincidence that, after all those years of Rae obsessing over a book about witches that Kellen had bought, a witch had now made off with his younger sister? If Davina was a witch, the ramifications were too much to handle. What might that mean for Rae, if she had an aunt with witch's blood?

She pushed the thought away and tied off the bandage. "We know it was them. The witch who took Davina was the one we saw in the crystophone projection."

"I know, but it doesn't make sense!" Kellen shouted.

Rae jumped and she gave him a dark look before sliding from his lap and returning to her mother. Genna sighed and turned her daughter's hands over, checking for scrapes.

"Even if they did crash the train, what about the missing solozite?" asked Kellen. "And that basalt dust caked in Braehurst's mouth?"

"They knew volchemical medicine. Who's to say they didn't know petrology too?" Genna dug through the medical kit and found a vial of herbal astringent. The mixture was cold on her finger and Rae flinched when she touched it to her bleeding cheek. "Why are you being so stubborn about this? We have an answer. Isn't that good enough? We don't know how all the pieces fit exactly, but isn't it—"

Kellen leaned close enough to her so he could whisper. "Morel didn't kill the witch."

The protests died on Genna's lips. "What?"

Kellen shrugged. Genna was about to ask him what he thought had happened, but the sound of boots thudding through broken branches made her stop. Genna turned to find Kira Westwick scowling down at them.

"How ready is everyone to walk?" she demanded.

"Walk where?" Kellen asked.

"You missed that while you were asleep." Genna lifted Rae off her lap so she could stand and help Kellen up. "Everyone decided we should try to find a village further north in the caldera. Though I thought we'd all agreed to leave in the morning."

"Dawn will come soon enough." Kira tapped her boots against the ground impatiently. "And I don't see any point lingering. I'd rather get somewhere safe before that witch comes back to finish us off."

"But isn't there a chance we'll encounter more witches if we go further north?" Kellen clearly didn't like this turn in direction, but he wasn't going to win Kira over.

"No one's pretending it's a perfect solution, but it was one we all agreed to," said Kira. "Unless you've got a better plan, I suggest you fall in line."

"I'm not arguing exactly," said Kellen. "But there's no way I could go along with your plan, even if I did agree with it. My brother can't walk and my sister is missing."

"We'll figure something out." Kira rolled her eyes.

"But Davina. She doesn't know where—"

"She knew the plan. If she manages to escape from that bloody witch, she'll know to look for us."

Kellen shook his head. "I'm sorry. If I'm going anywhere, it's to find her."

Genna folded her arms tight to her chest. She should have known it would come to this. "Don't you think we can wait until morning to leave?"

"What difference does it make? No one's going to find a witch out in the caldera in the dead of night. We're on *their* turf." Kira's words bore the sting of truth. She shifted her weight from one foot to another as her temper wore thin. "Look, I know I can't make you lot come along, but you should. Something still isn't right. You know my crate is missing and I doubt that witch would bother stealing solozite when she can rip up a mountain without it."

"I'm sorry, Miss Westwick." Kellen got to his feet, wincing when he placed his bandaged hand on the ground to support himself. "I can't leave Davina behind."

Kira tossed her hair over her shoulder. "Well, there you have it.

What about you, Miss Freath? Are you planning to stay here and die in this valley?"

Genna swallowed and reached for Rae. She pulled her daughter close, hoping that would give her some clarity before she made a decision. Her child's heartbeat pulsed through the layers of fabric between them, and she found her resolve. "We're staying too."

"Genna, you shouldn't." Kellen's jaw dropped in shock. "I can't promise it'll be safe, especially if we find Davina—"

"She's our family too. We'll try to catch up with the others once we've found her." Genna squared her shoulders towards Kira. "Go on without us."

Kira stamped her foot, and for a moment, Genna thought she might scream at them. Tears even began to form at the corners of her eyes.

"Morel said the same thing." Kira blinked and turned on her heel.

Kira's party left Kellen, Morel, Genna and Rae with a small collection of supplies—mostly the pack Morel had been expected to carry, since they lacked any men who could have managed it anyway. By the time they were fully packed to leave camp, the red of dawn was bleeding over the hills.

Genna helped Kellen spread Morel out beneath the sheet that had previously sheltered his brother. Quietly, she began to apply the lotion she'd found in the nurse's bag to the wound on his back. Kellen offered him his uninjured hand. "Need something to squeeze?"

"Not you," Morel grunted back, and Kellen laughed.

Kellen looked over his shoulder at the throng of people disappearing up the northern slope. The four of them fell quiet until Genna finished dressing Morel's wound. Rae found a large rock and dragged it over so he could elevate his leg. It was the best they could do to try to bring down the swelling.

They needed to decide what to do next. The answer should have been obvious since they had so few options. Usually, limitations made choices easier, but perhaps they'd lost too much. Instead, they gave in to silence and huddled together beneath the makeshift shelter.

They might have sat that way for hours if Morel's snoring hadn't broken the sombre mood. A smile creased Kellen's worn face and even Rae giggled. Her large eyes darted between the two men. Her father and uncle. It helped Genna feel better about the choice she'd made.

Finally, Kellen turned to her. "Why are you doing this? Now, of all times."

Because Rae deserved a family.

Because, for all his faults, Kellen deserved the chance to be a part of his daughter's life.

Because, for the first time, Kellen needed her. More, perhaps, than Genna had ever needed him.

Because even if this only lasted for a little while, a little while might be enough.

There were a million reasons.

But Genna wasn't good at putting those things into words.

She placed a hand over his and settled on the one thing the poets had taught her was customary to say at times like this. "I love you."

CHAPTER
✦✦ 34 ✦✦

Davina came to with sunlight beating down on her. It made her head throb, leaving her nauseated as she blinked herself awake. She tried to reach up and clear the sleep from her eyes, but her wrist strained against something—someone had tied her hands behind her back.

She jerked awake, only momentarily surprised by the sight of Hess perched on a rock a few feet away, the skirt of her nurse's uniform fanning out like she'd arranged the pleats for the greatest dramatic impact. She was as terrifying and majestic as the night before.

They were on a bluff, somewhere above the valley. The grey rain of the day before had blown away, leaving aching blue skies overhead. Davina needed to get down and rejoin everyone, but what direction was the camp in? Could she get away from Hess without losing her life? Wind swirled Hess's hair into red halos, her chin still pointed towards some distant horizon.

Davina swallowed and felt dryness in her throat. This was her chance. Before the witch could retaliate.

"Ashby!" she called out.

359

"You're up." Hess reached for a satchel at her side, pulling out a canteen. "You must be thirsty—"

"Ashby!" Davina tried again, but the truth settled in as Hess laughed, unscrewing the cap.

"Bless you, child. Very optimistic." Hess took a drink, then walked towards Davina with the canteen held out. "I'm afraid Ashby isn't my real human name."

Davina turned away, but Hess pressed the canteen closer. "Drink," she said. "It won't poison you."

"It's not poison I'm worried about." Davina struggled to stand, pulling against her bonds. Hess had fashioned shackles from strips of her skirt. With enough time or a sharp rock, Davina might be able to wear through them and escape.

Hess sighed, stepping back. "I forgot. You're Halgyric. I suppose I wouldn't touch an enemy's cup if I grew up in your culture either. How old are you, girl? There's so much that you need to learn."

"Excuse me?" Davina said. "I have no interest in learning anything from you."

"I wish you'd reconsider." Hess retreated to her perch on the rocks, scooping her skirt away elegantly as she sat. "I never meant for us to be enemies."

"Never meant… You blew up the train! And you attacked my brother and Carey…" But Davina was gasping to control her tears now. Those trees had been so large. And if something had happened to Morel… She sniffed, wishing her hands were free so she could hide her face.

"Yes, I *am* sorry about that. Your family, I mean. Not the train. Those men seemed a harmless sort." Hess tapped her nails against the canteen, then took another swig. "As for the train, all I can say is that putting your life in danger was never my intention. There are innocent casualties in war. More than anyone dares admit."

"Why are you telling me this?"

"It was always my plan to tell you everything," said Hess. "Once Allonia and I figured out who the other witch on the train was, we decided we'd bring her in and get out of that valley before the survivors were any wiser. But then people kept dying and things got so damn complicated—"

"What?" Davina felt a sharp edge in the rocks behind her. Subtly, she propped herself against it so she could work her wrists over the ridge. Hess seemed willing to talk, and so long as that remained true, Davina might be able to fashion her escape.

"I should start from the beginning," said Hess. "I know it's difficult to believe. Everyone sees witches as monsters, but from my perspective, I'm nothing but a patriot. Balter built that railway through our territory. It's land that belongs to the people of Rencha."

"Rencha fell three hundred years ago," Davina pointed out. It was ridiculous, citing an empire that collapsed so long ago. After the volcano blew, that civilisation had been wiped out by lava flows. The few settlements that survived were so blanketed in ash that their people were forced to flee to anywhere that would take them. Halgyr could trace more than a few bloodlines back to the refugees who'd crawled over the mountains to reach the safety of the northern shores. "No one's sat on the throne in generations. No one has any territorial claim—"

"Not the throne. I said her *people* do. The loyalists. The caldera belongs to us." Hess's mouth twitched as if she found Davina's obstinance amusing. "Balter has smashed itself across our lands, but just because they built their bloody railway there, it doesn't change the fact it's ours. I'd have thought you might be sympathetic to our situation. Our people would be better off banding together to keep Balter in check."

Davina scoffed. In truth, the Halgyric court was split on the matter. There were those who feared Balter and its expansion. But after what Balter's war machine had done as it pushed through the mountains, raining solozite down on the witches and spewing their modernised vision across the landscape, what wisdom was there in provoking them? It was better to play the ally. It made no sense for them to throw their lot in with the Renchans.

Unless…

Davina's gaze fell from Hess. Unless you were a witch. Witches weren't executed in Halgyr but strict legislation governed what types of witchcraft were permissible. Disobedience to those laws came with swift punishment. Since the Great Eruption, the Renchans had embraced the witches. Perhaps they'd only done so out of necessity. But, whatever the reasons, the result was the same.

"There are forces mounting against Balter even now," said Hess. "But if we have any hope of reclaiming the caldera, the railway needed to go. Allonia and I had our assignment. We tried to fulfil it in the most humane way possible. Allonia used her scryer's abilities to send the train crew to sleep, then we disconnected the caboose. They should all be safely alive on the other side of the canyon. Then we took out the bridge. The High Coven thought a few high-profile deaths wouldn't hurt the cause either. They wanted us to take out a luxury train."

"We were all just collateral to you?" Davina's wrists throbbed from jamming them into the rock, but she kept wearing down the fibres.

"You should have been. I won't pretend. But don't you see?

When I destroyed the engine, everyone should have been killed. But then *you* happened." Hess slid forward from the rock, until she was kneeling in front of Davina. "You turned the engine to stone and stopped me. It was a miracle. I knew there was another witch on the train, and I was sure—no, I *am* sure—that Ramona willed it this way. She let the High Coven conceive of the mission so I could find you. It wasn't a coincidence we all were on the same train."

"You're imagining things."

"Am I?" Hess came closer. "Think about it. You could have gone your whole life never knowing about your powers. Instead, Ramona brought us together. It's my job to take you to the High Coven and make sure you're properly trained."

"You're mad!" Davina knew she shouldn't lose her temper with a woman who could kill her, but she couldn't stand to listen to another word she said. "You destroyed the train, then you started killing us off for sport—"

"We kept you all alive!" Hess's voice was now a growl. "Or do you wish I hadn't set your niece's broken arm? Do you wish Allonia hadn't stopped your brother from bleeding out after you hacked his fingers off?"

Davina winced at the memory.

"Despite what you might think, killing doesn't come easy to me. I haven't harmed a soul since the train crashed. I'm not cruel. When I realised that Ramona thought it right to spare the rest of you—"

"Don't give me that bloody talk about your goddess," said Davina. "You helped because you were looking for me and wanted me to trust you. You're only telling me this because your partner's dead, and that's forced you to—"

"You're right about one thing. Allonia is dead." A tear glimmered at the edge of Hess's eye and it struck Davina that she, too, had lost someone in this tragedy. "And that means someone is killing people in that camp of yours. We both know that Morel didn't kill Allonia—he was following me last night."

Of course. The light that lured him away. Hess had distracted the night watch, while her partner cast the spell that had sent them to sleep, so she could... well, that Davina couldn't guess. They'd obviously risked something, since now one of the witches was now dead. Would Hess tell her? How badly did she want Davina's trust? "So, if it wasn't you or Morel who killed her... what happened last night?"

Hess shivered. "It should have been a simple task. Allonia is—*was*—a scryer, trained in mind manipulation. She was trying to extract a memory, but you Halgyrics aren't as pliable as we'd hoped, thanks to your damn mists and ruemoss."

"A memory?" Davina repeated.

Hess nodded. "From your eldest brother. Allonia sensed he knew your witch name."

It wasn't as though this was news to her, but Davina still fell silent. Some part of her had imagined that Kellen hadn't remembered it—that he might have needed to reread the letter from their mother to refresh his memory. But if someone could reach into his mind and take it, well, that meant he'd kept that secret closer than Davina had imagined. And judging by the fact that she was still sitting here, as Davina, he'd kept it safe yet again.

"We'll have to come up with another solution," said Hess. "The scryers in the caldera might know how to find your name, but until we get there—"

"I'm not going with you."

The rock cut through the final fibres around Davina's wrists, and she pulled them apart, triumphant.

Hess raised an eyebrow. "Do you think I only bound you with cloth, girl?"

Davina skittered further down the hillside, hoping that putting some distance between her and the witch would be enough. Hess might attack and force her to transform, she realised. Then, it would be up to her witch self whether she left her family behind. But Hess's plan didn't involve anything that dramatic. Instead, she took the scryer's ring from her pocket. In the clear light of day, Davina recognised the stone—obsidian. Perfect for manipulating memories and, with them, minds.

"Davina Linde." Hess swirled her finger across the stone's surface and Davina felt that pull again. "You will come with me, Davina Linde. You will come now."

Davina's eyes watered and she clamped her hands over her ears. She'd taken ruemoss. Why wasn't that enough?

"*Davina Linde,*" Hess repeated more sternly. "You will come with me—"

"No!"

"By the force of your name, *Davina Linde*, you will come with me now!"

Davina dropped to her knees. Her own name echoed like an incantation in her mind. *Davina Davina Davina.* Each repetition made it sound stranger. Less like her own. With each repetition, the nameless witch inside her stirred with hope, reached out to take over and banish her human consciousness.

It would be so much easier to give in. Her skull felt as though it might crack open with fire if she resisted much longer. *Go with her,* the witch inside seemed to whisper. *Go and you'll be wanted. Go and you'll never have to live up to the demands of a crown that never cared for you.* Hadn't she wanted this all her life? Hadn't she wanted to be valued and important? To be loved? Hess wouldn't pass over her the way her father had. The way Kellen did.

But if it was love she wanted...

Davina had spent so much of her life demanding that her family notice her. Begging for love. But all that time, she'd only been considering half the problem—what someone could give *her*. If she left, she'd save herself, but condemn her brothers. Morel, who'd taken her to Balter against everyone else's wishes. Kellen, who'd lied through his teeth a thousand times to protect her.

Kellen. Morel.

Her brothers. Their names belonged to her. And she to them. She couldn't let this monster take them away.

Kellen. Morel.

Though they had other names as well. Ones that were hidden in her heart. What if that dark ring found those too? Yet they rang through her now as well, swelling like an orchestra.

Prince Matthias. Prince Lawrence.

And finally...

Princess Rochelle.

Rochelle.

If she couldn't fight Hess as a witch or even as Davina, she could do it another way. She had a third name. For years, she'd been told the royal family wore masks to protect themselves from Soloz, a jealous, faceless god, but the mask wasn't her only defence. There was more than one vengeful deity to consider. Whether it was Ramona's will or not, Princess Rochelle couldn't be forced to follow Hess. She had a family to protect.

Rochelle. She clung to that secret name and pushed herself back onto her feet. For a moment, Hess looked triumphant. She held out her hand, expecting Davina to follow, no doubt, like an obedient lamb. But the princess turned and ran.

She scrambled away as fast as she dared, sliding down the precarious mountain slope. The gods help her if she was going the wrong way. Above her, Hess called out, "Wait!" But the spell had been broken. Princess Rochelle of Halgyr let out a wild laugh as she ran down towards the valley.

But her victory was short-lived. The slope below her buckled, rock flew upwards, and Davina barely had time to cover her face as a wave of brambles flew towards her. Who was she, thinking she could escape the wrath of a witch?

Hess was next to her in seconds. She yanked her up by the elbow. Even though she hadn't injured her chest, Davina struggled to breathe.

"What in Ramona's name? I told you to come! How can you…" But then understanding broke over Hess's face and she let out a peal of laughter. "Really? I suppose you are Halgyric, but if you're one of the royals, then your brothers… Oh, how marvellous."

Hess let go of Davina so suddenly that she stumbled to the ground. Heat warmed her cheeks as she understood what she'd just revealed. And to whom.

"Well, Princess Rochelle, we have a bargain to make." Hess folded her arms, a wide smile filling her face. "I'm going to let you choose one more time. Come with me, and I'll keep your secret safe. Or you can go back down that mountain and I won't do a thing to stop you."

"And why would you do that?" Davina asked.

"Because I enjoy having friends in high places. Let me help

you." With a flick of Hess's wrist, several trees fell to the ground, revealing a view of train tracks snaking through the mountains. It was enough for Davina to be able to work out which direction to head in. "Give my regards to Kellen. He'll be hearing from the High Coven soon, I'm sure. And remember… Halgyr would do better allying with *us* instead of Balter."

Davina glanced between the train tracks and Hess. Whatever she chose, it was a trap.

"If you're going to help them, I suggest you head back soon," Hess added.

"What do you mean?"

"For the thousandth time, girl." Hess sighed. "I destroyed the train. But I'm afraid the conductor, the gangster and Allonia were someone else's handiwork. Even the bloody avalanche that almost killed you and your brother had nothing to do with me."

"But… But who'd want to do all those things?"

Hess laughed at her. "*Think*, girl. Who did you see washing their hands of the crime?"

CHAPTER
✦ 35 ✦

Wᴴɪʟᴇ Mᴏʀᴇʟ ʀᴇsᴛᴇᴅ and regained his strength, Kellen asked Genna about everything he'd missed while he'd been recovering the day before. There were the missing soldiers, presumed dead in the avalanche that had nearly killed him and Davina; then there'd been the whole confrontation with Kira Westwick, when she'd assumed control over the survivors. Poor Morel must have hated being put in the spotlight like that.

Once Genna had finished, a drawn-out silence fell between them as she waited for his opinion on what had happened, but nothing came to him.

"So, now I've told you everything I know," she said, when he failed to react, "are you going to tell me what really happened when your sister cut off your fingers?"

The question was so abrupt that Kellen didn't have a response ready, and he simply gaped at her. He'd been at a loss for words the whole morning. It was so fiendishly unlike him, but he was finding speech agonising now there was nothing good left to say. His maimed hand, Morel's injuries, his missing sister, even Genna's declaration of love—all of them terrified him. Why had she chosen to love him now when he was so powerless to protect her or even return her affections? There had been a moment, following the amputation, when he'd been ready to say those words to her, then bleed out on the mountain. But she hadn't let him do either of those things. Frankly, he resented her for both.

Genna shook her head. "In normal circumstances, I'd gladly let you grieve and come to terms with this before badgering you with questions," she said. "But don't you understand? I can't help you unless I know what's going on."

"You don't know what you're asking." Kellen got to his feet, this time careful not to use his left hand for support as he stood. If they lived through this, there'd be a thousand small habits he'd need to relearn.

"Actually, I'm worried I do." Genna's gaze darted to where Rae sat a few feet away, tongue between her teeth as she flipped through *Lives of the Witches*. "If your sister is—is one of them, I have to know. As a mother, I have a right to—"

"Is that why you decided to stay? To find out if our daughter is a witch?" Kellen couldn't hold back the accusatory tone in his voice.

"Kellen! It's a reasonable question." Genna's voice was angry, and it was enough to make him ashamed of himself. Of course it was a reasonable question. But it had no reasonable answer. He turned on his heel and strode away from her.

"And now you're going to storm off like a child? This isn't helping anyone—"

"I know!" By the gods, he knew how bloody useless he was being. It didn't need pointing out to him. "A moment, Genna. I need a moment alone, and then—"

"And what are we supposed to do until then? Sit around and wait for you to act like a bloody man?" She was right to be angry with him, of course. Gods, why had she stayed? If she'd chosen to remain out of some sense of self-preservation, he wouldn't have minded, but it was clear she believed it would have been safer to head north in the hope of finding a village. The only explanation for her staying was her love for him, and that was so much worse.

He kept walking, more out of stubbornness than any sense of direction. Eventually he reached the train tracks. The rain of yesterday had turned the basalt dust to sludge, and it ran in grey tracks down the rocks. It would be inert now it was mixed with all the mud. Still, Kellen found himself squatting down to touch a spot in which some of it had caught and gummed up around the rails. It was the same texture as the residue they'd found lodged inside Jarvie Braehurst's mouth.

Kellen rubbed the mixture between his fingers, the brittle bits of stone getting into the cracks of his skin. Had the witches really been trained in volchemistry? Clearly they knew medicine, as well as their own craft, but it took some skill to use spent basalt dust, ground for another purpose, to attack a man. Had they really mastered petrology too?

"I found her." A small, determined voice materialised by his elbow.

Kellen jumped, turning to find Rae glowering at him with a massive book in her hands. "I'm sorry, you did what?" he asked.

"Hess." Rae shoved the book forward. "I found her."

Kellen stared back, unsure what to do. This was the first time the girl had ever addressed him willingly, and he didn't have the energy to respond. In a flash, he understood something about his father he never had before. It was so much easier to retreat into silence, to ignore people and stay wrapped up in grief rather than confront loved ones' expectations. Kellen could lock his own child out of his life too if he wanted. It was in his blood.

Rae's frown darkened, making her look so much like her mother. "Are you going to read it or not?"

"Oh." Obediently, Kellen held out his hand and Rae thrust the book at him. It was a good-sized volume—difficult to support with only one hand. The text was dense for such a small child, though there was an ink illustration on one of the pages to guide her. It depicted a woman with long flowing hair and a half-moon smile. The figure wasn't immediately recognisable, though Kellen soon understood why Rae had brought it to him.

Among modern witches, Hess has been quick to make a name for herself. Her origins remain unknown, though her apparent age suggests birth during the past fifty years. Many believe her an orphan of the Balterian expansion. Perhaps it is this that drives her fierce opposition to Balterian interests.

She came to attention fifteen years ago during the razing of Korio. Her destruction of a barracks caused widespread fires throughout the region, with estimated costs surpassing 120,000 finos. Following this, she was spotted near a military garrison, and was pursued by soldiers. Five died in the futile attempt to capture her.

She is believed to live in the caldera, where her many crimes are celebrated. And though her face is known to strike fear into the hearts of Balterian soldiers, descendants of the Renchans view her as a modern hero.

The description went on, but Kellen lowered it to see Rae, who was staring at him expectantly. "You can understand all this?" he asked.

"I thought I did." Rae's eyes dropped. "Ma helps me with the big words. But the book says she's a hero. How could a hero—"

She stopped abruptly, gasping as if she needed to stifle a sob. It caught Kellen off guard. Her hands clenched into fists and she swayed on her heels, as if holding all her fears in might knock her over.

"I'm so sorry." Kellen reached out a hand to grasp her shoulder and, to his amazement, she didn't flinch. "Making heroes out of people—well, it's difficult business. Heroes tend to exist because people have enemies. It sounds like, to her people, she's not evil or mean. She's a soldier. Like your Uncle Morel."

Her eyes flicked to his at the mention of Morel. Children always liked Morel. And while it was easy to be jealous, Kellen couldn't blame them. Morel gave more than he took and there were precious few men that was true of.

"But Uncle Morel... he wouldn't blow up a train, would he?" Rae asked.

Kellen shrugged. "Not one with children on it. But if it were a war and the train had soldiers on it—"

"But we *weren't* soldiers. Ma and I never did anything to the witches. I even liked them. No one on the train deserved it. No one—"

"Of course not!" He'd been too frank with her. There were things you didn't say to a seven-year-old. Even now, he was tempted to overexplain, because reading the book had reminded him of something—to some minds, the violence they had experienced was rational. "No one deserved to die. Not even..."

But Kellen's words died on his lips. He'd never been comfortable with moral absolutes. Even now, if someone asked him to condemn the witches for what they'd done to the train, it would be difficult. If the book was right, Hess hadn't killed out of spite, but out of dedication to her people.

"Not even who?" Rae prompted.

"Braehurst." His mind was working through something else now. Words someone had uttered to him during the Braehurst investigation rattled through him.

He was a hard, evil man. Everyone knew he was a monster.

"Jarvie Braehurst," Kellen repeated. "There was a man with connections to gangsters on the train. I doubt your mother told you, but—"

"Oh yes, I remember." Rae nodded in a long-suffering way. It was almost comical. "Well, if not even *he* deserved it—"

Kellen stood abruptly and reached for Rae, remembering a second later that he couldn't comfortably carry the book with his damaged hand. "Here. You'll need to carry this. Come with me."

Her eyes narrowed, but she obeyed. Ha! So there *was* something he had in common with his child. Just like him, she couldn't resist finding the solution to a puzzle. He led her back to the fire, where Morel was sleeping and Genna sat boiling the rainwater they'd managed to capture from the sheet above him.

"Genna? What happened to the boy?" Kellen asked.

"Pardon me?" Genna scowled, still annoyed with his earlier theatrics.

There was no time for apologies, though. "The beggar boy that the soldiers tied up," said Kellen. "I think his name was Dalton?"

"He'll be with the others, I imagine," Genna said.

"Are you sure? Because I didn't see him. Did anyone look for him after the avalanche?"

Genna turned to Morel, though he answered her with nothing but a snore. Eventually, she turned back to Kellen and shrugged. "I imagine the acolyte would have done."

"By Soloz." Kellen's breath grew shallow as another horrible realisation dawned on him "Genna, the boy *knew*."

"Knew what?"

"About Kira Westwick's solozite. Morel and I told him, so he'd help us look for it. We trusted him. If he didn't report to you or Morel afterwards, then something went wrong."

They'd told Dalton to keep it a secret, of course. Emphasised how little they were able to trust their fellow passengers. Clearly, their warnings hadn't been enough.

"You think the boy found the solozite?" said Genna. "But he was locked up when Braehurst—"

"No, not the boy," said Kellen.

How could a wretch like that have afforded the training necessary to operate solozite? Or activate spent basalt grindings? The person who'd caused the avalanche was someone who'd had access to elite schooling. Someone who'd listened to Dalton's tales of mysterious boxes being smuggled by Kira *before* Braehurst's death.

"Don't you see?" said Kellen. "Dalton told the one person he thought he could trust. He told Emeth Trudane."

CHAPTER
+ + 36 + + +

TWO NIGHTS EARLIER, Emeth had stared into a sky thick with the smoke of burnt iron. No one had fallen back to sleep after the initial train crash, so he'd looked upwards, wondering what it all meant. Perhaps the gods were intervening in Ambrose's plan to open a new solozite mine? Maybe they knew he and Drawley would get their hands on the lethal mineral and this was their last desperate attempt to stop it.

Why then had the gods left things incomplete? If the witch goddess was presiding over the night, why were Drawley and Ambrose still alive? They would pursue their aims as soon as they were back to safety. The intervention was half-done at best.

In the aftermath of the crash, there had been plenty of people and work to keep Emeth distracted. Everyone needed help. But, as the nurses took over tending the wounded and Penny Aldridge and her dance troupe took control of the luggage, Emeth's role became less clear. He wasn't needed by the Lords' Council and he had no family to care for. He'd racked his brain for what small service he could provide, and his thoughts had gone to the boy the soldiers had carried away.

By then, the dancers had broken open the food stores, so Emeth had crept in to grab something to feed Dalton Rai, who was obviously malnourished. When he visited the boy, the soldiers had already added another bruise above his eye and he lay shaking on the cold ground. Anger flamed in Emeth's stomach, but he tamped it down.

Captain Sewell swaggered forward before Emeth could get within ten feet of Dalton, his gaze sharp with distrust. "Something the matter, Mediate?"

"Please, I'm only an acolyte." Emeth offered a small bow, hoping the deference would earn him access to the boy. "I've brought food for the prisoner."

Captain Sewell shook his head, though he still stepped aside. "It's a waste on him. Go ahead. Listen to his troubles or whatever it is you lot do."

Dalton perked up as Emeth sat down beside him. He shoved the entire portion of bread and cheese that Emeth had brought into his mouth, as if he were afraid it might be taken away if he didn't eat it straightaway. For a moment, Emeth waited silently as Dalton chewed and swallowed. Then his patience was rewarded as Dalton turned to him with hopeful eyes.

"If you please, Mediate. I promise it wasn't me who attacked the train. But I think I know who did." Dalton did his best to whisper, but Captain Sewell was hovering two feet away.

"Gods, not this drivel again." Sewell raised the butt of his rifle and Dalton winced. Clearly, he'd been struck that way before. "Don't pay him any attention, Mediate. He wasn't on the passenger list. He's not supposed to be here."

"Captain, it's my duty to listen to the destitute in times of trial." Emeth held his ground, enjoying the way it made Sewell squirm.

A vein in the soldier's neck twitched. "Very well," he said. "At least *we* don't have to listen to it for once." Sewell motioned to his men to step away and Emeth turned back to Dalton.

"What was it you wanted to tell me?" Emeth asked.

"There are two of Selnick's goons on the train. I heard them myself." Dalton leaned closer. "I even got their names: Kira Westwick and Jarvie Braehurst."

Braehurst.

Emeth knew that name. His time working in his father's accounting office had given him a glimpse into Magnus Selnick's operations. And if the boy had overheard a name belonging to one of the gangster's enforcers, his story clearly held some kernel of truth. Emeth listened to the whole tale with interest, all his suspicions confirmed. Not only were a slew of greedy lords aboard this train, but so were the abhorrent criminal class that supported them.

Armed with the boy's story, Emeth went searching. While he didn't know what was inside the crate, he could guess. First, he went to the nurses and asked if anyone was looking for spiritual guidance, and Ashby had been only too happy to point him towards a collection of fretful survivors. Quietly, as he moved among the patients, he lifted a volchemical knife from the head nurse.

He found the crate before Westwick or Braehurst, but unfortunately not before Carson Neuwirth. The greedy conductor had seen an opportunity to make some serious money and the temptation to sneak off with some of Selnick's goods had got the better of him. But, when Emeth found him, he hadn't managed to drag the crate more than a few feet from camp. He even asked Emeth for a hand moving his goods.

It had all been all too easy. Emeth helped Neuwirth carry the crate a safe distance from camp, out of sight of where the survivors were gathering. Then, on the walk back, just as the conductor was explaining how important it was that no one else knew about what they'd just hidden, Emeth put the blade through the man's throat. He knew his window for detection wouldn't be long, but the night was dark and he managed to slip back into the camp and change from robes splattered with blood into clean vestments. Then he headed back to the nurses, hoping to look inconspicuous. That went even better than he could have hoped, as they later told Davina Linde he'd been helping them the whole night.

Once the Halgyrics had finished interviewing everyone about their whereabouts on the night of Neuwirth's death, Emeth finally had an opportunity to open the box he'd killed for. Now that all the surviving passengers had been pulled from the train, he was able to get his hands on a crowbar that was no longer needed and wrench the box open, exposing his prize. More than a hundred pounds of raw solozite.

Emeth broke down in tears. He could finish the gods' mission after all. He was part of it. Once he activated the solozite, he could isolate Balter from its eastern ports and secure a major victory for the Renchans. His plan came together gradually. The gods had led him to an incredible weapon—something far more powerful than anything he'd ever had at his disposal. Did they actually want him to use it? That much solozite would transform the entire valley, probably killing everyone who'd survived the crash.

But wasn't this—a way to stop Drawley and his schemes— exactly what he'd prayed for? Yes, he had his answer. The gods had stranded them in the wilderness and now it was up to him to finish the job.

First, he needed basalt dust. Lots of it. Over the course of the day, he made several trips to the train tracks to fill his satchel, then he emptied it next to where he'd hidden the solozite. He tried to remain inconspicuous, but eventually he was spotted.

Jarvie Braehurst was a man who was paid a lot of money to notice even the most subtle of clues, and it didn't take him long to wonder what possible reason a young acolyte would have to keep heading out into the scrubland beyond the eastern edge of the camp. Braehurst approached Emeth, making himself as tall, wide and intimidating as possible. "I think you've got something of mine," he said.

Emeth sized up the man and immediately yielded. "Oh… I… Please, come this way."

He led him straight to the solozite, and as Braehurst chuckled at both his own success and the acolyte's audacity, Emeth took hold of the knife in his satchel. There were still grindings inside it and he swirled the knife rapidly, agitating the basalt dust until it formed a whirlwind inside his bag.

"Now," Braehurst had turned around, a confident grin on his face, "you aren't going to say anything about what you've seen, are—"

Before he could finish, Emeth flicked his blade and the dust sped into his target's face. As it clung to his eyes and mouth, Braehurst instinctively reached up to try to dislodge the thick grime, leaving his throat exposed. Emeth lunged, knife at the ready. He slid a hand around Braehurst's neck, then pressed his knee into the big man's chest, unseating him. They landed in a tangle, but Emeth's aim was true and the blade slid deep into Braehurst's windpipe.

Emeth stood in shock for just a minute. He'd devised this

strategy years ago, as a joke, a mental exercise. It had been a laughable idea—*how would I kill a man, if I really needed to, using nothing but basalt?* Well, the need had come.

He dragged the solozite a little further east from Braehurst's body, but not as far as he would have liked. He barely had time to cover his tracks before the bloody Halgyrics returned from their trek to find the caboose and everyone started milling about with questions. Emeth changed his attire once again— praise be to Chanri that all his vestments were identical—then headed to the makeshift kitchen, intent on helping serve supper. It was the perfect occupation, and thanks to a few well-placed spills of soup down his robes, he soon looked as grubby as the other stranded passengers.

It was a good thing he'd made himself busy, too. It gave him an alibi when the Halgyrics came at him with that damn mist during the investigation. He'd barely been able to hold his thoughts together, but years of practice had helped him resort to half-truths. Had they asked their questions a little more thoroughly, he'd no doubt that he would have owned up to the whole affair. But with so many more obvious suspects around, they never prodded him too hard.

Then they asked Dalton for his testimony and freed him, which confirmed to Emeth that he was now truly on the right path. A guilty man had died, and an innocent boy was now free. Better yet, when the Halgyrics went looking for the solozite, Dalton told Emeth immediately and asked him to help with the search.

"But you can't say nothing about it to anyone," Dalton whispered sharply. "They think whoever's got it blew up the train and might do worse with it soon. But you're a holy man, Mediate. I figured if I could trust anyone, it would be you."

"Of course." Emeth swallowed against the dryness in his mouth. "Why don't you go and search the west side of the camp, and I'll take the east?"

"No need. One of those Halgyrics and that Kira Westwick have already headed west," said Dalton. "I'll come with you."

Emeth didn't want to hurt the boy. He poked around for as long as he could, trying to ditch him. But then Kellen Linde and his sister approached the area where Braehurst had died and began rifling through the bushes, so Emeth raced back to where he'd hidden the crate and began to prepare the basalt dust, so he could activate it and set off the solozite. He was lucky the pair were so distracted by their argument. They never saw him.

But, like a loyal dog, Dalton had followed him. And those idiotic soldiers who still believed the boy to be a threat to the remaining survivors followed Dalton.

As the soldiers came into view, Emeth threw the activated basalt dust into the solozite crate. The rocks within hissed and shot into the air as a column of lava. Emeth grabbed the last handful of activated dust and blew it into the plume of molten rock, nudging it forward. The liquid solozite bucked and pitched itself towards the soldiers, but in the tumult, the boy did a stupid, lamentable thing. He ran away from Emeth, back towards the soldiers and their guns.

They were all caught in the lava flow. As the molten rock collided with the ground, it ripped open the mountain, transmogrifying the forest that scaled its side into a raging river. The neighbouring cliffs collapsed, triggering an avalanche, and the world cracked open. Emeth clung to a tree branch at the edge of the chasm for as long as he could, expecting to be sucked under as the mountain crumbled.

This was it. They were all to be consumed, so that others might live in peace.

But for all the might he threw at the mountain, something stopped it. No, *someone*. A magic as powerful as his volchemistry had interfered and rendered his work useless.

It made no sense. Why would the gods allow Dalton to die, but leave the likes of Drawley alive yet again? As the shaking stopped and Emeth staggered back to camp, he was horrified to see how little had changed. How had these people saved themselves yet again? How were the lords still alive after everything they'd done? Why were the wicked always spared? Someone must be interfering with his mission.

As everyone tried to get the camp back in order, Emeth paced along the railway tracks, studying the wrecked train. For the first time, he recognised his mistake. The stone around the engine was evidence of a witch on board, but one who'd *defended* the passengers rather than attacking them. It was obvious to him now. This witch—this traitor to her own kind—was the one who'd interfered. *She* was why the gods had led him to the solozite.

Only now he didn't have the materials to finish the job.

He had to act fast and come up with a reason for the survivors to head north, into the volcanic heart of the caldera. There, he'd have what he needed. Luckily, he remembered Ambrose saying something had happened to the bridge, so, as quickly as he could, he ran down the tracks in the direction his friend had gone with the Halgyrics the day before. There, he found the proof they were stranded. How the bridge had been destroyed, he couldn't say, but it didn't matter. He had what he needed.

When he got back to camp, he went straight to Drawley with what he'd learned and told him how scared he was they would die in the mountains if they didn't seek help. That thunderous old buffoon had been all too eager to whip up the crowd, and, with a conspiratorial wink, was only too happy to keep quiet about how the information got out.

"I never should have doubted you, boy," said Drawley, beaming at Emeth appreciatively. "It's good to have you on our side. You're a Trudane through and through."

Emeth had to resist the urge to murder Drawley right there and then.

From that point on, everything had gone better than Emeth could have hoped. Kira Westwick was desperate to get away from the threat of the Balterian authorities—even the Continental Rail employees who might turn up to rescue them—and she and Drawley were able to persuade the remaining survivors to leave the camp. Soon they were packing for the trek north. The only task that remained for Emeth was to get rid of that witch.

He hung well back from the perimeter of the camp as night fell, reasoning that she'd do her work under cover of darkness. So, he was unaffected when Allonia cast her spell and put the rest of the survivors to sleep.

Killing her had been as easy as doing away with Jarvie Braehurst. Easier, in fact. She was too busy fleeing Kellen Linde, distracted by the fact that her target had somehow managed to wake up. She never anticipated the basalt dust that blinded her, the hand that caught her chest or the knife that slid into her ribs.

Emeth wiped the blood from the blade, then changed his clothes again, while the Lindes raised the alarm.

Of course, as soon as the red-haired witch dragged Davina Linde away, he realised he'd killed the wrong one—a shame, yes, but one that proved he wasn't acting alone. Everything locked into place. The gods had given him allies after all—the nurses. The witch who'd been ruining the plan was *Davina*. Of course. He'd always known that girl was more than Ambrose took her for. Hopefully, the red-haired witch would dispose of her. But, if she didn't, at least he now knew who his enemy was.

The gods had guided him this far. Now, with a satchel full of basalt dust, he'd have everything he needed to activate a volcano. No one would escape justice this time.

CHAPTER
+ + 37 + +

GENNA PULLED A set of bloodied robes from the brush, the birds around her squawking in frustration as she took away what must have smelled like an easy meal to them.

I followed the crows.

The nurse Ashby had said something similar, hadn't she? Genna read that in Kellen's notebook. Ashby had found Jarvie Braehurst's body because she'd followed the birds who'd been pecking at it. Looking back, knowing the woman had been a witch, Genna saw so much more to the strangeness in her words. Who followed crows around, for instance?

"Kellen!" She shook the robes free, fighting the bile that rose in her throat.

"Yes?" He ran to her, instantly silent when he saw what she was holding. The crows raged around them as he reached for the bloodstained fabric, stitched with the markings of Chanri.

Genna clenched her jaw, willing herself not to break down in front of him. The silence grew unbearable, as she waited for whatever Kellen was thinking behind that closed gaze. "But why would he do something like this?" she blurted out. "He was a holy man. He was…" She trailed off. Clearly they hadn't known anything about him.

"He was also the son of a lord. He suits the profile, doesn't he? Well-educated. Familiar with the finer points of volchemistry," said Kellen.

"Gods, of course." Genna's hand flew to her brow. "Lord Carey…"

"What's he got to do with this?" asked Kellen.

"Someone leaked that the bridge had been destroyed to the Lords' Council. Carey swore it wasn't him, but—"

"He was friends with Trudane," Kellen groaned.

A wave of guilt crashed into her. Kellen had been asleep, so of course he hadn't known, but why hadn't she seen it? "He resisted my perfume. How would he have done that?"

"Most religious orders use mist on occasion. He must have built up some resistance. We were both foolish not to question him further." Kellen attempted to run his fingers back through his hair—it was an old habit of his that he did when he was thinking—but he quickly got his good hand caught in the matted tangles. "But this settles it. We have to warn—"

"No." Genna shook with the unfairness of everything. From the moment Kellen told her his theory about Emeth, she knew it would lead to this—some wrongheaded act of heroism that would help the remaining survivors, but plunge them into further danger. "They left us here to die," she said angrily. "After everything you did for them, they still left us. Frankly, they deserve that lunatic."

"Genna, he tried to blow up a mountain. He can kill people with nothing but basalt dust. If he gets his hands on more materials—"

"If he gets his hands on something dangerous, there's nothing anyone can do about it. None of us!"

Kellen's eyes fell. "There might be someone who can stop him. I have to find Davina."

Genna swallowed hard against her tears. In so few words, he'd confirmed the last of her fears. "I can't go with you, Kellen," she said. "I'm sorry, but I can't leave Rae and there's no way I'm rushing headlong towards a murderer with a child in tow."

"It's all right." He lifted her hand to his lips and a tremor passed through her as he caressed her calloused fingers. "I wouldn't want you to leave her. I know I don't have the right to ask anything of you, but… if I don't come back, I need you to get Morel home. He's next in the line of succession and he's…" Kellen's voice cracked, betraying his fears. Genna leaned her forehead against his chest, listening to his heartbeat.

Kellen pulled her close, his usually elegant tongue stumbling over his words. "Morel—he's really the only friend I've ever had. He's…"

"Your brother." Genna trailed a hand down his arm. "You're going to come back. And you're going to tell him all this yourself."

"Please, Genna. Promise you'll help him."

She nodded. She could do that much for Kellen.

Together, they gathered up items that might help him in his quest to bring Davina back: Morel's shotgun; misting vials he'd confiscated from Lodi Barnaka's luggage; some volchemistry ingredients from Genna's bag. It was hard to believe any of this would be enough.

Then, once everything was in a bag or slung over his shoulder, he kissed her goodbye and headed off in the direction that Hess and Davina had gone. He didn't say his farewells to Morel or Rae. Genna realised it was easier for him to simply walk away from the people he might be giving up. No doubt his love for the girl spurred him onwards, too.

No, not a girl. A *witch*. The memory of Kellen lying on the mountainside, his hand gushing blood, came back to Genna. But instead of lingering on the gruesome details, she thought instead of Davina, clutching her knees beside him. Genna now understood what had made the girl sit in that guilty stupor.

All their hopes now lay in the hands of a witch who had tried to murder her own brother.

CHAPTER
✦✦ 38 ✦✦

THE AFTERNOON SUN beat down on Davina's neck as she finally reached the valley floor and the train tracks that wound through it. Hess must have dragged her a long way from the crash site while she'd been unconscious the night before. As she walked, Davina went over and over her final words to her. If they did make it off the caldera alive, how would Davina bring herself to tell Kellen that a witch now knew the secrets of the Halgyric royal family? If Hess told the High Coven their true identities, then the monarchy would come to an end. The threat of that alone would force Kellen to bend to the witches' will—and it was all Davina's fault.

First, however, she had to find her brothers and make sure they were still alive. She hitched up her skirts and ran. Her heeled shoes meant she had to spend far too much time focusing on keeping her footing on the rocky floor, but it was a soothing distraction. The landscape passed by in a blur as she headed south, and she thought about Hess's words to her: *"Think, girl. Who did you see washing their hands of the crime?"*

She was insensible to the passage of time. Only when the sun started to set did she notice the aching in her feet. As she began to worry how she'd be able to run in the dark in her impractical shoes, she noticed a curl of smoke rising on the horizon and nearly cried with relief.

She slowed to a stagger. "Morel?" she called, but after running for so long without water, she broke down coughing. "Morel? Kellen?" she croaked.

A distant figure appeared. Davina waved, but if the person saw her, they didn't acknowledge her. They darted towards where the plume of smoke was coming from instead. Then, as Davina staggered closer, someone else emerged, the evening light illuminating a halo of blonde hair. For a moment, Davina thought it was Kellen. But, as she stepped closer, it became clear the figure was a woman. Davina finally recognised it as Kira Westwick when the smuggler raised a pistol and levelled it towards Davina's head.

"Don't come any further," she shouted.

Davina halted and put her hands up in a display of innocence, but that didn't seem to set Kira at ease. Davina felt something bubble inside her. Her witch self knew a threat when she saw one. She simmered in the back of Davina's mind, hoping for Kira to unleash a bullet so she could take over. But Davina wasn't in enough danger. Yet.

"I don't want to shoot," said Kira. "So let's make this as simple as possible. I stay here and you stay there, and we'll both keep it civilised."

"Very well." Davina took a step back.

"How did you escape that witch?" Kira didn't bother with niceties, though at least she lowered her gun.

Davina felt her witch self settle back into the shadows. "She let me go," she said. As improbable as it sounded, it was true.

A handful of other survivors were gathering behind Kira, but not the faces Davina yearned to see.

"Where are my brothers?" said Davina, scanning the crowd.

"Further south, down the tracks," said Kira. "They couldn't make the journey. Your witch friend injured Morel." Her finger moved back over the trigger of the gun.

"She wasn't my friend!" said Davina. "She kidnapped me. I wouldn't have anything to do with someone who attacked my brothers." Again, this was all true, but Davina could see that no one was buying her story. They thought her a witch, too. Hess had outed her.

"What about Ms Freath? If I could speak to her—"

"She stayed back with your brother, of course," interrupted Kira. "Why didn't you go to them rather than come here?"

"I didn't know they were injured! Please, I don't mean anyone harm. I'm only looking for my family."

"Kira?" Penny Aldridge stepped forward from the crowd. "All the Lindes were absent when the conductor was murdered. They're about the only ones who are definitely innocent of that crime. Pinning all this on her—"

"Oh, and that doesn't strike you as convenient?" said Kira. "All absent. Their only alibis each other. Isn't that always when the killings start?"

"When the killings start? What do you mean by that?" Without thinking, Davina moved closer, worried where this was going. But Kira's hand flew up with the gun and Davina shrank back. "There aren't more dead, are there?"

"You tell me," Kira growled.

"Kira, please!" said Penny. "Perhaps she can help us. The witch, Miss Linde. Do you have any idea which way she went?"

Why, wondered Davina, was Penny coming to her defence? Was she just after information? After she'd told her what she knew about Hess, would she then let Kira fire? There had to be someone she could trust besides these two women, but without her brothers around—

"Carey!" Davina cried, the idea coming in a flash. "Please, can I speak to Lord Carey? He knows me well. He'll vouch for my character and—"

Kira frowned and her tone carried a touch of pity, but it was hardly enough to soften the blow of her next words. "Lord Carey is dead," she said. "The witch took care of that."

For a flash, Davina didn't understand her words. Morel had survived, so didn't that mean...?

But it didn't. Her last image of the two men came back to her. They'd been running straight towards her as Hess tore up the ground and sent that massive pine hurtling at them. Morel had been trained to react quickly, but Carey hadn't even been light enough on his feet to dance well. She could imagine him, staring upwards in dumb shock, and then...

She doubled over. The man who'd sat beside her in the aftermath of Kellen's injury and kissed her was now dead, thanks to Hess. More collateral damage. Another life that didn't matter to the witch.

It was too much. Tears came thick and fast, and Davina collapsed to her knees. Like slate on a steep slope, she slid down, down, down.

Harmless, foolish, wonderful Carey was dead.

+ ✦ +

After Davina's breakdown, most of the remaining survivors agreed that she couldn't possibly be putting on an act. Even though some remained suspicious of her, she was permitted to enter the camp. Penny came forward to guide her towards the fire, and once she'd been settled there, Kira sat with her and assured her that Morel's injuries weren't severe. She told her he'd only received a scrape on his back and a dislocated knee in the witch attack, but Davina didn't trust the woman. The memory of her pointing a gun at her head was too fresh.

By the time Davina had gulped back her tears and brought her emotions under control, it was fully dark, with just a sliver of moon glowing in the night sky. She wanted to continue down the train tracks, to where Kellen and Morel were, but the other passengers insisted she stay.

"I know you're worried, but there's no sense in leaving now you're here. Not tonight anyway." Penny rubbed Davina's shoulders as she spoke. The leader of the dance troupe seemed to be one of the few people left who was capable of compassion. "It isn't safe. Especially in the dark. What if you were set upon by a catamount?"

Davina brushed tears from her face. "Then I'll set out first thing in the morning," she said.

"You might not want to. Every time someone wanders away from the group, they don't come back," said Kira, examining her gun for dust. It struck Davina as performative; a reminder to her that she had it.

"So, there have been more murders?" asked Davina.

"Deaths," Penny said. "We don't know what caused them or—"

"Well, we've either got the worst bloody luck imaginable, or yes, it was murder. Again." Kira narrowed her eyes at Davina. "The witches aren't done yet."

Davina had the sense to nod solemnly. If Hess was telling the truth—and granted, that was a substantial *if*—then the deaths of the passengers had nothing to do with the witches. Davina squinted at those gathered around the fire, noticing something for the first time. There were almost no men left. Every woman who'd survived the crash was there. Penny and Kira appeared to be the leaders, but alongside them was everyone from Penny's dancers to Lord Gamth's wizened mother and Lodi Barnaka. But aside from Lord Gamth himself, tending to his mother's fragile cough, there were no men. Where were the members of the Lords' Council? Or that sullen acolyte? The soldiers? Were all of them dead? Or were they keeping their distance, in case another one of the women transformed into a witch?

"What happened today?" asked Davina, glancing between Penny and Kira, not sure which one carried more authority.

"Do you think we should show her?" asked Penny.

"Maybe." Kira holstered her gun. "She might know something."

Kira dipped a torch into the fire and held it aloft, and the two women stepped away from its warm glow. Davina gathered up her skirts and followed.

Kira's torch illuminated the face of a man, digging in the ground with a shovel. "What are you lot doing here?" he grunted, looking up from his work.

"The girl wanted to see what had happened to the Lords' Council." Kira swung the torch so it cast its light directly on Davina's face. In turn, she could now clearly see the scowling figure was Emeth Trudane—Carey's best friend. Her heart plummeted again, but she managed to hold back her tears.

"And do you think it's wise to trust her?" he asked. "She could well be a witch."

"Emeth, please…" Penny said.

"Oh, I won't get in your way," said Emeth, leaning on his shovel. "I'm not one to tread on a witch's toes. Besides… if no one here knows her witch name, then she's harmless."

There was some truth to that. Davina shuffled forward and saw why he'd been working so far away from where the other survivors had gathered—he was digging a grave.

Kira moved her torch to the right, and Davina saw that the lump to the side of the grave which she'd initially thought was a pile of earth was, in fact, the body of Lord Drawley. He was covered in welts, as if his whole body had been boiled in a pot.

"He wasn't the only one," said Penny sadly. "We lost the whole council except for Lord Gamth, but Drawley's was the only body we could recover. All in all, we lost Lord Zerick, Lord Solthus and Lord Raxton."

"We'd only hiked for half a day," Kira said, moving the torch slowly over Drawley's face, the flickering light accentuating his hideous injuries. "Everyone was tired, so we decided to set up camp for the night. The Lords' Council headed off for a private discussion about whether or not to send on an advance party— people strong and fast enough to find help and bring it back here. They'd only been gone half an hour when the ridge blew."

Before Davina could ask what she meant, Kira gestured for her to follow. Another hundred yards away, a fog rose in front of them. Davina almost walked into it, but Kira held a hand out to stop her. The mist felt hot against Davina's cheeks and the strong scent of sulphur stung her nose.

They were at the edge of a thermal pool, the crumbling lip just a few feet away. Thanks to the darkness and the mist, she could see nothing, but the soft sound of water bubbling told her more than enough. As she studied the ground beneath her feet, she saw the crumbling terrain of a geyser plain. It was very likely there were even more pools like this nearby.

"The geyser exploded right beneath the lords." Penny's voice trembled. "The ground gave way and they were all swallowed by the water. We found Drawley gasping and twitching next to this pool. He lasted less than an hour."

"Did it happen naturally, do you think?" Davina asked.

Kira shook her head. "No, there's another witch about, I'm sure of it."

"Or a volchemist," Davina said instinctively.

"Where would they get basalt all the way out here?" Kira gestured out into the darkness.

"They could have carried basalt dust from the tracks," said Davina. "We found loads of the stuff there. If they were a skilled volchemist, they'd only need a couple of handfuls of dust to ignite…" Even though the rising mist was hot and sticky, a chill passed through Davina. "…to ignite the volcano."

Davina trailed off as she looked behind the women and saw the most damning evidence of the night.

Emeth had vanished.

A chill ran down her spine.

"Where did the acolyte go?" she asked.

"What?" Kira turned to look. "I don't know. I expect back he went back to camp to—"

"Wash his hands of the crime." The image finally came back to Davina. When she'd gone to the medical ward to question the survivors after the conductor's death, she'd found Emeth washing his hands before he helped the nurses prepare someone for surgery. "It was him! It was—where is he?"

"Miss Linde, is everything all right?" Penny held her shoulders, as if trying to calm her down.

"Don't touch me! It was *Emeth*!" Davina shoved her away. The dancer shrieked and Kira's face contorted with anger as she reached for her gun.

"Stop!" Davina stumbled away from them. "I'm not trying to hurt her! I meant—"

Kira fired. Davina screamed, but the bullet flew over her shoulder. She turned to see what Kira had been aiming at. A male figure darted away as she rushed forward, letting another bullet fly. Emeth. It had to be.

"Kira!" Penny cried out. "Why are you—"

But in answer to her question, the ground beneath them buckled; and, forty feet away, a column of water rocketed into the air. A wall of heat slammed into Davina's face before the witch roared to life, giddy with fury.

CHAPTER
·+ 39 +·

The witch moved on instinct, raising her hands to greet the water before it could fall on her. Where it landed on her open palms, it crested away, transmogrifying into a stone wall that soon formed a solid, protective shell around her. A groan lurched through the earth. The geyser was clearly destabilising the ground. She'd find herself plummeting down into boiling water if she didn't act soon.

She pressed her palms into the shifting surface and joined the rocks together until they formed a thick, supportive crust. The shaking steadied.

As she rose to her feet, the nose of a gun pressed against the back of her head.

"I knew it!" A voice the witch had no memory of trembled behind her. "I bloody knew it!"

"What are you doing?" A second voice joined the fray, and the gun was knocked away from where it rested against the witch's skull. "She saved our lives!"

"She's a witch, Penny! Look at her!"

The witch turned to see two women, grappling over a pistol.

She could kill them easily if she wanted to. But did she? "Who are you?" she demanded.

"What kind of bloody question is that?" the woman with the gun shouted.

"Kira means you no harm, ma'am," said the other. "She's frightened, that's all. She'd never—"

"I would if you'd let me! She's a witch!" The angry woman—Kira—threw the smaller one off and began to raise her gun. But before she could fire, the witch took the barrel in her hand and flung the pistol away. It slid into a thermal pool and sank.

Both women raised their hands as the witch got to her feet. The one who'd had the sense not to attack her begged on their behalf. "Please, Miss Linde. We didn't know."

The witch felt the words flutter around at the back of her mind. Was that her name? "I asked who you were," she snapped.

"You honestly don't know?" Kira asked.

"Kira," said the small woman. "And Penny." She pointed to herself. "We're friends. Truly, we are."

The witch stared at them, wrestling with doubt. Where were Hess and Allonia? Why was it that every time she became her witch self, she was faced with a new cast of characters? Where were the people who could tell her what was going on and who she was?

Another blast rumbled through the sky as a second geyser erupted. The witch had to lunge to stop another torrent of boiling water from cascading down on them. She extended the rock wall, encasing them in all directions, leaving a narrow exit. There wasn't time to waste on these women. Someone out there was set on breaking the whole geyser plain apart.

"Where is he?" the witch demanded, turning to Kira and Penny. "The man with the long sandy hair. Did he do this?"

Their eyes grew wider. "Do you mean Kellen?" asked Kira.

"We don't know," said Penny.

They were useless, but at least she had a name for the man now. "I suggest you stay here," she said. "I'll decide what to do with you later."

The witch squeezed through the opening she'd left in their shelter, trying to devise a plan. The sandy-haired man—Kellen—was weak against her magic, but he did know her name. She'd have to surprise him and gain the upper hand.

Outside the protective shell she'd created, the geyser plain trembled and distant shouts streamed through the darkness. A torch smouldered on the ground a few feet away and the witch picked it up. The glow revealed a distant figure, loose robes obscuring the shape of his body. That must be him.

She grabbed a fistful of her skirts and hurried towards him. With each step, her feet throbbed. At least some things were constant across her memories. She was still stuck in these horrid, impractical shoes. Her view of the man swayed in and out of focus as she struggled to run with the torch in her hand. One moment there would be total blackness, the next a brief sighting of a hunched figure. Darkness again. Then the man, a little closer now, bending over his satchel. Another wave of night. And now she was only steps away. He came into focus.

He held a long, dark knife that glinted purple-black in the glow of her torch. Short, dark hair and thick eyebrows defined the shape of his face.

It wasn't Kellen.

Her pause was the chance he'd waited for.

His wrist flicked, but instead of a column of steam erupting from the ground, a cloud of coarse, black dust assaulted her.

She threw her hands up, trying to transform it into something harmless, as she had the boiling water, but the enchantment he'd used this time was of a more refined sort. The dust swerved around her hands and flowed relentlessly towards her face. It sank into her eyes and coated her mouth in a brittle, choking cake.

The witch retched and coughed out some of the dust that lined her throat, but before she could get her bearings, the force of a man's body collided with hers. Still blinded, she reached for his arm where his elbow bore down sharply into her sternum. But try as she might, she couldn't burn holes through his robes or thick gloves. Hess's words by the campfire came back to her with horrifying clarity.

He'll kill you with inconvenience. Make it difficult to cast magic or to breathe. He'll wear you down until you die at a knife's blade.

"You won't interfere with my calling again, witch." His breath slid hot against her cheek as he pressed her hands low with one of his arms, but no matter how hard she persevered, she couldn't reach his face. There was a practised confidence to the way he restrained her. A calculated wisdom to his gloved hands. He'd clearly killed witches before.

His blade dug into her neck, and she recognised the texture of obsidian.

The witch thrashed against him, deflecting the blow for now. But without the advantage of her magic, his weight and grip meant it would only be a matter of time before he won. Cold understanding gripped her heart. She would die out on this plain, nameless and alone.

Seconds stretched out into eternity. She twisted and grappled, dragging out every last moment of life she could. She dug her fingers into the earth, trying to transform it in desperation, but she was too weak. Her magic flickered at her fingertips, useless. Time blurred as she began to lose consciousness.

Gradually, calm resignation settled over her. All resistance left her body and her head lolled back, waiting for the slit to her throat. Yet the death stroke didn't fall. Her attacker's knees still pinned her body down on both sides, but his grip around her throat relaxed. For the first time since he'd thrown the dust cloud at her, she was able to cough until her throat unclogged and she breathed in the misty air of the geyser plain.

Mist. A trickle of understanding broke over her. *Halgyric* mist.

As she held that thought, she reached to rub the sand from her eyes. Her vision was still obscured by the darkness of the night, but she saw now that the robed man kneeling on top of her wore a slack expression. His shook his head, clearly fighting the soothing, disarming nature of the enchantment, but he was less practised in it than the witch.

No, less practised than her human self.

For it was that side of her that recognised this scent, and her familiarity and resistance to it echoed like a memory through the witch's bones. She *knew* something about herself. She was Halgyric. It wasn't enough. It wasn't a name—but it was somewhere to begin.

She couldn't tell where the Halgyric mist had drifted in from, but she had to use the opportunity while she had it. The obsidian blade still hovered over her throat, but this was her chance. Carefully, she shifted her heels, wedging them into the ground to give herself better leverage, then she took a deep breath and rolled.

The motion unseated the man on top of her, but it also knocked him loose from his trance. She'd barely scrabbled a foot away before he caught hold of her ankle. He yanked her backward, forcing her chest to slap on the ground. What now? She could turn the entire mountainside to liquid if she wanted to, but that would kill her as surely as it would him. Instead, she grabbed a nearby stone.

It was a laughable defence, but before she could connect the stone with anything solid, a crack of gunfire echoed through the air. She winced, half-expecting a bullet to strike her, but instead the hands on her leg relinquished their grip. Had the man been shot, then? No, he was scrambling away. He'd only been frightened off.

"Get away from her!" A familiar voice echoed over the plain— one of the few that the witch recognised. Several feet away, a wisp of smoke rose from the nose of a rifle.

Kellen had found her.

CHAPTER

✦ 40 ✦

KELLEN HAD AIMED wide on purpose. Emeth was too close to the witch for even the best marksman to avoid hitting her, and Kellen's aim was far from exceptional. But now he had the option of firing again. *Could* he kill a man? Maybe for Davina's sake. But that hint of doubt stopped him. His hands shook against the unfamiliar shape of Morel's rifle, his grip on the barrel made worse by the bandages that were wrapped around what was left of his hand.

"Get away from her!" He channelled all his anger into his voice. Perhaps with the influence of the mist, it would be enough. Lodi Barnaka's rosewater mist wasn't as strong as muddling haze, but it was designed to soothe the mind in a similar way, so he'd decided to try it. It needed to be enough. He had no other plan if it wasn't. "It's over, Trudane," he called.

"The gods will decide when this is over." Emeth's hand went to his satchel and Kellen twisted away. The basalt dust still found him, carried on a wind designed to target his eyes and mouth, but Kellen closed both before he could be overwhelmed by the gust. Still, it bought Emeth time.

Kellen spun around, aiming into the distance, but now Emeth was nothing more than a blur in the darkness. He fired anyway, but the acolyte was fast on his feet and had fled further away across the caldera.

A movement caught in Kellen's peripheral vision and he turned again. He swung the rifle around so that the witch came squarely into his sights.

At the sight of the raised gun, she took a step backward, hands raised.

Bile rose in his throat at the sight of this twisted version of Davina, who wore on her face every reason he'd ever given his sister to hate him. Flashes came back of the day before when she'd torn at him with those hands, damn near killing him. Her mouth was set in a brittle line that bore no resemblance to Davina's bored or playful expressions. And yet it *was* her. The girl in front of him was as much his family as anyone.

She could kill him. Perhaps she would.

Kellen dropped the gun.

The witch's eyes widened, but she didn't hesitate for long. A second later, she'd picked up the gun herself and had it aimed at him. "Who are you?" Her own voice trembled with uncertainty. "I know your name, but who *are* you? You tried to kill me the last time we—"

"I never tried to kill you." Kellen stared down at the dirt.

"You dragged me off a ledge!" She pushed the tip of the gun into his forehead, forcing him to look up at her. "You—you tried to throw me—and now you're stopping him? *Who are you?*" She was quivering with fear and anger. "Are you a trophy hunter? Do you want the world to know you're a witch-killer? Or do you want to take me prisoner? WHO ARE YOU?" Tears ran down the witch's face. "And—and why haven't you said her name?"

Davina. It would be so easy to call her back to her human self.

But Kellen forced himself to stare at the witch. As much as he wanted to see Davina's familiar face, this was the girl he needed. The girl who needed *him*.

"The real question." His voice trembled as he prayed she let him speak these few precious words. "Is… who are you?"

"Go on," she said, lifting the rifle from his forehead.

"I'm going to get something from my jacket. It's a letter. It belongs to you. I promise I won't do anything else." Kellen lifted his hands so she could see them.

When she nodded, he reached into his breast pocket and removed a worn envelope. His final lie. He'd told Davina the letter was back in Halgyr, when, in reality, he'd carried it everywhere since his mother had handed it to him at the age of thirteen.

He held it out to the witch now. "You're Cerise Linde. My little sister."

+ ✦ +

Cerise.

Sister.

Something stirred in her, but it wasn't the wave of recognition and understanding she'd hoped for. He could be tricking her. Still, she lowered the gun and reached out.

The witch's fingers closed over the envelope. The paper was warm from where it had been pressed against his chest, for more years than she could guess.

My sweet Kellen—

"But it's your name on it," she said as she opened it.

"Keep reading." Kellen made no move to take the gun.

She glanced around, looking for anyone else, but the people she'd seen around the campfire in the distance earlier had now dispersed. No doubt they were trying to escape with their lives before the robed man could blow up the entire plain.

She and Kellen were alone.

She swallowed and began to read the letter.

My sweet Kellen,

I'm leaving you much sooner than any mother should. I could fill this page with words of regret and longing. How I wish to see you as a man! What I wouldn't give to hold my children and kiss your foreheads as you all grow old. But the gods have taken those opportunities from me. And, instead of comforting you, I must give you an incredible burden.

I wish I could trust someone else with this, but your father and uncle have, at times, frightened me with their prejudices. You are, above all things, a gentle, even-tempered boy. And I trust this means you will become a reasonable man. How I hope you do.

My final wishes concern Davina. She is, like me, a witch. Upon my engagement to your father, I resolved to put away my powers and pray for only sons. In most instances, my pleas were answered. I had hoped Davina would escape Ramona's touch, but the goddess intervened and forced me to gift her with her witch name.

I wish I could take it to my grave, but something could happen, and if Davina's life is threatened by force, she might change to her witch self. When she does, she'll be confused and violent, and it will be your job to help her. She is too little to understand these things yet or handle the challenges that such talent will inflict upon her. So I give you her name.

To bring her witch self to life, call her Cerise Linde.

Cerise Linde.

There was more. Pleas to the boy to be a good brother, meandering stories about a childhood of witchcraft, but Cerise could no longer read through the tears that blurred her eyes. Instead, she traced the letters of that name over and over again. Cerise. Cerise Linde.

All her life, Davina had yearned for her mother and now Cerise held her tender words in her hands. With a start, Cerise realised what this memory meant. The curtain that cut her soul in two was drawn away and they were united. Cerise and Davina— the same girl longing for the love of the same mother.

Cerise turned towards Kellen. Even after reading the letter, she still didn't feel that wave of love and acceptance she'd imagined would come when she encountered her family. Instead, she faced a broken man, worn down by fear and loss. Tentatively, Cerise searched the corners of her mind, hunting for her human self— this Davina—to ask the girl about him. A wave of guilt struck her, which Cerise couldn't understand until an echo of Davina's voice sounded in her mind, clearer than ever before.

Look down.

Cerise was greeted with the sight of Kellen's damaged hand. She studied its malformed shape, noted the missing fingers. She—they—remembered now. Cerise had attacked him and it had been Davina's job to cut off the fingers turned to stone by her spell.

Yes, the guilt was a shared memory too.

Cerise sensed that the maimed hand wasn't the whole story. There had no doubt been other transgressions the girl regretted, just as there would have been slights against her that Davina blamed on her brother. Whatever was broken between Kellen and

Davina had been that way for a long time. And Cerise had only made things worse.

She supposed he had every reason to hate her. But he held both her names and, so far, he'd chosen to let her live.

Cerise tucked the letter into her dress. "Thank you," she said, brushing away the last of her tears.

"I should have told you a long time ago…"

"Yes. Well… perhaps." She honestly didn't know. There was still so much for her to understand about him.

Carefully, she laid the gun on the ground beside them. His eyes followed her motions, but he made no effort to pick it up. She extended a nervous hand. Maybe he wouldn't take it. After all, she'd nearly killed him. "Kellen?"

But he chose to slide his right hand into hers. "Cerise."

A shiver twisted down her spine. He'd said it again. *Her* name.

"I…" So her tears hadn't gone entirely. Her throat tensed around her words. "I've missed you."

And mercifully, she didn't need to speak anymore. Instead, he pulled her towards him. His long arms wrapped around her in the first embrace of Cerise's meagre lifetime and she buried her face in his long, fair hair. He smelled awful, but she wouldn't have moved away for all the world. She had a name. She had a brother.

And he loved her.

CHAPTER

·+ 41 +·

$\int$HE WAS SO like Davina: so certain she was right about everything; so brazenly confident.

She was so unlike Davina: so quick to ask his opinion; so willing to forgive.

For the first time in days, hope stirred inside Kellen. He didn't have a solution for their present problems, but he did have a partner, and she had more than enough ideas for how to stop Emeth.

"You're sure he's going to come back?" Cerise asked after he'd explained their situation as quickly as he could. Kellen had barrelled past a thousand details, but she'd been able to repeat the most essential parts—they were stranded out on the caldera, thanks to the actions of a group of revolutionary witches, and now a deranged acolyte was trying to kill off the survivors.

"He's attacked over and over, but he relies on surprise," Kellen explained. "He's clearly a skilled volchemist."

Cerise nodded. "Did you see what he did to the ground? He must have activated some of the geysers below the surface with that basalt dust of his." She furrowed her brow. "How do I know about basalt? Did *she* know volchemistry?"

They'd had to talk around Davina's existence carefully for the past several minutes. Cerise couldn't speak her name even if she wanted to, but Kellen had to expend far more effort into making sure he didn't let it slip—otherwise the witch would be forced to change form. "It was something she always wanted to study. Knowing my sister, I'm sure she found a way to learn a thing or two."

Cerise smiled, clearly pleased with herself. "I'll force him out of hiding."

"He might do something rash if you do. He was willing to destroy the entire mountain with solozite only a day ago," said Kellen. "Volchemistry takes materials, and he doesn't seem to have much besides basalt dust left. Still, if we're over a geyser plain, that's probably enough. I don't think anything will stop him from activating the whole volcano if he has to."

"That's fine by me," said Cerise, lifting her chin. "I'd like to see him try. I'm at my best in a catastrophe."

"Yes, I suppose you are." Kellen smiled. "But please remember the other survivors are made of far more breakable stuff than you."

"And you think I should save them too?" She wrinkled her nose, as if to show how inconvenient she found that restriction.

Kellen stifled a laugh and nodded.

"Then they should get as far away from here as possible. I'll try to keep him contained on the geyser plain."

Kellen glanced around. "I think most of the survivors have scattered."

"There are two women still out there. Kira and Penny." Cerise pointed towards a dark, stone pyramid. "Though they saw me transform, which complicates things. Do you still think we should save them?"

"Cerise, you are not going to knowingly kill *anyone*." By the gods, she was terrifying.

"What about Emeth?" she asked.

Kellen shook his head. "We need someone to hand over to the Balterian authorities or this whole thing could get pinned on you."

"Fine." She grimaced. "But I think you should deal with the women. They don't trust me."

"Agreed."

Cerise passed him the gun. "Go and get them," she said. "Then I'm doing it. I'm going to find him."

Her tone was so final. Kellen couldn't deny that it frightened him. Once Cerise unleashed her full power, what would happen? Would she be able to control her magic enough to protect everyone who depended on her?

But his misgivings didn't matter. She was his last hope.

Kellen hugged her one last time, then he shouldered Morel's rifle and headed across the plain to the stone shell that sat incongruously on the flat, barren ground. As he drew closer, he heard nervous panting from within. Kira and Penny must have stayed put during the confrontation, too terrified to move.

"Is there anyone in there?" he called.

There was no response, until he came to the small opening in the rock and looked in. The women were huddled together, gaping at him in either relief or horror.

"Mr Linde?" Penny squeaked. "*You* came after us too?"

"My sister needs you to move. I doubt this ground will be solid for much longer." He extended a hand, but neither one budged.

"You mean that witch you kept hidden?" snapped Kira.

"Please. If you don't get out of here, you'll be in danger," Kellen said, holding out his good hand. "Trudane's sure to come back."

413

Kira's back straightened. "Trudane? There's a Trudane nearby?"

"I think it was the acolyte's last name," said Penny. "Does that mean something to you?"

Kira looked between Kellen and Penny, clearly processing this new revelation. "It's a name I don't trust. That's for certain."

The women exchanged a look.

"All right, then." Kira grabbed Kellen's hand and allowed him to pull her through the narrow passageway in the rock. Penny followed at her heels. "If that bloody witch kills me, I'm telling the gods you deserve every curse known to man."

Kellen led them across the plain to where their campfire was still smouldering. As they gathered at its edge, Kellen could see the faint outline of Cerise tracking their progress. He threw another log on the fire so it would be easier for her to see their position. Hopefully, she'd be able to direct her magic away from them.

Penny crouched next to the fire, balanced on the balls of her feet like an animal ready to spring. Kira stood nearby, hands on her hips. In the distance, a handful of torches appeared. The sight of new flames from the fire had drawn some of the other survivors out, and dark forms began to approach cautiously.

"Can you help me convince them not to leave the fireside? She's going to try to keep this area safe, but if we get in the way—"

Kellen was cut short by a snort from Kira.

"You're very good at giving us no choice but to listen to you, Mr Linde," said Penny, not looking up from the flames.

"Well said." Kira crossed her arms. "Sure. We'll play along. Any idea what that sister of yours has in store for us?"

If there was ever a time for a lie, it was now. But Kellen

couldn't muster anything. It was out of his hands. To his amazement, he felt a freedom he hadn't experienced since before his mother died. Finally, someone else was watching over him. May the gods protect her.

He shrugged. "No idea."

+ ✦ +

Cerise pressed her hands against the ground. Below her, the earth hissed as steam forced its way through cracks in the brittle crust. Damp air warmed her cheeks, then the wind stole the heat away. It was as if Soloz himself was crouched by her side, breathing down her neck, challenging her to break apart the ground and release him.

In the distance, the campfire sprang back to life, a signal that Kellen and the others were safe. Cerise dug her fingers into a clump of stubby grass. Should she pray to Ramona or did the witch goddess even care what she did? Her existence was still rife with questions, but she would have to still them for now. She clung to the clarity of the truths she did know. She was a witch, with a brother who loved her. And she would be damned if she let some deranged Mediate-in-training steal that from her.

The ground shivered beneath her flattened palms. If there was one thing she needed, it was light. The thin moon did little to guide her towards where Emeth might be. The scope of her powers didn't give her much choice. It was time to set the world on fire.

Cerise sent out a tremor, turning acres of rock from solid to molten in seconds. Ripples of melting earth snaked across the plain, burning amber against the dark night. It didn't take long for the fresh lava to spread all the way to a cluster of trees and ignite them, casting an orange light over the whole plain.

She pulled back, focusing her attention on stabilising the ground upon which she stood. She cast a counter spell in a circle around her, hoping the thick granite crust she'd created would be enough to keep the molten rock from coming too close. She'd directed her magic away from Kellen and his camp, but it was far from a controlled process.

As the heat of the lava intensified, the groundwater beneath her shrieked. Soon, dozens of columns of scalding water pierced the sky as the pressure beneath the earth gave way and the caldera roared. Cerise transformed the falling water that came closest to her into a rock wall to protect those around the campfire, and as she did so, she couldn't fight the urge to smile. She too was a volcano; destruction and creation, joined together in one.

But where was Emeth? She looked between the trees she'd set ablaze and the campsite, trying to make up her mind. If she moved too far away to search for him, he would almost certainly go after Kellen and the other survivors. They'd be vulnerable without her.

Finally, a figure emerged from the burning trees. Cerise breathed deeply and moved towards it, but, as she drew closer, it became clear it wasn't human. A black stag walked out onto the plain. Cerise would never have seen it if not for the blaze, as its coat was all but swallowed up by the night. What was it doing walking towards the towering geysers? Every other animal for miles around had scattered.

The stag turned his head back and checked over his shoulder before taking another step onto the plain. A moment later, the shadows shifted again and a second figure emerged from the burning trees. Cerise froze. She recognised the figure immediately. It was *her*.

She was clothed in loose robes, giving her the appearance of a relic from an earlier time. The fire cast a hazy glow around the sharp angles of her face. Her smile was as thin, bright and wicked as the new moon. Her robes were tied in place by a cloth belt from which hung a large wooden mask. Its features were carved into a petrified scream, and with her every movement it bounced against her hip, yawning wordlessly into the night.

The figure turned and looked towards Cerise; the mask gaped at her as well. Two gods stared at her. One who had lost his face and the other who had won everything.

Cerise fell to her knees.

"My lady Ramona—" she began, but whatever plea she'd intended to make was cut short, as the witch goddess turned away and swung herself up onto the back of the stag in one fluid leap. She dug in her heels and rode him bareback across the writhing ground, between jets of water that burst from the rock, and flames and lava that licked at the deer's hooves. She rode past Cerise, past the campfire beside which Kellen and the others waited, and on into a distant wood on the far edge of the plain.

Cerise grabbed her skirts in a bunch, hoping she understood. If anything could be construed as a sign from the gods, this was it. She hurried after Ramona, her mind whirring with possibilities. Until now, the whole conflict had been confined to the mortal realm. Ramona watching the proceedings wasn't a comforting thought, but she didn't dare disobey her. Whatever was required of Cerise waited for her in that wood.

She moved quickly over the twisting terrain. When she reached the edge of the plain, trees loomed in front of her, blocking out the narrow sliver of moon overhead. Cerise listened intently for some sign of the goddess and her stag, hoping they'd guide her forward. But they had vanished. Should she go on into the wood to search for them, or look for some other sign? Or would that leave Kellen and the others too vulnerable?

She'd felt so certain when she'd followed the goddess that Ramona was leading her towards her target. But there was no sign of Emeth among the dark trees. Cerise looked back towards the geyser plain, still quaking with force as plumes of water erupted from it. On the other side Kellen's fire glowed steadily, and she took a step back from the edge of the copse. She shouldn't go on alone. She couldn't leave him defenceless. She turned her back on the tall, dark trees.

He lunged.

So Ramona had led her to Emeth. Right into the arms of death.

Like the last time, black dust flew into her face, filling her eyes, ears and mouth. A second later, the weight of a man landed against her chest. Emeth's hand went straight for her throat.

But this time, Cerise knew what to expect. Instead of trying to protect her face, she shielded her neck with her hands. When Emeth tried to choke her, his gloves scrabbled against a mess of fingers. It bought her enough time to cough up the black sludge and take a deep breath of fresh air. She rolled away from him and his murderous hands.

She expected him to grab her feet again, as he had back out on the plain, but he'd realised how well-prepared she was this time around. As she got to her feet, she saw the blur of his shadow receding into the woods.

Dammit! He would do this over and over again. Retreat, then wait for another opportunity to slit her throat. Ramona could lead her to him a thousand times, but the confrontation would always unfold the same way unless Cerise was somehow able to prevent him from escaping.

With a scream, she thrust her hands into the ground. A rumble that could have woken the gods ruptured the air as the caldera beneath her cracked and shifted. Old fault lines woke and screeched as they ground against each other. The woods in front of her buckled and huge pines twisted free from their roots. They toppled like the columns of old temples, radiating out in a circle from her hands. Birds shrieked in terror as their nests were wrenched from beneath them.

Through the commotion, Cerise kept her gaze fixed on Emeth as he darted and stumbled through the chaos. He narrowly avoided being flattened by a thick trunk, but there were too many branches for him to navigate. They snarled together, pinning him against the undergrowth. Cerise brushed the dirt from her hands and strode forward.

Emeth struggled to free himself from the tangle. His robes were torn, and the strap of his satchel twisted his neck to the side until he was forced to drop the bag. Cerise scrambled over the mess she had created. One of the heels on her shoes snapped as she placed too much weight against a flimsy branch. Davina and her ridiculous footwear! Now was her chance, while the basalt dust was out of reach. Her wrists still ached from where he'd grabbed hold of her a few moments earlier. By rights, she *should* kill him. He deserved every cruelty. Only Kellen's words had stopped her from razing the woods to the ground in order to burn him alive. As she neared him, she broke off a large branch from one of the fallen trees.

The gap between them closed to only a few feet, and Emeth turned, no longer struggling. He stood atop a fallen birch tree, panting with exertion. He held his knife up where she could see it. "I understand now. We're both an act of the gods, you and I." When he spoke, his words came in a rush, as if his last hope was to argue for his life. "They created me to destroy evil. And they created you to destroy me."

Despite herself, Cerise stopped. Did the gods communicate with him too? Had he seen Ramona and her stag as well?

He went on. "For a long time, your family was the one variable I couldn't account for. Balter infringes more onto Rencha's lands with each passing year, and every villain on that train deserved to be punished. But you Halgyrics? You sit in your northern perches, frozen and apart from the rest of the world. You're nothing but a useless cast of observers."

"Enough." Cerise slammed her palm against the ground and the earth shook again.

The tree beneath Emeth rolled. He twisted, trying to keep his balance, but soon toppled over and landed in a heap on the ground.

Cerise's grip tightened over her branch and she strode forward, picking her way over the tumbled terrain. "You're coming with me."

Emeth dragged himself out from beneath the tangle of branches. Blood streamed down his left side, yet he still wore a grin on his face as he pulled himself up to a standing position. "I kept asking myself," he continued, "does inaction deserve death as much as the likes of Lord Drawley did? I suppose I have my answer. Ramona has spared you. I harbour no illusions now. As a girl, you transform at the slightest hint of danger. And I need a little more than basalt dust to do away with you when you're a witch."

"Stay where you are." She brandished the stick again. "Or by the gods, I will kill you. I can live with your death, even if Kellen can't."

Emeth's smile widened. "You'll do no such thing." And then he raised his hand, as if toasting her for a fine performance. He unleashed the greatest weapon he had. "*Davina.*"

Cerise collapsed to the ground as her consciousness slipped away.

And Emeth turned his back on her and crept off into the night.

CHAPTER

+ + 42 + +

"SHE'S OVER HERE!"

Kellen circled back at the call from one of the dancers.

"Is she alive?" he called as he pulled himself over an uprooted pine.

"She's still breathing, sir."

Torches bobbed over the maze of fallen trees. No one had found Emeth's body yet, even though they all agreed they'd seen him and the witch struggling at the edge of the trees earlier. Kellen still wasn't sure which of the pair had flattened the forest. *Flattened* the forest. What a misleading turn of phrase. The ground was a warren of holes left by upended roots that had risen to dizzying heights as trunks piled up on top of each other.

Kellen wove his way through the mess of branches as quickly as he could. He would have preferred to come and find Cerise alone, but there had been no convincing the other survivors to stay behind.

But when he arrived at the spot in which his sister lay, he found it was Davina whose body the dancer had discovered. She lay crumpled over one of the trees, the dull colour of her hair and skin making it clear that Cerise had gone. For a moment, he was certain she was dead, but then her chest puffed upwards. She was unconscious, but still breathing. Bless the gods.

Kellen dropped to her side. "Any idea what happened?" he asked.

The dancer shrugged. "I don't know for sure, sir," she said. "But it looks like a bump to the head."

Kellen lifted Davina's hair and found a large lump at the back of her skull. He checked her for cuts or other signs of trauma, but found nothing except the cut Emeth's blade had made along her neck earlier in the evening. Gingerly, Kellen slid his arms around her.

"I'm going back to camp," he said. "You might want to tell the others to head back too. If Trudane is still out here, we'll be at a disadvantage."

The girl nodded, but her brow was furrowed in a way that communicated that she, like so many others, wasn't totally sure how much she could trust him.

Davina was bigger and heavier than he expected. How much she'd grown over the past few years! But he managed to carry her out of the forest, back to the safety of the fire. As he laid her next to the flames, she groaned and her eyes fluttered open for a moment. "Kellen?" Her voice was groggy and tears welled in her eyes. "You're here?"

He nodded, slipping his good hand into one of hers so she had something to hold onto. "I'm here. You're safe."

Davina sighed and curled closer to him. She squeezed his hand as she fell back to sleep. He looked at his sister, tucked at his side. A witch, as powerful as a volcano.

Perhaps they *were* safe.

+ ✦ +

"He said he couldn't kill me." Davina struggled for details from the previous night. She woke after dawn, disoriented and unsure if her dream about seeing Kellen the night before had been real. But he was there, waiting by her side. Around them were a handful of the other survivors, and Kellen promised that, as soon as she felt well enough, they'd fetch Morel, Genna and Rae. But her head throbbed—and she wasn't sure she could walk very far now that the heel on one of her shoes had snapped.

Kellen clearly wanted her to return to her witch self and give him a full account of what had happened, but, for now, there were too many people around. Davina thought that a relief. The witch had never been in control of their body for so long before, and the fact that so many memories now belonged to her other half frightened her more than she dared say.

At the same time, it surprised her how much she did remember. Since learning her witch name, the shroud that had obscured Cerise had begun to lift. Though the images were shadowy, like she was putting together scenes from a play she'd watched while seated at the back of a theatre. But when she surveyed the flattened forest and the pillars of stone on the geyser plain, she confirmed to herself that, yes, she had been there.

"I guess he'd tried three times by then," said Davina. "First, when he blew up the ground and set off the geysers, then when he attacked me with basalt dust and you saved me, and the third time, well… I think I was winning."

"I don't doubt it," said Kellen. "You put on quite the show. He must have been desperate to get away from you."

Kellen was grinning at her in that insufferable, self-satisfied way she'd seen so many times throughout her life, and she almost rolled her eyes. Then it dawned on her that, for once, she understood the look. He was *proud* of her.

Davina flushed and looked away. She wasn't sure she deserved his love and forgiveness. Not yet. Especially as she hadn't been able to catch Emeth. But still, she leaned into Kellen's side and let him wrap an arm around her, his squeeze a thank-you for everything she'd done the night before when she was her witch self. "Emeth said some other things too," she said. "I don't remember all of it."

Kellen nodded. "Do you think he's coming back?"

"Maybe?" Davina wished she could give a firm answer. "He's afraid of me. The witch wanted to kill him."

She gripped the letter Kellen had given Cerise, an anchor to that time when, for a moment, both sides of her consciousness had been able to inhabit the same body. It had been a fleeting, blissful minute of clarity. Once all the commotion died down, Davina would be able to sit and read her mother's words and recapture that.

Letters. That was a good idea, wasn't it? When they got somewhere with pen and paper, Davina resolved to write one of her own. An account, in her words, of her life and memories. Cerise could read it and that would be the start. They would figure each other out and, some day, they would be one.

"Mr Linde!"

Davina looked over to see Penny hurrying towards them. She gave Davina a wide berth though, never quite looking at her. Davina tried—and failed—not to take the slight personally. She'd saved the bloody woman's life. The least she could do was make eye contact.

"There's someone here to see you," said Penny. "Well, they

want to see whoever's in charge. Frankly, I don't know who else to point him to."

"I'd say you're in charge as much as anyone, Penny," said Kellen, but he still got to his feet. "What do you mean *someone*? Where did he come from?"

"A village further up the valley." Penny gestured north, past the geyser plain. "He's Renchan. He says he's trying to decide if he wants to help us."

Davina's jaw popped open. A village? They had been stuck in this cycle of death for so long she'd all but given up on the possibility of rescue.

"Of course!" Kellen was equally wide-eyed. "We'll come straight away."

"We?" Davina repeated.

"Well, I thought—but if you don't want to—"

"No, I do." Obviously. But it was a pleasant surprise to be invited. Kellen offered her a hand up and she swayed on her uneven feet. Her poor broken shoes. They'd been her favourite pair, too.

Kellen held her upright her with his good hand, and they followed Penny over to where the embers of the fire still smouldered. Most of the steam from the night before had dissipated, but small clouds still drifted across pools left over from when the witch had cracked open the earth. An old man waited for them there, staring out over the reshaped landscape with a frown. Next to him was a lanky youth, carrying a large bag on his shoulders. The old man turned his head towards them as they approached.

"Good day, sir," Kellen said. "I'm Kellen Linde. I'm sorry, but I don't know your name."

"No. You wouldn't. We don't hand those out to everyone."

The old man's gaze was sharp, his lined face like a weathered mountainside. "So you're the Halgyrics the girl mentioned. You look the part, young man."

"So I've been told." Kellen attempted to push his matted hair behind his ear, but it fell down next to his chin in a clump.

"That woman said you lot came from the railway," said the old man. "Been stranded here going on four days."

"Is that all?" Davina muttered.

"She also said," the old man went on, "that you, girl, are the one I'm looking for. Are you a daughter of sky?"

It wasn't a turn of phrase she was familiar with, though she could guess the meaning. Ramona was goddess of sun and moon, after all. But why would she admit that to a stranger? Even if Penny had told the man about her being a witch, saying it out loud was something else entirely.

Kellen offered no direction, for which she was grateful. Davina wasn't in a mind to listen. As the silence dragged on, the old man nodded, as if he understood enough. "You're wise to keep your secrets," he said. "But don't fear me, child. I won't ask your name. Either of them. I only came here because it's our custom to do right by Ramona's children. Last night, we could see the geysers erupting from our village. It was as good a clue as any that there was one of your kind in our lands. And, that being the case, we'd hate not to offer you hospitality."

"Am I to understand," said Davina, "that you'll help us if I *am* a witch?"

"We owe a great deal to your kind and nothing at all to the Balterians," he said. "The choice is yours."

"In that case, yes." Davina curtsied, a foolish gesture when she was dressed in rags and broken shoes. "I'm a... daughter

427

of sky. And we need the help. There are other survivors further down the rail tracks who are still waiting for rescue too."

The old man nodded. "Then we thank you for blessing us with your visit."

Visit. He said it as if the whole affair had been voluntary.

The old man did eventually introduce himself as Branthus. He asked far fewer questions than Davina had expected, and took the news that there was a homicidal acolyte from the order of Chanri still running about the caldera with considerable grace.

"Balterians," was all Branthus said. "Always making a mess of something. We'll be ready for him."

"I don't think he's targeting your people," Kellen tried to explain. "But the other passengers—"

"Not targeting us *yet*." Branthus shook his head. "*Balterians*."

As the remaining survivors packed their bags for one last journey, Kellen and Davina prepared to head back south to find Morel, Genna and Rae. Branthus offered to send the boy who'd accompanied him along with them, but in the end Kellen talked him out of it.

"If it's at all possible, though, we could do with a horse," he said. "I doubt my brother can walk yet."

"We'll send one along," Branthus promised.

Davina and Kellen walked mostly in silence, Davina wearing a borrowed pair of the ugliest work boots she'd ever seen in her life. Her head was still throbbing from her fall the night before, and with every movement she discovered more bruises and scrapes that Emeth had given her. Her neck, in particular, ached when she twisted it too far to the left. Perhaps it was for the best that she couldn't remember fully what had happened.

She couldn't imagine Kellen felt much better. Every so often she'd look at him and feel a pinch of guilt. A whack on the head was a temporary hardship, but Kellen would never get back those fingers she'd hacked from his hand. She couldn't understand how he still tolerated her.

But the answer Cerise whispered at the back of her mind was the only one that made sense: he really did love her.

"When we reach Morel…" Kellen broke the silence, his tone cautious. "After we've told everyone the good news, there's something I want to do. For the witch."

"Yes?" Davina raised an eyebrow.

"I want to introduce her to them. She's very lonely and—well, they're her family too."

Davina frowned. It would be one more thing she wouldn't be able to remember properly.

"I think it would be good for her," Kellen continued. There he went again, with his earnest stares and always being right about everything. But for once, that thought made her smile. So did Kellen as he went on. "And I think it would be good for *you*. She's a part of you, after all. But I don't want to summon her without your consent—"

"Let me see Morel first," Davina said. "As me. I need to know he's all right."

In the back of her mind, the witch stirred, jubilant at the thought of truly living.

Kellen squeezed her shoulder. "It's a deal."

CHAPTER

✦✦ 43 ✦✦

Since Mr Linde had left them to go warn the other passengers about the nasty acolyte, Rae Freath had reached a horrible conclusion. As it turned out, she'd rather have a father than not. Even if it was Mr Linde. Even if he didn't measure up to the lost fisherman she'd thought about for so many years. Ma had told her over and over that he'd come back soon, but Rae saw in her face that Ma didn't believe it.

All these years, Rae's father hadn't been dead. But now he probably was.

Night came and went, and in the morning Mr Linde still wasn't there. They were stranded, alone, trying to convince Uncle Morel to rest. Every hour or so, he'd announce he was well, jump to his feet, and then collapse after a few steps due to the pain in his knee. Ma tried to tell him to calm down a hundred times, but he never listened.

Rae stared at him. Would Morel be enough? If she couldn't have a father, would an uncle do? She hadn't had either until a few days ago, so why did she feel as though she'd lost something when an uncle was more than she'd ever had? But no. He wasn't enough. Other children got to have fathers. Was it so wrong of her to want hers to come back?

There were other things to be worried about. Sensible things that Ma kept track of as she rationed their supplies. They were running out of food. They were running out of water. There was still no sign of rescue coming from either direction along the train tracks. But all Rae's thoughts went to the father who should have been there.

The sun was high in the sky, warm and brilliant, when Ma spotted two figures walking down the valley towards them. She let out a scream and Rae wondered if it was from horror or joy. But then Ma ran towards them, laughing and calling their names. And before Rae could dare believe it was true, Uncle Morel launched himself to his feet, rushing towards Aunt Davina.

Rae struggled to keep up. The grown-ups were as giddy as children, pulling each other close and talking so fast that Rae could hardly catch what they were saying. *She* should have thought of something to say. Witch's hair, it was so silly of her. Here she was, wanting a father, but she still didn't have any clue what to do with one.

She drew up next to Mr Linde. Her father. She wrinkled her nose as he took his time kissing Ma. An unpleasant display, but it was probably better than them hating each other. As they broke apart, his grin was so wide that it could have flown off his face. "Where's—" He started, but then turned as he felt her hand on his leg. "Oh, there you are."

He bent down next to her. His eyes were hazel. Like hers.

"You came back," she whispered.

"Always."

Rae threaded her arms around his neck, burrowing her cheeks

into his shoulder as he lifted her up. She'd figure out what to say to him later. For now, it was enough he was here.

"I'll be honest." Ma's voice bubbled with relief. "I didn't think you'd make it back. Is he dead, then? The acolyte? Gods, I have so much to ask you."

"Well, there's a lot to tell. But I want to introduce you to someone first," said Mr Linde.

Rae looked up. She couldn't see anyone else coming towards them, though Aunt Davina had a knowing look on her face.

"I suppose it's only half an introduction," he went on. "I'm not sure she'd want you all to know her name yet, but we're family. And I think it would do you good to meet her."

No. He couldn't mean… But Aunt Davina took a deep breath, as if she was preparing for something very difficult.

"Oh." Ma's breath caught. "Ah, yes. We'd love to meet her."

"You're all right with this, Davina?" Uncle Morel asked his sister pointedly.

"Yes, Kellen and I agreed." Davina folded her arms. "Come on. Whisper her name already."

Kellen nodded and leaned in close to his sister. Rae strained to hear, but for now, he kept the name a secret. Then, right before her eyes, it was as if a layer of film melted away from Aunt Davina, revealing a sharper, hungrier face. The witch swooned for a second, though Uncle Morel caught her before she could fall.

But she twisted away from him. "Who are—oh, Kellen." She relaxed as she spotted someone she knew. "You're safe. And you're… holding a child?"

Kellen grinned at the witch. A *witch*. Rae could barely believe it. If Aunt Davina was a witch, then that meant there were still good witches.

"I wanted to introduce you to a few people," Kellen said. "This is your family. This is our brother Morel. My—ah… this is Genna. And my daughter, Rae."

"Hello." The witch waved awkwardly.

Uncle Morel moved as though he wanted to hug her, but she shied away.

"It might take me a little while to remember your names," said the witch. "Except yours." The witch locked eyes with Rae.

"Oh," said Rae. "Well, I guess my name isn't very long."

"No, it's not that." The witch took a step forward and placed a hand on Rae's shoulder. "It's because I get to be the one who gives it to you. We aren't alone anymore, Eloise."

In that moment, Rae slipped into a beautiful dream. And when she—Eloise—opened her eyes, a brand-new witch smiled back at her Aunt Cerise.

· EPILOGUE ·

Hᴇss ᴘᴜʟʟᴇᴅ ᴛʜᴇ hood of her cloak tight, shielding her face from the mountain rain. By her estimate, it would take her a fortnight to walk to the High Coven. With a bit of luck, there would be help along the way. Perhaps there'd be a village in which she could exchange her services for a donkey. She'd happily knock down some trees or tear up the ground for Renchan villagers to sow their seeds. She could save them weeks of work with just a flick of her wrist.

But even a horse or a donkey would only get her to the High Coven a few days sooner. In the meantime, she needed a companion—someone she could trust to know her names. Witches travelled in pairs, and Hess had learned a long time ago that wasn't always by choice.

His trail was easy to follow. The remnants of his battle with Davina—or whatever name the girl bore as her witch self—were everywhere around the geyser plain. For a day, Hess shadowed the remaining survivors of the train crash until it became clear to her that Emeth wasn't with them and they didn't intend to hunt him down. They were too busy enjoying being rescued. Too injured. Too tired to be curious. But they could have found him if they'd wanted to. After all, he was bleeding all over the caldera.

It took Hess less than a day to follow the trail of blood, footprints and spent basalt dust that lay in his wake. He'd used it to knock over obstacles that lay in his path, clearly more concerned with making a quick retreat than a subtle one, but it didn't matter. This was Hess's caldera, and he was a fool if he thought he could escape her on it.

When she came across Emeth's campfire, his face contorted into shock at the sight of her. Clearly, he'd never expected to see her at all. He reached for his satchel, but she held up a hand in warning. "Oh, don't do that," she said. "Neither of us want it to come to *that*."

He paused, considering his options. For all his foolishness, he was an intelligent young man. Too convinced of his own intelligence, in fact. But he must have noticed the calm way she moved towards him—the way her face showed contempt but not anger. An expression she saw mirrored in his own features. "Am I to understand," he said slowly, "that you don't intend to kill me? You killed Ambrose."

"And you killed Allonia." Hess surveyed his campsite, looking for somewhere to sit, but nothing presented itself. He'd settled for a rather pathetic setup beneath the shelter of a gnarled birch tree. His fire looked as though he'd started it with basalt dust, and the grindings shimmered in the flames. He was using magic to survive, she realised. This boy wasn't built for living out on the caldera. Ramona spare her! What a pathetic companion he would be, but what other option did she have? "I think our accounts are even," she said eventually. "The dandy was your friend, then?"

Emeth's eyes dropped. That modest display of affection reassured Hess. She didn't need an ally who killed without compunction. A man like that couldn't be controlled.

"I'm sorry about him," Hess offered. "He seemed a harmless sort, and if I could—"

"He wasn't a good man. He was weak-willed. He…" Emeth wouldn't meet her eyes. He seemed to be trying to convince himself of his own words. "I should be thanking you. He was one of the lords, the same as the rest of them."

"Same as you?" Ah, *now* he was looking up.

Anger boiled in him at the accusation. "I renounced that life. I swore myself to—"

"Chanri, Goddess of Gentle Creatures. Yes, the irony of that hasn't escaped me." Hess relished being honest. "You might worship Chanri, Mr Trudane. But you don't serve her. And don't squirm like that when you hear your name. Your upbringing has made you who you are, just like the rest of us. You were born to power, not servitude. It makes us more alike than you might think."

"And you'd have me revel in that power?" said Emeth. "My father approved hundreds of building projects on conquered caldera lands. You want me to be like him?"

"By Ramona, don't be ridiculous," she said. "But the way you activated those geysers? And blew up the Lords' Council? You were born to power, Emeth Trudane. And you know things. You've mastered a whole form of magic that my sisters and I have never known."

He turned his wide, dark eyes towards her, and she was reminded of that night not long ago when she first met him—a terrified boy searching for meaning while a train burned on the caldera. At the time, they'd both been disguised. She as the jolly

437

nurse, him as the trembling priest in training. They were free of pretence now.

Their true natures were clear. Hess was her people's soldier; this boy could be her weapon.

She leaned closer, feeling his yearning for her approval. She gave him what he wanted, the words well-practised. "Don't you see?" she said. "It's no coincidence that you and I were on the train together. Ramona set this whole thing up. It's my job to take you to the High Coven, so you can train the witches in volchemistry."

"By the gods…" Emeth sat in shock for a moment before a smile of relief broke over his face. "And then… then we'll help the Caldera Peoples—"

"We'll destroy Balter. All of it." And any other nation that resisted them.

Emeth's shoulders shuddered, as if a tremendous weight had lifted from them. It had gone better than Hess could possibly have imagined. She'd absolved him. She would have his loyalty yet. "The gods have work for us," he said.

"Exactly."

And as delight spread across the young man's face, Hess almost believed in the gods herself.

ACKNOWLEDGEMENTS

I'VE WANTED TO be an author since I was five years old. As such, I've built up a massive list of people who helped me get here. Brevity was never my strong suit, so buckle in.

First will always be my family. To Mom and Dad, who believed in me so completely since I was a wee one, stapling printer paper together in order to make "books". I don't know how you put up with me, but I'm eternally thankful you do. Katie and Matt, you're the best siblings a kid could ever have. Thank you for marrying wonderful people and having wonderful kids. Andrew and Jessica, thank you for joining the Paxman fray.

To the friends who shaped my writing over years of imaginative play, thank you for listening to all the winding, intricate lore I attached to our stuffed animals. But especially thanks to Miranda Leavitt, who talked me into digging up some of my oldest stories and writing those characters again. *Death on the Caldera* simply wouldn't exist without you.

This book also wouldn't exist without the people who took a chance on me. Penelope Burns—agent extraordinaire—I know you're always on my side. Thank you for never giving up on this story and being its champion. And a huge thanks to Rufus Purdy of Titan Books, who understood what this book was trying to be and did so much to help me make it into that. Your steady support has meant everything to me.

An enormous THANK YOU to the teachers who guided me down this path: Diane Chartrand, who taught middle school English and firmly believed I would be a published writer one day; everyone at Chatham University, who helped me find my drive to finally publish my stories; Katherine Ayers and Johnathan Auxier, you taught me more about writing than anyone else ever has.

I've been lucky enough to get involved with several wonderful writing communities over the years. To the class of Pitch Wars 2017, look at us, still getting new books out there! Most of all, thank you to the group of you who banded together with me to form our Writer's Alliance critique group in 2020. You got me through a pandemic, query trenches, submission and a dozen other smaller trials along the way. Diana, Heidi, Cass, Jenn, Bori, and Molly—you are all superstars! Talking with you in crit group is the highlight of my week.

An extra special shout-out to my sub-alliances. Eliza Langhans, who stuck it out with the muddy middle of this book when no one else could make it to crit group aside from the two of us. You kept me on task, and we both know what a thankless job that is. Ipuna Estavillo Black, you are one of my very best friends. You constantly remind me of the joy books can bring and there's no one who cheers me up better when I'm frustrated with the creative process.

Next, my Storymakers community! Finding this conference was a turning point for my creative life. The friends and connections I've made by becoming more involved each year have brought me joy, insight, and (let's be honest) spreadsheets. I wish I could name every last one of you, but there are dozens, so this is going to have to be a highlights list:

Risto Snow, my arch nemesis—I mean, best friend. I adore you and am so grateful for your support, writing feedback, and video-making prowess. Jaime Theler, mentor above all other mentors! Thank you for your sharp, insightful critique and for being there when I needed to talk out agent calls and the fifty million emotions that come with that. Emily Inouye Huey, thank you for taking chances on me and making it so I could come and be part of Storymakers year after year. Jessica Guernsey, you've been with me through some of the weirdest ups and downs of my writing life and never fail to make me laugh. Jamie McHenry, I can't wait to grab dinner together the next time I'm down for the conference. And finally, Margaret Seeley, you make me feel smarter than I actually am and I'm so glad I get to work with you.

There are hundreds of others; people I met through Discord groups; friends who read my earliest manuscripts and didn't throw them across the room in disgust; authors whose books inspire me and make me try to reach further; dozens of aunts, uncles, cousins and so forth who buoy up my spirits. So here is just a grab bag of some of the people I love best.

Agatha Christie, whose books gave me the best nightmares.

Grandma, who loves a good "crimmie".

And Colton Blum, who I know is with me in absolutely everything.

To all of you, God be with you 'til we meet again.

ABOUT THE AUTHOR

EMILY PAXMAN is an author and artist from Vancouver Island in beautiful British Columbia, Canada. She's a huge fan of gardening, cats, watercolour painting, and several other hobbies that befit an octogenarian. She has her Master's of Fine Arts in Creative Writing from Chatham University, has written for indie video game company Wizard Games, and splits her time (unevenly) between creating comics and writing novels. You can read her webcomic, Neptune Bay, on Webtoon. *Death on the Caldera* is her debut novel.

Follow Emily on Bluesky: *@emmypax. bsky. social*; and on
Instagram: *@emmypaxman*

For more fantastic fiction, author events,
exclusive excerpts, competitions, limited editions and more

VISIT OUR WEBSITE
titanbooks.com

LIKE US ON FACEBOOK
facebook.com/titanbooks

FOLLOW US ON TWITTER AND INSTAGRAM
@TitanBooks

EMAIL US
readerfeedback@titanemail.com